TREASURE BOX

Also by Orson Scott Card

Lost Boys

Pastwatch:
The Redemption of Christopher Columbus

Saints

The Folk of the Fringe

Ender's Game

Speaker for the Dead

Xenocide

Children of the Mind

Seventh Son

Red Prophet

Prentice Alvin

Alvin Journeyman

The Memory of Earth

The Call of Earth

The Ships of Earth

Earthfall

Earthborn

Cruel Miracles

Flux

Monkey Sonatas

The Changed Man

TREASURE BOX

A Novel

Orson Scott Card

HarperCollins*Publishers*

HarperCollins books may be purchased for educational, business, or sales promotional use. For information please write: Special Markets Department, HarperCollins Publishers, Inc., 10 East 53rd Street, New York, NY 10022.

FIRST EDITION

Designed by Christine Weathersbee

Library of Congress Cataloging-in-Publication Data
Card, Orson Scott.
    Treasure Box : a novel / by Orson Scott Card. — 1st ed.
      p. cm.
    ISBN 0-06-017654-7
    1. Married people—New York (State)—Fiction. 2. Family—New York (State)—Fiction. 3. Supernatural—Fiction. I. Title.
PS3553.A655T75 1996
813' .54—dc20   96-16248

96 97 98 99 00 ❖/RRD 10 9 8 7 6 5 4 3 2 1

*To Russ and Tammy Card,
dear friends and beloved family,
for the faithfulness that carries you
along roads rough and smooth*

ACKNOWLEDGMENTS

For the first time in many years, I actually wrote an entire novel at home. Thus every page was wrung from the patience of my family. Kristine and Emily read every chapter as the first draft emerged from the printer, and Geoff was not far behind; the fax lines hummed as Kathy Kidd in remotest Sterling, Virginia, received and read each night's work the morning after. To all four of you, thanks for your responses, which helped me know what I had written and how it needed to be improved.

Later, when the first draft was completed, I had great help from other advance readers, most notably my friend David Fox and my wise editor at Harper, Eamon Dolan; they also have my gratitude. Any flaws still remaining are probably due to my stubborn disregard of good advice.

My thanks to Kathleen Bellamy and Scott Allen for good work under all circumstances. Thanks also to Clark and Kathy Kidd, for giving me DC and northern Virginia.

And last of all my thanks to Charlie Ben and Zina, for reminding me always of the joyful striving of childhood.

CONTENTS

1
Harvest

Quentin Fears never told his parents the last thing his sister Lizzy said to him before they pulled the plug on her and let her die.

For three days after the traffic accident, Lizzy lay in a coma, her body hosed, piped, pumped, probed, measured, medicated and fed so the doctors could keep her organs in good condition for transplant, while Mom and Dad struggled with the question of whether she was really dead.

Not that they had any doubts. The doctors showed them the flat lines of Lizzy's brainwaves. The doctors reverently assured the Fearses that if there were the tiniest spark of a hope that Lizzy was actually alive inside that bandaged head, they would cling to that hope and do all in their power to revive her. But there was hope only for the people whose lives might be saved by Lizzy's organs, and then only if they could harvest them before they deteriorated. Mom and Dad nodded, tears streaming down their faces, and believed.

But eleven-year-old Quentin did not believe the doctors. He could see that Lizzy was alive. He could see how the huge bruise reached out from under the bandages, blackening Lizzy's eyes; he watched the bruise change over the three days of the coma, and he knew she was alive. Dead people's bruises didn't change like that. And Lizzy's hands were warm and flexible. Dead people had cold, stiff hands. The machines that measured brainwaves weren't infallible. And who was to say there wasn't something deeper than the electrical activity of the brain?

"Quen understands about brain death," said Dad to one of the doctors late on the first day of her coma. He spoke softly, perhaps thinking Quentin was asleep. "You don't have to talk down to him."

The doctor murmured something even softer. Maybe it began as an apology, but it ended more as a question, a doubt, a demand.

Whatever it was the doctor said, Dad answered, "He and Lizzy were very close."

Quentin murmured his correction: "We *are* close."

It was just a word. A slip of the tongue. Only it meant that Dad had given up. She was already dead in his mind.

The men moved out into the corridor to continue their conversation. That happened more and more in the hours and days that followed. Quentin knew they were out there plotting how to get him out of the way. He knew that everything any grown-up said to him was bent to that purpose. Grandpa and Grammy Fears came to see him, and then Nanny Say, Mom's mom, but all conversations seemed to come to the same end. "Come on home, dear, and let Lizzy rest."

"Let them murder her, you mean."

And then they'd burst into tears and leave the room and Dad and Mom would come in and there'd be another fight in which Quentin would look them in the eye and say—not screaming, because Lizzy had told him years ago that scream-ing just made adults think of you as a child and then you'd never get any respect—he would look them in the eye and say whatever would stop them, whatever would make them leave the room with Lizzy still alive on the bed and Quentin still standing guard beside her.

2

"If you drug me, if you drag me out of here, if you murder her in my sleep, I will hate you for it for the rest of my life. I will never, never, never, never, never . . . "

"We get the idea," said Dad, his voice like ice.

"Never, never, never, never, never . . . "

Mom pleaded with him. "Please don't say it, Quen."

"Never forgive you."

This last time the scene played out, on the third day of the coma, Mom rushed crying from the room, out to the corridor where her own mother was already in tears from what Quentin had said to *her*. Dad was left alone with him in Lizzy's room.

"This isn't about Lizzy anymore," said Dad. "This is about you getting your own way. Well, you're not going to get your own way on this, Quentin Fears, because there's no one on God's green earth who has the power to give it to you. She's dead. You're alive. Your mother and I are alive. We'd like to be able to grieve for our little girl. We'd like to be able to think of her the way she was, not tubed up like this. And while we're at it, we'd like our son back. Lizzy meant a lot to you. Maybe it feels like she meant everything to you and if you let go of her there'll be nothing left. But there *is* something left. There's *your* life. And Lizzy wouldn't have wanted you to—"

"Don't tell me what Lizzy would have wanted," said Quentin. "She wanted to be alive, that's what she wanted."

"Do you think your mother and I don't want that too?" Dad's voice barely made a sound and his eyes were wet.

"Everybody wants her dead except for me."

Quentin could see that it took all of Dad's self-control not to hit him, not to rage back at him. Instead Dad left the room, letting the door slam shut behind him. And Quentin was alone with Lizzy.

He wept into her hand, feeling the warmth of it despite the needle dripping some fluid into a vein, despite the tape that held the needle on, despite the coldness of the metal tube of the bedrail against his forehead. "Oh, God," said Quentin. "Oh, God."

He never said that, not the way the other kids did. *Oh God* when the other team gets a home run. *Oh God* when somebody says something really stupid. *Jesus H. Christ* when you bump your head. Quentin wasn't raised that way. His parents never swore, never said God or Jesus except when they were talking religion. And so when Quentin's own mouth formed the words, it couldn't be that he was swearing like his friends. It had to be a prayer. But what was he praying for? Oh God, let her live? Could he even believe in that possibility? Like the Sunday school story, Jesus saying to Jairus, "She isn't dead, the little girl is only sleeping"? Even in the story they laughed him to scorn.

Quentin wasn't Jesus and he knew he wasn't praying for her to rise from the dead. Well, maybe he was but that would be a stupid prayer because it wasn't going to happen. What then? What was he praying for? Understanding? Understanding of what? Quentin understood everything. Mom and Dad had given up, the doctors had given up, everybody but him. Because they all "understood." Well, Quentin didn't want to understand.

Quentin wanted to die. Not die *too* because he wasn't going to think of Lizzy dying or especially of her already being dead. No, he wanted to die instead. A swap, a trade. Oh God, let me die instead. Put me on this bed and let her go on home with Mom and Dad. Let it be me they give up on. Let it be my plug they pull. Not Lizzy's.

Then like a dream he saw her, remembered her alive. Not the way she looked only a few days ago, fifteen years old, the Saturday morning her friend Kate took her joyriding even though neither of them had a license and Kate spun the car sideways into a tree and a branch came through the open passenger window like the finger of God and poked twenty inches of bark and leaves right through Lizzy's head and Kate sat there completely unharmed except for Lizzy's blood and brains dripping from the leaves onto her shoulder. Quentin didn't see Lizzy with dresses and boys who wanted to take her out and a makeup kit on her side of the bathroom sink. What Quentin saw in his dream of her was the old Lizzy, his best friend Lizzy whose body was as lean as a boy's, Lizzy who was really his brother *and* his sister, his teacher and his confidante. Lizzy who always understood everything and guided him past the really dumb mistakes of life and made him feel like everything was safe, if you were just smart and careful enough. Lizzy on a skateboard, teaching him how to walk it up the steps onto the porch, "Only don't let Mom see you or she'll have a conniption because she thinks every little thing we do is going to get us killed."

Well it *can* get you killed, Lizzy. You didn't know everything. You didn't know every *damn* thing, did you! You didn't know you had to watch out for a twig reaching into the open window of your car and punching a hole in your brain. You stupid! You stupid stupid . . .

"Mellow out," Lizzy said to him.

He didn't open his eyes. He didn't want to know whether it was Lizzy speaking through those lips, out from under that heavy bandage, or merely Lizzy speaking in the dream.

"I wasn't stupid, it was just the way things happen sometimes. Sometimes there's a twig and there's a car and they're going to intersect and if there's a head in the way, well ain't that too bad."

"Kate shouldn't have been driving without her license."

"Well, aren't you the genius, you think I haven't figured that out by now? What do you imagine I'm doing, lying here in this bed, except going over and over all the moments when I could have said no to Kate? So let me tell you right now, don't you dare blame her, because I could have said no, and she wouldn't have done it. We went joyriding because I wanted to as much as she did and you can bet she feels lousy enough so don't you *ever* throw it up in her face, do you understand me, you tin-headed quintuplet?"

Quentin didn't want her to tell him off right now. He was in the middle of a war trying to save her life and the last thing he was worried about was Kate. "I'm never going to see her again anyway."

"Well, you should, because if you don't, she's going to think you blame her."

"I don't care what she thinks, Lizzy! All I want is *you* back, don't you get that?"

"Hey, Tin, there's no way. I'm brain dead. The lights are out. The body's empty. I'm gone. Toast. Wasted."

He didn't want to hear this. "You . . . are . . . alive."

"Yeah, well, right, and it's a lot of fun."

"They're trying to kill you, Lizzy. Mom and Dad, just like the doctors. Grammy and Grandpa and Nanny Say, too. They want to unhook you from everything and then cut out your kidneys and your eyes and your heart and your lungs."

"My chitlins, you mean."

"Shut up!"

"My giblets."

"Shut *up!*" Didn't she know that this wasn't a joke? This was life and death going on here and she was still *joking* like it didn't matter.

"It does matter," she said. "I'm just trying to cheer you up. Just trying to show you I'm not really gone."

"Well don't tell *me*, tell *them*. If I try to tell them you talked to me, they'll put me in the loony bin."

"They're coming to take me away, ha ha, hee hee, ho ho—"

"Stop it!"

"Tin, I'm here, not there, not in that body. *Here*."

But he wouldn't look up. Didn't want to see whatever she wanted him to see.

"All right, be that way. Stubbornest kid ever spawned of man and woman. You're driving Mom and Dad crazy, you dig, you dig, you dig?"

He did the next step in the ritual. "I dig, I dig, I dig."

"Well, well, well," she said, and giggled.

"They're trying to kill you."

"My body's no good to me anymore, Tin. You know that. And even when it's gone and buried or whatever, *I'll* still be here."

"Yeah, right, like you're going to come talk to me every day."

"Is that what this is about, then, Tin? What *you* want? I'm supposed to stay around so you can cuddle me like a stuffed animal or something?"

"Mom and Dad should have been the ones trying to save you!" That was the crux of it, wasn't it? Mom and Dad shouldn't have believed the doctors so easily. Too easily.

"Tin, listen to me. Sometimes your Mom and Dad are the only ones who know when it's time for you to die."

"That's the sickest lousiest most evil thing I ever heard anybody say! Parents don't ever want their children to die!"

"They didn't put the tree there. They didn't put the car there. They didn't put me in the car. They didn't put me in this bed. I did all that myself, Tin, or chance did, or fate or maybe God, he hasn't said. The only choice I left for them was whether my death was going to be completely meaningless or not. Give them a break."

"I'll never forgive them."

"Then I'll never forgive *you*."

"For what!"

"For keeping me tied down like this, Tin."

He couldn't help it then. He opened his eyes. And she wasn't there. Nobody was there except that still body lying on the bed, breathing into and out of a mask. Her voice was silent.

Quentin got up on rubbery legs and walked to the door. Was it still trembling from his father slamming it? He pulled it open and stepped outside. They were all there, looking at him in surprise: Dad, Mom, Grammy and Grandpa, Nanny Say, and the three main doctors. One of the doctors was holding a hypodermic syringe. Quentin knew what it was for—to tranquilize him so they could get him out of the room. Well, too late. Lizzy had sent him out of the room herself.

"Go ahead and kill her now," said Quentin. Then he turned his back on them and walked down the corridor toward the elevators.

Father came out to the car and talked to him before they harvested Lizzy's organs. In that conversation Quentin broke down and cried and said he was sorry and he knew Mom and Dad weren't killing Lizzy, that she was already dead, and they could go ahead with the organ-taking and he took back what he said about never forgiving them and could he please just wait in the car and not have to talk to grandparents or any of those doctors or nurses, who would be unable to keep the triumph out of their voices or their faces and he couldn't bear it.

"Nobody feels any triumph over this," said Dad.

"No," said Quentin, still trying to say whatever it was Dad needed to hear. "Just relief."

Dad took this in. "Yeah, I guess so, Quen. Relief." Then Dad leaned over and put his arm around him and kissed his head. "I love you, son. I love you for standing by your sister so long. And I love you for stepping away from her in time."

Quentin stayed alone in the car until after his sister's body died. And he never told them that Lizzy had come and talked to him. At first because he was too angry to tell them something so private. And then because he knew they'd put him in therapy to try to get him to understand that it was just a hallucination born of his grief and fear and stress and fatigue. And finally he never said anything because even without therapy he pretty much came to believe that it was, in fact, a hallucination born of grief, fear, stress, and fatigue.

But it was not a hallucination. And deep inside himself, in a place he didn't often go, where he kept the things he didn't like to think about but dared not forget, he knew that

Lizzy was still alive somewhere, and somehow she was watching what he did, or at least looking in on him from time to time.

How did he grieve?

He read her library—she always called it that, four shelves on cinderblocks, packed with paperbacks she had bought or been given by friends. He picked up the most–thumbed, most–bent, most–brokenback books and read them first. *Lord of the Rings, I Sing the Body Electric, Chronicles of Narnia, Fountainhead, The Crystal Cave, Pride and Prejudice, Rise and Fall of the Third Reich, Stranger in a Strange Land, Gone with the Wind, Childhood's End, Breakfast of Champions,* Quentin read them all, and yet when he thought back he remembered it differently, remembered hearing them all read aloud to him in Lizzy's voice. Lizzy reading the incantatory cadences of Bradbury, the delicate politeness of Austen; Lizzy telling of the ring slipping accidentally onto Frodo's finger as he fell from a table in Bree; Lizzy reading out the measurements of every male character in *Breakfast of Champions* and howling with laughter when the narrator declared his own. Lizzy enchanted with Merlin's magic, Lizzy grokking, Lizzy sobbing as she read of a Nazi soldier dashing out a Jewish baby's brains against a wall, Lizzy caught up in the tragic awe of the human children being carried off by the pied piper devil aliens, Lizzy mercilessly ambitious as she built buildings no one else would dare to build or married Frank Kennedy for his money even though he was engaged to her sister. All the voices of all the books were hers. It was the only time Quentin could hear her speaking to him. He read them all and then started over, read each one again and, again, started over.

His parents gave him other books for Christmas, his birthday, as a reward for good grades (Lizzy always had good grades, so Quentin would too). Finally, after Quentin was well started on his fourth passage through those shelves, he came home from school one day and the books were gone.

The shelves were gone. Lizzy's room was gone. Just an empty shell—walls, ceiling, carpet. Only the thumbtack holes in the walls and the red spot in the carpet where she spilled fingernail polish during her one and only attempt at self-decoration remained to prove that she had lived there. Cleaned-out, swept, vacuumed, the room was like her death all over again. For Quentin, perhaps it was really her death for the first time. The silencing of her voice.

He walked into the kitchen where Mom and Dad were sitting at the table. Waiting. They knew what they had done, they knew what it would mean, they were waiting to deal with him together. Quentin walked into the kitchen and got a drink of water and drank it all down and then poured another and emptied it onto the floor.

"Quentin," said Dad, "There's no need to . . . "

Quentin opened the refrigerator and began pulling things out and heaving them back onto the floor behind him. Milk cartons, egg cartons, leftovers, half-empty bottles. His father's arms caught him from behind, gathered him into an embrace. Quentin writhed his way free and ran for the back door leading out into the yard. Dad started to follow.

"Let him express his anger," said Mom. "I can clean this up."

Quentin ran to the flower garden and kicked the tops off the tulips and then began to pull them up, pull up every plant. The hard rootthorns of the roses carved at his palms but he got three of them out before Dad and Mom both came out of the house and struggled to hold him. He kicked and flailed with his arms, not caring how they cried out in pain at the blows that landed, until finally he lay facedown in the grass, his arms held behind him, the weight of his father's body on him. Mom was weeping frantically, Dad was panting with the exertion.

"You've got no right to destroy things like this," Dad began.

You've got no right to kill Lizzy.

"It's time for us to move on and live. Including you, Quentin. We asked you not to swallow yourself up in Lizzy's life. We hinted, we begged, we ordered. You don't have any friends, you don't do anything but sit in that room and read the same books over and over again."

Her books. Her voice reading to me.

"And it's going to stop. We can't let you live in this . . . haze, it's not right, it's going to *stop*—"

At that moment, when he said the word *stop,* Dad's voice changed, just a little; an undercurrent of uncontrollable fury rose to the surface and, as had happened only a few times in Quentin's life, he was actually afraid of his father, of what this rage might do now that it was in control.

And, just like those other times, Mom immediately picked up on the change in Dad and suddenly her tears stopped and she began to talk calmly, rationally. Soothingly. "We've already lost one child, Quen. Don't make us lose the other."

Immediately the rage receded and Dad's voice also calmed. "I don't know what the garden has to do with this anyway. Or the fridge."

Now Mom became downright intellectual about it. "They're our things, dear. We took away his world, so he's going to take away ours. Metaphorically speaking."

"Well, whatever the official psychological terms might be, it's pretty damn childish."

"Yes, and he's a child."

The crisis was over. The well-worn script had been acted out. Mom weeps; Dad goes into protector mode; his rage frightens her and she begins to talk like a college graduate, which she was and Dad wasn't; and so Dad backs off and hands the authority back to her. Conciliation and analysis are the order of the day. Quentin couldn't have explained the pattern in words, but he knew the flow of it, knew that there would be no serious punishment. Instead Mom and Dad would be careful with him and with each other for several days, tiptoeing through all conversations, sidestepping all conflicts, both of them vaguely ashamed of themselves and afraid of each other and unsure why. In the electric space between them, Quentin would be left alone. He didn't remember learning this pattern. It had always existed, and both he and Lizzy had used it for years, the one scrap of power that children had; but used it rarely, because it was too frightening to realize that Mom and Dad *could* be controlled, or at least gotten around. Sometimes it was better not to get your own way than to face Mom's and Dad's frailty.

"If I let you up, Quen," said Dad, "will you stop this nonsense and go to your room?"

Quentin nodded. The song the junior high choir was learning ran through his mind. Let there be peace on earth, and let it begin with me. Dum, dum, ta-dum, ta-dum.

Dad let go of his arms and rolled off him. Quentin sprang to his feet and walked to the house, to his room. As he passed the open door to Lizzy's room he closed it. He closed the door to his own room, too, and lay down on his bed and faced the wall.

After a while Mom knocked on the door. "Quen, will you be wanting some supper?"

He didn't answer.

"Quen, you have to eat."

He didn't answer.

"Quen, do you really intend to never talk to me again?"

He didn't answer and she went away.

Apparently they decided not to force the issue. He ate nothing that night, but the next morning he got up and had breakfast with Mom before he went to school. He talked to her. Normal stuff. No mention of the events of the day before. It never came up again. The kitchen smelled for a couple of days from the one pickle jar that broke, and then it didn't anymore. Father replaced the dug-up plants and only one of the roses died from the trauma. They turned Lizzy's old room into a combination sewing room and household office. The only hint of the strain between them that remained was that Quentin simply would not go into the room, would not speak to anyone who was in the room, and whenever the door to Lizzy's room was open he would close it as he passed, no matter who was inside, no matter if they asked him not to. Eventually his parents simply gave in and kept it closed all the time, whether they were in there or not; and if they wanted to talk to him, they got up and left the room and closed the door behind them. It was a small accommodation, really, considering. His one tiny act of permanent revenge for their having stolen Lizzy's voice from him.

Slowly, over the months and years, one by one Quentin found copies of the exact paperback edition of each of those books Lizzy had owned. He bought them and kept them in boxes in his closet, until he had replaced them all. If his parents knew about it, they said nothing. After all, his grades were high, he wasn't getting into drugs or booze or smoking like the bad kids at junior high and high school. The psychologist that they talked to told them that, while it would be nice if he could speak with Quentin and make sure, nevertheless it seemed that the boy had dealt with the loss of his sister rather well. Considering.

Eventually all the people who had gotten parts of Lizzy's body died. Eventually everybody dies. Quentin became quite philosophical about it. Everybody dies. What matters is what you do between now and when it happens to you. It was especially important to Quentin, because he was living for two.

2
Groceries

Junior high, high school. Quentin's days were full and then were forgotten, or at least not much thought about. There were friends. There was laughter. The wild kids held no attraction for him; the rich kids wouldn't have him because he wouldn't suck up; so he drifted in among the smart kids, the play-by-the-rules kids. Quentin soon became the witty one in his circle, the one who didn't say much but always had the deft put-down, the bon mot, the new catchphrase. Perhaps it was all the dialogue stored up inside him from Lizzy's books. He became both desirable and dangerous to have as a friend. No matter how close you thought you were to him, no matter how often you had laughed with him, he could still turn around and sting you, and you had to smile and take it. So he had friends, yes, but they were always held one barb away.

He finished high school with awards in Spanish and math in the final assembly of his senior year. Grades that brought him just under salutatorian. He was passed over in the official "most likely to" balloting, but in the unofficial ballot in homeroom class he was voted "most likely to be the guy your mom wishes you were dating" and "most likely to own the company you end up working for when your first-choice career falls through." Liked, even admired a little by his fellow students, though never fully trusted. They knew without knowing it that he didn't belong to them.

Funny, though, their voting him the guy that moms wanted their daughters to date. Because he didn't really date anybody. He didn't even do the tuxedo proms, except the preference dances, when he was asked each year by a sweet and only vaguely unattractive intellectual girl. He said yes each time and rented the tux and bought the corsage and then never asked her out afterward, which probably hurt her feelings but he just wasn't interested in pursuing anything. Four dates in four years. Not much of a record. If his parents worried they didn't say anything.

He certainly didn't worry. He wasn't blind—he knew which girls were attractive. He had his share of interesting dreams and pleasant fantasies. But when it came to thinking of maybe asking a girl out, he'd start watching her a little bit in class or between classes or at lunch or wherever, and pretty soon she'd say something or do something that was . . . wrong. She didn't measure up. To what, he couldn't really say.

Maybe it was like Lizzy had said when boys started asking her out. "Why waste time with a guy when I know there's no point?" Mom used to say, "But he's a perfectly nice boy, why not go and just see the movie? Eat the pizza." And Lizzy would roll her eyes and say, "Mom, please, are you really saying I should let them spend money on me when I know I'm just leading them on?" and then the two of them would burst out laughing and Quentin would sit there unnoticed at the kitchen table or in the living room or wherever he was and he'd think, What is this thing between women, like men are a joke that women all told each other long ago but men never get it.

Only maybe now he *did* get it. The joke wasn't men, the joke was people who didn't know what they wanted to give or to get and so kept disappointing and being disappointed.

Quentin didn't know what he wanted, but he did know what he didn't want. What he didn't want was any of the girls at school. He had lots of friends who were girls. He liked them. Nice girls. Just not for him.

And not for him were the girls at Berkeley, either, as he majored in Spanish and then math and then history, grinding away and getting good grades so that even with all the changes in major he graduated right on time and hadn't had more than ten dates in all four years of college. The first couple of years Mom and Dad didn't say anything, but by his junior year Mom had begun asking in every phone call and every visit home to Santa Clara, "Have you been meeting any nice girls? Are there any nice girls in any of your classes?" And there was that one excruciating conversation with Dad in the garage helping him mix the paint for the wood trim around the doors and windows, when Dad's weird questions finally coalesced enough for Quentin to blush furiously and reassure him that yes, Quentin liked girls and not boys, he simply hadn't found the right girl yet but he was looking and don't worry, Dad, when I do bring somebody home she'll wear a dress and she'll have two X chromosomes, now can we please just paint the trim?

He graduated with a double major in Spanish and history and promptly got a job back home in Santa Clara with a company that was actually trying to sell computers for people to use at home or in small businesses. He came into the company because a friend from high school got a job there and thought maybe he could be an adviser on a home history program they were developing, but in no time Quentin fell in love with programming and discovered he had a real knack for it. By the end of the year he had sold out his stock in the hardware company and jumped to a software house that was developing a word processor for the new IBM PCs. A year later that company was bought by an even bigger company that made operating systems and programming languages and spreadsheets and word processors and pretty soon he had risen high enough in the hierarchy for them to move him to Washington State where he officially lived on a rented houseboat but actually slept most nights in his office because he was indispensable to several major projects. He had nothing to spend money on, and so he poured it all into buying stock in his own company as it increased a hundredfold in value, and then doubled and doubled and doubled until anybody who had started working for them in the seventies was a millionaire many times over, and Quentin richer than most.

One day in 1987 he realized that he wasn't interested in programming anymore. Yesterday it was still a challenge. Today it wasn't. Nor did he care about business or marketing or even the people he worked with. They had all changed, the job had changed, the company had changed. It wasn't any fun and if he just sold his stock he'd never have to work another day in his life. When you win the lottery, do you go back to sweeping the supermarket aisles? That's all his job had become to him.

He cashed out all but about ten percent of his stock and there he was at age twenty-six with twelve and a half million dollars. Fifty software and hardware companies offered him ludicrously high salaries that no one could ever really earn, and he turned them all down. So there he was with a rented houseboat, no career, and, to put it candidly, no life. It was as if he had been running a long, long race and finally realized that there was nobody else in it with him, he had crossed the finish line years ago and didn't notice it because not a soul was there to cheer for him and clap him on the back and say, "Good run, Quen! Good run!"

Or, come to think of it, maybe they *were* there, only Quentin himself didn't care what they thought of him and so he sloughed off their praise and their friendship because he was still waiting for the one voice he'd never hear again.

What do you do with 12.5 million bucks? Quentin put most of it into safe stocks and bonds, a nest egg which he never touched except to move from one safe investment to another. In his worst year, the recession of '91, he still made a million in interest, dividends, and capital gains. He paid off his parents' house and bought them a nice car and then couldn't think of anything else to do with his money. Even renting a very nice apartment, he still needed only about fifty thou a year to live on, which included a car of his own (nothing outrageous, just a Nissan Maxima). He traveled a little at first, until he found out that hotels in Cancún and Paris and Hong Kong were pretty much alike. So there he was with a lot of money coming in and it seemed completely pointless just to plow it back into more investments and make more money that he had no particular need for. Besides, after you've churned your own portfolio until even your broker is telling you enough already, what is there to do with the rest of the day, the rest of the week, the month, the year?

Home for Thanksgiving in '92, after Dad had finished railing about the election of Bill Clinton, the conversation took kind of a serious turn. Quentin just sat there staring into the fire and in the silence Mom said, "Quentin, did it all happen too easily for you?"

At once Dad leapt to the defense of capitalism and explained again why it was that Quentin had worked hard and guessed right and the free market had rewarded him, quite properly, with wealth which really wasn't extravagant, not by the standard of Ross Perot or Bill Gates, anyway.

But then Dad ran out of steam and there was a silence again, and some more wordless fire-staring, until again Mom spoke up. "If you don't have any dreams of your own, Quentin, why don't you borrow somebody else's?"

Dad snorted. "Dreams." But of course he had always been the dreamer of the family, and as Quentin thought about it he realized that when he got so extravagantly wealthy he had really been fulfilling his father's dream. A few years' work in a job he enjoyed, and he had snapped that tight wire inside Dad's heart and the old man was

19

happy now, at ease. The system had worked for his son, and that was almost better, in Dad's eyes, than if he had earned all that money himself.

The next Monday, Quentin turned over a few hundred thousand dollars of his portfolio to his father to manage for him, of which his father would keep half as his commission. But that was only the beginning of his response to his mother's remark. There were other people with dreams who needed only a few thousand or a few hundred thousand dollars to have a shot at making them come true. It was something to do with his excess money.

He ran an ad for one week in the *San Jose Mercury News*: Small investor looking for hardworking partner with good ideas. He was flooded with letters. From among those not written in crayon he chose a few dozen that seemed worth looking into. Quentin ended up forming fourteen partnerships, in which he supplied all the capital and the salary of an accountant who reported to him; Quentin himself remained benignly silent until it was time to either fold a failing business or offer to let a successful partner buy him out. The picture was usually pretty clear within a year. More than half of the businesses did well, and some made serious money. Two of them went public and Quentin's gain on each of them more than repaid his entire investment in all fourteen partnerships.

It had been the best year of his life. He could share in the happiness of the successful partners, and as for the ones who failed, they might be disappointed but they knew that at least they had given it a good shot. And since Quentin covered all the partnerships' debts and losses, they all walked away clean. Nobody lost. Some good things were accomplished.

But why limit his new project to the south bay? Quentin began traveling again, renting an apartment in a metro area, putting an ad in the local paper, sorting through the responses, forming the partnerships. It took a few months to get things under way; then he'd move on, keeping the apartment for another year or two so he'd have a place to stay when he came back for follow-up visits. He didn't quite choose each new destination by closing his eyes and stabbing at a map with a pushpin, but his method wasn't much more scientific—he'd look through the travel section of some bookstore and go wherever a picture intrigued him. There was nothing predictable about it. His stay in Vermont wasn't in beautiful Montpelier, it was in bleak and dirty Burlington; but when he went to Texas he skipped the bustling cities and drove east from Dallas into the lush savannah country until he came to Nacogdoches and thought, for a while, he might have found his home for life.

But a few months later he was on his way again. Durango, Missoula, Kennewick, Seneca. Asheboro, Mandeville, Oakland, the Bronx. There was no shortage of dreamers, no shortage of interesting dreams. Dayton, Concord, Grand Junction, Grand Island. Flagstaff, Johnstown, Boise, Savannah.

Spring of 1995. Herndon, Virginia. The weather was finally warm and Quentin had just placed his ad, not in the *Washington Post* but in the local shopper. So it would be a few days before it came out and he had time to kill. He went to Worldgate and saw a Wednesday afternoon showing of some movie about the Ebola virus starring Dustin Hoffman as the hero who somehow finds a way to synthesize a serum that can be manufactured so quickly it can cure people with advanced cases of the disease. He came out of the movie wondering why he was so upset. There had always been stupid movies. Why should this one bother him so much?

He stopped at the frozen yogurt shop at Worldgate but the place had been taken over by extraordinarily smelly gourmet coffees, which meant that all the yogurt would be mocha no matter what flavor it was supposed to be. Why did such a minor annoyance make him want to yell at somebody about how you don't put something with a dominant smell into a shop that depends on having a variety of different flavors? It was absurd. It didn't matter. But when he got to his car he slapped the roof so hard his hand stung and for just a moment he felt a little better.

Maybe my life isn't so great after all, he thought as he drove up Elden Street to the Giant food store. It was just before five. The local rush hour wasn't too bad, and the DC commuter wave wouldn't hit for another half hour. Maybe I'm already getting tired of living on borrowed dreams. But if I stop doing this, what will I do next? And how long will the next career last?

Meat pies, apricot nectar, and Teddy Grahams pretty much accounted for his diet these days. He contemplated buying stock in Marie Callendar's, Libby's, or Nabisco, but decided that when it came to food he'd rather be a consumer than an investor. He wondered what the markup must be to allow Giant to accept American Express, or did the food store maybe have some sweetheart deal with Amex so the rakeoff wasn't as steep as it was for everybody else? And then he thought, Is my life so empty that this is the best thing I can think of to think about?

Think of a thing to think about. It became his mantra as he pulled meat pies out of the freezer compartment.

And then a whiny child's voice pierced the nonsense in his mind.

"If you were ever *home* you'd know that I eat healthy things all the time and all I'm asking for is some *real* ice cream instead of that fakey stuff."

It was a girl, maybe ten or twelve, blond hair done up in that smooth too-sophisticated way that always made Quentin vaguely sad, as if somebody was letting the kid throw away her childhood.

Only this one was obviously a real harpie. A pouty face, a voice too loud, and the parents all aflutter trying to placate her. "We just want you to be happy, dear," said the mother.

"You told us to help you watch your waistline," said the father.

Could these people *hear* themselves? They sounded like some movie star's toadies.

"Well I didn't mean *ice* cream, did I?" said the girl, as if her parents were the stupidest people who had ever lived.

"I don't think there's anything wrong with a little Ben and Jerry's, do you dear?" said the mother. "It doesn't have as much fat as the Häagen-Dazs, does it?"

"Whatever," said the father. He, at least, seemed to understand what a monster this child had become. How weak they seemed, to let her manipulate them like this.

All at once a memory flooded back—lying in the grass, Dad's body pressing down on his. Dad getting angry, and Mom suddenly being conciliatory, and Quentin getting away with something. Just as he had done a dozen times before.

So what? So all children are manipulators—at least he had always had the decency not to humiliate his parents in public like this little dipwhistle.

Of course that could also be taken to mean that he was a hypocrite while this little girl was simply open about what all children try to do and all but a few parents are too weak to stop them from doing.

Thank heaven I never married or had kids, thought Quentin. Who needs to get into a lifelong power struggle with your own kids?

He had all the pies he needed for a couple of weeks—all that the freezer in his rented townhouse would hold. He wheeled the cart down the aisle past the girl and her tame parents. He made a point of not looking at them—why not let them pretend that nobody noticed their humiliation? But he couldn't resist a long hard glare of contempt at the girl.

She met his gaze with a saucy look; but there was a twinkle in her eyes that surprised him. Could it be irony? Could it be that she knows exactly how bratty she seems?

Well what if she does? Knowing you're a jerk doesn't mean you're any less a jerk; probably the opposite. Lizzy never looked like that. She had too much pride to act like

23

this girl, or look like her, or talk like her. This girl was alive and Lizzy was dead and all of a sudden it rolled over him how many years of life she had missed and how much better she would have lived those years than this snotty little girl. Better than Quentin, too. She wouldn't have found herself thirty-four years old and sick of the emptiness of her life. Because her life wouldn't have been empty. She would have loved somebody and married him and had children. And they wouldn't have been children like this, they would have been good kids, decent kids, kids you could be proud of. She would have made her life mean something. While Quentin had—what? Money? And this girl . . . she had that irony in her eyes. Knowledge without wisdom. Power without purpose. Like me.

He stood in the checkout line. The clerk bantered a little with the dressed-for-success woman in front of him. Quentin gazed around the store listlessly, seeing everything, noticing nothing.

Until he saw a woman in the express line, bent over her purse, digging for coins or a pen, and there was something about her, about the way her hair fell, about the slope of her shoulders, the clothes she wore. He knew her, absolutely knew her, only it couldn't be her, but she was so perfectly like his memory of Lizzy that he couldn't breathe. And when she stood straight and handed money to the cashier, she did it with that straight-armed, elbow-locked movement that was Lizzy's own.

"Sir?" said the clerk.

The woman ahead of him was picking up her bags and leaving. Quickly Quentin finished moving everything from his cart to the conveyor belt, glancing up as often as he could to see if he could catch a glimpse of her face. Not that there was any hope that it could be Lizzy, but if this woman really was somehow Lizzy's double, then maybe he could see her face, see what she would have looked like grown up, only that was crazy, all he would see was that it *wasn't* Lizzy, and it would hurt him all over again that she wasn't there. Already it hurt him. Already something deep and long denied was stirring inside him. The grief that he had never expressed except on one miserable afternoon of throwing jars on the floor and pulling up plants.

She turned around just as he was bending down to get the last of the pies out of the cart. When he looked up again she was almost at the door, but he caught a glimpse of her face and gasped aloud at the face, at the exact, the perfect copy of . . .

"Sir, where are you—"

"Just ring it up, I'll be back in one second—"

But she was gone. Standing there at the railing that kept carts from going out into the parking lot, he scanned for her, for that walk, that hair, that light spring sweater, walking to some car, walking to another store, but she wasn't there. No sign of her.

He pressed his hands to his face. The woman couldn't have looked that much like her, it was just his mind playing tricks on him. He returned to the store, to a clerk who was looking annoyed, to a line of shoppers—refugees from the DC rush hour now—who seemed about one step from a lynch mob. He swiped his card through the machine, signed the slip, gathered up his frozen food and headed for his car.

The one thing I can't have in all this world is Lizzy. But she's what I've wanted, all day, all month, all these years. Coming out of that bad movie today I wanted to jammer to her about how stupid the science in it was, how pathetic it was to see Dustin Hoffman in a role so dumb, a Stallone castoff. She would have laughed and quoted some line from *The Graduate,* which of course she had snuck off to see even though Mom and Dad declared it a dirty movie and off limits. "It wasn't dirty to *me,*" she said. "I just came home and proved that it takes bigger boobs than these to do that tassel thing." And the yogurt place, it was Lizzy he wanted to tell his diatribe to. And in the store, he needed Lizzy beside him

25

so they could laugh about that bratty little girl and then hatch some bizzarre plot to kidnap her and then see how low the ransom would have to go before her parents would finally pay it and take her back.

But I can't have Lizzy.

And as he plunged his car out into the heavy traffic of Elden Street, it occurred to him for the first time that even if Lizzy hadn't died, he couldn't have had her with him at age thirty-four in Herndon, Virginia, in the spring of 1995, because she would have been thirty-nine years old and undoubtedly married and probably she would have had a couple of kids in high school by then and a husband who adored her because she wouldn't marry anybody stupid enough *not* to adore her and *he* would have been the one talking to her and listening to her and sharing jokes with her and inflicting his diatribes on her. Not me.

If she had lived, she would have gone away to college before he even got to high school. The closeness between them would have faded. He would have grieved a little, maybe, but he would have turned to his friends then, the way other people did. He wouldn't have kept comparing every girl he knew to his perfect image of Lizzy because Lizzy would still be home for holidays and he wouldn't be so needy for her; some other girl's fresh and un-Lizzyish style or look or attitude would have intrigued him instead of putting him off. He would have fallen in love the normal dozen or so times and right now if he had these millions of dollars he wouldn't be wandering North America borrowing other people's dreams, he'd be at home, and everything he did and made and built and won would have been for his wife, his children, their future. Together they would have invented dreams of their own, dreams to spare, enough dreams that they could freely share them with strangers instead of his having to go shopping for them.

Grownup men don't share their lives with their sisters, they share them with their wives.

He felt sick with the sense of loss. What have I been doing all these years? How stupid can a reasonably bright guy be?

The realization struck him so hard that he had to pull off the Herndon Parkway into a condo parking lot and rest his head against the steering wheel and what was he doing? Why was he crying like some ten-year-old kid? It wasn't Lizzy he was grieving for after all. It was himself. It was his own lost years.

It was Lizzy whose organs they harvested, not mine. So why have I made myself as solitary as the dead?

Finally he got control of himself, pulled a Kleenex from the box he kept on the perpetually empty passenger seat, dried his eyes, wiped his glasses, put them on again, and leaned back to look at the bright evening all around him. Cars pulling into the parking lot. People getting out and going into their condos, where some of them lived alone and some of them had roommates and some of them had a wife or husband and some of them had kids and every damned one of them had more sense than Quentin Fears had.

There she was, climbing up the stairs to the end townhouse of the building right next to him. He could see her face clearly as she dug in her purse for her keys. No, she didn't look like Lizzy after all, not really, not as much as he had thought in the store. But her movement *was* the same, or very similar; he hadn't imagined *that*. And her hair, it was almost like Lizzy's, wasn't it? When Lizzy had worn it that way, or almost that way? Long, anyway.

Not Lizzy at all, really. But—and here's the thing that surprised him—she was still attractive. Still interesting. The way she stopped searching, stood up straight, rolled her eyes heavenward in exasperation, and then made one final dive of the hand into the purse, to have it emerge a moment later, clutching the keys on a big brass ring. How could she have missed something that size in her purse? She slipped it into the lock, went inside, and closed the door behind her. Lights went on. She was home.

But I'm not home. Not here, not anywhere.

More than anything else Quentin wanted to get out of his car and walk up to that door, knock on it, smile sheepishly when she opened the door and . . .

And what? Lie? I'm sorry, I seem to have locked my keys in my car, can I use your phone to call triple-A? Beg your pardon, but I noticed you in the grocery store and you look so much like my dead sister that I really want to spend some time with you, thinking about her and crying—do you have a few evenings free?

She probably had a husband in there waiting for her, or coming home soon afterward. But as he sat in the parking lot, nobody else walked up the front steps. There was no husband. Somehow there was no husband. And the certainty grew: I should be the one to walk those stairs, to open that door, to laughingly call out, "Hi, honey, I'm home." To tease her about a purse so cluttered she couldn't even find a two-pound eight-inch brass ring of keys.

Hello, I'm a multimillionaire who is pathologically lonely and so filled with pent-up longings that you have only to think of a desire and I'll satisfy it. Mind if I come in?

He restarted his engine and drove away. It was dark. He had sat there for nearly three hours. When he got back to his apartment the meat pies weren't even cold, let alone frozen. He spent a half hour slopping them out of their pieplates and grinding them down the disposal. Then he went to the Rio Grande and over a plate of pork tamales and a bottle of sangria-flavor Peñafiel at the bar he plotted how to find out who she was and, more to the point, how to arrange to meet her before the end of the week.

3
In the Garden

The first thing Quentin's lawyer found out about her was that she didn't own the townhouse—a property-management firm was renting it out for an investment group in Atlanta that owned twenty condos in the complex. So she was renting.

Only she wasn't. The condo was empty.

Then did she work for the property management company? Nobody from the firm had visited the property except the yard guys, and they had no employee who fit her description particularly well anyway.

A previous renter? A relative of a previous renter? An ex-spouse or former lover of a previous renter? A roommate or subletter of a previous renter?

The condos were fairly new. There had been only one renter before, a Pakistani family of four who had been waiting for their house to be built out in Oak Park. No roommates, no sublets, no ex-spouses or former lovers, and even if one of their relatives had looked like her, they'd never given anyone a key because the wife was home all day so who locked the doors?

The research had cost him about a thousand dollars in lawyer and private investigator fees and the result was zilch.

She didn't exist. No woman could possibly have walked up to that door and turned a key in the lock and gone inside. He didn't see it, it didn't happen.

He sat in the parking lot for half an hour on Saturday, trying to figure out how he could have been wrong. And came at last to the obvious conclusion—he was one seriously lonely man. Conjuring hallucinatory images of a woman very much like his dead sister, just so he could imagine meeting her and talking to her and having somebody to build a life with. It was definitely time to start dating.

The trouble was he had no idea how to go about it. He'd been a witness of the singles scene at restaurant-bars like Rio Grande and Lone Star and T.G.I.Friday's, and it always looked so pathetic to him. Come here often? You look *good* and I haven't even had a drink yet. Buy you a drink? Want to help me celebrate my promotion? I hope you just broke up with your boyfriend so I don't have to kill him. Did any of these lines actually work? And even if they did, what came of it? One-night stands? Quick torrid affairs? Did any of these deliberate encounters lead to something that cured loneliness instead of simply easing the symptoms for an hour or two? Quentin wasn't interested in meeting the kind of woman who would come to one of those places looking for the kind of man who hoped to meet women there.

But this was the DC area, wasn't it? There were serious parties going on every night; Quentin knew it because some of his new business partners moved in those circles—the guy who was trying to start up a serious fund-raising business, for instance. The lobbyist who was trying to get out of the lobbying business and into publishing. They had both invited Quentin to the kind of party where congressmen and generals and admirals and undersecretaries showed up. He had turned them down as he always did.

He drove home and called them both. Two parties on the same night, one in Georgetown at a second-tier embassy and one in Chevy Chase at the home of a once-famous hostess.

"These are people on the make, Quentin," said the lobbyist. "They're going to figure out fast that you aren't power, so you must be money. I hope you won't mind that."

"Are you saying they're *all* cynically looking for people to exploit?"

"All the eager-looking ones are. If they're really vivacious or fervent or, you know, *on*—they're trying to get something out of the night. So if you want pleasant company, just look for somebody who's bored but not drunk and you'll probably do OK. Of course, that's usually a description of somebody's spouse who isn't, you know, inside the beltway. So they're probably not just bored but boring. And devotedly married."

"I just want to see what these parties are like. Tell me what to wear."

The first party was cocktails before dinner; the would-be fundraiser didn't have the clout to get him a seat at the table, but that was fine with Quentin, he had the other party to go to. The first one was a bust—everybody was on the make or, worse, on the way down and desperately clinging to prestige. Quentin kept count of the snubs he got until he ran out of fingers and then he concentrated on eating the really fine hors d'oeuvres and avoiding the cocktail pushers.

The second party was much nicer. The hostess hadn't really faded, Quentin quickly concluded. It was Washington that had faded; she had an elegance that felt pre-war. Not World War II, either. More like World War I. Could that graceful era possibly have survived in this house? The age when undersecretaries were all men of good families with old money, serving their country as a civic duty and not as a rung on the ladder? That's how it felt, for the first hour at least. But then he began to see that his lobbyist partner had been right. Even in this old-fashioned gathering, there were those who tried just a little too hard and those who remained just a little bit too aloof. It was as much about status as the other party had been, except, of course, that the other one was more nakedly obvious about it.

31

I might have been like these people, Quentin thought. If I hadn't just stumbled into money by being a pretty good programmer at exactly the right time for that to bring millions of dollars down on the heads of unsuspecting geeks. I might have been on the outside looking in; at the bottom looking up. Now I'm on the outside, all right, but above, looking down. I don't need anything these people have to offer. What I need, they don't even care about. Some of them probably even have it, and are wasting it, losing it—an adoring wife or a husband who gets taken for granted, ignored, hurt, left behind on the upward climb. He spotted a couple of these—women who were clearly uncomfortable in their designerish or designeresque dresses, women who belonged at a PTA social like Quentin's mom, bringing cookies to the bake sale. There was nothing for them here. Not even their husbands. Their husbands were here, yes, but not for them.

There was a high-ceilinged library with a ladder that rolled around the walls hanging from a rail. Quentin had seen such places in movies and the urge to climb the ladder was irresistible. He pulled out a book at random from the topmost shelf.

"All right, you can borrow that one, but don't lose my place."

Quentin turned to see who had produced that strong but aging woman's voice and nearly lost his footing.

"Oh, don't fall, please, the family fortune couldn't stand another lawsuit. That's why I gave up gossip."

It was the hostess. Quentin put the book back and climbed down. "I didn't mean to meddle," he said. "I've just never climbed a library ladder before."

"And I'm too old to do it anymore," she said. "That's why I have my assistant put all the mystery novels up there, so I won't forget and read them a second time by accident and then get disappointed when I realize that it's only *that* one again. Except that it happens anyway, even with the brand new ones. I've read them all. Seen them all. Met them all.

Served expensive alcohol to everybody, and they all look the same."

"How many times have you met *me*?" asked Quentin. As always, he found himself sliding into the style of conversation that seemed appropriate. Polite, self-deprecating wit, that's what was called for, thrust and riposte but no one ever bloodied. He didn't analyze it, he just slipped into the role.

"Let's see," she said. "Lonely, bored, hoping to connect with somebody but unwilling to believe that you're actually good enough for anybody."

"Oh, I'm good enough," said Quentin. "Male, mid-thirties, no pot belly, all my hair, good teeth, and money."

"But you don't want the kind of woman who keeps that list, am I right?"

"So I guess you're the one I'm looking for."

"Me? Don't be silly. I married my husband for money and I've done rather well at hanging on to it in spite of taxes, recessions, inflation, and those people who make you look at pictures of starving children before they let you say no to their charity."

"Did he know? That you married him for money?"

"My dear, in those days it didn't occur to decent people to marry for any other reason. My family was old money and his was newer. Mine had more prestige and his had more zeroes after the two and the four. His mother traded on the connection to get a better grade of guest at her parties, and I was able to help my sisters live in the style to which they were accustomed until they married even richer men than my Jay. Everybody won."

He hadn't realized that there were still people who lived in such a Jane Austen world. "Did you love him?"

"Jay? I thought not until he had an affair with a secretary during the war, and then I was insanely jealous for a while and I thought that meant I loved him. Later his libido calmed down and we gardened together for a few years before he got Alzheimer's at sixty and faded away and died.

Those few years in the garden, I think I did love him then. That's really above average, in my experience. Not everybody gets those years in the garden."

"I don't even have the garden."

"Neither did we, till we planted it together." She smiled, but he could sense that the intimate moment was over. She was ready to move on. So he made it easy for her.

"I'm feeling guilty. I'm monopolizing the hostess."

She studied him for a moment, as if passing a verdict on him. "There's a clever young woman out on the back porch, admiring a gnarled cherry tree that hasn't borne fruit in years but I keep it because my Jay and I planted it together and he kissed me there. It's a magical spot, and I've been prowling the party looking for someone to send there to join her."

"I've kept you talking so long, I doubt she's still there."

"Oh, I told her if she stirred from that spot before you got there, I'd never let her back in my house."

"You told her you were sending me? But you don't even know me."

"I told her I was sending a young man I wanted her to be nice to for my sake because he was so lonely at this party."

"Was I *that* obvious?"

"No. There's always a lonely young man at my parties. It's in the nature of young men to be lonely. Did you think you were unique?"

"So you're a matchmaker."

She turned and headed for the door, slow of step but making rapid progress all the same. "I have a garden that doesn't get used enough, that's all. Think of yourself as plant food." And then she was gone, back to the party.

The young woman was in the garden, just as the hostess had promised. For a moment, seeing her from behind, he thought he knew her. He even thought, madly enough, that it was *her,* the one he had seen in the grocery store and then at the door of the townhouse. But then she turned and her hair was reddish and her face was really nothing like Lizzy's or even the other woman's, but she seemed nice enough. Bored, but nice.

"So you're the lonely young man?" asked the woman.

"And you're one who's supposed to cheer me up?" asked Quentin.

"She's such a matchmaker. She forgets things though. Such as, this is the third time she's sent me to wait under the cherry tree."

"I take it the previous times didn't work out?"

"One of them did. I didn't find true love, but I did find a candidate for Congress from a Philadelphia suburb."

"Is that where you're from?"

"No, it's where *he* was from. I'm a headhunter, Mr. . . ."

"Fears."

"Oh, you sound dangerous. Or at least hostile."

"Yes, it sounds like 'fierce,' but it's spelled *F-E-A-R-S*."

"What an interesting contradiction," she said. "Written down, you're timid; spoken, you're dangerous."

"Unfortunately, I'm not a candidate for anything."

"Neither am I," she said. "I'm not working tonight. I'm really here for old time's sake. I love the grande dame, *and* her garden, *and* her matchmaking. I had to come to one more of her parties before I leave."

"The beltway has lost its charms?"

"I suppose," she said. "Both parties are simply too ideological for me anymore. They insist on nominating horrible people because they have the correct opinions on the key issues. They don't want the kind of candidate I like to find."

"And that is?"

"Well-balanced. Open-minded. Ambitious but principled. Reasonable. Telegenic and electable but also hardworking and bright and honest enough that I'm proud to have helped them get started."

"This really was a career? Finding candidates?"

"I always think the best people for public office are the

ones who really never thought of themselves in public office. Somebody has to put the bee in their bonnet."

"So what will you do now?"

"To be honest? I haven't a clue."

"But with all the candidates you found, surely there's one who can help you land in a career—"

"To be honest, Mr. Fears, the only candidate I ever found was the one I met here under this cherry tree, and he quit after one term. It wasn't really my career because nobody paid me for it. It was my . . . vocation."

"What's your career?"

"Middle level bureaucrat. But I have this face and I look good in evening attire and I got invited to parties by bosses who needed a partner for an out-of-town visitor—all legitimate, I assure you. I kept my eyes open, hoping to find the candidate for office that I could vote for with a clean conscience. My dream was to find a president."

"And now you've given up?"

"The parties are controlled by screamers from the left and the right. There's no room for my dreams in this town." She shivered, though the night was merely cool, not chilly. "I can't believe I'm telling you all this. I don't tell this to people. I guess you're hearing my swan song."

"I'm kind of curious why you have these dreams of politics in the first place."

She looked at him with a kind of fierceness in her eyes and took hold of his arm tightly. "Because I love power, Mr. Fears. Power used wisely and well, power used to make people safer and freer and happier. But it's power that I love, even though one is supposed to pretend that it isn't. As if anyone would ever come to this benighted town for any other reason."

"So why don't *you* run for office?" asked Quentin.

She smiled. "Voters don't take pretty women seriously."

Quentin almost said, You're not *that* pretty.

She laughed as if she had heard him. "I'm telegenic. The camera loves me. You should see my driver's license. My yearbook picture. I swear I can't take a bad picture. It's a curse. I'm much less attractive in person."

Quentin laughed and felt something inside him relax for the first time in twenty years. Something that he hadn't even known was clenched. "Well darn," he said. "I wish I'd seen your picture before I met you."

"No, it's better this way. You would have felt too intimidated."

"Now I've got to see your license, you know."

She shrugged, opened her little evening purse, and took out the plastic card. He looked at it, angling it to get moonlight on the picture. "Am I correct in thinking that you actually crossed your eyes for your driver's license picture?"

"I stuck out my tongue the first time but they made me take it over again. They were very angry."

"This may be the ugliest driver's license photo I've ever seen."

"Do you think so?" she said. "Have you seen a lot of them, or are you just saying that?"

"What did you do in your high school yearbook, put your finger in your nose?"

"I had friends on the yearbook staff. They managed to sneak in a picture of the back of my head. Just my hair in curlers and the back of my neck. They got in *so* much trouble till my parents finally believed me that it was all my idea."

Her name, according to the license, was Madeleine Cryer.

"Ms. Cryer," he said, meaning to ask if he could see her again.

"Call me Madeleine, please."

"Then you have to call me Quentin."

"Is that your name?"

"Yes."

"But how unbearable. That's a terrible name for someone when you're already going to be stuck with a weird last name. Didn't your parents love you? Didn't you get beaten up in school a lot?"

"Everybody called me Quen."

"Quentin. Isn't that a prison?"

"Somebody actually asked me recently if I was named after the guy who did *Pulp Fiction*. Even though I must be fifteen years older than he is."

"I have to call you something else. Tin. I have to call you Tin."

Lizzy's old nickname for him. It hit him so hard that he caught his breath.

"Don't be mad at me," she said. "I shouldn't have teased about your name."

"I'm not mad," he said. And then laughed. "Actually, *you're* Mad."

She got the pun at once and winced. "I guess if I can call you Tin, you can call me Mad." She raised an eyebrow. "I *can* call you Tin?"

"Only if you'll have dinner with me. Monday?"

"I was going to fly back home tomorrow."

"Where's home?" he asked.

"The old family manse is way up the Hudson. I usually fly to Newark. I've already sent home most of my stuff. Not that I had much. I travel light, I live light."

"Upriver on the Hudson. I don't know any good restaurants there. So you'll have to pick."

"Oh, don't be absurd. You wouldn't fly to New York just to have dinner with me."

"Oh, is that excessive?"

She studied his face for a moment, perhaps trying to find the irony in his words. "You're really sweet."

"My homeroom class voted me the most likely to be the guy your mom wishes you were dating."

"I think you might just be the one my mother would like me to date. My grandmother won't agree, of course, but who cares about her?"

"Let me meet your grandmother and I promise, I'll win her over."

She smiled vaguely and looked away. "Maybe I won't go yet."

"But if you've shipped all your things home . . . "

"As I said. I travel light. Where are you taking me to dinner?"

"I'm new around here. I've been living in Herndon. You tell me."

"What's your budget? Because you *are* paying, you know."

"I can eke out at least one good dinner at a really nice place."

"I don't even know what you do for a living."

"I'm between jobs, but I have a little saved up from my last one."

"If you're serious about a really nice place, there's a French restaurant near Herndon. Some-French-word Chez François. Close to the Potomac. I've never eaten there, but I hear it's good. The kind of place where they scrape the crumbs off your table between courses."

"Wow," said Quentin. "Is that class or what."

"Give me your number, I'll call you when I get the reservation."

"I can take care of that, you know," said Quentin, writing his local number on his business card.

"But I'm not going to give you *my* number, and then what would you do with the reservation?"

"Take your grandmother." He handed her the card.

"I don't have a phone number and I'm not sure which friend I'll crash with when I don't take my flight tomorrow. So I'm not being unfriendly. I *will* call."

"I've heard that line before."

"No you haven't," said Mad. "That's the guy's line, so I know you haven't heard it, and I don't think you've even said it."

"Am I so obviously naive?"

She touched his cheek lightly. "I think you're sweet."

"But not powerful."

"I told you—power was my dream. You're real."

She turned and walked away from him.

"Can't I take you home? Take you wherever you're crashing tonight?"

But she kept walking as if she hadn't heard him. He took a few steps after her, then thought better of following her, then thought again and followed her anyway, only she had already made her way through the crowd and she wasn't anywhere in the house, top to bottom.

Of course she wasn't going to call, he knew that. But still, it had been a wonderful half hour there by the ancient unblooming cherry tree. She might not have looked like Lizzy, the way his hallucination did, but she bantered with him in the same easygoing playful way that Lizzy always had. It was the first time he had actually enjoyed the company of a woman as a woman. It was *possible.* That's what this evening meant. There was hope for him to find someone. There really were interesting women out there and there were even some who might find him interesting, not for his money, but for his conversation, his company. He refused to be disappointed that this particular encounter hadn't led anywhere. It was enough that Madeleine Cryer had opened a never-opened door.

And then the next day, Sunday afternoon, she did call. They had dinner that night. They met for lunch the next day, a picnic by the Great Falls of the Potomac. They broached the delicate subject of money and each confessed to having some. Her fortune was much older, his was much larger, but it wouldn't be a barrier between them. That afternoon he bought them both English racers and the next morning they rode the whole length of the W&OD bike trail from Purcellville to Mount Vernon and at the end, with rubbery legs and covered in sweat, he asked her to marry him and she said yes, as long as he promised never to make her ride a bike that far again.

4
Prenuptial Agreement

Everything seemed to be going so well. Yes, he still had a vague worry in the back of his mind about how this all started—hallucinating a grown-up version of his dead sister—but with Madeleine in his life Quentin was beginning to realize how deeply unhappy he had been all these years. It took such small things, just her smile, her hand resting on his, and he would get this glow inside and he'd find himself wearing a goofy grin and nodding at everything she said and he'd realize: This is pretty good! This is what other people have known about all these years and tried to tell me! This is what kept my parents going even when their daughter died, even when their son became this weird wandering recluse, because they had *this* between them, this secret that you can't guess from outside, you have to be inside it, and then it's all so clear, it transforms the world like getting your first pair of glasses and suddenly you can read all the signs and recognize people from far off and pick out individual birds in the sky, that's how it felt and as far as Quentin was concerned, he wouldn't mind a bit if it kept going like this pretty much for the rest of his life.

Then he flew to San Francisco for meetings with some of his older partnerships. At the end of the trip he stopped in to see his lawyer, Wayne Read, to take care of the changes the marriage was going to require, like rewriting his will and changing the beneficiary on his insurance policies.

"Does she have a lawyer?" asked Wayne.

"I don't know."

"Does she have money? An estate?"

"I don't know."

"I need to know if I'm supposed to unilaterally write the prenup or negotiate it with another attorney, and if she has an estate that needs protecting or if it's just yours I need to worry about."

Quentin was annoyed. "I don't want my estate protected. When we're married it'll be *our* estate."

"You've known her what, a week and a half?"

"But I've been waiting for her all my life."

The lawyer just looked at him.

"That was humor," said Quentin.

"No, you meant it," said Wayne. "Listen, Quen, I've been your lawyer ever since you could afford one. I know that you've been miserably lonely that whole time. Now you've fallen in love and you don't want to believe anything bad can happen. But all these years you've been paying me to be the friend who will always tell you the truth. The friend who can give you bad news."

"The friend who charges me three hundred bucks an hour."

"The friend whose job is to know a lot more about how the world works than you do, and keep you from falling into heavy machinery."

"Metaphorically speaking."

"Sometimes people aren't what they seem."

"I know that, Wayne."

"No you don't, Quen. Because you *are* exactly what you seem, and so you always assume that other people are, too."

"I've had partners who cheated me."

"Who *tried* to cheat you. I draw up too good a contract for them to actually succeed."

"They got away with the money."

"Only because you let them. Only because you never let me sue or bring criminal charges."

"It was only money."

"No, *after* they embezzled it from you it was only money. When *you* had it, it was something more than money. It was fertile seed. It was the power of life. In your hands money makes things grow. In their hands it bought new cars and TV sets and some nice dinners out and then it had disappeared and nothing came of it."

"My point is that I don't care enough about money to need a prenuptial agreement. If Madeleine turns out to be a fake or even if the marriage just turns sour or something, don't you think *that* will be much more devastating than losing a few million bucks in a lousy divorce settlement? If I lose the woman I love, who cares about the money?"

"Quentin, you only say that because you've never lost either. Broken hearts heal. But when a fortune is gone, it stays gone forever."

"I'm still employable."

"No you're not, Quen. They're programming Pentiums and PowerPC chips and they're doing it in C. You don't know anything about that."

"She's not going to divorce me and she's not after my money. Can we get to the business I came here for?"

They got down to business and it didn't take long. On the day the marriage became valid, the new will would take effect, and Madeleine would become cobeneficiary of his insurance policies, along with his parents.

Wayne rose from behind his desk. "I'm very happy for you, Quentin. True love is rare."

Quentin stood up and shook his hand. "I hope I'm not being billed for *that* bit of counsel."

Wayne laughed dryly. "Since you're not listening to me anyway, I'll go ahead and ask the really lousy question: Have you got her HIV test results?"

Quentin took back his hand. "Wayne, you deal with my papers, not my sex life."

"Forget the HIV test, then, but at least tell me you've been using protection."

"Wayne, you're way over the line here."

The lawyer offered no hint of apology, just regarded him, waiting for an answer.

"But to ease your mind," Quentin finally said, "Mad and I haven't slept together."

Wayne looked genuinely stunned. "Are you living in a time warp?"

"The sixties never got to my house, and that means the nineties have nothing to scare me with."

"You've never even *tried* to sleep with her?"

"Wayne, you can shut up any time now." Quentin was still smiling, but it was getting thin.

"She's probably wondering by now if you're gay."

Quentin stopped in the doorway and said, "Wayne, you may think of yourself as a paid friend, but I think of you as my lawyer. Everything that happens with my business is your business. But what happens with my pants is between me and my dry cleaner."

"Marriage is a contract, Quentin. And my business is to warn you when you're walking drunk along the edge of a cliff. Congrats on the wedding, though. I'm sure you'll be very happy."

Quentin let the door make just the tiniest slam as he left.

But Wayne had said what he said, and now Quentin couldn't get it out of his mind. These *were* the nineties, after all. He wasn't so disconnected from the world around him that he didn't know how things had changed since he was in high school and the guys he knew had to work themselves up just to hold hands with a girl, let alone kiss her. The whole sexual revolution and then herpes and AIDS, he knew about them. They simply hadn't touched his life because he was one of the good kids who didn't play around. What about Madeleine, though? Somebody like her, it was impossible to think that in the nineties she hadn't had plenty of guys make moves on her. Had she moved back? Somebody on NPR about five years before had said something about how when you slept with somebody, you were also sleeping with everybody they had ever slept with. How many guys had Madeleine slept with? Up till he talked with Wayne Read, he had assumed that Madeleine was a virgin just like he was. When he thought about it, he realized that he had pretty much assumed that all nice women were virgins.

Wayne was right. He *was* in a time warp.

This was absurd. Wasn't the double standard supposed to work the other way? A guy who was all worried about whether his fiancee was a virgin was supposed to be a hypocrite with plenty of notches on his own belt.

And it wasn't just a question of past partners and sexually transmitted disease. Quentin was hopelessly naive. There were magazine articles at every grocery checkstand talking about techniques for satisfying a woman every time, but Quentin hadn't read any of them. Was Mad expecting him to know all these techniques? Did they even work? Was it hard to learn them? How romantic would it be on their wedding night if he had to keep stopping to check with a manual?

He had a couple of hours to kill before his flight. Instead of turning in his rental car he kept going down Bayshore and got off the freeway at the Hillsdale Mall, planning to pick up a book on how to be a good lover—he knew that no self-respecting American bookstore would be without a few of those. But to his chagrin Hillsdale was apparently the one mall in America without a single bookstore.

45

He ended up at the airport newsstand, which had an issue of *Cosmopolitan* that offered to explain how a woman could satisfy a man; but that wasn't really the subject matter he was looking for. On the flight east he tried to watch the movie, gave up and tried to sleep, and finally ended up trying to imagine what it was that he remembered from high school locker room talk and from being at Berkeley in the early seventies and from movies and television shows. Touching breasts was a big deal, he knew that. But was it a big deal for the guy or for the girl or both?

He was in a cold sweat, there in the airplane seat, just as if he had woken from that dream of being on a stage, expected to say lines in a play, only he didn't know what the play was and he'd never been to a single rehearsal. Sweating and trembling because he was going to have to take off his clothes and get into bed with a woman who had high expectations of him and he wasn't going to be able to deliver. He was going to botch everything. He remembered a couple of movies in which some teenage kid had his first chance at sex and got so excited he finished before the girl had even started, and this was apparently the most degrading, humiliating thing that could happen to a man. The woman's contempt would destroy him on the spot. At the time he had assumed this was all comic exaggeration and that such things either never happened at all or if they did, it was no big deal. But now he knew that it would happen to him and it would be a huge problem and she would despise him.

It might have been OK when he was young, being sexually inert in a culture—his parents' culture—that valued chastity. But it was certainly doing him no favors now.

And then there was the last thing Wayne had said. That Madeleine might be wondering if he was gay. He had kissed Mad a few times, and it had felt very good, and every one of those times he had a pretty good indication that he was oriented toward heterosexuality. But *she* wouldn't know about that. Would she? Do women look for that kind of thing?

The man sitting next to him came back from the airplane lavatory and looked at how Quentin was gripping the arms of his seat. "Yeah, I used to be a white-knuckle flier, too." Quentin smiled wanly and looked away. He didn't bother explaining to a stranger that the plane crashing sounded like a pretty good idea, compared to his terror of having sex with the woman he was going to marry. Thirty-four years old.

He had to resolve the question before the actual marriage. Not have sex with her—you don't jump off the cliff the first time you go rappelling. He just had to try something. Make a move.

From Dulles Airport he drove down the toll road to the Reston Parkway and found a plentiful selection of books about sex in the self-help section of the Little Professor Bookstore just before it closed. He went home and was already reading, trying to imagine himself and Madeleine doing these things, when she called.

"Weren't you going to phone me?" she asked.

"I meant to," he said. "I'm just wiped out. I didn't think you wanted to talk to somebody as stupid as I am right now."

"Does this mean you don't want me to come over?"

That was how things went—she always came over to his apartment because she was moving around from place to place, camping on couches in friends' tiny apartments. Her phone was a cellular so the number was the same wherever she was staying. He had offered to put her up at a hotel but she laughed at him. "I don't want you spending money on something as stupid as that when I can stay with my friends for free. They all owe me, so don't worry about it." He never met any of the friends. Was she ashamed of him? Or of them? No matter—it was her he wanted, not her friends.

So if they were to get together, it meant she would come to his place.

"It's after ten," he said lamely.

47

"I have two tubs of Ben and Jerry's chocolate chip cookie dough ice cream."

"I have dishes and spoons."

"Then we belong together. See you in a minute, Tin."

Not even during exam weeks in college had he ever read so fervently and rapidly and intensely as he did during the twenty minutes he waited for her to arrive.

By the time she got there he had already decided against most of the things the books suggested. Maybe people who had been married for ten years might be comfortable enough to do stuff like that with another person, but no way could he imagine trying it with Mad. All he wanted to do was see if he could, as the books suggested, give her any kind of pleasure during mild foreplay; and, of course, by so doing assure her that he was in fact straight, if inept. And maybe he was also hoping to see if she, in turn, was at all interested in *him* as a sexual partner. That would be, all in all, a great deal of very useful information for them to gain from what would be quite a minor event, taken in its proper perspective. Besides, skimming the books, however rapidly and urgently, had left him in a state of dazed arousal. Or, to use the more technical term, rampant horniness.

They talked, they ate ice cream, they laughed, they sat down to watch the news and then maybe catch Letterman before she went home, and there on the couch with the weatherman occluding his fronts and alofting his lows, Quentin touched her cheek and turned her face toward him and kissed her and realized for the first time how chaste all their kisses had been, and so he tried the thing where you slide the tip of your tongue along your partner's lip during the kiss and—

And that was the end of the kiss. She looked rather startled and laughed nervously and put her arms around him and hugged him with her face against his shoulder.

Did he do it wrong? Even pimply teenagers used their tongues when they kissed, for heaven's sake—couldn't he manage even *that* much?

48

No, no, it just startled her, that's all.

He ran his hands up and down her back. She giggled.

"What?"

"That tickles. What are you doing?"

"I'm trying to, uh, introduce a new level of physical closeness in our relationship."

She looked at him like he was crazy.

"Look, I'm just—I just thought it was maybe time we—"

We what? The only image that could come to his mind was the most weird of the suggestions the sex manuals offered. That wasn't at all what he wanted to do, at least not today, but still there was that picture in his head and it pretty much drove out of his mind the words he had meant to say.

But apparently she interpreted his silence in the worst possible way. She shuddered with revulsion and leapt up from the couch. "No!" she shouted. "Do you want to make me puke?"

This reaction was way beyond anything his dread had conjured up.

"All I did was—"

"If you think I'm ever going to do anything so disgusting with you for love or money—"

What did she think he meant? Since he had said nothing—did she mean she didn't want to have sex at all? "We're getting married," he said. "Married people generally touch each other without one of them puking. Most people assume that getting married means that somewhere along the line you—"

"I hate you!" she screamed at him.

He had never seen her like this, as she frantically picked up her purse and put on her flats—or rather, halfway put them on—and hobbled to the door as she finally settled her heels into her shoes. She slammed it on the way out, or at least an attempted slam, since the weather seal around the door kept it from making a satisfying noise. By the time Quentin could get to the door, she was already pulling away from the curb in her Escort.

* * *

He tried to call her that night and all the next day but only got the voice mail on her cellular service. All the time, he kept trying to think what he had done wrong. What had she thought he meant to do? They were engaged, weren't they? It wasn't as if he meant to have sex with her that very night—he intended to wait till they were married. He had been raised that way. But couldn't he touch her? Or was he so bad at it that it physically revolted her?

Or was it him at all? Maybe she was—what, frigid? Was there such a thing really? He thought that feminism had declared frigidity to be a myth that men made up to explain why women didn't want to have sex with sweating ignorant louts. Admittedly, he was ignorant and probably had been sweating. But—a lout? That was harsh. Had something happened in her childhood that made her interpret all sexual advances as something vile? By afternoon he had a couple more books, this time about sexual dysfunction, and read intently until he fell asleep by the still unringing phone, the fifth of his abject apologies and pleadings still unanswered on her voice mail.

The next morning he awoke to the doorbell ringing. Insistently, ring, ring, ring. Groggily he tried answering the phone, which was not ringing, and then got up, slipped on a robe, and went to the door.

It was Madeleine, carrying a bunch of daisies and looking as if she hadn't slept much the night before. "You must hate me," she said.

"I thought you hated me," he said.

"Can I come in?"

"Yes, of course, come in."

"You have to understand that I—I know I overreacted the other night. I thought you were—oh, who cares what I thought? I do want to marry you, you know, and of course marriage means physical intimacy and I just—I've never

50

been with a man that way, you know, and so I—I'm just so sorry."

"Mad, it's all right, you don't have anything to apologize for, I was insensitive I guess, I just—"

"No, it was my fault, I—"

"Didn't you get my messages?"

"I listened to them over and over. I couldn't believe you still loved me after the way I acted. I just—I couldn't call you because I didn't know what to say, I—"

"At least let me put these flowers in water. And your coat, is it that cold this morning?"

He pulled a glass pitcher out of the cupboard and put in the daisies. He meant to fill it with water but first he turned around to speak to her and saw that she had unbuttoned the coat and under it she was wearing nothing.

The coat was sliding off her shoulders but then she saw the look on his face. It must have seemed like a look of horror—not that she wasn't beautiful, her body was perfect, but from the way she acted two nights before this, it was too much, and besides, Quentin was terrified, he didn't know what to do. He dropped the pitcher onto the counter, just a couple of inches' drop so it didn't break, and the handle kept it from rolling off.

Her face changed from a smile to embarrassment, consternation. She shrugged the coat back on and wrapped it around herself and sank down onto the couch into a near fetal position and began to moan. "I've blown it again. I'm so stupid! I can't believe I—"

"No, no, Mad, it's all right, I just—I mean it was sweet of you, but that isn't what I wanted the other night, I just—"

"But that was supposed to be a real turn-on or whatever, that's what the article said—"

He laughed out loud.

"Don't laugh at me," she said miserably. "I'm sitting here naked in a coat with a polyester lining and polyester gives me a rash."

"No, come here, come with me." He got her up from the couch, trying not to notice how the coat fell open and she couldn't really close it efficiently with him holding one of her hands. "Come here."

He led her into his bedroom. "You have to see this," he said. He bent down and picked up the whole stack of sex manuals he had been studying. "Were you reading, perhaps, one of these?"

She looked at the titles and it dawned on her what they meant. She laughed, too. "Oh, you're kidding. You, too? There's another person on this planet as naive as me?"

"Maybe most people are like us," said Quentin. "They're just ashamed to admit it."

"No, nobody gets to their thirties as ignorant as we are. How did two freaks like us ever get lucky enough to find each other?"

"Listen, Mad, let me tell you something. I'm glad to know you have such a beautiful body. Such a . . . terrific body. Such a . . . "

"I get the idea."

"But I don't need to see you like that again until we're married, OK? Pressure's off for now. We can sort of work up to this. Pretend we're teenagers or something. Put off the dreadful day."

"That's fine. That's good," she said.

"And when you remove the startlement factor, whatever it was you read—I have to tell you, it really wasn't a bad suggestion."

"It was an article in *Cosmo*. A bunch of ways to please your man."

"Bummer. If only I'd bought that issue when I saw it in the airport in San Francisco. I would have known my part of the script."

"They don't give the man's part in *Cosmo*. They just sort of take it for granted that you already know your lines and stuff."

"Well, I don't," said Quentin. "I'm just winging it."

"So am I."

"The blind will lead the blind."

"Until we fall into a pit."

They laughed. He kissed her. She went home to get some clothing. Later, at lunch, they laughed about it all over again. "That's going to be such a great story to never tell our kids," said Quentin.

She rolled her eyes. "Of course we'll tell our kids. Just not in front of each other, that's all."

"Do parents tell kids things like this?"

"This is the nineties, Quentin," she said. "Isn't it?"

"Next time I fly to the coast, Mad, I want you to come with me."

"I'm unemployed and homeless. I think I can fit a trip to the coast into my schedule."

"I want you to meet my parents."

"Won't they hate the girl who's going to take away their little boy?"

"Are you kidding? They'll kiss the ground you walk on. They gave up hope of having grandchildren years ago. And the bonus is, with any luck the kids will look like you."

"I'd love to meet your parents," she said.

"And when do I make the trek to the Hudson River Valley to meet your folks?"

Her face darkened and she looked away. "My family isn't like yours, Quentin. I think I want us to be married *before* I take you home."

"Are you kidding?"

She shook her head. "Let's not talk about it, OK? Not today."

"You don't want me to meet your family and you don't want to talk about it?"

"Just picture me naked in that stupid coat and it will take your mind right off my family."

"Not true. It just makes me imagine your father holding a shotgun."

She giggled. "My father holding a shotgun. Now *there's* a picture. He'd never *touch* a weapon."

"A pacifist?"

"No, a klutz. He'd shoot off his own leg." She laughed again, but in a moment that dark, distant look was back on her face. It wasn't until Quentin moved the conversation far away from parents and families that the mood cleared and she was happy again.

5
Bliss

Was it possible that his parents liked Madeleine *too* much? Quentin expected them to be delighted that he had a fiancée at all and that he had brought her home to meet them, and he expected her to charm them because she was, after all, charming. But within hours they seemed to have lost all sense of proportion. Everything she said, they laughed or oohed or tsk-tsked or whatever the appropriate response was. Their attention toward her never flagged. They offered her drinks, food, their own bed—it was way beyond hospitality.

They were obsequious. It was as if they were servants and Madeleine was the mistress of the house. It embarrassed him, but he couldn't seem to get either of his parents alone to tell them to lay off a little; nor could he seem to find a moment alone with Mad to explain that they didn't always act like this, that they must be compensating for all those years that they had given up on the idea of his marrying.

Poor Mad must be going crazy with them fawning on her all the time, but she was a trouper, she didn't show a sign of irritation. Just acted as though it were the most natural thing in the world.

Quentin tried to take her out to dinner.

"The four of us?" asked Mad.

"Nonsense," said Dad. "The two of you just go."

"The lovebirds need some time for tête-a-tête," said Mom, smiling.

"But you *must* come," said Mad. "How often will we be together like this? We have to make memories together."

"And I'll bet the crockpot chicken I was making will be just as good tomorrow," said Mom.

"Oh, that's right, Tin," said Madeleine. "I forgot that I helped her pound the chicken this morning."

"But it doesn't matter, if Quen wants to take you out."

"I wouldn't dream of missing out on the chance to taste your crockpot chicken when it's just so."

Quentin wanted to scream. It wasn't just his parents gushing over her, she was also gushing over them. If everybody would just stop trying so hard, maybe they could have a civilized visit. But that apparently wasn't going to happen without some kind of intervention.

"Listen," said Quentin, "I don't really care if we eat in or out. I don't care if we have chicken or Big Macs. I brought my fiancée here to meet my parents. And the way it looks right now, we're going to leave here without ever having done that."

They all looked at him as if he were insane.

"Quen," said Dad, "here we are. There she is. We've met."

"That's my point. *My* parents have a personality. They have habits and customs. They have a life. I wanted to bring Madeleine into the life. So she could see who you are, the family we are together. But you two are being so completely, insanely accommodating that—it's like your own personalities have been completely erased."

Tears filled Mom's eyes. "We've just tried to be nice."

Madeleine looked desperately embarrassed. "Tin, I thought it was all going really well."

"We only want you two to be happy," said Dad. He put his arm around Mom.

"Look, I'm sorry, I didn't want to make a scene," said Quentin. "Tell you what, you three stay here and have the crockpot chicken and tell each other how perfect it is and then spend the rest of the night insisting that the other person choose what TV show to watch or game to play. I'm going to the movies."

He turned and headed for the front door. He had his hand on the knob when he heard something that stopped him cold.

Laughter. Warm, throaty laughter. Lizzy's laugh.

He caught his breath. He turned. It was Madeleine. But now the laughter had changed. Still low, still warm, but no longer Lizzy's voice. Mad didn't look at him.

"Well, shucks," said Mad, speaking to no one in particular. "Maybe there *is* such a thing as getting along too well." She looked at Dad and winked. "Let's have a fight, Mr. Fears. It'll make Tin feel so much better."

Dad smiled and nodded. "Well, maybe not a fight. Maybe just a tiff."

"I know we're all joking and we're embarrassed and all," said Mom, "but there *is* just the one thing, just the tiniest thing—I know you have a right to call him by whatever pet nickname you want, but . . . calling him 'Tin' . . . "

Mad put her hand to her mouth. "Oh, I should have known. I should have realized."

"How *could* you have known that our Lizzy called him . . . "

"But he *did* tell me that," said Mad. "It just never crossed my mind, after all these years, that it would—but of course, it was this very house where she—it *did* seem all right with Tin—with Quentin—and so I just—please forgive me."

"No, no," said Mom. "Now I feel just awful for mentioning it. Because it *is* all right. I just—I just thought that—"

"Acknowledging her," said Dad. "That's all that was needed, maybe. To acknowledge her. That she called him that. And then it's OK."

"Yes," said Mom. "You can call him that, really. It won't bother me now, because I've, because I've spoken of her."

"But you should have spoken of it before," said Mad. "Two days I've been driving you bonkers with—"

"No, no, nothing like that," said Mom, "I just—every time you said it, you called him that, I wanted to speak, to say, 'That's what Lizzy called him,' and it wasn't even going to be a complaint, just a comment, just to say, I don't know, that she still has a place in our home, in our memories. But when I thought of saying it, I just, it just felt like something clamped down inside me and I couldn't *speak*."

"Well," said Dad, "you're speaking *now*."

"See?" said Mom. "Quentin *was* right to just bring things out in the open. We *were* being on our best behavior a bit too much, weren't we? Why, I'm—I'm almost *exhausted* with politeness. And yet I really *do* like you, Madeleine, dear. I just wanted so much to make a good impression, I suppose."

"The main thing," said Dad, "is this: Dinner in or dinner out?"

It was dinner in and now, at last, it was as if his parents had come out of hiding. There was chatter and banter and some catty gossip about neighbors and other church members, and the laughter was genuine and Mad actually got to see what life in his home was like.

And when, about ten that night, he suggested that he and Mad might take a walk around the old neighborhood, Dad yawned and said, "About time we got rid of you for a few minutes, you two. Let these old bones go to bed." And that was that. Mad and Quentin would be alone together.

They held hands walking from streetlight to streetlight. "They used to just be mounted to the telephone poles," said Quentin. "Then when they were building the expressway over the old creekbed behind the house, they buried all the phone lines and put up these aluminum poles. Shame, too. Because Lizzy and I had scratched graffiti into all the old poles. Like marking our territory. No good trying to mark anything on *these* things." He slapped the pole and it rang metallically.

"It's *her* shadow in the house that made everything so tense, wasn't it?" said Madeleine.

"Not her shadow. Her memory isn't a shadow," said Quentin.

"Losing her was a shadow," said Mad. "That's what I meant."

"I don't think it had to do with her," said Quentin. "My parents—I've just never seen them act like that. Like complete strangers."

"I wouldn't know," said Madeleine. "I've never known a normal family."

"What, your parents have eight legs each?"

"Life in the Family Arachnid," she said, laughing. "No, my parents were fine. But . . . well, to be honest, they acted like your parents *were* acting, all the time. When I actually saw them, of course. Just always sort of—what—*on,* I guess."

"On what? Cocaine?"

"More like on stage." She jabbed him. "They weren't *that* hyper."

"I didn't mean to make a scene like that," said Quentin. "But I couldn't seem to get you alone. Or them either."

"I was so afraid that I wasn't doing it right," said Mad.

"Well, it wasn't you, anyway. *They* were the ones acting strange. *You* were a hero about it all."

They walked on to the corner. "That way was where I used to ride my bike to junior high. The elementary school was back that way, through an orchard. Now it's a park. The orchard. The school is gone. My Scout Troop once took on the job of distributing flyers for a supermarket through the whole neighborhood. I had two hundred of them to tuck into people's screen doors. I did about twenty and then dumped the rest in a culvert, right down there."

"There's no culvert there."

"That used to be a bridge over a creek. Everything's changed. I wish I could show you the place I actually lived in. You're lucky that way—didn't you tell me your family had lived in their house forever?"

"Not forever. We're all descended from immigrants."

"It must be nice, though, to go back and have nothing changed."

She laughed but it was nasty. "Oh, yes, it's so *nice*."

"Is there really some major problem between you and your family?" said Quentin.

"It's not a feud or anything," said Mad. "There was a rift for a while, but I've had it under control for years now."

"But you still won't take me to meet them."

"Oh, in good time." She turned and faced him. "After we're married."

"What, you think they'll come between us if we're merely affianced?"

"I want to be part of *your* family before I take you into the bosom of mine."

"Do I hear the sound of somebody moving up the date of our wedding?"

"We haven't *set* a date yet."

"I meant from 'let's talk about it sometime' to 'let's get married pretty soon.'"

"Sooner than that."

"How soon?"

"I suppose tonight wouldn't be practical."

Quentin kissed her. "There's the matter of a license."

"As soon as possible. Here, in this town. At your family's church. Surrounded by your parents' friends."

"Nothing would make them happier."

"And you? Would that make *you* happy, Tin?"

He nodded.

"And yet you still look sad."

He shook his head, smiling. "Not sad at all. Very happy. The sooner the better—you know that's how I feel. Short engagement, yes, but then I've been waiting twenty years for you."

"Do you love me as much as her?" asked Mad.

Quentin made a show of looking over his shoulder. "Who?"

"As Lizzy. Your sister."

"Let's put it this way—I never would have married my sister."

"No, I was wrong even to bring it up. But I've felt it—I've felt it almost from the start. Another woman. And yet you kept insisting that there *was* no other woman, there had never been another woman, only every time you had a memory of childhood Lizzy was in it. *She's* the other woman, the one in your past. And because she's . . . dead . . . I can never measure up to her."

Quentin kissed her, long and thoroughly. "You're not being measured against Lizzy. She's my childhood, my memory, my past. But you're my future."

"It's selfish of me, isn't it? But you have to love me. More than anyone, you have to love *me,* or I can't . . . can't anything. Can't be happy."

"Mad, you're already off the scale. I love you more than life."

She clung to him under the streetlight.

But as he stroked her hair he wondered—was it true? Did he love her more than Lizzy? Was there still some crazy part of him that clung to Lizzy and wouldn't let her go? After all, he had never hallucinated seeing Madeleine.

He shook off the thought. It was Madeleine who had opened up his life and given it meaning. He was excited for the future now. That was something that his memory of Lizzy had never been able to do. Hallucinations, but no dreams.

It took longer than they thought, because a proper church wedding required some lead time—invitations, if nothing else, took a week. But by the end of August they were married, full church wedding and all, the bride like a goddess in white, the groom grinning like an idiot, or so Dad assured him just before the ceremony.

The honeymoon was Hawaii, of course, because neither of them had ever been there and from the bay area, that was the only place you could go with a more pleasant climate. They made love for the first time on their second morning in the Turtle Bay Hilton, after recovering from jet lag and post-wedding exhaustion. They were both shy and awkward but it worked pretty well. "After all," said Madeleine, "if it was really hard, stupid people wouldn't have so many children."

They snorkeled, they visited Japanese Buddhist temples, they flew to Maui and the big island, they ate fresh pineapples and shopped in the open-air mall in Honolulu and stood at the pass where hundreds of warriors plunged to their deaths in an ancient Hawaiian story. They watched the show at the Polynesian Cultural Center and tried out some of the dances back in their room, minus the costumes, of course. Quentin noticed during the week that he actually had something of a knack for having fun.

But there was still a shadow between them, and it wasn't Lizzy, because the shadow wasn't in Quentin, he was sure of that. It was in Mad. They would make love and he would hold her in his arms and she would smile at him and he would say, Yes, it was wonderful, it was sweet, I love you. And she would assure him, too, only he knew, though he wasn't sure how, he *knew* that he was telling the truth and she was lying. It wasn't good for her. Something was wrong with this part of their marriage and she wouldn't tell him what. He couldn't even ask her, because she really wasn't giving any outward sign of dissatisfaction. It was more as if there were some inner pain that she couldn't shake off, that nothing he did could ease. A pain that became most painful in those moments after sex when she should have been happiest, should have felt most loved, most worshiped by her husband. Something was stealing joy from them, something in her past.

Something in her family. Something in that mansion on the Hudson that she was determined not to let him visit.

Was she molested as a child? Beaten? Emotionally starved? If she didn't want to tell him, how could he find out? This was certainly one case where it wouldn't help for him to get his lawyer working on finding the answers. Besides, Wayne would have such a smirk. Married a week, and already you're having me investigate her family? Maybe if you had let me investigate them *before* the wedding . . .

No, he wanted *her* to tell him. When she trusted him enough. And so he would make sure she never had cause to doubt his love and loyalty, his strength and honor. When she knew that nothing she told him could shake his bond with her, then she would speak.

At the end of the week, she was the one who brought up the future. "Our week is almost up," she said. "And it occurs to me we haven't said anything about what happens next."

"We could stay another week. Another month, if you want. I made kind of an open-ended reservation."

"This was a wonderful week, but the best part of it was you, Tin, and I get to keep *you* wherever we go. Have we even decided where we're going to live?"

"I have connections in most cities in North America. But don't feel limited by that—I'm sure that we could find a way to get along in England. Or France. Paris? Provence?"

"I don't think I'm cool enough for Provence."

"But you have the body for the beaches of the Riviera."

"Nobody would even notice me there."

"I wouldn't be able to keep the Frenchmen's hands off you."

"Really, Tin, where will we live? Your stuff is in Virginia, and mine is still packed, my family can ship it wherever we decide to live. Have you finished your business there? Are you ready to move on?"

"I don't know," said Quentin. "I mean, that wasn't exactly a career. It was more of a pastime. I was marking time till I met you. So now . . . I don't know."

"It was a wonderful pastime," said Mad. "Making other people's dreams come true."

"Helping them make their own dreams come true, you mean."

"What I mean is, Tin, why stop?"

"Well, for one thing, too many of them have succeeded."

"What does *that* mean?"

"When I talked to my lawyer about revising my will to include you, he had me get my accountant to provide me with a complete inventory of my assets. Some of my partnerships are now worth more than the fortune I started with. My point is that I'm now rich on a whole different scale. Maybe it's time to help somebody with a truly extravagant dream."

"Who?"

"You."

She looked at him as if he were crazy. "*You're* my dream, and here you are."

"No, that's not what you told me. There in the garden. Under the cherry tree."

"*En château de la grande dame.*"

"Remember? You coveted power, you said. To pick your candidates and help them get started. What you didn't have was money."

"But what do *you* care about politics?"

"That's why it's a partnership. You pick the candidates, I fund them."

"It doesn't work that way. There are election laws. Limitations on contributions, that sort of thing."

"We'll form PACs. Foundations. We'll contribute to local party organizations and encourage them to support the candidates we favor. Mad, if there's one thing I've learned, it's that when you have enough money the law is a reed that will always bend your way."

"You make it sound possible."

"Not only possible, but completely legal. And if we can't contribute directly, so much the better. The goal wasn't to have candidates beholden to *us*, was it? The idea was they should be independent and wise and sane and—telegenic, wasn't that part of it?"

"Do you mean it?" she said.

"As I said, I have connections in every city that matters. Let's make the grand tour. Attending the parties that I've avoided for all these years. You'll dazzle them, and I'll talk turkey with the local politicos. We'll pick our candidates and start the ball rolling. Isn't there an election next year? Is it too late to find candidates for Congress?"

"If only it weren't too late to choose a candidate for president."

"President schmesident," said Quentin. "We could probably make more difference if we concentrated on state legislatures."

"You're right, Tin. What I care about is finding good people and getting them started. And it might very well be state legislatures. County commissions! City councils! School boards!"

"We have our work cut out for us."

They fell back on the bed, laughing. "We sound like a silly old movie," said Quentin. "Mickey Rooney and Judy Garland. 'We can put on our *own* election.'"

"I have no idea what you're talking about," said Madeleine.

"You've never seen an Andy Hardy movie?" asked Quentin. "You can't be serious. You're—you're not even an American!"

"No, I'm just not an *elderly* American. You really *did* grow up in a time warp!"

It was only later, as she slept beside him on the plane, that it occurred to him that Wayne Read had accused him of living in a time warp, and he had never told her about *that* conversation. Had he?

He must say a lot of things without realizing what he

was saying. Because he had never told her that 'Tin' was Lizzy's nickname for him. He wasn't stupid—when she first called him that it was in the garden, under the cherry tree, and the last thing he had wanted at that moment was to get prickly and say, Don't call me that, it was my dead sister's nickname for me. And later, he didn't want her to change, it felt right having her call him that, so why would he have told her that Lizzy used that name for him? When would he *ever* have told her? And yet she knew. Before Mom explained, she knew.

Maybe she just put things together. Picked up clues, reached a conclusion, and then *thought* he had said it outright. So she was observant. He couldn't hide things from her. It was a good thing he intended to be a faithful husband.

Their new political career wasn't as easy as they had thought. Oh, their initial plan worked very well. A man of Quentin's wealth and a woman of Madeleine's beauty and grace had no trouble at all being admitted to the highest circles of political activity in either party, in any city. The trouble was that in those circles they never met anyone that fit Mad's criteria for a good candidate. That was the basic contradiction of their plan: If the ruling cliques already knew a person, he or she was already too "inside" to qualify.

They needed to find people who weren't politically aware, or at least not politically *self*-aware. So through the autumn of 1995 they widened their net. They established their credentials with the insiders, yes, but they also went to service organizations, to activist groups, to charities and churches; they took newspaper reporters and city bureaucrats to dinner and asked them who really made a difference in the community, the men and women they actually admired. And slowly but surely they began to find people. Not in every city, but now and then one face, one name would come to the fore.

It was exhilarating work, and Quentin could see why Mad loved it, even though it wasn't something he would ever have chosen to do on his own. And watching her do it, that was almost miraculous. His money opened political doors and made campaigns possible, yes, but she was the one who persuaded these reluctant candidates, who kindled the ambition that had lain dormant within them, or had been turned outward to some cause. You can make a difference. If you don't run, who will? Instead of fighting city hall, you can *be* city hall—and you won't be beholden to anyone. You'll have the courage and strength that come from not caring—because you *don't* care whether you get reelected, do you? So you won't always have your eye on the polls—you'll be free to follow your heart and mind. And if you lose—well, you tried, didn't you, and you'll only have made more connections to help you in the work you're already doing.

They bought it. They absolutely bought into her dream and made it their own and after a while the only thing that continued to surprise Quentin was how little it cost. National politics might cost millions, but local politics could still be paid for out of pocket change, as long as you had willing volunteers—and Madeleine had the knack of finding people who really could inspire others to spend hundreds of hours stuffing envelopes or knocking on doors or manning booths or phoning people. And once the candidate began to emerge, other financial supporters gathered.

"Mad," Quentin said to her, as they drove from the airport to his parents' house for Christmas. "Mad, this politics thing isn't working."

"Are you kidding?" she said. "I think it's going great!"

"Oh, sure, for *you* it's going great. But it was supposed to help me get rid of all this money, and we're just not spending it fast enough."

"That's because you're in the wrong country," said Mad. "America isn't corrupt enough yet. There are some Latin

American countries where you have to compete with drug lords when you want to buy an election, and you can soak through a hundred million in no time."

"Well, I'm going to have to start another hobby. Something *really* expensive. Donating to universities, for instance—I hear that's a bottomless hole."

"A Fears Building of Something on every campus, is that it?"

"Or a Cryer Building," he said. "They don't have to be named for me."

"Not that name," she said. "I don't want my name on anything."

"Too late. I've got it on a marriage certificate."

"You tricked me! Just to get my autograph!"

Christmas was wonderful, even though Mad complained a little about the green lawns and the lack of snow.

"We can't all live in the perfect climate of the Hudson Valley," said Dad.

"Californians are climate-deprived," said Mom. "The things that *do* go wrong aren't seasonal. There's no earthquake season, for instance."

"There's a mudslide season," suggested Dad.

"But not every year."

"Next year," said Dad, "Madeleine should invite us all to Christmas with *her* family. So we can tramp around on snowshoes. Do you have any nieces or nephews, Madeleine? Or—heavens, you're young enough—you might still have younger brothers and sisters at home!"

"No believers in Santa Claus, if that's what you mean," said Mad, laughing.

Quentin watched her, waited for her to sidestep the issue. But she didn't.

"Maybe I *will* have you all come out."

"No," said Dad immediately. "I was just joking. We don't go inviting ourselves to other people's Christmases!"

"Not Christmas Day, maybe," said Mad. "We don't do much for Christmas anyway, I think you'd be disappointed.

But the week after. Don't you think, Quentin? Wouldn't that be a good holiday next year?"

"Sure," he said. "Sounds great."

But it bothered him. She wouldn't take him home to meet her family, after all these hints. And yet she'd invite Dad and Mom to come along with them. Of course, she was inviting them a year in advance—she might find a thousand excuses for canceling before then. Or maybe whatever she dreaded there might be easier if his parents came along with them. Or maybe she had simply overcome those fears, right now, today, in this conversation.

"You don't sound very enthusiastic," said Mom. "Are you afraid we'll use the wrong fork, Quen?"

"Oh, it's just that Mad has told me such terrible things about her family. Visitors have been known to arrive and . . . disappear."

Mad looked at him in consternation. "No such thing."

"That's why she's never taken me there. And her house is haunted. And it was built over an old chemical sludge factory. People get cancer just flying over, the airlines have to route around it."

"There *were* no factories making chemical sludge when the family manse was built," said Madeleine. "All the rest is true, though."

"Don't forget the Indian burial mound, Mad," said Quentin. "Her family bulldozed a whole burial mound because it blocked their view of the river. But on the spot where the mound was . . . *nothing grows.*"

"That's not true," said Madeleine. "It's always a jungle of briars and poison ivy."

"Which your mother harvests and uses to make those unforgettable prickly salads."

"All right," said Madeleine, laughing. "I'll take you home first, to meet my folks."

Mom and Dad were appalled.

"Quentin hasn't even met your parents?" Dad asked.

"How does he know idiocy doesn't run in your family?" He was trying to make a joke out of it.

Mom's reaction was sympathetic—but not to Madeleine and Quentin. "Oh, but your mother must be so *hurt* that you married without telling her!"

"Oh, don't worry. I *told* her. I just didn't invite her."

"Oh, worse and worse!" cried Mom.

"My family's very odd," said Madeleine. "You have to understand—they would have thought it presumptuous of me to expect them to come. You simply have to understand that . . . I mean, when I came here—did you people pose for Norman Rockwell or what?"

"That depends," said Dad. "Do you like Norman Rockwell paintings?"

"I dreamed of Norman Rockwell paintings when I was a child," said Mad. "I thought they were a wonderful fantasyland. Or heaven—if I died, that's where I'd go, to a Norman Rockwell Thanksgiving or Christmas. Like the one we just had."

"Well, what does *your* family do, beat the servants and burn down the neighbors' house?" said Dad, carrying the joke too far, as usual.

Madeleine smiled wanly. "Servants always used to quit before we had time to beat them," she said. "They finally gave up hiring them."

Mom was outraged at Dad, though of course she put a jesting face on it. "I can't believe he's teasing about your family, Madeleine, dear, he just has no sense of tact, he never *has*." She playfully punched her husband on the arm; but Quentin could see that it hurt, and Dad didn't like it. It was a pattern already familiar from his childhood—Dad always got a small, painful bruise when he went too far. And yet it didn't stop him from going that far. As if painful jabs were the medium of exchange in the economy of their quarreling. Would he and Madeleine evolve ways of hurting each other and then ignoring it and going on?

"Oh, please," said Madeleine. "Let's just take it as a given that my family is weird. I'm simply the normal-looking one who can go around in public. But I'll tell you what. Quentin has been dying of curiosity and I think he's sort of hurt that I've never taken him, so this is it. Next week. After New Year's. We'll drive up the Hudson Valley and I'll take him into Château Cryer and when he comes back here he can tell you *all* the weird things he saw. Believe me, you can't stay there for three hours without having a dozen very bizzarre tales to tell."

"Tell us some now," said Quentin.

"You see?" said Madeleine. "Now that I've actually agreed to take him, he's afraid and he wants me to prepare him in case he wants to back out. Well, I'm not going to tell him a thing. He'll just have to come with an open mind."

"I'm sure your family is perfectly wonderful," said Mom, "and that's what Quentin will tell us."

"Maybe," said Madeleine with a knowing smile. "And maybe not. But I'll tell you *this*. Nobody in my family makes a banana cream pie like yours, Mother Fears. And the half-pie in your fridge is moaning my name."

"The pie doesn't know your name," said Quentin. "That was me you were hearing. But we'll settle for the pie for now."

"Quentin," said Mom reprovingly. "You're not such a newlywed anymore that we should have to put up with your innuendos."

"Innuendo?" said Quentin. "Why, whatever do you mean, Mother dear?"

After the pie, as Mom cleaned up in the kitchen and Dad signed on to America Online to send after-Christmas e-mail to his brothers, Quentin gave Madeleine a chance to back out of her invitation.

"But I don't want to back out. I'd already decided it was time for you to meet them. I would have told you privately but then the conversation just went that way and—you don't mind, do you?"

"Not at all. In fact I'm relieved. That you trust me enough to take me home."

"It wasn't a matter of trusting *you*, Tin, my pet, my poo. I know *you* can handle it. They just have a way of getting under my skin. With you to hold on to as an island of sanity, I think I can get through a day with my family. Just a day, mind you."

"And then a night at the Holiday Inn?"

"Well, of course we have to stay overnight, but you know what I mean. Twenty-four hours and then we *go*, no matter how my family pleads with you to stay, do you understand me? Because even if I'm wearing a plastic smile on my face and saying, 'Oh, yes, Quentin, let's *do* stay,' trust me, I do *not* want to stay, I want you to get me out of there before we reach the witching hour."

"Which is?"

"If we arrive at noon, then by the next noon we must be gone or I will turn into a puddle of mucus on the floor."

"That's an attractive image. If I kiss it, does it turn back into a princess?"

"No, it just turns into a cold." She kissed him. "Your kiss has already turned me into a princess."

6

She Loves You, Yeah

The limo met them at La Guardia in the late afternoon on New Year's Day and they started out on the drive up the Hudson. "Shame we won't be able to see the river," Quentin said. "It'll be dark before we get over the Triborough."

"You can't see the river anyway," said Madeleine. "Not the way you can from the bluffs. The great houses were all built to be seen from the water. That was the highway then, the steamboats up the Hudson."

"The house is that old?"

"A fireplace in every room. The kitchen is an add-on. The bathrooms are carved out of hallways and stuck under stairs. All afterthoughts."

"They built these huge gorgeous mansions and then went outside to the privy?"

"Don't be silly," said Madeleine. "They had fine porcelain chamberpots. Which were emptied by the servants."

"Let me guess about the toilet paper."

"Every room had a water basin and towels. What do you think they were for?"

"Oh, for the good old days," said Quentin.

"I suppose *your* people all had flush toilets from the fifteenth century."

"No. But they dug their own latrines and built privies and used the Sears catalogue. Nobody handled anybody else's sewage."

"The idea of money was different then," said Madeleine. "If there was a filthy job, other people did it, and you paid them."

"My people believed in independence. You did for yourself, beholden to no one."

"The snobbery of the poor."

"The helplessness of the rich."

"Only *you're* the one with money."

"What, your family's broke?"

"We have what we need, I guess. Nothing on *your* scale."

"My money's an accident, Mad. It fell on me while I was doing what I cared about. I was lucky to be in a company run by a marketing madman. And once I *had* money, I couldn't stop it from growing."

"That's what I love most about you, Tin. You have no ambition whatsoever."

"One ambition. To make a future with you."

She smiled at him.

He pulled the *Beatles Anthology* CD out of his carry-on bag and put it in the player in the limo. "I haven't had a chance to listen to this since you gave it to me."

"I thought you might want something from your childhood."

"It's not like I remember them. I was three years old when they did the Sullivan show."

"It's all ancient history to me."

"You're not *that* much younger than I am." On the marriage license she had put 1965 as her year of birth.

"I lived on another planet then," she said. "We didn't even have a radio in our house."

"Chamberpots, no radio."

"I did love to crank the Victrola."

"Seriously?"

"No. I suppose there was a radio somewhere, but it's not as if anyone would dream of letting *me* choose the station. We didn't get out much."

"Why not? Didn't you go to school?"

"Tutors. Family tradition."

"Were they *trying* to isolate you?"

"I think perhaps so," said Madeleine. "Grandmother ruled with an iron fist. She never liked me."

"Grandmother? Will I meet her?"

"I don't know. She *ought* to be in a rest home, with tubes sticking out of her."

Quentin had never heard such venom from her.

"Alzheimer's?" he asked.

"Advanced bitchiness," she answered.

"Give me a little preparation. Who is it I should try hardest not to offend?"

"Tin, don't you get it? I don't care who you offend. I've been free of their control for years now. I'm bringing you here to show them that there are good people in this world and I found one of them and if they don't like you, screw 'em."

Quentin digested this for a while, listening to the music, then looking at the booklet that came with the CD. "It's funny how all their early stuff sounds so much like Elvis. Only not as good."

"What?" She looked baffled.

"The Beatles."

"Oh, sorry, I wasn't listening."

"Listen to it now. That's Paul singing, only listen to what he's doing to his voice. Distorting it like crazy. They don't even sound like the Beatles."

"He can't hold his pitch very well, can he."

"That's what I mean. It's like they haven't found their own sound yet. Not one of these cuts before their first studio singles even sounds like the Beatles. It's like they walked into the studio as a club band that did Elvis and Ink Spots imitations, and came out as the Beatles."

"I thought you said you were only three when the Beatles came along."

"Yeah, well, when I was old enough to listen to music, what was there? England Dan and John Ford Coley. 'I Put My Blue Jeans On.' 'She's Gone.' And who can forget Fleetwood Mac?"

"I guess they must be forgotten because I never heard of any of those groups. 'I Put My Blue Jeans On' sounds like a commercial."

"It was a song, by this squiggy little guy from England I think. And they *did* make it into an ad jingle. Or maybe it started that way, what do I know? And 'The Year of the Cat.' Man it was bad. Lizzy and I went back and listened to the old stuff. My parents were Elvis nuts but they also liked the Beatles. It was in their closet."

"Well, if the Beatles were Elvis clones at first, that's understandable."

"The recorded stuff wasn't. What did *you* listen to?"

"I told you, nothing."

"Had to be disco. Let's see, you'd've been fifteen in 1980. Oh, I know. Michael Jackson! 'Billy Jean'! 'We Are the World.' Or maybe Springsteen."

"What is this, a test? A final exam or something?" She looked really annoyed.

"Look, I'm just talking about music, that's all."

"Well I don't know any of it! And there's no reason that I should, so stop it!"

She looked furious and frightened as she turned to look out the window into the deepening night. Lights and signs whipped by on the freeway.

"It wasn't a test," said Quentin quietly. "Why would I be testing you?"

"I don't know," she murmured.

"Well I wasn't. I love you whether you care about music or not. I was just trying to think what would have been current when you came of age. People usually know the music that was hot when they were about fifteen or so, and then for a few years till they get married. I got into it early because Lizzy took me with her when *she* was that age. And I never stopped because I didn't get married till now. You have friends in DC, didn't *they* play any music?"

"It never sounded like music to me. Nine Inch Nails." She shuddered.

"But they didn't play you any Counting Crows? Martin Page? Natalie Merchant?"

"We were bureaucrats. And what I cared about was government." She turned back to face him. "The Beatles. They were rich, weren't they? Famous, right?"

"More popular than Jesus Christ, I think the saying was."

"Yeah, well, what did they do with it?"

"Do?"

"With their money and fame. What was it for?"

"Music, I guess. Songs."

"No, that's what it was *from*. What was it for?"

"For itself." He studied her face, wondering if someone he loved so much could be so blind to something as simple as this. "They did music because they loved the songs. Writing them and singing them."

"Like you loved the programming, is that it?"

"Sure. You do what you love, and sometimes money happens or fame happens, but mostly it doesn't happen but that's OK because you were doing what you loved."

She shook her head. "Like a kid who's given this big wonderful present, only when he unwraps it, all he can think to do is play with the the box it came in. With the wrapping paper and ribbon."

"OK, so what's the present?"

She leaned toward him and spoke with such intensity that her words scoured his heart. "Running things."

He remembered what she had said in the garden. About power.

"But that's just the box, too," he said. "Power, I mean."

"No it isn't."

"Sure it is. What's *power* for?"

"I don't get what you're asking me."

"You asked the same question about money and fame — what are they for? Well, what about power? Running things? Running them for what? To accomplish what?"

"Whatever you want." The answer was so obvious to her that she clearly didn't understand a word he was saying.

"That's the point? What do you want?"

"To run things," she said.

"But all these candidates we've been encouraging, Mad, didn't we pick them out because they had purposes? Causes?"

"*They* had causes," she said. "That doesn't mean *I* have to."

This attitude was so baffling and unpleasant that Quentin wished he hadn't got into the conversation. "I thought you chose these people for their causes."

"I did," she said. "Nobody's easier to control than a politician with a cause."

He shuddered. "That doesn't make any sense."

"Sure it does," she said. "I assumed you understood that. As long as he's accomplishing his cause, he'll do everything *else* you tell him to. Like you do with the people you got into partnerships with."

"What is it you think I'm doing with them?"

"They have their dream—as long as they get to accomplish that, then you get everything else your way."

He could certainly see how it might seem like that to someone with her perspective. His partners brought their dream, their drive, their expertise—but everything else was done Quentin's way, which is why he never lost much money with even the worst failures. He had control. And as soon as they weren't accomplishing his purpose, he cut them off and set them adrift. Uninjured, but they were no longer useful to him and so he had nothing more to do with them.

That's how it looked, yes, if you chose to see it that way. But that wasn't what he meant, or who he was. He wasn't using these people, he was helping them.

"Get real," said Madeleine. "Nobody ever helps anybody except in order to help themselves. Not even you. Not even when you do your best lying to yourself about it."

"I don't like this conversation," said Quentin.

"It's your conversation, Tin. But I thought we both understood this. I haven't lied to you. I told you from the start it was power that I wanted most. You knew that's what you were signing on to when we went into partnership."

"Partnership?" The word was sour in his mouth.

"I don't mean our marriage. I mean our partnership. The candidates. We're building up a network of people we can control without their even guessing we're controlling them. Maybe only two or three times in their career will we have to make them do something, and when we do, it won't violate any of their principles because it'll have nothing to do with their pet cause. We'll just ask them to help us out on this or that, whatever it is, and they'll know that they owe us everything and so they'll do it. And never think twice, because it'll be so small, so *nothing*. An appointment. A single vote. Locking something up in a committee. Confirming an appointee their party opposes, or opposing one they're supposed to support. As a favor to us, the ones who got them started on their wonderful career that's been so *good* for their cause."

"So we're the fat cats after all," said Quentin.

"No, not at all!" She laughed at the idea. "Tin, you've seen the fat cats, they strut around getting in petty catfights about stupid local matters that amount to nothing. They show off their jewelry and their tans at local fundraisers. They pride themselves on mingling with the common people and then pride themselves on being more 'inside' than the common people. We're not like that."

Quentin shook his head. It was as if he hadn't really

known her. And yet she was the woman he loved. He had to think about this. It wasn't anything like what Wayne Read had warned him about. After all, he'd known her for months now. And maybe she was right, maybe he should have understood this attitude of hers from the start. What did it matter, anyway? So she was more open about wanting power than most people, what of that? It was honesty, of a sort. Integrity.

Or else it was cynical manipulation, so deeply evil that few politicians could bring themselves to conceive of it.

He shook off that dark thought. This sweet, naive, child-like woman beside him simply had a childlike, naive view of the romance of political power. It was an outsider's vision, that's all. Just as he had found with money, she would soon find with power—that it got boring once you had enough of it, and then you had to rethink everything in order to find something worth doing with it.

Evil indeed. What dark thing dwelt in his heart, to make him think of such a word in relation to his Mad? He would say nothing to her to imply criticism. Better to treat it lightly, as a game, and then help her gain a wiser view later, as she gained more experience in the political world.

He leaned over and kissed her. "When you rule the world, Mad, do I get to be prince consort?"

She laughed. "Why do you think I married you?"

He laughed with her. He was relieved to see that she could mock herself. As long as she could see the humor in her own desires, they would never get the better of her.

The Beatles sang about how they wanted money. The other stuff, you can give it to the birds and bees. You really got a hold on me. Roll over, Beethoven. And the CD ended.

Silence filled the car for a while. Except that he could hear his own heartbeat, pounding like Ringo's relentless drum. With her head on his shoulder, could she hear it, too? His heart? Now that it belonged to her, did she hear it?

* * *

They never would have noticed the entrance to the estate if she hadn't been there to point it out. Even as it was, with her saying, "Right here, turn here, right now!" the driver overshot it and had to back up.

"Sorry," he said. "I couldn't see it till we passed it."

"No sweat," said Quentin.

"I can see how it's easy to miss in the darkness," said Madeleine.

The lane they drove up was so overgrown that branches scraped both sides of the car, and sometimes limbs hung so low that it seemed the lane ended entirely.

"Tearing up the side of the car," the driver murmured.

"I paid for the insurance coverage, didn't I?" asked Quentin.

"Oh, yes sir, no problem, sir, just talking to myself."

"I suppose they've been forgetting to have the gardener come out to the lane," said Madeleine. "Or maybe it's just Grandmother's idea of privacy."

At last the lane opened up onto a large field of snow. Not a tiretrack or footprint disturbed it, even though it had been days since the last snowfall. Only a slight depression in the snow showed where the lane went.

The house emerged from the great ancient trees that surrounded it, but could never have hidden it in the daylight, for it rose five rambling stories above a sweeping front porch with a stairway surely as wide and high as a Greek temple.

"How many hundreds of people live here?" asked Quentin in awe.

"In its heyday, there were probably half a dozen families. Nobody moved away. We were such a tightknit clan back then." She laughed. "Money requires a big house, anyway, Tin. No matter how many people actually live there. You're the only one who doesn't understand that."

A silent servant stood waiting for them, a tall thin man, the cliché of a butler. He wore only a lightweight jacket but didn't seem bothered by the cold.

"How did he know we were coming?" asked Quentin.

"I'm sure someone noticed the lights coming up the lane."

Quentin wasn't quite sure what the servant was there for, since he didn't open their car doors or help them get their luggage out of the car—the driver did all that. Quentin tipped the driver and sent him off. The tires crackled in the gravel and the engine sounded like a windstorm as the car swept away, its taillights streaking the snow with red.

"Much more Christmasy than anything in California," said Quentin.

"It doesn't feel Christmasy to me," said Madeleine. "It feels oppressive."

"Welcome home, Miss Cryer," said the servant softly.

"You see?" said Madeleine. "They know I'm Mrs. Fears now."

"Beg your pardon," said the servant. "Habit of decades."

The servant led them up the stairs. He must have come out of the house another way, since theirs were the first feet to break the crust of snow on the steps. Quentin carried his own bags; the servant was carrying Madeleine's. Was this a sign of things to come? Madeleine belonged here, and Quentin was barely tolerated? Or maybe if Quentin had simply left his bags, the servant would have come back down and picked them up later. He had no idea, really, how the whole business with servants worked. And from what Madeleine said, it might all be different here anyway. Her family followed its own rules.

Which was all the more apparent when not a soul from the household came to greet them. They were led up silent, empty stairs to a room on the third floor—a huge room, well furnished, but lighted by only two lamps with cloth cords that plugged into ancient two-prong outlets. "I guess nobody's brought this old place up to code," said Quentin.

The servant looked at him as if he were a newly noticed crack in the plaster, and then left the two of them in their oversized but ancient bedroom.

"Well, Mad, is there a bathroom attached to this room or do we wander down a hall?"

She laughed. "There's a bathroom attached to *all* the rooms now—somebody went on a modernizing kick back in the 1920s. When they put in the electricity they also put in the plumbing. But you can see up on that wall how the moldings aren't exactly right. That's because the wall didn't used to be here. This is a false wall added on so they could fit in two bathrooms, ours and the one attached to the next bedroom over." She showed him in to the quaint old bathroom, with a clawfoot tub and a toilet with the tank high on the wall. And a pull chain.

"Oh, really," said Quentin. "Surely this was old-fashioned even in the twenties."

"My family cultivates an air of eccentricity."

"I feel like we've walked into the castle of the beast."

She raised an eyebrow. "I know the place smells musty, but—"

"In the story of Beauty and the Beast. How she lived there but never met a soul for the longest time."

"Oh, they're all in bed."

"It's not that late."

"I didn't say they were asleep. The house keeps Grandmother's schedule. Quiet time begins right after supper. Everybody to their bedrooms. Including arriving guests. We can go on down to the kitchen and make sandwiches, though. As long as we don't slide down the banisters or shout through the halls. Everybody will stay out of our way until tomorrow."

"Who's everybody?"

"How do I know till I've taken inventory in the morning?"

So they divided up the drawers and closet space and unpacked and changed out of their traveling clothes into pajamas and bathrobes and padded downstairs in slippers to the basement kitchen. "This must be convenient for the servants," said Quentin.

"That's what dumbwaiters are for," said Madeleine. "It's *so* low-class to have the food prepared on the same floor where the family and company live." She laughed. "Oh, Tin, are you beginning to see why I didn't want to bring you here right away?"

"I remember the grande dame telling me that in the old days, everybody married for money. New money married old money. Is that what I am? New money?"

"No," said Madeleine. "You're nothing but a love machine to me."

"You have mustard on your lip." But while she was still looking for a napkin, he kissed it off. They carried their sandwiches upstairs.

7
No Place Like Home

In the morning, watching through half-open eyes as Madeleine staggered from bed to bathroom, Quentin wondered why he had been so emphatic about wanting to meet her family. Not because he actually wanted to feel this nervous, worried about whether he'd measure up to their expectations—or, worse, fit them exactly. It didn't help that Madeleine had been so maddeningly vague about what was wrong with her family. Or even, for that matter, who they were. The only one she ever mentioned specifically in connection with this house was her grandmother. Quentin's own grandmothers were so funny and loving and kind, each in her own way, that it was hard to imagine that any grandmother could be awful. What would an evil grandmother do, bake cookies without sugar? Refuse to babysit?

"Wake up, Quentin."

"Did I doze off?"

"I wasn't *that* long in the bathroom. I think you're just hoping to avoid meeting my family."

"Maybe. Unconsciously, I assure you."

"You still haven't opened your eyes."

"Who else am I meeting today? Besides your dreaded grandmother?"

"Whoever's in residence, of course."

"I'll meet your parents, won't I?"

"I doubt it."

He felt his insides twist. "Then why are we here? Mad, I wanted to meet your parents."

"You never said that. You said you wanted to meet my family."

"And are those two separate entities?"

"My parents don't live here. My mother had a falling out with my grandmother."

"Well, why don't we go meet your mother, then?"

"Because this is home," said Madeleine. "This is my inheritance."

"You're the only heir?"

"Tin, I think you're stalling."

"I just don't get how your family is related."

"Grandmother begat Mother, and Mother begat me. Like in the Bible."

Quentin pulled the pillow over his head. She jerked it off at once, then pulled off the covers. There was a definite chill in the room.

"Come on, it's cold."

"You should have put your jammies back on last night."

"After you went to all the trouble of pulling them off with your teeth?"

"In your dreams."

"You mean I was dreaming?"

"The glass of cold water comes next, Tin. Rise and shine."

Quentin immediately quoted: "'Whenever I hear you saying, Rise and shine, rise and shine, it makes me think how lucky dead people are!'"

"What are you quoting?"

"*Glass Menagerie*. Tennessee Williams. High school English class."

"Get. Out. Of. Bed." She began pulling on his foot. He let her drag him to the floor, then tried to pull her down on top of him. But instead she planted a foot on his chest and said, "Rise or die, Tin."

"Oh, well, if *that's* my choice."

The bathroom floor was icy. The water from the tap was icy. He ran and ran the hot water. The temperature didn't change. He stuck his head out of the bathroom door. Madeleine was shimmying into a dress. She never wore dresses in the daytime.

"How long do I wait for hot water?"

"There's no hot water in the morning here. Didn't I tell you? Grandmother believes morning baths are bad for the health. The hot water is turned on at two in the afternoon so that you can have a hot bath between four and six, in time for supper."

"Are you joking?"

"Was it funny?"

"So cold water is all I get?"

"It's good for what ails you."

He splashed the stuff onto his face and shivered into the face towel. He toyed with the idea of not shaving—his beard wasn't all that heavy and the color was light, and he often went a day without shaving. But Grandmother—he had to make the right impression on her, didn't he? If Mad was wearing a dress . . .

A few minutes later, dressed in sweater and slacks—she had warned him not to bring jeans, as there would be no occasion for which they would be regarded as appropriate— he gave Madeleine his arm, opened the door, and led her out into the corridor.

A man was standing there, arms folded. He had a beard, dark and cut to a point at the chin. His bearing was military, but his clothing was civilian. A suit, and rather an old-fashioned one. "About time the two of you came out of there."

"Why should it have bothered you, Uncle Stephen?" said Madeleine in a sickeningly sweet tone. "Did you need to use our bathroom?"

"Your grandmother wouldn't let anyone eat breakfast till you came down."

"So she's in a good mood. Glad to hear it."

Uncle Stephen scowled and marched down the stairs.

"She waited breakfast for us?" asked Quentin, incredulous. "It's noon!"

"It's actually a good sign, believe it or not," said Madeleine. "If she were angry at me, she would have made everybody else eat at dawn, and then make sure there was nothing in the kitchen for us to eat."

"So she makes everybody else fast, because she's feeling well-disposed toward you?"

"It's never a question of whether there will be suffering, Tin. The only question is who's going to be the victim. So far so good."

"Who's Uncle Stephen?"

"My father's brother."

"*He's* here, but your father isn't?"

"My father has a life."

"So Uncle Stephen isn't even a blood relative of the family? Just an in-law?"

"I didn't say that. My mother and father are cousins."

"Second cousins?"

"Wouldn't you like it better if I told you yes? But no. Uncle Stephen's father and Grandmother were brother and sister."

"But Grandmother got the house?"

"Grandmother gets what she wants. Except me."

Madeleine's parents were first cousins. Well, that didn't necessarily mean anything. Cousins marrying didn't mean there *would* be birth defects, only that the likelihood was increased.

They reached the main floor and Madeleine nodded

toward a pair of doors standing only slightly ajar. "During the winter we always have breakfast in the library. The sun warms the room."

"Sounds cheerful."

As they walked toward the doors, Madeleine added, "I should warn you that Grandmother probably won't speak to you."

"You've got to be kidding."

"Don't take it personally. She likes to disorient people. She can go weeks at a time without speaking a word."

"Then how do people know what she wants?"

"Oh, trust me, she makes her wishes known." Madeleine was still chuckling as they passed through the doors into the library.

The walls were lined with books, floor to ceiling, just as in the grande dame's house, but there was no ladder. Apparently no one ever needed the books on the top shelves. Quentin got the feeling that this wasn't a living library, constantly being added to, borrowed from. Rather it was a library by custom. Some ancestor had bought the books, but no one had actually read any of them in a century. They were wallpaper.

The heart of the room now was the long table that ran parallel to the array of floor-to-ceiling windows. It was of a dark wood polished so deeply that the scant morning light from the windows shone every bit as brightly in reflection as in reality. The bone-white china also had a deep luster, and the crystal was so fine that it seemed not to exist except as bright sparkles of light in the air.

Seated in formal array around the table were six adults, with two empty chairs for Quentin and Madeleine. The empty chairs were at opposite corners of the table.

Everyone's eyes were on them, of course, except for the bent, gray-haired woman, shawled and stooped, who sat with her back to them in the tall chair at the head of the table. Grandmother, obviously, since no one else in the room could possibly be a candidate. The only other woman at the table was in her fifties at the oldest, which made it impossible for her to be the ruler of this roost.

Madeleine led Quentin forward quite boldly until her hand was resting on the tall back of Grandmother's throne. "How lovely to see you all. May I present my husband, Quentin Fears. You may call him Mr. Fears. And you may call me Mrs. Fears. Quentin, darling, allow me to introduce my family."

She was going to have her family call her Mrs. Fears? Only with difficulty did Quentin keep his broad smile riveted to his face.

"Uncle Stephen you met in the hall upstairs."

Uncle Stephen half-rose from his chair. "Charmed, I'm sure."

"The pleasure is mine," said Quentin, relying more on dim memories of dialogue from high school Spanish class than on any actual knowledge of formal manners. "Am I to call you Uncle Stephen?"

"If you should have occasion to address me, Mr. Fears," said Uncle Stephen, "you may feel free to call me 'sir.'"

"Thank you, sir," said Quentin, trying to keep the irony out of his voice.

Madeleine laughed lightly. "Uncle Stephen was in the military for a few minutes during the Korean War and he allows no one to forget it—though I'm never sure whether he understood the difference between the Korean and Crimean wars. He's a Light Brigade-ish sort of soldier at heart. Ours but to do and die, right, Uncle Stephen?"

"Only Madeleine may speak to me so jocularly," said Uncle Stephen coldly, addressing Quentin. "In case you thought her jaunty airs might be tolerated in someone else."

"I'll try to avoid error, sir," said Quentin.

"The charming lady next to Uncle Stephen is Aunt Athena. She is Grandmother's youngest sister, the one who never married. Her real name is Minerva, but she hated it and chose the Greek version of the name when she was in her twenties. Aunt Athena is noted for her wisdom."

Aunt Athena smiled broadly. "Oh, Magdalena, I've missed you so much. Where have you been?"

"Busy busy busy," said Madeleine. "Isn't my husband a fine one?"

"Husbands are usually so overrated. But as long as he makes you pregnant and you produce an heir to this great empire of love." Aunt Athena suddenly realized what she had said, blushed, and pressed her hands to her cheeks. "Did I say 'pregnant'? Oh, what a tongue I have."

"The next empty chair," said Madeleine, "is yours, Quentin, but I fear that my chair, which is next to it at the foot of the table, is inappropriately occupied."

The young man sitting there—he could be no more than thirty—looked up and grinned saucily. "Grandmother lets me sit here all the time now, Mrs. Fears."

"But not when I'm home, Paul. We've had this discussion before."

"It's a chair, darling," said Paul. "Just a chair. You can sit anywhere."

"Paul is my mother's younger brother," said Madeleine. "He's really forty-five. He only looks so young because he wears makeup. He's also very short and wears lifts in his shoes. I have no doubt that he's sitting on a dictionary right now."

"Charming as ever, aren't you, darling?" said Paul. "Maddy was always my favorite niece, Mr. Fears. You can call me Paul, by the way. And don't go near the bluffs with Maddy. She's a pusher."

"Move," said Madeleine. "And try not to lick the forks before you do."

Paul got up and walked around the table to the other empty chair, at Grandmother's right hand. At the same time, Madeleine led Quentin around the table the other way, waiting for him to help her into the chair at the foot of the table. There really was a dictionary sitting there. She handed it to him. Heavy. After a moment's hesitation he set it on the buffet a few paces beyond the table. He rushed back to help Madeleine slide gracefully into her chair and push it up to the table. Not until he was seated himself, at her right hand, did he get a chance to look up to the head of the table and see the face of the fabled Grandmother.

She was asleep.

Madeleine continued the introductions. "To my immediate left is Simon. Simon is a friend of the family. He's been living here since . . . when was it, Simon? 1950? Was Truman still president?"

Simon looked bashful and confused. In his seventies, he had only the barest fringe of white hair. He ran one hand and then the other over his scalp. "The Cryers have always been extraordinarily generous to one who has nothing to offer but his meager friendship, which, despite its little value, is at least constant."

"I'm pleased to meet you," said Quentin, starting to rise from his seat.

"No don't!" cried Simon. "Don't get up! Not to me! Pretend I'm not here!" Then he hunched his head toward one shoulder and grinned as his body shook and his tongue darted in and out at the corner of his mouth. Apparently this was what passed for laughter in the obsequious Simon.

"Keeping Simon here is one of Grandmother's aesthetic statements," said Madeleine.

The comment stung Quentin with its viciousness. "Mad," he said softly.

She grinned and patted his hand. "He's deaf as a post, darling. And dumb as a stump."

Since Simon had just finished speaking, he could only assume that she meant 'dumb' in the sense of 'stupid.'

"And last but not least," said Madeleine, "is my cousin Jude. I'm not sure where on the convoluted family tree he actually fits, but he's long been a favorite of Grandmother's and as long as she lives, he'll have a place at her side."

"Oh, Mrs. Fears, you're always such a lark!" cried Jude. He was a bushy-eyebrowed old codger, even taller apparently than Uncle Stephen, but stooped so far that his head was rather near his plate, and he had to lift his head to bring the goblet to his lips. "Howdy, Mr. Fears. We're glad Madeleine—Mrs. Fears—found her a fine young man like you. *Welcome* and *glad* we are to know you. Are you really richer than God?"

"Now, Cousin Jude," said Madeleine, "you know that God's millions are counted in a more dependable currency than American dollars. There's no comparing."

Cousin Jude thought this was the funniest joke.

As the old man laughed, Quentin's eyes wandered to the head of the table, where he was startled to see that Grandmother's eyes were wide open, staring at him like headlights on bright.

Quentin turned to Madeleine and spoke softly. "Your grandmother . . . "

"Yes, Tin?"

But glancing back at the old lady, he was chagrined to see that her eyes were closed again.

"I thought she was awake."

"Oh, she's hearing everything, be sure of that. In and out of sleep, but aware all the time. And she has the hearing of a bat, so she's listening to our little whispers right now. Aren't you, Grandmother."

But Grandmother's eyes remained closed, her face slack with sleep.

At her right hand, Uncle Paul leaned forward with a grin. "Going to introduce me again, darling? I can change my name if you'd like."

"No need, Uncle Paul," said Madeleine. "Shall I ring for breakfast?"

"Please," said Uncle Stephen. "Some of us need to take nourishment at regular intervals."

"It's your bell, dear," said Aunt Athena.

Madeleine reached out and rang a small bell that sat beside her place at the table. It occurred to Quentin that hers was the place where Uncle Paul had been sitting. So he really had been an interloper there.

As soon as the bell rang, the same quiet servant from the day before opened the door from the butler's pantry, and two footmen came in with steaming plates, one of biscuits and one of scrambled eggs and bacon. Both began serving with Madeleine, and worked their way down the two sides of the table, crossing behind Grandmother and working up the other way. But no food was put on Grandmother's plate.

The collection of people around the table was odd, Quentin supposed, and there were certainly family tensions, but he couldn't help noticing that it was Madeleine who seemed to rule here, not Grandmother. It wasn't an idea he liked much, that Madeleine herself was the main source of family tension. And it wasn't fair, either. He had no idea of what had actually gone before. All the hostility might well have been earned. What did he know of these people? Uncle Paul, with his smarmy smile and ingratiating manner, was only fifteen years older than Madeleine but looked her age. For all Quentin knew, Paul might have molested Madeleine when she was a girl, or tried to; he might richly deserve Madeleine's goading. Not that Quentin took such speculation seriously, but after all, Madeleine *had* recoiled from his first attempt at any kind of serious physical intimacy with her. Wasn't it possible that Paul—or someone—had done something which made even a husband's caress at first repellent to her?

No, no, it wasn't right to start assigning unspeakable crimes to strangers. If Madeleine hadn't accused them, why should he?

The eggs were hot, the bacon cooked perfectly. The biscuits were steaming, freshly sliced, the butter still melting inside them. Whatever other failings this house might have, the cuisine had the simple perfection that approached the platonic ideal. Not scrambled eggs, but *the* scrambled eggs that all other scrambled eggs were imitating. The bacon of bacon, the biscuit of biscuits.

"Delicious," said Quentin to Madeleine.

She smiled, then leaned close to him and whispered, "Tin, in the upper classes one doesn't compliment the food. It's assumed that the food will always be perfect, and it isn't to be discussed."

He started to laugh, but caught himself when he realized she wasn't joking. All he could do was look at her oddly for a moment and then dig in to eat more. This was the food she was used to; he cringed to think of where he had taken her, what he had cooked for her. He had never wanted to live rich, but when they built a house, it would have to have a kitchen where a first-class chef would be glad to cook; and the chef would have to have a budget that would allow the acquisition of such ingredients. He could do no less for Madeleine, even if she said she didn't need such things.

The footmen came back for a second pass, this time with fruit—slices of pear so ripe they dissolved sweetly in his mouth almost without chewing; chunks of fresh pineapple with not a trace of acid sting to them; raspberries so plump and tart that the flavor seemed to dart through his whole face the moment he bit down on one. He closed his eyes to enjoy the perfect flavor without distraction.

"He's asleep!" crowed Simon. "Put him right out!"

Quentin opened his eyes, startled.

Simon looked crestfallen. "Oh, shame! No nap after all! Poor boy! Newlyweds get no sleep at all, do they!"

Madeleine put her hand on Quentin's knee under the table, to still his response. "Now, Simon," she said loudly, presumably to pierce Simon's deafness. "Mr. Fears is still a young man. He doesn't think of a nap as recreation yet."

"Not recreation!" cried Simon. "A feat! The great Olympic monathlon! To sleep, perchance not to dream! To obliviate one's dire sins in the wine of night!"

Grandmother was looking at Quentin again. And this time her eyes didn't close when he glanced at Madeleine and touched her sleeve.

"Grandmother," said Madeleine. "I hope he meets with your approval. He's everything I need, don't you think?"

Grandmother said nothing, but her eyes continued to drill into Quentin's soul, or so it seemed. He wanted to beg her pardon. He wanted to leave the room.

"With him beside me, I can open the box, don't you think?"

Grandmother's eyes slowly closed.

"Grandmother is annoyed with me," said Madeleine.

"Box?" asked Quentin.

"My inheritance. My grandfather left it for me. But by the terms of his will, I was forbidden to open it until my husband stood beside me."

The words cut him to the heart. She had never spoken of this before, never a hint that she stood to gain financially as soon as she brought a husband home.

"Oh, relax, Tin," she said. "I don't actually care about the inheritance. Not like I did when I was a girl. It bothered me *then*, of course, to see that box every day and know I couldn't open it. I grew out of that. I would have been happy never to come back here, never to open it. But since I *am* here, and *do* have a husband. . . ."

"I knew you weren't marrying me for my money," said Quentin. "It never occurred to me you might be marrying me for *yours*."

He said it with a smile and a laugh. But it was only barely a jest.

"It isn't money, I'm quite sure of that. Or if it is," said Madeleine, "it isn't much because the box isn't all that large." She laughed and patted his hand. "Quentin, you're taking all this too seriously. I called it my treasure box when I was little. I even made maps of the house to where it was buried, though of course it isn't buried at all, it just sits there in the open."

"That seems a cruel temptation to a child. You might just have opened it."

"If I open it prematurely, I can't keep what's inside," said Madeleine. "I think Grandmother always hoped I *would* open it, and lose it. That dear old temptress." Madeleine's laugh was light and not unkind-sounding. Yet it *was* unkind, Quentin thought. She can be unkind without even noticing it. Do I know my wife at all?

Madeleine leaned over and rested her head on his arm. "Quentin, I don't like who I become when I'm here. And you don't like me either. You would never have loved me if you had met me here. But when I go back outside with you, I'll be myself again, you'll see. My true self, my best self. Not this awful . . . whatever you think I am."

"I think you're my dear wife," said Quentin. "But going outside sounds like a good idea. You were going to show me the river."

"You had enough breakfast?"

"Full as a tick," said Quentin.

"Grandmother, do excuse us to take a walk along the bluff."

Grandmother's eyes followed Quentin as he rose to his feet and pulled back Madeleine's chair so she could also rise. But she said nothing.

Simon's voice piped up loudly. "Everyone here who is actually real, please raise your hand!"

Madeleine murmured to Quentin, "When they get to a certain age, I think they should be locked up somewhere."

Quentin laughed and shook his head. "Why, when he's already locked up in a dream?"

"Oh, you put that so beautifully." She squeezed his arm. "I *love* you."

The library had only the windows to link it with the outdoors. They had to cross the entry hall and go into the official dining room in order to reach a door leading out onto the back portico. It was a broad expanse of flagstones with five wide steps leading down to the snow-covered lawn. The lawn itself, interrupted only by an occasional tree that was invariably surrounded by a circular bench, flowed on to the bluff overlooking the river. The river itself was, of course, below the level of the bluff, but in the clear, weary light of a winter afternoon, they could see the dark shadows of trees against stark and shining snow on the bluffs on the opposite side of the river. Miles and miles away, it seemed, though it could hardly be that far.

"It's a little bleak," he said.

"Imagine it with leaves," said Madeleine. "Imagine it filled with life. Imagine it when the country was still young and you might hear the tootle of a steamboat on the river below, and the sound of children laughing as they ran along the bluff."

As she spoke, the pictures she conjured in his mind delighted him, and he smiled. "All right," he said. "I'm willing to admit that winter has its own beauty, too."

"This house wasn't always filled with strange old people, you know," said Madeleine. "It was once alive and bright."

"When you were a little girl here?"

"I was a solitary child when I lived here," said Madeleine. "And Paul—he was no company for *me*."

Quentin wondered again whether Paul might have molested her, or tried to.

"But Mother told me what it was like when she was young. She and Paul were little here, and even though that was well after the age of the steamboats, of course, they knew the stories—Aunt Athena told them—and they'd play steamboat captain down by the river or up in their attic playroom."

"The idylls of childhood."

"Whatever that means. Exactly."

"But Aunt Athena can't be old enough to remember steamboats, either."

"Oh, of course not. Just a conduit for old stories. Family memories. She has to use her head for *something*. Keeping the old tales alive isn't a bad occupation for it."

"Mad, you're so *nasty* about them."

"I'm sorry," she said. "I'm always so frightened when I come here, I'm not at my best."

"What are you afraid of?"

She didn't answer and she didn't answer, and then they were at the bluff and the river scene unfolded below them. Even with patches of ice along the edges of the river, it was formidably wide. Quentin remembered paintings by the Hudson River School and tried to apply those magnificent pastorals and landscapes to the scene before him. It wasn't hard. Before the river was a highway, it was a habitat, and now that the traffic was gone, perhaps that old life was coming back. Some old docks still touched the icy river edge, but at other places the verge of the river had been given back to the woods. How many squirrels were living off stored nuts in those trees in the lee of the bluffs? How many coons and rabbits, field mice and weasels lived without the sight of man for months on end?

Her hand stole around his waist and she leaned into him. "Oh, Quentin, I do love this place, I *do* love it. This is what brings me back, even though I hate who I become when I'm here."

"So let's open the treasure box and go. I can buy you another place on the river with a view just like this. Or better."

"There *is* no place just like this."

"You don't want me to look for another Victorian mansion?"

"Pre-Victorian, dear," said Madeleine. "Victorian is so . . . nouveau."

They laughed.

They walked on the path along the edge of the bluff. In a few places the drop-off was rather steep, and the path did skirt rather close. He couldn't help remembering Uncle Paul's jocular warning: Maddy's a pusher. And he was walking on the side by the river. But she wasn't pushing, she was holding him, and he loved the feel of the way their bodies moved, not quite together, but rubbing against each other, hip to hip, his arm across her shoulders, her arm around his waist. The breeze was a little chilly, but the sun was warm.

They reached the end of the family property and turned back to the house. They took a different path this time, and it led around a small stonewalled graveyard with an arched entrance. "Isn't it kind of morbid, keeping the family dead here on the property?" asked Quentin.

"It depends on how you regard the dead," said Madeleine. "They were part of us in life. Shouldn't they be part of us in death?"

"Will *you* be buried here someday?" he asked.

"*I* intend never to die," she said.

"Statistically, almost every woman who marries is signing on for widowhood at some time in her life."

"Do *you* want to be buried here?" she asked teasingly.

"Not unless I'm really dead," he said. "No fair burying me while I'm still snoring."

"You admit you snore?"

"Everybody snores," said Quentin. "But they only hear the other guy's snoring."

"And sleep through their own," said Madeleine. "Isn't that the way it goes."

"Does my snoring annoy you?"

"I think it's sweet," she said. "And when it keeps me awake, I pinch your nose and then you think you woke up to go to the bathroom and while you're in there trying in vain to aim somewhere near the toilet, I fall asleep very very quickly."

"What an efficient system. By the way, I may miss sometimes, but I've never yet peed on my feet."

"Or if you did, it didn't wake you," she said.

"You're as gross as a kid," said Quentin.

"It's one of the things you love best about me, though."

"Maybe," said Quentin. "But you have to promise to act shocked when our children talk gross. It's no fun if your parents can match you, ick for ick."

100

"I promise to be shocked."

They were back at the house. The dining room was empty. So was the library, and the table had been de-leafed and turned the other way, so it didn't take up the whole space between the vast walls of books. It wasn't as warm and inviting as the library in the grande dame's house had been. Instead of ladders, there was a balcony around three sides of the room, with a narrow spiral staircase leading to it. It all looked cold and uncomfortable, like a high canyon that you could only scale by taking your life in your hands climbing up a rickety narrow ladder. He went to the shelves to examine the titles, but Madeleine caught his arm almost at once. "Quentin, there's *nothing* readable there."

"In a house this old," he said, "there are bound to be some real finds."

"There aren't, trust me. Nobody actually reads. When this room was remodeled into a library, they bought books by the yard."

"Oh." Quentin was disappointed. He had once held a first edition, first printing of *Uncle Tom's Cabin*. In his hands, a book that started a war and changed the world, perhaps one of the very copies that had done it. But if the library was recent instead of old . . . still, even books bought at estate auctions sometimes had gems.

Nevertheless, he understood that Madeleine was more eager to open her treasure box than she wanted to admit. He let her lead him out into the entry hall and then into a parlor in the northeast corner of the house. It was lighted only by the windows, which on a winter afternoon meant the room was dim indeed, especially because heavy brocade curtains were closed at the top and swagged open near the base, so they more than half covered the glass.

Everyone was gathered here, though all but Uncle Paul and Grandmother seemed to hang back as close to the walls as the furniture allowed. Grandmother stood firmly, despite her shrunken, ancient appearance, her hands atop an intricately engraved mahogany box that stood on a small table in the middle of the room. Uncle Paul hovered near her, looking down at the box and then up at Madeleine and Quentin.

"Oh, darling, do hurry," said Uncle Paul. "I'm *so* eager to see what's left for you in there."

"I can bet you are," said Madeleine dryly. "Try to contain yourself."

Nevertheless, Paul's hands kept darting down toward the box, though he never quite touched it.

Grandmother's eyes stayed fixed on Quentin.

"Tin, dear," said Madeleine. "Why don't *you* open the box?"

"Oh, it's really not my place," said Quentin. "*Your* treasure, after all, and wanting to open it all these years."

Grandmother's eyes bored through him.

"Tin, I know it's silly, but now that it's come down to it, my hands are trembling so much I—isn't it silly? I guess this meant more to me than I thought. Won't you please help me out?"

"Is there a key or something?"

"No key!" Uncle Paul offered.

"Do keep your helpful information to yourself, Uncle P," said Madeleine.

"Oh, I know, darling, it's *your* prize."

"It *is*," said Madeleine. "There's nothing in there *you* can use. Count on it."

"Oh, I know," said Paul. "But we're all just so . . . *intrigued* with it. Like Christmas—you're dying to find out what's in everybody's packages, not just your own."

"Quentin," said Madeleine. "Please don't say no to me."

Quentin sighed and stepped to the box and put his hands on it. The wood was warm and smooth, the surface clean and polished. The geometric etching was intricately done, almost lacy in places. It was a beautiful box.

It was also a box with Grandmother's hands on it. Not to block him; her fingertips touched only the back corners of it.

But her eyes still drilled into him, and even though she said nothing, he couldn't help but assume she was forbidding him to open it.

"I don't think your grandmother wants me to open it."

"Did she say so?" asked Madeleine.

"She hasn't been very chatty so far today," said Quentin, "but as you said, she lets people know what she wants."

"Quentin, everybody else here knows it's my right to open it. And my husband's right—what's in there is as much yours as mine, isn't it? You didn't ask me to sign a prenup, and I didn't ask you to sign one, either."

"You know what just occurred to me?" Quentin said, laughing. "Wouldn't it be a kick if it turned out that the box itself was the inheritance? You know, a keepsake. Nothing in it at all, just the box itself. The magical dreams of childhood, preserved forever."

"There's something in it, all right," said Madeleine.

"It's just chock full of stuff," said Uncle Paul.

"Something is chock full of something, anyway," said Madeleine. "You're not helping, Uncle Paul."

"I'm not?" said Paul. "Oh, foo. Fum. Fee fie foe."

"Tin, aren't you going to open it for me?"

"Sure, of course," said Quentin.

"Then do. Just open it."

"I am," said Quentin.

"You are what?" said Madeleine.

"Opening it."

"The evidence of my eyes says otherwise," said Uncle Paul, leaning close and looking him right in the eyes. "Open the damn box, you impotent lickspittle."

The venom in his voice almost stung. Quentin took a step back, removing his hands from the box.

Grandmother was still looking at him, but was she smiling a little?

"Tin!" wailed Madeleine. "Just go to the box, take hold of the corners of the lid, and lift it up. There's not even a latch!"

103

He stood there in embarrassment, unsure of why he couldn't quite bring himself to do this simple thing for his wife. "Is this a joke? Is something going to pop out at me?"

Madeleine abruptly began to beat the air with her fists like a tantrum-throwing child. "Open it open it open it!" Her face twisted into a grimace of weeping.

"Good heavens, Mrs. Fears, what a display!" cried Uncle Paul.

"Madeleine," said Quentin. "What's going on? This is too weird for me."

Abruptly she stopped the tantrum and was in control of herself, but the damage had been done. Quentin had seen a side of her he didn't know existed. Like a spoiled child. That's how she had acted ever since coming into this house. Like a bratty kid who was used to being able to say anything to anybody and no one would reprove her.

"It's *her* stopping you, I know it," said Madeleine. "Grandmother won't let me have what's rightfully mine."

"Madeleine, I just don't feel right about opening it," Quentin said. "Can I help that? If it's so easy, you open it, not me. I want you to, really. I'm just not part of this. Open it."

She slapped at him, though she was too far for her hand to reach him. Bursting into tears she screamed, "Why did I marry you if you can't do the one thing I want most for you to do!"

"Look, I'll open it!" Quentin said. "But I hope you know this isn't the most attractive you've ever looked in your life."

"Open it!" She was frantic now, almost panicked.

Quentin touched the box again. It was so warm. His fingers tingled. This whole business is turning me into a basket case, he thought. Obviously this box was far more important to her than she had let on. And yet she had kept it a secret from him through their whole engagement and these months of marriage. Plotting and planning. It meant that he had been manipulated and he hated that. Hated manipulating and being manipulated.

104

"Mad, I really think this isn't a good time to open the box," Quentin said. "You're upset and I'm upset and we need to have a talk about this first."

She wailed at him, sinking to her knees. "There's nothing to talk about! It's mine!"

"I know it's yours. But it's waited all these years, can't it wait till we talk this out?"

"Do you think talking will *help*?" she retorted. "She's stopping you. She's getting her way and I hate her for it! I'll kill her, I swear it."

"She's *not* stopping me, for heaven's sake, Mad!" But in a way she was, those fingertips on the box, those piercing eyes.

"What do *you* know about it!" Madeleine wailed. "All this work, all these months, I'm so *tired!* All for *nothing!*"

"I hope you're not referring to our marriage," said Quentin, trying to sound like he was joking. But of course he was not joking. He was frightened.

"If you loved me," said Madeleine, rising again to her feet, her face a mask of fury. "If you *loved* me like you say, you would open this box right now. This minute. This *second.*"

Quentin turned to the box again, put his hands on the lid. The box trembled. "My hands are shaking," he said. "I don't think—right at this moment, Madeleine, I'm wondering—you make me wonder if our whole marriage is a sham, just so you could get me to open this box. Tell me that isn't true, Mad. This whole thing is so crazy, it can't be true."

"Open," she whispered, her face a mask of fury. "The. Box."

Quentin took his hands away from the trembling box and pressed them to his face. "Mad. Mad, what's happening to us?"

She screamed. Not the scream of a child in tantrum, but a high wail that sounded like a woman keening with grief. He turned to her, reached out his hands in pleading. She recoiled from him, spun around, and ran, staggering, from the room.

Confused and frightened and hurt, Quentin turned back toward the box. "I'll open it, Mad! Come back, I'm opening it, see?"

But Uncle Paul's hand was on the box now. "Not without Mrs. Fears in here, Mr. Fears," he said, smiling. "It's in the will."

Quentin looked around the room. Somehow, without his noticing it, all the others had slipped out of the room. Well, he wasn't surprised—this hadn't been a pleasant scene to watch. Only Uncle Paul and Grandmother remained, both of them touching the treasure box. Quentin looked Grandmother in the eye. "Doesn't she love me, Grandmother?" he asked.

The old lady's lips began to move. Slightly, no sound coming out.

"I should follow her," Quentin said. "I'm going to follow her and bring her back and we'll open the box and then we'll get *out* of here and everything will be all right. That's what I should do, isn't it?"

Her lips moved again. He leaned close, to hear her.

"Babbling old woman," murmured Uncle Paul, but he removed his hand from the box and stepped back out of the way.

Grandmother, almost nose-to-nose with him now, whispered to him. "Find me," she said.

It made no sense at all. The woman was senile. She was no more in control of this house than Quentin was.

Madeleine. Somehow she could explain it all. She could make sense of it. She was his wife, after all. She loved him, he loved her, they had everything in common, they had their lives together, she was his and he was hers forever. This was just some insane quarrel, some stupid misunderstanding.

Where was she? He ran out of the parlor into the entry hall. He checked the library, the drawing room, the dining room. The door to the back portico was open, the winter chill already skimming the floor so his feet went cold as soon as he entered the room.

He ran to the French doors leading out to the portico. She wasn't there. He cast his gaze out across the lawn of snow just in time to catch a glimpse of her, her hands at her face, as she ran awkwardly into the walled graveyard.

Immediately he took off after her across the snow.

8
Footprints

Quentin couldn't see her in the graveyard. He ran among the headstones, looking left and right, but she wasn't kneeling anywhere, wasn't standing behind anything. There were bushes, but all of them were leafless. If she was within the graveyard walls, he would see her.

There was no other gate. He ran to each of the far corners of the enclosure, to see if her footprints led to the wall, if by some chance she had climbed it.

How absurd! She was wearing a dress, she was angry, upset—why would she climb a wall?

But then, where was she?

He must have looked away as he ran toward the graveyard. While he was watching his footing in the snow she must have seen him coming and slipped back out again, wanting to avoid him. And maybe she was right. Let her calm down, let him calm down. They could face this problem rationally. She had warned him that there would be problems when she went home. She had told him that she didn't like the person she became when she was here. Well, she had been right all along. He didn't like the person she became, either. But the person she was outside of this place,

109

the person she *really* was—he loved her, and they could get away from this place and go back to their life and this would become a half-funny memory, to be told to no one. It would become in-references between them. They would call some longstaying visitor a "friend of the family" and both of them would think of Simon. Someone would be obnoxiously formal and they would wink and whisper, "Uncle Stephen." Someone would say something foolish in the attempt to be wise, and they would say, "Athena," and remember this breakfast and the dear foolish spinster aunt who sat at table with them.

But they would never joke about Grandmother. Or Uncle Paul. Or the treasure box. There was real pain there, and if Quentin ever understood it, fine, but if he never did that was also fine, as long as he had his Madeleine and they never had to come back to this place.

He had run the circuit of the graveyard, looking for her footprints. They weren't there. She hadn't come in here after all.

He stood in the entrance, looking down at the snow. Only one set of prints led into the graveyard. His own.

But he had seen her run in here. From the portico he had watched her before he ran across the lawn to meet her here.

He looked out onto the lawn. There were the footprints the two of them had made that morning, the distant ones leading down to the bluff, the near ones that marked their return journey. He walked over to the near prints. Only one set of shoes had broken the crusty surface of the snow. Again, they were his.

She *was* with him. He had his arm around her; she held him by the waist. They jostled together as they walked. He remembered it. It was impossible that she left no prints in the snow. But then, he had also seen her enter the graveyard.

As he had seen a woman who looked something like Lizzy unlock the door of a townhouse in Herndon and walk in and switch on the lights.

He returned to the graveyard and leaned his back against one of the legs of the stone arch of the gateway. He was hallucinating again. This was disturbing, but not terrifying. It happened the first time out of loneliness, out of longing. This time it was a different kind of stress. But both times he had seen what he needed desperately to see: the first time, Lizzy grown up and leading a normal life; the second time, Madeleine going into a place where he could find her and talk to her and make things right between them. Where he could make sure of her, that she was the woman he knew and loved and not this stranger, this tantrum-throwing, greedy child who had to have someone open up her treasure box.

Of course, normal people didn't hallucinate, even in times of stress. It meant that he had some sort of mental illness. But it wasn't really impairing his functioning yet. They had drugs now to help schizophrenics control their psychosis. That must be what was going on with him, the early symptoms of advancing schizophrenia. But he could go to a psychiatrist and get the drugs he needed to continue functioning. This could be controlled. There was no reason to be afraid.

No, come to think of it, there *was* a reason. Because he hadn't been under stress when he walked with Madeleine along the bluffs, and that had to have been a hallucination, too, because she left no footprints.

Unless it was a hallucination *now*. Unless his mind was erasing footprints that really *were* there, because he couldn't bear to have her with him if she was the person he saw in the parlor. That would explain it. He was in the middle of a serious psychotic episode but it would pass. Even without treatment, these episodes passed, didn't they? Especially in the early stages of the mental illness. He had read a book about this a few years ago and he thought that was how it worked. Once he had control of himself, he would walk out of the graveyard and see two sets of footprints, and he would go back to the house and find Madeleine in the bedroom. That's where she had to be. He hadn't even looked for her upstairs. His need to find her had been so great that he had looked out the open dining room doors and seen her outside when in fact she was probably up on their bed, crying and waiting for him to come to her.

He turned to head for the house, but there was that trail in the snow, and her footprints had not reappeared. He couldn't go back yet. He would take a few moments to collect himself. The world had to return to normal. He had to get a grip on reality. He thought of those old tire ads where fingers grew out of the treads to snatch at the asphalt of the highway. He was skidding along, skipping over things; had to turn into the spin and control it, like driving a car on ice.

He began walking among the stones in the graveyard, looking at the names so that he could get his mind off what was happening to him. Of course there wouldn't be any Cryer names here. The house had been in Madeleine's mother's mother's family, and he had no idea what their name was. There was such a mixture of names on the stones, none preeminent. But the first names were recognizable enough. Families naming new babies after older family members, and the first names passed down generation after generation. There was a Jude. A Stephen. No Athena, but that wasn't her real name, was it? Ah, here was a Minerva. And off in the corner, even a Simon.

But Simon wasn't in the family, was he? So of course it was just coincidence that his name had a match in the graveyard. He looked closely at the stone:

SIMON WISTER

UNKNOWN–FEB. 2, 1877

"I WAS A STRANGER, AND YE TOOK ME IN."

The heat of blood rushing to his face came even before the thought entered his conscious mind. Simon was a visitor who stayed. And here was a headstone belonging to a Simon whose birthdate was not known, and whose epitaph was to a stranger who was taken in.

Well, Quentin, he thought, as long as you're losing your mind, why not throw in some dead people walking around and eating breakfast with you?

He went back to the Minerva headstone.

MINERVA MUELLER

1 JUNE 1866–12 JULY 1918

BELOVED OF ALL

WISDOM IN SIMPLICITY

Summer 1918 would suggest that this Minerva was carried off in the flu epidemic. At age . . . fifty-two. Wisdom in simplicity. Could this be a kindly way of referring to dimwittedness? If the Aunt Athena he had met this morning were to keel over, could he imagine a more appropriate inscription than this?

But they sat at table and ate with him. They talked with him and with Madeleine. They were *real*.

"Everyone here who is actually real, please raise your hand."

Uncle Simon's words came back to him with painful clarity. Everyone had ignored him, of course, as if he were a madman. But then, no one had raised a hand, either.

COL. STEPHEN ALAN FORREST

DEC. 22, 1910–DEC. 24, 1951

HE DIED IN DISTANT SNOWS

IN SEARCH OF PEACE

ON HIS GRAVE THE LILY GROWS

113

PURE WITHOUT CEASE
THE LILY KNOWS, THE SOLDIER KNOWS
HOW SHORT IS LIFE'S LEASE

His military bearing. Someone—Madeleine—said that he had served in the Korean War. But he was *not* old. Forty-one, the age of the Stephen buried here, that was a good approximation of the apparent age of the Uncle Stephen at breakfast. But even an 18-year-old who fought in Korea, if he was alive today, would be sixty at the youngest. And Uncle Stephen did not look sixty, not with that dark beard, that ungraying hair. Maybe he dyed it. Or maybe he was dead.

Cousin Jude's namesake, Philip St. Jude Laurent, was born in Yorkshire in 1799 and died in America in 1885. Hadn't there been a hint of some kind of accent when he spoke?

No, no, this was madness.

He did not know Grandmother's name, and so he could not look for her headstone, if she had one here.

The only Paul in the graveyard had died as a baby, not a man of forty-five, as Madeleine had said Uncle Paul was, or of thirty, as he seemed to be.

And without admitting to himself that he was looking for one, he found to his great relief that there was no headstone for anyone named Madeleine.

Names ran in families, that's all. Names and family lore. Mad was goading them, introducing them with links to names from the graveyard whose stories they would have known. She was being a brat this morning, that's all, and he was simply the only one who didn't get the joke. The others would all have known about these headstones.

But there were no footprints here in the snow except his own.

He walked out of the graveyard, but instead of returning to the back portico, he walked around to the front of the house. There were the tire tracks from the limo, coming around the driveway. Here's where the car stopped and the driver got out and walked around to the right side and the left side of the car, to open doors for them. On the left side, where Quentin had been sitting, his own footprints dutifully appeared, showing how he walked around to the trunk, where he stood as he took his bags from the driver, where he walked as he headed around the other side of the car to walk on up the front stairs of the house.

But there were no footprints at Madeleine's door except those of the driver as he shuffled to open it for her. There were no footprints where the servant had stood. And only one set of prints, Quentin's, led up the front stairs to the door.

If this is a hallucination it's awfully selective, thought Quentin.

He was rather proud of how calmly he was taking the clear evidence of his own mental breakdown.

Somewhere inside that house was Madeleine. She would help him sort this out. She had married him in sickness and in health, hadn't she? Didn't they say that in the old church wedding vow? She would get him to a shrink and they'd get this under control and life would go on.

He climbed the steps, adding only the second set of footprints to break the snow, opened the front door of the house and stepped inside.

It was not the same house.

Oh, the rooms were arranged the same. Even the furniture was in the right place. But dustcovers were on all the major pieces of furniture, and the floor was half an inch thick in dirt and dust, except where his own peregrinations of last night and this morning had carved paths in it. Every step he took stirred up dust clouds and in only a few moments he was sneezing and coughing. If he had come through here before, why hadn't he sneezed and coughed before? Or had he? He had vague memories of wondering last night if he was coming down with a cold. Or was he merely inventing that memory to try to make these things make sense?

He opened the library doors. The windows had had several panes broken out, and snow had drifted across the cloth-covered table. Hundreds of books had been scattered across the floor. The room was freezing cold. His footsteps alone marked a passage across the floor, to what was obviously the only chair that had been moved and sat upon in many years. The others were tied to the table and floor and each other by cobwebs and spider webs. Even the chair he had used was bewebbed and dusty, and now he looked down at his own clothing for the first time and realized that strands of web and patches of dust were drawn across his jacket, his trousers. He brushed at them, and they came away; how could he not have noticed them before?

I am not going through a psychotic episode right now. The certainty grew even as he framed the words in his mind. This morning I was seeing things that were not real. People at breakfast. This room clean, this furniture lustrous. The footmen bringing perfect food here—not a single footprint led from the butler's pantry to the table. What did I eat, then?

The answering churning in his stomach told him that he had eaten nothing. The dryness in his mouth told him that he had drunk nothing. Not since yesterday in the limo, the Icelandic bottled water he had poured for himself and Mad. Had she drunk it? Was there anyone there to do the drinking? Had there ever been anyone there?

Yes, there had to have been. The limo driver *did* go to her door to open it—he saw her, too! His parents had seen her. His friends, the people at parties and meetings all over America—they all saw her, talked to her. They couldn't all be insane, or if they were, then insanity had lost all meaning.

Madeleine! He felt a sudden terrified yearning for her. Madeleine, how could I even for a moment have stopped believing in you!

He ran from the library, out into the entry hall, then up the two flights of stairs to the room they had shared. He flung open the door. There were his two bags, the suitcase and the carry-on. His side of the bed had been disturbed and slept in. But there were no sheets, just a single white dust-cover thrown over the mattress, and webs fringed the bed on every side. Only his drawers in the bureau had been disturbed. Only his clothing hung in the musty wardrobe.

He ran into the bathroom. There was no water in the toilet, just his own urine at the bottom of the bowl. The floor of the bathroom was grimy. The tub was vile—at some point the sewer must have backed up and left grime all over the bottom of it. Had she known? Had she known what the bathroom was really like, and had enough compassion for him to steer him away from trying to bathe in it? The taps in the sink gave no water. His toothbrush still had toothpaste embedded in it—he hadn't rinsed it, but he had brushed his teeth. And now that he thought about it, he could taste the toothpaste in his mouth, could feel the graininess of it between his cheek and gums.

His heart beating madly, his mind racing yet thinking of nothing, he quickly gathered all his clothing out of the wardrobe and the drawers, his kit out of the bathroom, and crammed them all into his luggage. I slept alone in here last night, he thought. And yet we made love, Madeleine and I. We made love and then finished our sandwiches. But there was not a crumb to be found, and only a disturbance of the dust and grime on the small night table where his fingers must have brushed across the surface as he thought he was setting down the plate with his sandwich on it.

Luggage in hand, he left the room and clattered down the stairs. He did not even bother to look for a telephone. If this house had one, it would be as disconnected as the electricity and the waterlines.

The electricity. Today he could see because of light from the windows. But last night there *was* no light. And yet he hadn't bumped into anything. Someone had led him.

Madeleine had led him. She might leave no footprints, but someone who knew this house had been with him or he never could have made his way inside in the darkness, up the stairs, into the bedroom in the pitch black that must have prevailed. The thick bedroom curtains had been closed.

I was not making it all up. Hallucinations can make you see things that aren't there, but they can't possibly let you see things that *are* there in pitch darkness. Schizophrenia doesn't give you a flashlight.

He set down his bags beside the door. He had been brought here by someone for some reason. The illusion had continued right up to the time when he didn't open the treasure box. Then Madeleine had fled and everyone disappeared except Uncle Paul and Grandmother. The ones whose headstones he had identified in the graveyard had disappeared.

What was real? The cleanliness of the place had been illusion, the food and servants were false, the people were—what, ghosts?—but the table had been real, the chairs, the doors, the bed, even the toilet and sink and tub in the bathroom. Maybe, in the parlor, on a small table, there really was an engraved wooden box that someone, for some reason, needed his help to open up.

He turned and headed for the door leading to the parlor. But as he approached it, two bright white letters appeared on the door.

NO

"I'm not making this up," he whispered to himself.

The letters disappeared. He took another step toward the door.

More letters appeared, faster this time, smaller, each word taking the place of the one before.

DON'T

COME

IN

GET

OUT

GET

OUT

DEATH

DEATH

LIVES

HERE

He backed away from the door, looked around at the gloomy walls. In the cold dark fireplace something flickered. A light. He did not move closer; rather he recoiled from it, fearing what it would be. Yet he couldn't take his eyes away.

A rat emerged and perched atop the pile of ancient lumber stacked there. It looked him piercingly in the eye. As Grandmother had done. It opened its mouth.

"Find me," it said.

This was not madness, Quentin knew that now. It was not his mind creating a false reality. On the contrary, his mind was correctly apprehending that the rules that he had always believed reality to be governed by did not apply in this house. Something had made a rat speak, had made

119

words appear on a door to a room he must not enter. Something had led him through this house in the dark. Something had made him believe that the woman he loved was at his side as he walked alone along the bluffs. Someone had introduced him to a group of dead people at breakfast and convinced him that he was eating the best food he had ever tasted in his life, while leaving his stomach empty.

All this he understood rationally. But his body was not rational. His heart was pounding, his limbs were cold, his fingers trembled. He dared not turn his back on the rat, on the parlor door, and yet dared not stay in this place another moment. So he did turn, and walked briskly to the front door where his luggage waited for him. He opened the door, picked up his bags, and stepped out onto the snowy porch.

At the foot of the stairs, where the car had stopped last night, Madeleine stood waiting for him, her face calm, even sad.

The terror fled, swept away by his relief. Madeleine was real. Madeleine was here. His love for her washed over him again. It would be all right. She would see him through this episode of—of whatever it was.

"Mad," he said. "You won't believe what I've been going through."

She shook her head. "Oh, Tin, I'm not Madeleine. Not anymore. She's gone."

He walked down the stairs toward her. "Call yourself whatever you want, you're here. I thought I had lost you."

"You lost me years ago, Tin. When I died in that hospital. When I told you to mellow out. When I told you not to keep me tied down."

He stopped, not believing the words coming out of Madeleine's mouth.

"You dig, you dig, you dig?" she said.

And then it wasn't Madeleine's mouth. There was no transformation. It had never been Madeleine.

"Lizzy," he whispered.

120

"Now you see me," she said. "But you're still not seeing me. It's your own mind putting this shape on what I am."

"Was it you all along?" At once he remembered seeing her in the grocery store, and going into that townhouse.

"That wasn't me," she said. "But that was part of why I came. You have the power to call me. When you thought you had seen me, your need for me brought me back here. Most of us are tied to our bodies, our relics, but I'm tied more to you. I don't mind, really I don't. Especially because when I came, I saw the danger you were in."

"But if it's you, Lizzy, I'm not in danger."

"It wasn't me, don't you get it? It was someone else who found my image in your mind and used it. When I came to you she was making you see that hallucination of me going into the townhouse, but I wasn't inside the thing you saw, Tin, I was with *you*. There in the car beside you, feeling you call to me. You're so strong when you call to me like that. Even if I wanted to, I don't think I could stay away."

"Why didn't you speak to me then, the way you're doing now?"

"Because *she* was there. The dead don't have any strength compared to the living. If she wants me silent, if she's paying attention to me, then believe me, Tin, I can't speak."

"*I'm* alive, Lizzy. *I* wanted you to speak."

"Yes, you had the strength to call me, but, Tin, if you're strong, she's—well, she's beyond strong. When she noticed me, she saw the opportunity. She used me, kept me close by, so she could raid my memory the way she raided yours. Use me as part of that Madeleine thing she made. She's a master at manipulating the dead. I thought it was mortuary reunion week at breakfast here this morning. All last night she was rummaging through the graveyard, calling those poor saps back from wherever they were and forcing them to attend her little banquet."

"Why? Who is she? Is *she* Madeleine?"

"I told you, she *made* Madeleine. Out of nothing. Out of

your desires. Whatever you thought was beautiful and charming, that's what Madeleine became. The way she found the perfect taste and smell and texture for every food you ate today. She also drew on me, of course, forced me into the illusion. I was like clay to her, I couldn't do anything but what she wanted as long as she watched me."

"So I guess she's not watching now."

"You failed her. She left raging. And for the time being, she forgot me. For the first time since you called me back, we're alone together."

Quentin remembered how it was when he first took Madeleine home to meet Mom and Dad. How Madeleine never left them alone.

"Yes," said Lizzy. "Like that. Because she's mortal, she has power over me. She could paste little bits of me into Madeleine. My memories of you. Little habits of mine that you would respond to without realizing it."

"And I believed it all."

"Of course you did. Everyone did. When you went out in public with Madeleine, she pulled me in and used me as the core of her, so the illusion could fool hundreds of people all at once."

"That must have been hard for you."

"Only because I hated what she was doing to you. As for me, I had no urgent appointments. The dead never do. It's not that we're apathetic, we still care about things as much as ever. We're . . . patient."

"And yet you're here."

"Because *you* have a deadline. Because there are worse things than death."

"Losing Madeleine?"

"Opening that box."

"Why? What's in it?"

"I don't know what it is, Tin. I only know that it's very strong and the others are all terrified of it."

"The others?"

"The other dead ones. The dead ones at breakfast. The only one who doesn't fear it is the one who's been using us. *She* hungers for it. That's why she's so angry now. Why she isn't paying attention to us. We aren't useful to her at the moment."

"So she *is* human. She can only do one thing at a time."

"She's stronger than you and definitely stronger than me, but she can't do everything. I don't think she was able to keep her true self from leaking into Madeleine. Especially today. Today she was so busy keeping her dead puppets under control that she wasn't as careful about making Madeleine act like Miss Perfect all the time. Especially when she had the servants in the room. There weren't any real people behind those servants, dead or alive. She was just making you see them. That's a lot harder than building an illusion around a real soul. Making those servants about wore her out. And while she was maintaining them, some of the others got to sneak in a few things they wanted to say to you."

"Lizzy, I don't understand this."

"And you think I do? It's not like they give us a manual: How to Be Dead. The answers to everything don't become clear the minute you die. I mean, now I know there's definitely a life after death, but we don't look like humans to each other. You see me like this because when you recognize that I'm Lizzy, your mind adds the rest."

The moment she said it, he realized that she was looking a lot less definite. Wavering.

"Don't lose me now," Lizzy cried. "I have to tell you how this works, so you aren't completely helpless against her!"

He reached for her, but there was nothing there. She faded more. "I don't know how to hold on to you!"

"Don't look at me! Look away, listen to my voice until you have me in your head again. The way it was when I read to you out of my favorite books."

"That was real, then," he whispered.

"Listen to me. I don't think she's done with you. She

123

needed you for some reason, and she didn't get what she wants, so she *still* needs you, and I don't know how to fight her but at least I can tell you what I've figured out about how things work. That's something. It's all I can do."

He nodded, not looking at her. "I'm listening."

"Most mortals can't see us dead people, but she can. So can you, sometimes. She can also cut loose of her body without dying and go out and do stuff. You *can't* do that."

"Is she here now? Is she listening to us? Would you even know?"

"I would know, and she isn't, not right now. I can't even feel her rage, that's how far off she is. Maybe she went back to her own body, wherever that is. The point is that when she's loose and wandering, she's like us dead people. Only she's stronger because her body's alive. So let me tell you what I've figured out about souls, so you'll know what *she* is when she's loose. We don't even have a location, unless somebody mortal calls us the way you called me. When I'm not here with you, I'm nowhere in particular. We're still free to make choices, but without a body there aren't a lot of choices to make. We can't change anything in the physical world, and we're kind of weak in some ways. We can get tired—I'm about wiped out now. And we're still bound to our old lives, for a while at least, until the old ties dissolve away. The people she called to breakfast, they're tied to this house, to the family that holds this place. She's part of it, and she can use it to bring them and tame them. That's the list. All I Know About Death, by Lizzy the Dead Girl."

"Lizzy, who *is* she?"

"I don't know, Tin, that's what I'm trying to tell you. If I knew, do you think I'd keep it a secret from you? I only know that she's so strong she must be mortal. She's a living person. And she's so powerful that she's able to create illusions that you and everybody else can actually see and touch and—and all the other things you did with her."

Quentin thought of all that he had done with Madeleine.

"Lizzy, you said that sometimes you were part of Madeleine. . . ." He blushed.

"She only used me like that in crowds, Tin. And don't worry about what I saw. We don't have bodies here, we don't care about that stuff."

"Lizzy, I loved her."

"You loved a dream that had been made real by a person so cruel that—I hate her, Tin. She's vile. But Madeleine wasn't vile. Madeleine was wonderful."

"If this—person—if she's vile, how could she create something as . . . someone like Mad?" And he was filled all over again with longing for his wife, who he now knew was gone forever, even though he needed her as much as always.

"She didn't invent Madeleine. You did. She took Madeleine out of your head. You gave her the script and she acted it out for you. What you loved was your dream of love."

"Why was she doing this to us?"

"All I know is it has something to do with what's inside that box. Obviously she can't open it herself, or she wouldn't need you."

"But if she wanted me to open it, why were Grandmother and Uncle Paul stopping me? At least, she seemed to think Grandmother was stopping me, and he blocked me the last time I tried to open it—"

"Well, see, the Grandmother and Paul, she didn't call them. They just came. The old lady is a wanderer, like *her*. Not dead. Uncle Paul—I'm not sure what he is."

"Lizzy, I'm crazy, aren't I? You've never been real and even there in the hospital I was out of my mind with grief and so I hallucinated your voice and I've been crazy ever since."

"Listen to me, Tin! Don't get weak on me! You are not insane. Everything you saw, you were made to see. And what went on in that parlor today, that was real. She didn't choose you accidentally. Like I said, you're strong. Not like her, but strong enough that she can't just do whatever she wants to you. You see through her sometimes. Like when she was controlling Mom and Dad, you saw it, you saw there was something wrong, and it really scared her, I could feel that. She needed you for some reason but she's also just a little bit afraid of you because she can't control you. So you're not without resources."

"Then teach me how to use them!"

"I don't *know* how. I never had power like that when I was alive, and I certainly don't know anything about people like this . . . this *user.*"

"What about this Grandmother person? You said she was alive, too. And she told me to find her. Is that so she can teach me?"

"I don't know anything except that she's in a mortal body somewhere in this world, and she and the User hate each other. Whatever it is that the User wants, Grandmother's trying to stop it. And if she said for you to find her, well, maybe you should."

"But why doesn't she just find me? Madeleine did."

"I don't know, Tin. I've told you everything I know."

"What about Uncle Paul? If she didn't call him, who is he?"

"I don't understand what he is. The User got all upset and excited when he showed up. And Grandmother hates him and fears him even more than she fears the User. He's tied to this house much more tightly than any of the others. And the User and Grandmother were both fighting him the whole time at breakfast, keeping him under control. That's what I know. That's all of it."

"Lizzy, what am I going to do?"

"I don't know. Maybe they'll all leave you alone now. Maybe you can pick up your bags and walk out of here and go back to your life."

"What life? Madeleine was my life. It's like she's died, only she never lived. Lizzy, it's like losing you all over again."

"Only you haven't lost me. And as for her—what you found in her was yourself."

"Oh, that's great, now I don't have to write to Ann Landers or go on Oprah."

"Don't be a snot, little brother. I'm telling you the truth. Everything you found in Madeleine is still in you. Waiting for you to love a real woman and give all that to her."

"Yeah, well, apparently women don't come with signs announcing which ones are flesh and blood and which ones don't leave footprints in the snow."

"I don't leave footprints, either, Tin. But I still love you. That's why you have the power to call me. And maybe this User, whoever she is, maybe while she was busy trying to control you to get you to open that box, maybe she also fell in love with you a little. If she has any spark of humanity in her, I don't see how she could help it. So maybe you have some power over her, too."

"I don't want power." He sank down to the snowy step and buried his head in his hands. "Lizzy, I want my life back."

"Don't we all," she whispered.

He felt something touch him, warm and deep, like a candleburst inside his heart. Like a soft breath of joy that swept through him and brightened him, and he looked up to ask her what it was she did to him, how it was she could give him such a gift of light. But she was gone. He was alone on the front porch of an empty house.

Empty, but not empty. A house where writing appeared on doors and rats talked and a wife more dear to you than your parents, more loved than your beloved dead sister, a wife who was the whole meaning of your life could simply disappear. Could run away without leaving a footprint in the snow.

9
Missing

Quentin had a lot of time for thinking as he trekked through the waning afternoon to the nearest town, which was not particularly near. He had time to think as he waited for a car to come up from New York to pick him up. And on the drive down to La Guardia, and as he flew on the shuttle to Washington, and at last when he walked into the apartment where he had lived when he fell in love with Madeleine, he had plenty of time to think.

He thought of all kinds of things. About Grandmother. Lizzy had said she was a mortal, a living person. And she had said, once with her own mouth, or the image of her mouth, and once with the mouth of a rat in the fireplace, "Find me." Should he? Why couldn't *she* find *him*? And if he did find her, what then? Did she expect him to get involved in some kind of struggle between the kind of people who could do what had been done to him? Who could call the spirits of the dead and make them seem alive to some poor sap of an ordinary mortal? Would Grandmother make him face her again, face the User? No, he wasn't going to do it. The old lady could rot, the User could rot, they could all rot, they should all go down into that graveyard and stay there. Deep and cold under the snow. Stay there.

He also thought of Lizzy, of what she had said about life after death. The dead still existed, with all their memories, but the way she was living didn't sound like any theology Quentin had heard of. Why didn't anybody else know about this? He couldn't be the only one who had spoken with someone from beyond the grave. He *knew* he wasn't. So why wasn't there some book about this? And if the dead just hung around and mortal people could call them and control them and make them do things, what sense did that make? What was it all for? And why did he have to spend so many years without Lizzy?

The one thing he could not permit himself to do was think of Madeleine. The pile of books about sex was still on his nightstand—he hadn't been back to this apartment since they got married. He had never slept with her here. But her face was everywhere in this place. He blotted her out. She wasn't real. But he remembered the feel of her under his hand. How perfect her skin was. How cool and dry, and yet how warm when she should be warm.

Of course she was perfect. So were the berries and the pineapple and the pears. So was the luster of the table and the dishes and the goblets. Everything was perfect because the User took it out of his head. And she knew all the right things to say and do because the User stole it out of Lizzy's memory or trapped Lizzy inside the illusion. Forced Lizzy into this hideous fantasy in which all that Quentin amounted to was a pair of hands to open up the lid of a box.

Well, why go to all this trouble? Why *him*? With the kind of power the User had, why not just take some poor sap from up the road, walk him on down to the big house on the Hudson, and tell him to open the box?

The box was the big deal. There was some kind of barrier protecting the treasure box, locking the User outside. She apparently had thought that Quentin could get past that barrier and was furious when he didn't.

But what stopped him? He felt no barrier. He was about to open it when she ran out. Why did she give up so soon? Questions that had no answers.

Who was the User? Where was she? And how much power would she have with a .45 bullet boiling through her skull?

He lay there in the bed. Three in the morning. Trembling and cold. Check the thermostat. Already hotter than he normally kept his house. He must have taken a chill this afternoon on the road. Last night at this time he had been sleeping in a bed full of cobwebs after making love to his imagination. Last night he had slept in a stone-cold house that he only thought was warm. Why didn't he freeze to death? Did the User have the power to keep him warm? Four in the morning. He was starving. He had tried to eat the crackers in the cupboard, the only food in the apartment that hadn't passed its expiration date, but they were like dust in his mouth. He got up now and ate them anyway, and drank tap water, it felt like gallons of tap water. He showered. He took all his clothes out of his suitcases, clothes that had been put into dusty drawers and a filthy wardrobe, and laid them out to air. The clothes he had actually worn, the day he arrived at the house and today when he left, he threw them all into the garbage. He threw away the toothbrush from his kit. Five in the morning, he slipped back between the sheets and now he could sleep, still not letting himself think of Madeleine.

But sometime in the night, his mind went where he dared not let it go, and he woke up sobbing in grief for her. Madeleine, Mad, Mad. I don't care if you were a lie, I loved you. I loved you and you left me and I didn't do anything to deserve it, I was good to you. He cried himself back to sleep.

When he woke again it was five in the afternoon. Dark outside already. He got up and called the garage that kept his DC car. In the time it took them to bring it over, he showered again, dressed. He came out to meet the driver, tipped him, then got in the car and drove to Tysons Corner and picked up some shirts and slacks, socks and underwear. A new pair of running shoes. A new razor, new kit, two new suitcases exactly like the ones he already had. A new winter jacket. He drove home and changed into new clothes, then put everything that had been in the house on the Hudson, including the clothes he had stuffed in the garbage in the wee hours of the morning, packed them into the old suitcases, and carried them out to the dumpster. It was nine o'clock. He drove to Lone Star and ate peanuts and steak soup and it was all ashes in his mouth but he went on and ate the salad and the filet because he was not going to let this thing kill him. He was going to go on with his life.

He got home and the message light on his answering machine was blinking. Someone had called.

But that wasn't possible. When he was away from one of his residences—which was most of the time—he had all the calls automatically routed to a single answering service in Nebraska. When he got to one of his residences and wanted to start receiving local calls on his own phone, he would call in and punch in the code to release calls to that particular phone number.

Only his parents, his lawyer, and Madeleine had the codes that would allow them to override his answering service and reach the answering machine in this residence. And his parents and his lawyer had no idea he was here. They would assume he was still at Madeleine's family house on the Hudson River.

Which meant that the message on his machine had to be from Madeleine. Except that Madeleine didn't exist. Which meant that it had to be from the person behind Madeleine. The person who made her. The User, who could wander free from her body and follow him wherever he went, who would know where he was, who would know he was away when the phone call was made so her intention was to leave a message on the tape, and not talk to him directly.

He could hear Lizzy's voice telling him that the User wasn't done with him yet. She hadn't got what she wanted. If she needed him before, she still needed him. Only now it wouldn't be love that she used to motivate him.

He didn't want to hear the message. But he reached out and touched the PLAY button.

"Quentin Fears? This is Ray Cryer. We're worried that we haven't seen Madeleine since you ran out on her yesterday. We have the local police looking for her, but it occurs to us she might be out looking for you and you may find her first. If you do, we'd appreciate a call. Her mother and sister and I are worried sick. Just worried sick. I know you were very angry yesterday, but I hope you'll still help us find our little girl. The local police here might call you to ask you some questions. I hope you'll cooperate with them. You have our number." There was an emotional catch in his voice at the end.

Ray Cryer? Madeleine's mother and sister? These were people Madeleine had never spoken of. Quentin had certainly never met them. Nor did he have their number. But he had no doubt that they would be completely convincing to the police. That was what the User did best—completely convincing people.

The implications were clear. Quentin had better do what they—no, what the User—wanted, or the police would be looking far and wide for a woman they would never find because she didn't exist. And when they didn't find her, it would start looking very bad for Quentin. Her parents say that Quentin had a fight with her. He snuck away with his suitcases, and ever since then they haven't seen their daughter. Why did he sneak off? Where is Madeleine? Your Honor, you don't have to find a body to know that there was foul play.

No. A murder trial was out of the question. There had to be *some* evidence. The mere disappearance of a person wasn't enough. But that didn't mean that the police wouldn't be convinced that there was a murder. That they wouldn't be dogging Quentin's heels for months and years looking for Madeleine. And the publicity. No, it wouldn't even take publicity. It would just take visits from police investigators to all of his partners and all of the political people he knew in every city where he did business—Madeleine had met them all, and if the User forgot any of them she could just drop in on Quentin's own mind and take the list out of his memory. He had no secrets from the User. The cloud of suspicion would grow around him. His parents. They would question his parents.

"You have our number." No doubt the police would hear Ray Cryer say that. Even if he erased this tape, there was probably also a recording on the other end, and then they would wonder *why* he had erased his copy. And since he didn't have the number, what choice did he have? He had to go back to New York, back to the house on the Hudson. Where the police would ask him about that night he spent in the house. If he said he slept in the house with Madeleine and had breakfast with her family, they'd go in and find a cold, dark, waterless house with only his footprints in the dust and only one side of the bed slept in. If he said the house was empty and dark, the police would doubtless find it sparkling clean and well lived-in, with Ray Cryer expressing his bafflement that Quentin would tell such an obvious lie.

He couldn't win. There was no escape from her. He might as well give up and head back there first thing in the morning. Or get in his car right now and drive all night and . . .

No way. That's what the User wanted. For all he knew, she was putting these thoughts in his head right now to try to bring him back. Well, Lizzy had told him he was strong. He had some power to resist her. And the User wasn't all-powerful, Lizzy had said that, too. It strained her there in the library at breakfast to keep six dead people under control, maintain the illusion of Madeleine, and show various servants bringing in imaginary food, all at once. During the police investigation the User wouldn't have half so much to do. She wouldn't have to produce the deep illusion of Madeleine at all. As for this Ray Cryer, he might be a real person and not a mental construct at all. Making the house look clean and lived-in would be a cinch. But could she create the illusion of detailed chemical evidence? Bloodstains? Anything that would convince a court that a crime had been committed? Maybe—but wouldn't she have to know exactly what the lab technicians would need to look for? Could she make her illusions show up on a photograph? Or would she have to follow the photograph constantly to make sure everyone saw the right things when they looked at it? If she knew enough and had power enough to do all that, then there was no point in his even trying to resist her.

But she wasn't infinitely powerful. Her limits could be reached. And he was not going to roll over and play dead.

It was eleven at night. He called his parents in California.

"She left me," he said. Almost his first words.

"No," said Mom.

"Aw, Quen, I'm so sorry," said Dad. "I never would've thought. She was so—you two were so perfect together."

"I don't know where she is. She didn't tell me where she was going."

"How could she do that?" said Mom. "You just don't do that. Decent people don't . . . "

"Does her family know where she might have gone?"

Here it came—the beginning of his counterstory. Since he had never met or heard of this Ray Cryer, he wasn't going to go along with the User's story that they knew each other. "I never met her family. She took me to the house on the Hudson, but there was nobody there." That was dangerous, he knew, since they were telling the police that he *had* met her parents. But if they gave him a lie detector test about meeting Madeleine's parents at the house, he could pass it. "And then today, this afternoon, she left."

"But that's so odd," said Mom. "She was taking you there to meet them."

"Did you fight?" asked Dad.

"I had questions. She had no answers. She knew I wasn't happy but no, we didn't fight."

"Oh, son, it'll work out, I know it will," said Mom. "When she realizes you love her no matter what—"

"I do love her, Mom."

"Well there you are. She'll come back, Quen. How could she not? The way you two looked at each other, it was so sweet, you're so much in *love* with each other, for pity's sake!"

"Dad, Mom, it's not just that she's gone. I'm worried."

"What about?" asked Dad.

"What if something happened to her? She just walked out. I don't know where she went. I didn't see her on the road as I walked to the next town. I didn't see her footprints in the snow."

Silence on the other end of the line.

"Quen, I know this is out of line, but I have to ask. You didn't hit her or anything, did you?"

Mom was furious. "How dare you even suggest such a thing about Quentin!"

"Calm down, Mom, it's all right. If she doesn't turn up soon, the police are going to ask exactly the same question, and they ought to. Dad, I never raised a hand to her or hurt her in any way. The last time I saw her she was fine."

"Why do the police even have to be involved in this?" said Mom. "Wives leave husbands all the time."

"I never met her parents, but now all of a sudden I have a phone call from a man claiming to be her father and he probably is. But he's lying and saying that I met him, which I didn't, and he has the police looking for her and they're going to question me."

"This is so strange," said Mom. "You should be calling to tell us you're going to have a baby, Quentin, not that the police are going to question you."

"You never met her parents," said Dad, "and now suddenly her father is phoning you and they've got the police looking for her. Quentin, is there a chance that Madeleine was setting you up for blackmail all along? You pay up and suddenly there she is, and what was all this missing persons investigation about?"

"I don't know. So far nobody's asked me for money. It's all really confusing and I'm not sure what's really going on. But in case you're contacted and questioned, I wanted you to hear about this first from me."

"That was very wise of you, son."

"What should we tell them?" asked Mom.

"The absolute, complete truth, Mom. I didn't do anything wrong and there's nothing to hide."

"Quentin, I'm so sorry that this is happening," said Dad. "If it's any consolation, we thought she was as wonderful as you did."

"Yeah, well, we're all suckers for the perfect woman, aren't we, Dad? The difference is, the one you married is real."

"Oh, Quen," said Mom.

"Listen, there's a chance that this will hit the papers and if it does, they'll make it look like I'm guilty of something horrible because that's what sells papers. You know, Software Millionaire's Wife Missing, Husband Can't Explain Disappearance. If it's a con, and I think it is, you can be sure there'll be some evidence that supposedly contradicts things I've told you. No matter what other people are saying, though, you can be sure of this: I did no harm to Madeleine, and if I could have her back right now, as my wife, flesh and blood, right here beside me, I'd be the happiest man alive." And then, because this was true, and because he was tired, and because he had never had a chance to mourn for the wife he lost, he wept, his parents listening to him on the phone, believing him, comforting him.

And why not believe him? Everything he had said was true. And he had told them all that they could possibly believe.

Afterward, physically and emotionally drained, he fell asleep in front of the TV in the living room before Letterman got to the top ten list.

Next day he phoned his Virginia lawyer and asked him how to go about reporting a missing person. He explained that his wife had left him in New York State, but he had come home to Herndon assuming that she would find her own way back to one of their residences, only she wasn't answering the phone anywhere and until he located her he had to assume that something *might* have happened to her and he wanted the police to be on the lookout just in case—wasn't that the right thing to do? And his lawyer assured him, definitely, that was the right thing to do.

So he did it, but they didn't seem to think there was any urgency. "She'll turn up, Mr. Fears. Just give her time to cool down."

"I'm sure you're right," he answered. "But please just put out the word, won't you? Call the police up there and ask them to be on the lookout?" They assured him they'd see to it. He knew that the New York police would assume he was launching his own search because of the phone message from Ray Cryer, but if he didn't start searching it would look even worse.

That afternoon he boarded a flight to San Francisco and by evening he was in his lawyer's office.

"Only for you do I cancel dinner at my favorite restaurant in San Rafael and drive down into the city."

"You should have told me," said Quentin. "I would have come up and joined you there."

"I didn't want you there," said Wayne Read. "I wanted me and my wife there. Being married to me wouldn't be easy for any woman, and it's particularly hard for my wife. So this is costing me, Quentin."

"Madeleine left me."

"Oh." Wayne looked nonplussed for a moment. Then he

put his head down on his desk. "I'm trying really really hard, Quentin."

"Go ahead and say it. You told me so."

"Quentin, I'm not happy to be right. I wanted *you* to be right."

"Yeah, well, she's gone. And I need your help."

"I assume she's got a lawyer. Do you know who yet? Because I'm not a divorce lawyer and—"

"Wayne, you're not getting it. She's *gone*. Not just leaving-me gone, I mean *gone*. I've filed a missing persons report in Virginia. I got a phone message from a man claiming to be her father, and he says they've also got the police looking for her up there."

Wayne's demeanor changed. A little bit more serious. A little bit suspicious, too, though he was trying to conceal it. Well, Quentin didn't blame him.

Quentin gave him the whole story he had told his parents.

"Well, somebody's bound to have seen her leave the house. She'll turn up somewhere."

"I doubt it."

"Why?" Again the suspicion.

"Because I never met this Ray Cryer but he left me a phone message implying that we knew each other. He had the code that let him switch off my answering service and leave a taped message on my machine in Herndon—and only Madeleine had those codes. Well, besides you and my parents."

"So she's not missing."

"Let's just say that this guy who calls himself Ray Cryer knows more about her disappearance than I do."

"Then let's find her," said Wayne. "Between the investiga-tors we can hire and the police, we'll find her."

"No we won't. Nobody will ever find her."

Wayne thought for a while, tapping his pencil. "Quentin, are you telling me the truth?"

"Everything I've told you is true."

"That's not exactly what I asked." Then, as Quentin was

139

about to speak, Wayne raised his hand to stop him. "Wait a minute, Quentin. Don't get mad at me, but I have to tell you. If you have committed some crime, and you wish me to be involved with your defense in any way, don't confess that crime to me. If you confess a crime to me, then my advice to you will be to turn yourself in and make a full confession, and I will not represent you in your defense. Do you understand me?"

"Relax, Wayne," said Quentin. "I didn't kill her. As far as I know she's as alive as she ever was."

Wayne relaxed a little.

"And I do want to begin a search. But not some little penny-ante search. It's going to have to cover every city where I have residences, which is a long list, as you well know. But she might have gone to any of those places and I have to at least go through the motions of a serious search. Don't I?"

"Go through the motions?"

"I told you. We won't find her."

Wayne shook his head. "I really hate paradoxes, Quentin. Do you know where she is or don't you?"

"I know she's nowhere."

"If she's buried in the basement of that house, Quentin, the police are going to find her."

"She's not buried anywhere because she's not dead. She's also not alive. She never existed."

"That must have been an interesting wedding, Quentin."

"The real search is for her true identity, Wayne. I want to be able to prove that the Madeleine Cryer I married has no birth certificate in any of the fifty states. That she never went to school anywhere, that she never had a job. The other investigations are because I have to look like a worried husband searching for his vanished wife. But my attorney has to know that what I'm really searching for is the identity of the person who deceived me. Or someone who might know the truth about her."

Wayne leaned back in his chair. "Now, that's interesting. I wonder where the investigator should start."

"There's almost nowhere he *can* start, Wayne. Like you said, I was a fool. The whole time we were engaged, back in Virginia, she claimed she was staying with friends, moving from house to house. We talked on her cellular phone. I never had a phone number for any of those friends. Never met one. Never heard a single name. She said she was in a job somewhere in the bureaucracy, but I don't know what it was, and frankly I don't believe she ever had such a job, though of course I'll pay to have the federal personnel files searched to see if she worked for them."

"What about this Ray Cryer?"

"Whoever he is, I doubt he'll be real helpful to us—if he talks to our people at all."

"But we can investigate him and *his* background," said Wayne. "Either he really is her father or he's faking, and either way, checking up on him will help us."

"And the house, Wayne. The deeds. And I mean going back generations. She knows that house. That wasn't a fake. She knows it in the dark. She's connected to it somehow."

"We'll do it, Quentin. In the meantime, you won't mind if I strike her name off your insurance policies and out of your will?"

"Write it up and I'll sign everything."

"The police are going to be *so* suspicious of you."

"Of course they are. *You* are, and I pay you handsomely and listen to your wise and intensely personal advice. Think how much less likely *they* are to think I'm telling the whole story."

"Though of course you *are* telling the whole story." The irony in Wayne's voice was palpable.

"I've told you the whole story I'm going to tell the police and the whole story I told my parents and the story I'm going to tell everybody else forever, and every bit of it is true."

"But there are some bits you sort of left out?"

"Maybe."

"Are you going to tell me?"

"I want to. If I dare."

"Attorney-client privilege protects everything you tell me. I've already given you my don't-confess-a-crime-to-me warning. Please remember that I mean it."

"But what if the thing I tell you convinces you I'm out of my mind?"

"I'm already convinced."

"I'm not joking, Wayne. I've been questioning my own sanity, and unless you're crazy, you will too."

"Crazy people have as much right to a lawyer as sane people."

"But what if you thought it would be in my best interests to be committed to a mental hospital? To be declared incompetent?"

"I have no standing for that," said Wayne. "Your parents could try it, or your wife, or your children if you had any. Your heirs, perhaps."

"My in-laws?"

"They're running a different scam right now," said Wayne. "The point is, your attorney couldn't try to commit you on his own account. I'd be disbarred if I tried. My job would be to stop *them*."

"But if you—*when* you don't believe me, will you still work as hard for me as before? Or will you start handing my work over to underlings until you finally spin me off to some other lawyer?"

"Quentin, now you're bothering me. What is this, some alien abduction thing?"

"I wish." He took a deep breath. "Get out your recorder."

"I'll remember what you tell me."

"I want it in my own voice."

"Quentin, attorney-client privilege only protects you in court, not from public attacks on your reputation. Of course I'll do all I can to protect any tape you make here, but the best protection is for the tape never to exist."

"Tape it."

"Your call." Shaking his head, Wayne got out his recorder. And Quentin told him what really happened, starting with his sighting of a woman who looked like Lizzy at the Elden Street Giant food store in Herndon. From there he skipped to the events at Madeleine's family mansion. The midnight snack. The reason she gave him not to take a shower. The exquisite food at breakfast. The other people at the table. The walk on the bluff. And then the treasure box, Grandmother saying "Find me," Madeleine fleeing into the graveyard. No footprints but his own. The names on the headstones. The dark, cold, empty house, the dust and filth, the bed that only he slept in, the bureau that held only his own clothing. The words that appeared on the door. The talking rat. And then Lizzy, dead Lizzy come back to talk to him, to explain what she understood. And the long walk back to civilization.

Told all in a stream, Quentin didn't believe the story himself.

But there was Wayne Read, turning off the tape recorder, nodding. "I'll keep this tape, Quentin. In my safe. I'm not going to give it to a secretary to transcribe."

"Right."

"What I don't get, Quentin, is why you told me this . . . stuff."

"Maybe I just had to tell someone."

"Not you, Quentin. You're not a get-it-off-your-chest kind of guy."

"Maybe I'm afraid that somewhere along the line I'm going to get killed. And if I am, I want somebody to know why."

"Me? Your close, intimate lifelong friend?"

He was right. It wasn't Wayne Read he had told this story for. Quentin thought for a moment. "If I'm dead, Wayne, then I want you to play this for my parents."

"Quentin, come on."

"I want them to know."

"Quentin, it's one thing to tell me this stuff, but telling your folks this thing about Lizzy coming back—how is that going to do anything but hurt them?"

Quentin leaned across the desk. "Give me the tape and I'll find another attorney."

"I didn't say I wouldn't do it, I just gave you my best advice. I'm used to you ignoring me. But you *are* an ass, Quentin."

"Thanks."

"If you're not crazy you're the stupidest liar I've ever known. Dead people hanging around just in case somebody conjures them back? For *breakfast*?"

"I'm sure inventive, aren't I, Wayne?"

"The worst thing is that I can't even tell my wife because if she heard *this* story she'd know I was having an affair and didn't even care enough to come up with good lies."

"Are you having an affair?"

Wayne sighed and looked away for a moment. "I'm not, but she is."

"You're kidding."

Glumly, Wayne explained. "When she started getting suspicious of me, I figured *something* had changed, and it wasn't me, I was just the same as always. So I had her watched for a few weeks. She was giving—favors, I should say—to guys in the parking lots of bars."

"And she's still accusing *you* of having affairs?"

"Quentin, people are crazy. That's why I told you that. So you'd understand—I know that people do crazy things. But they do them in the real world. The guys my wife sees—they're cowboy types. She goes to cowboy bars. In Marin County, right in San Rafael, we have three kids, and she's blowing guys in the parking lot in exchange for a joint. How is that crazier than your telling me this horrible story that you actually want me to play for your parents if you suddenly croak. I once thought you were the only island of sanity in a screwed-up world. You had no connections except

144

your parents. You didn't get emotionally involved. Rational decisions kept doubling your fortune every three years or so. No waste. No lies. No illusions. Then you fall in love with a woman and she leaves you and you come to me with this *story* and I swear, Quentin, I've lost all faith in the human race. I've got only one question. Is there any way you can get *my* wife to disappear off the face of the earth? No, no, I don't mean that."

"I don't know if this is what you had in mind, Wayne, but at least you made me remember that I'm not the only guy in the world with problems."

"That's not what I had in mind. I don't know what I had in mind. I didn't really have anything in mind. I guess I *am* a getting-it-off-my-chest kind of guy."

"Why don't you divorce her?"

"Because she's still a good mother when she's home. And I love my kids. And I love my wife. Or at least I love what I thought she was."

"I love what I thought Madeleine was, too."

"Yeah, but at least your wife didn't exist." Wayne laughed but it caught in his throat. "Why aren't we drinkers, Quentin? Guys who drink can go to a bar at a time like this."

"Is Swensen's open? We can eat like a hundred scoops of ice cream and puke in the street."

"Well, that's *half* the fun of drinking, at least."

Quentin got up. "I'm sorry I spoiled your dinner with your wife."

"Yeah, well, maybe I would've stuck a fork in her eye, so you probably saved me from going up on assault charges."

"I hope nothing ever happens that's weird enough to make you believe me, Wayne."

"I hope the same thing. But I still like you and care about you and I'm the best lawyer you'll ever get, especially now that you're a complete loon."

"Thanks, Wayne."

"Come in tomorrow after two to sign the papers getting

her name out of your will and off your policies. You'll have to eat the ice cream alone."

And that was that. Somebody else knew the truth—somebody alive—even if he didn't believe it. Now it was just a matter of waiting. For his investigation to lead him somewhere. For the police to start getting suspicious of him. The trouble was that all he was likely to come up with was negative evidence—nobody knew her, nobody had seen her. But there was a paper trail. The User couldn't alter the paper trail. At least he didn't think she could. She dealt in illusions, in getting people to do what she wanted. She hadn't actually changed physical reality one bit. If she wanted that house to look clean, she could fool people. If she wanted it to *be* clean, somebody had to come in with a mop. The same applied to documents and records. It wasn't easy to fake a life. This Ray Cryer could be exposed. It could be proved, eventually, if he spent enough money, that Madeleine Cryer had never been born.

Which wasn't to say that the User would stay defeated. If one attempt failed, she'd make another—he knew that about her now. She needed him, for some reason. *Needed* him. And as long as she needed him, she would keep coming at him, and he'd never know it was her. He could never trust anybody again.

That was the worst. Knowing that the User could come at him however she wanted, in any disguise. He'd never guess it was connected to her. After all, there hadn't seemed to be any connection at all between his sightings of Lizzy and meeting Madeleine at the grande dame's party. Every single person he ever met for the rest of his life, he'd have to wonder if it was really the User, trying again and again.

In the long run, he wasn't going to get out of this until he found the User herself and confronted her. The night before, he had imagined, in his rage, finding the User's mortal body and putting a .45 slug in her head. Now, in the light of day, did he really have the heart for that? Was he a murderer, just waiting for the right provocation? He shuddered at the thought. There had to be a way to defeat her short of killing her. To get her out of his life.

Of course, the simplest way would be to go back to New York and open the damn box.

Only he didn't want to do that. If only because the User wanted it so much. Whatever was in there, it would be a very bad thing if the User got it. Because the User loved power, didn't she? That part of Madeleine, that disturbing part of her—that was the User talking. It had to have been. Certainly she didn't find it in Lizzy, or in Quentin's image of the perfect woman. That had been the User telling the truth about herself. The love of power. Whatever was in that treasure box was about power, and if there was one sure thing in this whole business, it was that the User should not get her hands on more power.

Power. Madeleine had told him that she was in Washington in order to be around power, to get some kind of influence. Was any part of that true? The User must have noticed him somewhere, and it was after he moved to the DC area that he started seeing things—Lizzy, and then Madeleine. The User might have grown up in the Hudson River Valley, but that house had been closed down for years. She had to be living somewhere, and it made sense that it was in the DC area. And if she lived there, somebody knew her.

He made a connection. The grande dame's party, where he met Madeleine. There *was* someone in DC who had known Madeleine before he did.

But he wouldn't send one of his investigators to talk to the grande dame. He owed her more civility than that. He'd go and talk to her himself.

10
Memories

"I remember you. Or do I?" She was as gracious as before, and the confusion of her words didn't show on her face.

"You were very kind to me at a party one night," said Quentin. "In fact, you introduced me to my wife."

"That would be clumsy of me, to introduce a husband and wife to each other."

"No, no, she wasn't my wife at the time, we—"

"Please, Mr. Fears, I was joking. I'm old, but I still understand the ins and outs of simple communication. I spoke to you for a while, didn't I? I think I ran on and on, but you were very patient."

"Conversing with you made me glad that I had read my sister's collection of Jane Austen novels."

"I was not around in the Georgian period, Mr. Fears."

"You converse as elegantly as if you had been. It makes a California boy like me struggle to keep up."

"Now I remember you. I caught you fingering the books in the library."

"I thought of myself as eyeing them."

"You were climbing the ladder, anyway. Did you come to thank me for introducing you to . . . what was the young lady's name? Not Duncan, anyway."

Not Duncan? "Madeleine Cryer."

"The niece, yes."

"Niece?"

"Well, of course to you she's your wife, but to me, she's the niece of my good friends the Duncans. They have been so kind to me in the last few years, since my husband passed on."

"And so you invited their niece to your party."

"How could I not? Such a lovely girl. Not at all like the Duncans' rather unfortunate daughter. Oh, but now I'm being a gossip."

"What's the Margaret Truman quote? 'If you can't say something nice, come sit by me'?"

"It wasn't Margaret, my dear boy. But these stories have a way of attaching themselves to the people the newsmen have actually met. Of course no one invites newspapermen to any *real* parties. So they never know the truly clever people."

"You aren't telling me that it was *you* who originated that—"

"How old do you think I *am*, young man!" She feigned horror. "That story was ancient before Margaret Truman was born. My great-grandmother's diary mentions hearing that line attributed to the wife of James Buchanan."

"He was the president before Lincoln, wasn't he?"

"Very good—you are in the top two percent of your generation, for knowing that."

"Do I make the top one percent for knowing that Buchanan was a bachelor?"

She clapped her hands together, hankie and all. "Oh, you are a delight, Mr. Fears! It's no *fun* teasing people who never understand they're being teased."

"Do the Duncans understand?"

She looked at him sharply. "So we're on a fishing expedition. But I think your purpose is either loftier or lower than mere gossip."

"Loftier, I think. My wife has left me."

"Without a claim check, it appears. So when she returns to reclaim you . . . "

"Oh, I'll be here waiting, if she returns. Her departure was sudden. I don't know where she is."

"Did you do her violence, young man?"

"I'm not a violent man," said Quentin. "But I appreciate your concern for her safety."

"Men do not come with labels, alas, clearly identifying those who harm women from those who are unfailing gentlemen."

"Then tell me nothing, but merely allow me to write a note to Madeleine, care of the Duncans, care of—"

"Care of me."

"Though many hands touch my message, yet may it still have power to touch her heart."

"In all my reading, I can't recall where I heard that gracious speech before."

"You heard it here."

"You invented your own? A lost art is revived before my eyes."

"That art cannot be lost as long as you are in the world. In you the river of time slipped its banks and took a different route from the rest of the world."

"Now *that* one you did not invent."

"The January *Atlantic*."

"The article on Madagascar." She laughed. "Oh, Mr. Fears, you're such a spoof."

"Madeleine and I read that issue on our last plane trip together."

Her face grew solemn. "The pleasure of your company has made me forget your errand. By all means, give me your message."

He patted his pockets for a pen. "I'm here unarmed, I'm afraid."

"Then you must rise to your feet and arm yourself at my writing desk. Perhaps you'll want to choose one of the second sheets, so you don't have my monogram on your note."

Quentin went to the writing desk, chose paper and a pen, and wrote.

> Dear M
>
> I love you and miss you. Please assure me that you're well. Tell me the future is still a treasure box which we may open together.
>
> All my love,
>
> Q

Since Quentin had no idea what the User wanted, he could not be sure that this note, if it even reached her, would have any effect at all. But if in fact the opening of the treasure box was her goal, this note had to leave her wondering exactly how much Quentin had understood of the things that happened at the house on the Hudson. It had to be good for him if she thought he understood less than he really did. And since he understood very little, it shouldn't be hard to persuade her that he knew nothing.

Except, of course, that the moment he called attention to himself, what would stop her from ransacking his mind and finding all his secrets? Lizzy said that the User had left him some independence. You are not without resources, Lizzy said. So maybe it was worth writing this note.

He folded the note in half, then carried it to the grande dame.

"Oh, Mr. Fears, you are cruel."

"Am I?"

"You could have sealed it. Then I would have steamed it open and read your note. But handing it to me folded shows such trust that I would die before I violated it."

Quentin laughed and read it to her.

"Oh, Mr. Fears, I will not deliver this note. Instead I will find treasure boxes of my own for us to open together. Why couldn't you have white hair and arthritis! Such a romantic!"

They laughed together.

"Young love is so hard, these days, Mr. Fears," she said, offering him her hand. He took it gently, and because of the way she rested her hand on his, he did not shake it but instead bowed over it, thinking that he should surely be wearing a cutaway for this scene. "If I see my friends' naughty niece, I will reprimand her for wasting such a fine young man—and after all the trouble we took to bring you to her!"

"Trouble?"

"I told you at the party how I felt about marriages and money. The Duncans are an old family. You are new money. Such a match is made in heaven."

"But the only person I knew at this party was a lobbyist who —"

"Who was invited to this party because he knew you."

"But I only called him a day before to ask him to take me to something."

"Really? Then the Duncans must have been watching you rather closely, because it was exactly the day before when they asked me to invite both that lobbyist and their dear niece."

"So you didn't just stumble across me in the library."

"Nor was Madeleine only by chance under the cherry tree. Oh, Mr. Fears, I thought I was helping create a good family, not setting you up to have your poor heart broken. Will you forgive me?"

"There's nothing to forgive. If I've had any happiness in my life, it's because Madeleine brought it to me. And even if I only had that happiness for a season, I'll always be grateful to you for sending me to her that night."

"I'm glad you're not in politics, Mr. Fears, for I should have to leave my home and vote for you, and I do hate going out."

"Yours would be the only vote I'd get, but I'd feel as if I had won."

She applauded him again. "If only you would pink some rival in a duel over me, I could die happy."

"I have to ask, even though I know the answer. You couldn't simply tell me the Duncans' first names and where they live, could you?

"If your wife didn't introduce you to them, and they didn't introduce themselves, it's hardly my place without their consent, don't you think?"

Quentin nodded. It was the answer he had expected. "I'll come back when it's all settled, to tell you how things came out."

"My door is always open to you, Mr. Fears. Good day."

Outside on the porch, he was almost surprised to see an ordinary overmoneyed street in Chevy Chase. There should have been carriages passing over cobbled streets, and rows of townhouses, and blossoming cherry trees. Instead it was winter, the trees were bare, and most of the houses showed that money and taste do not arrive on the same schedule.

Duncan. Friends of the grand dame—but for how long? And they arranged for his invitation to the party. She was already watching him, the User was. How had she found him? Rich men were thick on the ground inside the beltway. Why had she chosen him?

It was almost, almost worth it, just to have met the grande dame and won her friendship. If only he were really the courtly gentleman he had just mimicked in her drawing room. But somewhere along the line he suspected there would be a time when he stood toe to toe with an enemy, and there would be no pinking in *that* duel. Something bright red would flow, and someone would fall, and his thought at that moment was that it would probably be himself. But he would not go down easy.

Quentin got into his car. Once inside, he looked around to see if he could spot the surveillance teams that were supposed to be watching the house to see who entered and left after his visit. He didn't see anyone at all, not even a car parked on the street, which either meant that they had screwed up completely or they were very, very good. He pulled away from the curb and called Wayne Read on his cellular phone.

"You just pulled away from the house," said Wayne, by way of greeting, "and you're heading toward the beltway."

"I didn't want them to follow *me*."

"Just wanted you to know they were on the job."

"And calling you long distance to report on it."

"Well, hey, you can afford it and we both own stock in AT&T."

"I've got a name for you to look for. Duncan. That's a last name, a married couple and they have a daughter. Supposedly Madeleine is their niece. I'm willing to bet that Mr. Duncan is the guy who called himself Ray Cryer."

"Duncan. I'll bet there's only one Duncan family in all of the DC area."

"That's what the surveillance team is for, right? I wrote a note to Madeleine and left it with the grande dame. Either she'll send somebody to the Duncans or the Duncans will send somebody to pick it up. Either way, there'll be somebody to follow."

"Unless she puts it in an envelope and puts a stamp on it."

"People still do that?" Of course he knew they did, but since he hadn't personally licked a stamp in many years, he simply hadn't thought about that possibility.

"Still a bargain at thirty-two cents. And if we interfere with the U.S. mail, that's a felony for all concerned, so we won't do it, even for a guy we love as much as we love you, Quentin."

"Yeah, well, you still have the name Duncan to go on."

"I can hear the phone call now. 'Is this the Duncan family that has a niece who magically disappears after six months of marriage to a rich insane man because he doesn't open a box in time?' We'll find 'em for sure."

"If you're so smart, I'll bet you know who the only bachelor president was."

"Of the U.S.? James Buchanan, the guy right before Lincoln. A Virginian who did his best to screw things up for the North before the Civil War. You want more?"

"Have you found anything about her cellular phone number?"

"It's a Cellular One number, one of the ones they reserve for company use in that area. Needless to say, it hasn't been assigned to anyone during the past year."

"And here I was thinking the connection was always so clear," said Quentin.

So all his phone calls to her while they were engaged had probably taken place without anyone actually answering a phone anywhere. The User just made him think he was hearing Madeleine's voice come out of the phone.

He got out onto the beltway before rush hour started, so driving home was only mildly hellish. When he got inside the message light was flashing again on his machine. He wondered if it would be 'Ray Cryer' again or some other mischief from the User. Instead it was the police chief in Mixinack, New York. That wasn't the town Quentin had walked to when he beat his retreat from Madeleine's house; Mixinack lay to the north, and farther away. But who could fathom how jurisdictions were laid out? It was still midafternoon. He called.

"Chief Bolt here."

"I'm—you answer the phone yourself?"

"Everybody's at the coffee machine or using the john. Who's this?"

"Quentin Fears, returning your call."

"Well, hi."

"Hi." Quentin didn't want to say anything until he found out what Bolt already knew. So he let the silence hang, till Bolt picked up the conversation and went on.

"I got this fax from Herndon, Virginia, saying your wife was missing. You found her yet?"

"Not yet, no. I have investigators on it, but there's nothing yet."

"Oh, well, I'm sorry to hear that. Haven't seen your wife, Mr. Fears."

"I'm even sorrier to hear *that*."

"I can bet. Tough break. My wife left me once. Damned shame. Came back, too. Damned shame. That was a joke, son. But I guess you don't feel like joking."

"I appreciate your thoughtfulness."

"I'm a thoughtful kind of guy. I bet you're wondering why I bothered to call when I don't have anything to tell you. Well, what can I say? I'm a curious guy. My secretary just got married and with this stomach flu going around I've got to keep all the men I've got left out on the road running speed traps, or we won't be able to meet the payroll. That's another joke, but I've given up on you laughing."

"You're telling me you're all alone in the office."

"That's my point! You *are* listening! Well, you see, that's why I'm the one saw your fax. We get a lot of those hate the damn machine, you know, like to rip it out of the wall, since *we* have to pay for the paper for every boneheaded stupid meaningless fax that any moron in the country decides every police department ought to have. But your fax caught my eye, because of the address you gave for that house where you say your wife left you."

"You know the place?"

"Well, you see, this is a small town, and yes, I know it well. Drive past it quite a bit. Hasn't been a soul living there for five years since the old lady went to a rest home."

An old lady who had ties to the house, gone to a rest home. That might explain why Grandmother couldn't find him herself.

"I have my boys check it out now and then," said Bolt, "to make sure there's no vandalism. You know, broken windows."

"Are there any?"

"You tell me, son. You're the one says he spent the night."

"I didn't say that."

"No, I guess I'm saying that. Saw that fax from Herndon, and I thought, let's check it out. So next time I'm driving down that way in daylight, I pull up and sure enough, there's tire tracks going in and coming out. And footprints. Don't like footprints—that's vandals. That's bums trying to squat in an abandoned house. Or tracks can be bored teenagers looking for a place to smoke some weed or pass along some sexually transmitted disease, but whatever it was I figured it was my job to know. Drove on in, parked a ways back, and saw as how you must have had a driver when you got out of your car."

"We did."

"Yeah, well, I looked for a lady's footprints, but it seems she never got out of the car."

"Is that what it looks like?"

"Or you carried her in. It's damn sure she never set foot in that snow."

"Interesting observation."

"So far so good," said Chief Bolt. "So I remember how the owner asked me to look in on the place, so I think, Time to look in. Climbed up the steps and it's kind of dirty in there, isn't it?"

"Yes sir, I'd say so."

"And cold. A man could freeze his ass off in there. But somebody walked upstairs and spent the night on a filthy dustcover and peed in a toilet that doesn't flush and spit toothpaste into the dry sink. Walked to the basement kitchen, stepping on roaches all the way, walked to the empty fridge—am I getting this right?"

Bolt's cocky sarcasm was contagious. As always, Quentin picked up the tone of the conversation and played it back. "You're quite the Sherlock Holmes," he said.

Bolt's reaction was a brief "Ha." And then: "Well, I won't go through your whole itinerary. A walk out to the bluff. You did a real dance all over the graveyard. Walked around front.

And then I've got your tracks coming back out the front door. You sat down on the second from the bottom step and set your bags down beside you. And then you got up and walked on out to the road and went south. Have I about got it right?"

"Can't argue with the truth, Chief."

"And I ask myself, where was this woman who was supposedly last seen leaving the old Laurent place?"

"Laurent?"

"I guess the Laurents lived there longest so the name stuck. Anyway, the only thing I could figure was the missing woman you're looking for must have drove off in that car. Looked like the driver went around to open the door for her, but she never got out. And now she's missing."

"Definitely missing."

"So I really had only one question for you, Mr. Fears."

"Fearsss. Rhymes with pierce."

"Here's my question. Why did a man who the Herndon police tell me is richer than several third world countries combined, why would such a man go inside a freezing cold abandoned house and spend the night in bugs and filth?"

"Is that a crime, Chief?"

"Oh, if I caught you there, I could lock you up and put a vagrancy charge on you, but since you could show means of support and all, I don't think it would stick. Trespass, of course, but you didn't steal or vandalize. So no, we're not charging you with anything. I'm just curious, that's all."

"So am I. I want to know where my wife is. Doesn't sound like you know."

"I see," said Chief Bolt. "Kind of unfair for you to come up here, act weird, go away, and not answer questions about it."

This wasn't going at all well.

"Chief, let me ask you a question."

"Do you want me to answer it or just weasel around like you did?"

"Didn't you get an inquiry from a Ray Cryer about my wife, Madeleine Cryer Fears?"

"Ah, the father-in-law."

"I've never met him, but he says he is."

"Maybe it's in the paperwork somewhere, but—"

"No, it would have been called in during the last few days. You've been answering the phone, right?"

"Ray Cryer?"

"Right."

"Nothing here. I've got the old messy-desk filing system, so I can't swear to it, but no, nothing."

"Well, you see, this Ray Cryer called me and told me he had called you to tell you his daughter was missing. From that house. And that he already had the local police looking for her."

"We're the local police, and we aren't. Looking for her."

"Curiouser and curiouser."

"But if you were there when she left, Mr. Fears, why would he call to tell you she was gone?"

"That's my question, Chief. It sounded to me like maybe he was trying to set up a different version of events."

"Well, we'll never know, will we? Right now, all I've got is your word that your wife was there. And clear evidence that you've got really weird taste in lodgings."

"Well, thank you, Chief Bolt, you've been really helpful."

"So you're gonna blow me off?"

"No sir. On the contrary, I'm hoping you'll keep your eyes open and help my investigators when they get there."

"This Ray Cryer blackmailing you? Is that it?"

"Pardon?"

"Were you on drugs that night? Was it a drug deal or something, and they dropped you off and threatened you or something?"

"What are you talking about?"

"You won't tell me why you acted so weird, I got to rack my brain coming up with stories that fit the evidence."

"Chief, the house is haunted. I was invited in by ghosts, slept with ghosts, had breakfast with ghosts, went on out to the graveyard to say good-bye to their bodies, and then hiked along the highway to get home."

"You know, I may be a small-town chief of the tiniest police force this side of Maggody Arkansas, but I got as good a doorway into jail as any other cop in America. So why are you showing me such disrespect, son? Though I will say that at least you're paying for the call."

"Chief Bolt, I don't want to be your enemy."

"That's good to hear. I'm not a good enemy to have."

"Can you tell me anything about old lady Laurent?"

"Laurent? She's dead."

Dead? Then what was "Find me" all about? "I'm sorry to hear that."

"Happened about twenty years ago and she was older than God when she croaked, so nobody's broke up about it."

"I thought you said the old lady went into a rest home a few years ago."

"Son, it's plain to me you don't know squat about that house and the people who used to live in it, and yet you said your wife took you there to meet her family. Now you lay it out plain. Is this Ray Cryer blackmailing you about something? Did you do something criminal in that house? Or are you just insane? Because you sure as hell did *not* marry a woman who has anything to do with that house, since that family is *gone*. Old lady Laurent is dead. The current owner is her daughter, the old lady I mentioned who went into a rest home. And *her* only daughter is about thirty-five and married with a little kid, and she's never been back since the old lady moved out."

"I did nothing criminal in that house. If Ray Cryer is blackmailing me, he hasn't asked for money yet and if he does I won't give him any because I haven't done anything I need to hide. As to whether I'm insane, well, at my income level people generally call us eccentric."

"But you're still not answering my questions."

"Chief, I want very much to meet you."

"The feeling is mutual."

"I want to go through that house with you and find out everything you can tell me about it."

"What, am I a realtor now?"

"Believe me or not, Chief, my wife came to that house with me. She grew up in that house, of that I have no doubt. It's her people buried in the graveyard. And if I have any hope of finding her, it'll be through whatever I can learn about that house. So I will be there soon. And in the meantime, I'll fax you the receipt from the limo service that took us there, so you can find out whether I did in fact arrive with my wife."

"I'll be waiting for it, son."

They said their chilly good-byes. Quentin hung up the phone and called the limo company to have them fax Chief Bolt a copy of the bill. All the while, he kept telling himself that this was about the stupidest thing he could do. Since Ray Cryer was lying and he hadn't told the police anything, why should Quentin do anything to arouse more suspicion? Why didn't he just tell Bolt some cockamamy story and hang up and sigh in relief and call off the search for a missing wife that he knew would never turn up? And above all, why would he provoke Bolt into getting proof positive from the limo driver that yes indeed, Mrs. Fears got out of the car and went into the house with Mr. Fears? The fact that there were no woman's footprints coming *out* of the house could only make the chief suspect foul play.

And yet at the time it seemed like the right thing to do. A gut feeling. A sense that Chief Bolt was a decent guy whose trust was worth having. And there was something important about him.

Oh. Of course. Chief Bolt knew the old lady. And if there was any sense to the universe at all, the old lady in the rest home had to be Grandmother. Didn't she? Only she wasn't old lady Laurent, who was twenty years dead, which would make her Grandmother's late mother, which meant Laurent must have been Grandmother's maiden name and the chief would know her married name and where to find her. So knowing the chief was maybe a route to Grandmother.

It was also quite possibly a route to jail.

Quentin shuddered, and then thought of the thing that had made him shudder: When he felt so certain that he should say what he said to the chief, what made him think it was his own idea? For all he knew, he was acting out somebody's script.

No. The User doesn't do that. She's made me see things, but she hasn't made me *do* things. She can't make me say or do things because if she could, that box would be open and this whole thing would have ended back there by the Hudson. And if Grandmother could make me do things she wouldn't have made me see a talking rat in order to persuade me.

Quentin thought about it some more and realized why he didn't palm off some easy lie on the chief. It was because Quentin was a pretty good judge of people, Madeleine, of course, being a spectacular exception. After screening hundreds and hundreds of people responding to his ads, after working with many dozens of partners over the years, he could tell pretty quickly which people he'd enjoy working with and which would be nothing but pain.

And Chief Bolt was his kind of guy. It was that simple. If Bolt were asking him for funding to start some business, Quentin would hear him out, make sure the premise was sound, and have the papers drawn up, because he could do business with Bolt.

Except the business Bolt was in was the suspicious cop trade, and the only partnership the chief had in mind was the uneasy partnership of cop and suspect. The only thing the chief lacked was evidence of a crime and Quentin was helping him find some.

Maybe it's an unconscious attempt to thwart the User, thought Quentin. After all, I can't open that treasure box if I'm in jail.

11
Reunion

Something touched him in the night. As he lay on his side in bed, something light glided over his bare skin, above his hip. He woke with a start, slapping at it. Someone gave a cry. He lunged for the light and turned it on.

Madeleine sat in the bed, holding her hand as if it had been burnt, an accusing look on her face.

He couldn't think of anything to say.

"Miss me?" she said.

Suddenly it annoyed him, the way she was holding her hand, as if she were really in pain. "Don't bother holding your hand. I know you aren't hurt."

"You think it doesn't hurt when you slap me?"

"I thought a spider was crawling up my—yeah, well, I wasn't far wrong, was I?"

"Don't be mad," she said. "Please don't be mad."

The expression on her face was so genuinely sad, so full of longing, that he felt himself melting with compassion in spite of himself. But no, *no*, he refused to be taken in.

"Get out," he said.

She was wearing a nightgown. She plucked at the hem. "Tin, please, I . . . "

"Don't call me that. You sucked that out of my mind. Or Lizzy's—that name doesn't belong to you!"

"No, it's *your* name."

"It's my name when it's spoken by somebody who loves me. Not somebody who's trying to use me to open some . . . *box*." He got up and walked clumsily around the bed, out of the bedroom, into the kitchen. He got orange juice out of the fridge and poured a glass.

She stood in the kitchen doorway. "Enough for me?"

"No," he said. "You don't need it. And that's something I want to know. Since you're not really here, what did you *do* with everything you ate and drank? Where does it go?"

Her face went cold and she walked back to the living room. "I see," she said. "Your note meant nothing."

He followed her, the glass of juice in his hand. "So your real name is Duncan?"

She whirled on him. "My real name is Madeleine Cryer Fears. Your wife. There's a license."

"And how did you sign it? How did your name get on it? You can't *really* hold a pen."

"I can hold a pen. I can hold a glass. I can hold *you*. Remember how it felt?" She reached for him. Her hand, reaching to brush against his cheek, to cup his jaw and draw him close . . .

He grabbed her wrist and pulled her even closer, then poured orange juice over her head. It dribbled down her hair, over her forehead. She covered her face with her hands and wept. "All I want is to love you, Quentin!"

He stood there, looking at the juice, how real it looked. How it dripped from her hair onto her shoulders, some of it down onto the carpet.

"No," he said. "You're not there, and when I poured out that juice it went straight down to the carpet. It didn't go into your hair because you . . . aren't . . . real."

She took the glass and threw it against the wall. It shattered and fell. "Think the neighbors heard *that*?" she asked.

The shards of glass sparkled in the light from the kitchen.

She was crying. He was crying. "Madeleine," he said. "I'm so sorry, I'm—you wouldn't believe—these past few days without you—"

She held him. Her body fit perfectly against his, as it always had. "You think it was easy for me? I shouldn't have run out of there, but Grandmother—she hates me so much. I should have remembered, my love for you, it's stronger than anything, stronger than her hate, stronger than . . . Oh, Quentin, don't ever be angry with me again, please, it scares me, it hurts me . . . "

And as she spoke, he looked at the glittering bits of broken glass and remembered the shimmer of the perfect goblets on the table in the library. And then how bare and dirty the table looked, under its dustcover. The look of the water flowing out of the tap into the clean sink in the bathroom, and then the dirty dry sink with taps that didn't work.

"Tin, please let me call you that, please, let me come back and be your wife the way I should be. The way we promised before God that we would."

"You didn't want any cameras at our wedding, Mad," he said. "Why was that?"

She was toying with his hair. "I wanted to imagine that I was the perfect bride, beautiful as snow in sunlight." Her words were simple, and her voice was like low music. Her hand touched his skin, the same touch that had wakened him a few minutes ago and it was awakening him again. "I didn't want to see pictures that might contradict my dream. Do you believe all those Kodak ads? That nothing is real unless you have a picture of it to prove it to yourself? Maybe I should be giving you a Hallmark card right now, or calling you on AT&T so we can have a really touching moment."

He laughed. It *was* Madeleine, it was the woman he loved. The sound of her voice, the feel of her hair under his fingers.

Her hair.

167

And now suddenly her hair was sticky with orange juice. But a moment ago it hadn't been. His hand froze in place.

She looked into his eyes. "What?" she said. "What?"

He turned his face away. He thought of Lizzy. He thought of the false image of her, walking up to the townhouse that was rented to nobody.

He pushed her away and walked to the wall where the glass had fallen. He bent down and picked up a shard of glass and drew it along the wall. A scratch appeared in the wallpaper. Suddenly, without planning it, without knowing he was going to do it until he did, he jabbed the glass into the skin of his abdomen. Jabbed twice, three times. Only then did the pain come. He doubled over, it was so bad. Fell to one knee. But he knew it was a lie. He looked down at his belly. Blood was coming out, but there wasn't enough of it.

And then, suddenly, there was more. Too much. He hadn't hit an artery. There wasn't anything there that could bleed so much. In fact, he knew that there was no wound there to bleed. Nothing. No reason for pain. There wasn't even a piece of glass in his hand.

He still held the shard in his fingers.

Hadn't Lizzy told him he was stronger than most people? Why couldn't he fight off these illusions of hers?

On one knee, he sliced through the skin of the other. Sliced deeper and deeper. The glass cut deep. But all he could think of, all he *let* himself think of, was dissecting a frog in science class. The musculature of the leg when he peeled back the formaldehyde-soaked skin. And for the moment he thought of that, his leg was also a frog's leg. He peeled the skin off just as he had the frog's leg.

"No!" cried Madeleine.

There was no wound in his leg at all. No shard of glass in his hand. No stab wound in his belly. The orange juice glass lay on the floor where he must have dropped it when Madeleine made him think she had taken it out of his hand.

On all fours, he moved to the spot where she had been

standing when he poured the orange juice over her head. There it was, a single puddle, spattered, but only one stream of juice had fallen, uninterrupted by a human body. He had recovered reality.

Which meant that he had lost her again.

"Madeleine," he whispered.

From the couch, her voice sounded cold and angry. "I'm still here."

He recoiled, fell back onto the carpet, looked at her. She was on the couch primping her hair, looking into a small vanity mirror. "So your dead sister told you that you were strong," said Madeleine. "Bully for you."

"Who are you really?" he said. "Just be honest with me, can't you? Who are you and why did you pick me?"

"I'm Madeleine Cryer Fears," she said. "I'm your wife."

"You don't exist and you never did."

"Oh? Then who *have* you been making love to in beds all over America?"

"A lie," he said. "I've been loving a lie."

"Wrong answer, Quentin," she said. "I am the truth. I am the deepest truth in the most secret places in your heart. I am all your dreams come true."

"What do you want from me?"

"What every wife wants. Someone to love. Someone who'll love me. Trust. Faith. A future. Your babies."

"Shut *up*!"

"Do I take it this means you've changed your mind about children? Men are like that, so changeable. But I can wait. I won't trick you—no babies till you're ready to be a daddy."

"You never let up, do you?"

She leaned forward until she was spread like a lizard on the couch, leaning over the arm so they were nearly face to face. "Let me tell you a secret, my darling," she whispered. "I'm as real as *any* wife. What do you think marriage is? It's all pretense. Your mother pretending that your father's temper doesn't scare her. Your father pretending that he doesn't

169

ORSON SCOTT CARD

hate it when she gets him all riled up about something and then suddenly can't understand why he's upset. Pretending to be happy with each other when they're both so desperately lonely because along about week three of their marriage they realized that they didn't really know each other and they never would, they'd be strangers together for the rest of their lives. But they couldn't live with that, nobody can, I've seen thousands of marriages and they can't face it that they're paired up with a stranger and so the decent ones, the ones who want to be good, they pretend to be whatever they think their partner wants them to be, and then they pretend that they believe in their partner's pretense. The only difference between them and me is that I'm so good at it. When I pretend to be exactly the wife you really want, I *am* that wife. I *am*. It is my whole existence. And when I pretend to love you exactly as you are, I *do*. I'm totally focused on you, I'm witty when you want witty, sexy when you want sexy, weepy when you want sentimental, beautiful when you want to show me off. I am your true wife."

"You don't know anything," said Quentin.

"I know *you*."

"You know how to get power over me. And it worked, yeah, you had me dancing. Eating out of your hand. Give the boy exactly what he dreams of and he'll sit up and beg."

"I'm the one who's begging now," she said.

"You're the one who doesn't leave footprints in the snow," he said. "You're the one that orange juice pours right through."

"You think you don't believe in me."

"I don't."

"Then why am I still here?"

"You're not," he said.

He got to his feet. At first, for just a moment, he limped on the leg he had carved with the shard of glass. Except he hadn't cut it, there was no injury; he forced himself to walk without a limp.

170

"Even when you aren't looking at me, I'm here," she said.

She followed him as he walked through the doorway to his bedroom. He slammed it and it passed right through her. She stood there on the inside of the slammed door.

"I don't like it when you do that," she said.

"Slam doors?"

"I think that on the whole I've been pretty decent about this."

"You!" He climbed back under his sheets. "You're an indecency."

"I didn't have to come to you with love, you know."

He looked away from her, leaned over and switched off the light. Now only the faint light slanting in through the mostly-closed blinds illuminated the room.

"I can find other things in your mind," she said.

Suddenly he threw the bedclothes off him. A half-dozen huge shiny spiders were skittering rapidly along the sheet, over his legs. He flung himself off the bed onto the floor.

"I know those spiders aren't real," he said, panting.

A man's voice answered him, a bleak-sounding whisper. "What is reality?" And then a vast hand clamped him around the throat and picked him up and flung him back onto the bed. As he sprawled on his back, the huge, white, slimy figure with a pus-filled wound for a face raised its other hand and smashed it down into his groin. Quentin screamed in agony until the monster squeezed his throat shut.

This isn't happening, he told himself. The trouble was believing it.

If I believe it, he thought, she can kill me with my own fear. I have to stop fighting it because it isn't there. Like the broken glass wasn't there. Like the wounds in my leg. My throat is shut by my own panic, not by any hand because there *is* no hand.

Breathe slowly, let the air out a little, then bring in a little. There's nothing in the room with me. I'm alone here on my bed.

He opened his eyes. The monster was gone.

But Madeleine was lying on him, her head on his chest, her waist between his legs, her hair spilling onto the bedsheet. Her body felt warm. He could feel her heartbeat. And despite himself, he was filled with longing. He raised his hand to caress her. But he stopped himself. It would not happen. He brought his hands up and tucked them behind his head, fingers interlocking. Just like the monster, this image, too, would go away.

"Aren't you the strong one," she whispered. "Aren't you brave, to insist on reality. You never *could* face your own dreams."

She rose from his belly. But not as a normal woman might, raising herself up on her arms. Rather she rose like a marionette, pulled by strings. And yes, she *was* a marionette, with Madeleine's face, her naked body, but the joints were mechanical and her jaw moved on a string.

"Please. Someday, if I'm really good, can't I be a real girl?"

And then she was gone.

He lay there, panting, exhausted physically and emotionally.

"Oh, Lizzy, I did it," he whispered.

He rolled to one side, then onto his stomach, one leg drawn up, his fist doubled under his chin, the way he always slept, the way he had slept as a boy. But his eyes stayed wide open. Seeing nothing. Seeing everything.

12
Believer

"Sorry, Quentin, but he must have seen our surveillance team," said Wayne. "Doubled back twice and we lost him."

"Him?" That was something, Quentin figured, to know it was a man.

"A guy in a messenger service uniform. So you were right, she *didn't* just use a stamp."

"Guys from messenger services don't double back to avoid surveillance."

"Yeah, well, they assumed he *was* a messenger and the real quarry was whoever he brought the message to. And then he pulled his maneuver and he was gone."

"Well, the message arrived," said Quentin.

"You got a call?"

"A visit."

"And?"

"I learned nothing," said Quentin bitterly.

"How can you learn nothing? Who came?"

"Madeleine."

"So she's not dead?"

"Wayne, it wasn't the Madeleine you believe in, the flesh and blood one. It was the Madeleine who doesn't leave footprints."

"Quentin, how can I help you when you won't help me back?"

"Keep on believing I'm crazy if you want, Wayne. But don't let up on the investigation."

"Quentin, really. I'm trying to believe you. And you know me, I'm a lawyer, I can *act* like I believe my client whether I do or not. I learned that from watching the O.J. trial."

"OK, Wayne. It's cool."

"What is?"

"Madeleine visiting me. You not believing me no matter how hard you try. The investigators losing the messenger. Even if they don't find anything, I need them to keep going after everything."

"By the way, the deed to that house is in the name of a certain Anna Laurent Tyler. Seems she inherited from her mother, Delia Forrest Laurent, who got it from her late husband's will. It was originally built by a Laurent, though, back in the early 1800s."

"Any address for Anna Laurent Tyler?" Quentin was writing down the names. He remembered that in the graveyard there had been a Delia Forrest Laurent, Devoted Wife, sharing a headstone with Theodore Aurelius Laurent, Beloved Husband.

"Sure," said Wayne, "but it's the address of the house in the deed."

"Anna Laurent Tyler. That's something. The police chief in Mixinack said that she had a married daughter. Probably she didn't really marry a Duncan, but maybe we can get the true name out of the local papers. From the wedding announcement. A Tyler being given away by her mother, Anna Laurent Tyler."

"When?"

"I'd start about three years ago and work backward. How would I know? If I find out more from Chief Bolt today, I'll let you know."

"Today?" asked Wayne.

"I'm going back up to New York. To Mixinack."

"Why? Hair of the dog?"

"Yeah, well, this dog follows me around anyway, I might as well head for the doghouse."

"So you aren't missing the little woman as much as you thought."

"Let's say that last night's interview was painful."

"You have my sympathy, Quentin."

Chief Bolt's police department was in a graceful old city building, the kind made of huge stones with classical-looking pillars and lions in front. There were two police cars parked in back, in reserved stalls. Quentin pulled his rented Taurus into one of the Visitor spaces, went inside, and began wandering around in search of the police department. Apparently this was one of those small towns that lived by the principle that if you didn't know where something was, you had no business finding it. He would have asked for directions, but the place was deserted. Somewhere, though, somebody was typing. He finally found the source of the sound in the basement, behind an unmarked door. He knocked.

"Come in," said a woman.

He stuck his head in the room. "Just looking for the police department, ma'am."

"You found it."

"This? Right here?"

"Said so, didn't I?"

"I have an appointment with Chief Bolt."

She pointed toward a closed door behind her, then went back to her typing. Quentin hadn't realized that New York manners extended so far north.

Quentin knocked on the chief's door—which also had no sign. This time a man's voice told him to come in.

Bolt was a burly man with military-short hair, but he

didn't have the air of rigidity about him that Quentin had always associated with that look. His uniform was a little tight on him, a little rumpled. And his face looked to have some warmth, as if he might just have a sense of humor. Not usually a cop thing.

"Hi, I'm Quentin Fears."

Bolt nodded, but didn't look up from the form he was filling out. So much for the warmth.

After a moment, Quentin realized that it wasn't a form at all, it was a crossword puzzle.

"Five-letter word for anxiety, has a *G* in the middle," said Bolt.

"Angst," said Quentin instantly.

"Spelled?"

"*A-N-G-S-T*."

"Oh, angst," said Bolt, pronouncing the *A* to rhyme with the vowel in *rang*.

"Need help with any others?" said Quentin.

"I would've got it eventually." He looked up at Quentin. "Younger than you sounded on the phone."

"No, I sounded like a guy my age," said Quentin. Once again, as he had on the phone, Quentin picked up Bolt's off-hand manner, his bantering style.

Bolt grinned. The warmth Quentin had seen wasn't an illusion. "I figured I'd never see you, we got off to such a good start on the phone."

"Yeah, well, once you visit Mixinack, you keep on coming back."

"We ought to have that as a slogan. Put it on a sign out at the city limits."

"I got a million of 'em."

"Sit down, Mr. Fears." His tone was friendly now. Quentin's instinct had been right. Bolt liked a man who gave as good as he got.

Quentin sat down and looked around a little. The office was meticulously clean, despite the tattiness of it. And contrary to what Bolt had said on the phone, his desk had only a few papers on it.

"Looks like you're all caught up with your work," Quentin said.

"We're doing OK for the middle of a crime wave."

"Chief Bolt, I just wanted to ask you a couple of questions."

"Really? Just a couple? Couldn't you phone?"

"I figured fair was fair, and you'd have some questions to ask me."

"Still, there's a phone. Why are you here?"

"Because when I get the answers to my questions, I want to be able to act on them immediately."

Bolt nodded. "I always feel that way, too. Found your wife yet?"

"As a matter of fact, I saw her last night. She's not missing anymore."

Bolt nodded more slowly. "Well, good. Why didn't she come along?"

"I didn't say she was back with me. Just that she wasn't missing."

Bolt sighed and recited:

> The ways of love are strange and hard:
>
> The love you want is always barred;
>
> The love you have you want to change.
>
> The ways of love are hard and strange.

"I didn't want to change my love," said Quentin.

"Did you like the poem? I wrote it."

"Did you? I thought I'd heard it before."

"Yeah, well, that's why I'm working in a police department in Mixinack instead of being lionized in the New York literary scene."

"You want to hear my questions?"

"I'm all ears."

"Where is Anna Laurent Tyler?"

"In a rest home."

"And where is that rest home?"

Bolt nodded slowly. "Well, now, what are you going to do when you locate it?

"Go see her."

"Won't do you any good," said Bolt.

"You don't know what I want to say to her."

"I don't care if you want to sing her the 'Anvil Chorus'."

"I hope you know the tenor part," said Quentin.

"She's pretty much a vegetable, son," said Bolt. "So you can talk to her all you want, but I don't see how it'll do you much good."

Quentin felt as if the air had been knocked out of his chest. "Can't be," he said.

"Can so," said the chief. "Well, look at that. The word that crosses *angst* at the *N* is *anvil*. And I just said *anvil* a minute ago. Can you believe that?"

"Just one of the many marvels of an afternoon in Mixinack."

"You still want to see her?"

"I can find out where she is eventually, but instead of making me have my investigators call every licensed rest home in the state, why not just tell me?"

"Better than that. I'll take you."

"In a police car? Will you flash the lights and run the siren?"

"In your car. You think I'm going to use up part of my monthly mileage on giving a rich man a free ride?"

"When can you go?"

"Now," said Bolt, pushing back from his desk. "I haven't had lunch. You like chili?"

"No." Quentin followed him out into the hall.

"That's cause you haven't had Bella's chili. Is that really the coat you came in?"

"Yes."

"Nobody told you it was winter?"

"I don't plan to hike around outside a lot."

"In the north, in the winter, you should always dress as if you were going to have to walk home ten miles in a blizzard from a car stuck in a drift."

"That's how my driver should dress. I should dress for sitting in the limo drinking champagne while I wait for him to get back with help."

By now they were outside. Quentin led the way to his Taurus.

"Oh, I see," said Bolt. "That was a joke. You don't have a driver."

"You don't have a coat, either."

"Man, I must be stupid," said Bolt.

Since snow was falling steadily now, he had a point.

They came out of the parking lot and Bolt directed him until he was heading south on the two-lane road that led past the Laurent house. Quentin realized at once that they weren't heading for the rest home at all. Sure enough, when they got to the half-hidden driveway Bolt directed him to turn left and go on in.

"I see quite a few new tire tracks since I was here last," said Quentin.

"Yeah, they're all mine," said Bolt. "Had to come here and take pictures of the footprints before they got covered."

"Oh," said Quentin. "Evidence?"

"Definitely. I just don't know what it's evidence *of*. Now that your wife is back in the land of the living."

"If you can call it living," said Quentin. "A joke."

"I got it. First time I heard that, it was Andy Devine in some cavalry movie. Or maybe it was *Rin Tin Tin* on TV when I was a kid. Was he in that?"

"Before my time," said Quentin.

They got out of the car and Quentin dutifully tagged along up to the front door.

"Hope you don't mind the detour," said Bolt.

"I kind of expected it," said Quentin.

"Just wanted you to walk me through what you did the night you spent here."

"Do I need an attorney?"

"Don't you have one?"

"I meant with me."

"I'm not going to arrest you for trespass, Mr. Fears. Therefore you have no need for an attorney."

"Am I really that stupid-looking?"

"Humor me, Mr. Fears."

They were standing in the middle of the entry hall. Quentin looked at the fireplace but didn't see any talking rats. The door to the parlor had no writing on it. And the chief was a strong man with a pistol. All of this made Quentin feel much better about being in this room again.

"I never saw this room till I came to see Mrs. Tyler off to the rest home," said Bolt.

"Bet it was cleaner then."

"Much. The glaziers are supposed to have come this morning to fix the window in the library. It was broken, you know."

"I know."

"I used to come to the back door all the time. Downstairs. There's a ramp going down to the kitchen. Toolrooms are down there, too."

"You used to work here?"

"As a kid. Started helping out with weeding when I was little. That was before chemicals, so keeping the dandelions out of the lawns kept about a dozen of us kids in movie money all summer. But I kept hanging around, ended up mowing lawns and then I made gardener's assistant. That's how I put myself through college. Shoveled snow off that front porch out there so many times I hate to remember."

"So this house is more than just a neighbor's place to you."

"Had my first kiss here," said Bolt, sighing. "Come on downstairs, I'm curious about what you did in the kitchen."

Quentin followed him. Bolt flipped on lightswitches as he went.

"Lights are on now?" Quentin asked.

"Guess so," said Bolt. "I had them turned on yesterday. I wanted to see more than a flashlight could show me."

With the lights on, the stairs and hall looked to Quentin just as they had the night Madeleine led him down for a midnight snack. But the kitchen didn't. Quentin had distinctly remembered a table. Instead, there was a spot on the floor where someone had apparently sat down on the filthy linoleum.

"You walked in here—in the dark, or with a flashlight," said Bolt. "You went to the fridge, to those cupboards. But the fridge is locked shut, as you might notice, and nobody's opened it. So why walk there? Twice—see? Twice."

Quentin remembered getting out mustard, mayo, a couple of sliced meats, and a head of lettuce. Then going back for pickles when Mad asked for one.

"They used to keep bread in this cupboard," said Bolt. "And sure enough, here's where you walked. To the bread cupboard, and then to the silverware drawer. See? Only . . . no bread, no silverware."

He opened the empty drawer, the empty cupboard.

"Bummer," said Quentin.

"Then you sit down on the floor. But . . . right where the kitchen table used to be. Right where the chair at the head of the table used to be. Butler used to have the undisputed right to sit in that chair. The cook made damn sure nobody else—least of all a sweaty gardener's assistant—sat in it."

"Got to keep that furniture clean."

"Why did you sit on this floor, Mr. Fears? And what did you find in those cupboards?"

Quentin shrugged.

"Now, see, there we are," said Bolt. "You want me to answer *your* questions, but you won't give me tit for tat."

"Why give you answers you won't believe?"

"Well, answers I don't believe would be a step forward. Because right now what I don't believe is that you saw your wife alive yesterday."

Quentin shook his head. "When you watched all those old *Columbo* episodes, didn't you notice that he always had a dead body before he started the murder investigation?"

"I didn't say murder," said Bolt.

"You said you didn't think I saw my wife alive yesterday. And I tell you she was as alive as she ever was."

Bolt kept opening cupboards until they were all open. Then he hitched himself up to sit on one of the grimy counters. "This is where I had my first kiss. This room. I was sitting on this counter."

"The cook?" asked Quentin.

"The owner's daughter. Rowena Tyler."

"How old?" asked Quentin.

"Who?" He must startle the chief out of a reverie.

"Rowena. You."

"I was twenty-two. And don't ask why it was my first kiss at that age."

"My first kiss came later than that, Chief," said Quentin.

"She was fifteen."

"So were you her first kiss too?"

"I didn't ask. Judging from the chasteness of the kiss, I'd say yes. And thanks for not saying some smart remark about robbing the cradle."

"I was just thinking that it's sort of a young-adult version of *Lady Chatterley's Lover.*"

"Never read it. Sounded boring compared to the *True Confessions* magazines my friends and I snuck over and read in the pharmacy when we were twelve."

"So this room is full of memories for you."

"Rowena's about your age now, wherever she is."

"Never met her, I'm afraid."

"She married and left before she was twenty. I think Mrs. Tyler knew that something had passed between us, because for the first couple of years she didn't ever mention Rowena in front of me. And then one day she did, and I didn't flinch, and then she kept me posted about her. She had a child, a daughter, in 1984. She's going to turn twelve this year."

"The woman I married was older than that."

"But younger than Rowena."

"Definitely."

"Help me with this, Mr. Fears."

"See, here's where we're running into our conflict, Chief. You seem to think I understand what happened here, and that I'm just not telling you."

"Aren't these your footprints?"

"I'm willing to bet they are."

"And your buttprint on the floor?"

"Wouldn't be surprised."

"That stairway is pitch black, day or night, when the power's off."

"If you say so."

"But your prints are surefooted."

"Flashlight?"

"And the driver says that when he dropped you and your wife off out in front, the lights were on and a servant was waiting to take Mrs. Fears's bags."

"Odd what details will stick in a person's mind."

"And the servant knew her. Called her by name."

"No, he got it wrong," said Quentin. "He called her by her maiden name, Cryer."

"Tyler."

"Cryer."

"That's what he said, too. Amazing, don't you think?"

"I hoped maybe he'd remember."

"Lights on all over the house," said Bolt.

"Well, not *all* over. A few windows."

"Not possible," said Bolt.

"What a liar that driver is."

"Did you get to him first?"

"And bribe him to tell you a story that is so obviously false? Boy am I dumb!"

Bolt shook his head. "This family matters to me, and you're doing something here and I really, really want to know what it is because even though the old lady is about as alert as a lawn these days, I owe her. More than that—I like her. She's a friend. And when she dies, this house will go to Rowena. And her I more than liked. Even if I couldn't give her what she wanted most."

"What was that?"

"A way out of Mixinack."

Quentin nodded. "Small-town blues."

"Yeah, well, I'm a small-town guy. Small-town dreams. I told her I'd go to the city with her but she said, 'And do what?' and I didn't have an answer for her."

"They have cops down there, too."

"Yeah, but the cops down there *work* for a living. And I wasn't a cop then, remember? I was a gardener's assistant."

"Starcrossed lovers."

"My point, Mr. Fears, is that you look like some kind of computer nerd and I'm a really strong guy and unless I know that you aren't going to hurt these people with your millions of dollars and your private investigators and your lawyers, well, I'm going to beat the shit out of you right here in this kitchen."

"Actually, I was kind of hoping you could protect me from *them*."

"These are good people, you rich lying asshole."

"Chief, I know you won't believe the truth if I tell you, and you obviously won't accept my silence, so you just tell me the lie that you'll believe and I'll say it. Whatever it takes to keep from getting beaten up."

"You think I won't do it? You think just because I know

you'll come down on me afterward with every lawyer in the known world, I won't do it?"

"Oh, sure, maybe you'll do it, maybe you won't. If you decide to do it, I'll just stand here until you knock me down. I won't raise a hand against you because you're an officer of the law and besides, I've never raised my hand in violence against another person in my life."

"What are you, a Quaker?"

"A wimp," said Quentin. "Come on, Chief Bolt, I like you and you like me. I understand why you're threatening me but I'm not going to tell you stuff that I know will just make you madder. I'll accept how mad you are right now. I think if you beat me up when you're only this mad, I'll live through it without needing serious surgery."

The chief slid off the counter and took a step toward Quentin. He didn't flinch, though the chief's threats did scare him. Quentin had never been beaten up. He had, however, seen the Rodney King tape.

But Chief Bolt didn't hit him. Instead he slammed all the cupboard doors shut and kicked the fridge. Then he stood with his forehead pressing against the door of the freezer compartment.

"Chief," said Quentin, "thanks for not hitting me."

"You're welcome," said Chief Bolt. "It's not you I'm angry at."

"I figured that, since I'm such a nice guy."

"This place really screwed up my life. I should be happy. I've got a good job, a good wife, and some good kids. But I come back in here and it all comes pouring back over me. And I want to hurt somebody."

"I know the feeling."

"Do you? No, the real question—*did* you?"

"Chief Bolt, I don't know for sure who Madeleine is. But I do know that when I came here the other night, a servant met us outside in the drive, and the lights were on. Mad and I came down to this kitchen and sat at the table. I was at the head of the table, and she was beside me on the right."

"Housekeeper's chair."

"And we made sandwiches. My second trip to the fridge was for pickles."

Bolt reached down and snapped the lock open—it hadn't been fully engaged, apparently. He yanked open the refrigerator door. "Show me the pickles, Mr. Fears!"

The refrigerator didn't even have shelves.

"They tasted very good," said Quentin. "But the next day, after my wife disappeared, I was as hungry as if I had come down in the dark, sat on the floor, and eaten nothing but my imagination."

Bolt shook his head.

"Chief, after my wife left me, I saw this house as you see it right now. Not the kitchen, of course. The stairs were too dark to get down without a flashlight, and I didn't have one. But while she was with me, there were lights. There was food. Furniture. Everything clean and elegant. We sat down to breakfast—even though it was lunchtime—we ate in the library. No broken window. And eight of us at table. Grandmother—that's all that Madeleine ever called her—and . . . let's see if I can remember . . . me and Mad, of course, and then Uncle Stephen, Aunt Athena—no, her real name was Minerva—and Simon and Cousin Jude and Uncle Paul."

"Paul?" asked Chief Bolt. His voice sounded different. "There was a Paul who lived here."

"You know him?"

"I saw him a couple of times when I was a child. At the town Christmas party. The Easter egg hunt on the lawn out front."

"Really? What was he like?"

"Short," said the chief. "He was a toddler. He died when he was about a year and a half old."

"Must not be the same Paul," said Quentin.

"You went out to the graveyard," said the chief. "Let's go out there again. Let's look around."

"You got the heat turned on out there?" But the chief was already heading up the stairs. Quentin followed.

The snow was big flakes now, a Christmasy kind of snow instead of the nasty drizzly snow that had been falling earlier. All the old footprints were gone. But the chief seemed to have memorized Quentin's route through the graveyard.

"Like you're trying to catch someone at first, big strides," said Bolt. "And then you see there's nobody in here and you have to see if there's any other way out, or if they climbed over the fence—am I right?"

"Dead on."

"And then you start looking at the headstones. I checked every single one you stopped at. Simon, Minerva, Jude, Stephen."

"I noticed the coincidence," said Quentin. "But the dates were impossible."

"See this one?" He pointed out the grave of the infant Paul who had died at the age of a year and a half.

"Yeah, I saw it," said Quentin.

"Paul was Rowena's brother. She never knew him, though. He was older, and he died a couple of years before she was born. But she came here a lot, to look at his grave."

"Grim," said Quentin.

"After I kissed her that time, after she was sure I was in love with her, she told me a secret. The reason why she wanted to get away from this house."

Quentin said nothing. This was obviously a very difficult memory for Chief Bolt—he was trembling, and his voice was thick with emotion.

"She told me her brother had been murdered."

Quentin felt a chill run through him.

But the chief wasn't done yet. "She told me her mother killed him."

What a wonderful family, thought Quentin. Grandmother, with blood on her hands.

"I take it you never arrested Mrs. Tyler for the crime," said Quentin.

"I didn't believe her. I told Rowena that she must have overheard something and misunderstood it. What evidence did she have, I asked. How could she possibly know something that happened before she was born? And she just looked at me and said, 'I know what I know, Mike.'"

"And?"

"And when I didn't believe her, she didn't see me anymore. She wasn't in the kitchen when I finished my day's work. I hung around each day, waiting. Came early and stayed late. Worked especially hard, but I never saw her."

"She hid from you?"

"I couldn't even ask, because if I asked that would imply that I had some right to ask, and I was the gardener's assistant, for Pete's sake. But I didn't have to ask, I knew what she was telling me. After a couple of weeks I quit and became a cop in Albany, which was a bigger city than I wanted to live in, and after a couple of years the job I've got now was open and they hired me and I came back and I just couldn't stay away from this house, I'd stop by here and Mrs. Tyler would talk to me and tell me news about Rowena and how she was sorry I just missed her. And then she got married and I told you the rest."

"Do you believe her now?"

"I was five when Paul Tyler died. But I looked it up in the library. The Mixinack paper was a daily in those days and the story filled the front page for a week. A real tragedy. The chauffeur backed over the baby. Didn't see him toddle behind the car after he started it up."

"Doesn't sound like murder."

"Chauffeur left at once for England. Distraught, poor guy. Wasn't even here for the inquest. The family didn't blame him, they even paid his way. Out of the country. He was the only witness."

"But who would doubt what happened?"

"So here you are, with a New York limo driver to back up your story about seeing lights and servants here, and a wife who claimed to have grown up in this house. And you have breakfast with people whose names are all on headstones in the grave-yard. Including a boy that Rowena told me was murdered by his own mother. If that was true, how could she know? How?"

Quentin didn't answer.

"Because in this house," said Bolt, "the dead walk."

Quentin looked away. Walked to the entrance of the graveyard and looked out over the falling snow. He heard Bolt come up behind him, looked over his shoulder at him.

"So I'm crazy, is that it?" asked Bolt.

"Have you ever seen anything yourself?" asked Quentin.

"Only one thing," said Bolt.

Quentin waited.

"The door at the back of the entry hall, the back left—it doesn't open."

The parlor door.

"Your footprints led right up to that door, and then back out again, but I didn't see where you turned around," said Bolt. "You've been in that room, haven't you?"

Quentin nodded.

"It opened for you."

"I sure can't go through walls."

"The cook said that nobody ever went in that room," said Bolt.

"I'm not surprised to hear it," said Quentin.

"Can't see in through the windows."

Quentin looked over at the house. "Takes kind of a tall ladder to find that out, doesn't it?"

"The old lady asked me to keep an eye on the house."

"Apparently the parlor is an exception."

"Am I right?" asked Bolt.

Quentin nodded. "As far as I know. Yeah, you're right. I ate breakfast with some dead people."

"Except one," said Bolt.

"Grandmother," said Quentin.

"You see why I had to have your answer before I took you out to see her."

"Well what was that about beating me up in the kitchen?"

"Because I was hoping I was wrong and you were just a rich guy jerking people around."

"Why would that be better?"

"Because if baby Paul was murdered, that would explain why the house is haunted. And that would explain how Rowena knew that somebody murdered him."

"And you didn't believe her."

"And I lost her."

Quentin leaned against the arch. "Well, Chief Bolt, sometimes folks just screw up."

"I can't say I screwed up," said Bolt. "I love my wife and my kids. I have a good life. And if I'd gotten involved with the Tylers, well—look how good it's all worked out for you."

"Which is not to say that Madeleine fits into the haunted house theory," said Quentin.

"Does she have to be buried here to haunt it? Or maybe she was secretly buried."

Quentin shook his head. "There's just one little problem with the ghost theory, Chief. I met Madeleine in Washington, DC at a party. We traveled all over the country together. Must be five hundred people shook her hand at parties and fundraisers and dinners, not to mention our wedding. I don't think she's a ghost."

"Well, then, we're back to my original theory, and I have to wonder if you have any witness besides yourself who saw her alive last night."

"Can't we just agree that some really weird stuff happened here the night I slept over?" said Quentin.

"Mr. Fears, before I take you to see the old lady, I have to point out to you that one of the main reasons I didn't believe Rowena is because I knew Mrs. Tyler. She's one of the best people I know. And there is not a chance, not one skinny chance in hell that she would murder anybody, let alone her own baby."

"And my wife Madeleine loved me so much there's not a chance she'd ever leave me."

"She's a ghost, son," said Chief Bolt. "I mean for Pete's sake, she disappeared in this graveyard, didn't she? That's why you were looking for her here, wasn't it?"

Quentin nodded.

"Just cause her name isn't on a marker doesn't mean she isn't dead."

"Chief, you stick to your theory and I'll stick to mine."

"Well, hell, son, since we're both believing in the impossible, can't we at least get our stories straight?"

"Not till I figure out how your story fits in with my story."

"Well if you'd tell me your story, maybe I could help you make it fit."

Quentin considered this a moment. "All right," he said. "On the drive to Grandmother's house."

"I don't know as we'll have enough time. It isn't far."

"Over the river and through the woods, right?"

"That describes the route to every house in this part of the country, son."

"Quentin," said Quentin. "Please call me Quentin."

"I'm Mike," said the chief.

"Mike, I'm ready to try Bella's chili now."

"Not a good idea if you're going to tell me your story while you eat. Nobody can talk with a mouth full of Bella's chili."

"We'll work it out."

They went back into the house so Bolt could turn off all the lights. The entry hall was the last room, of course, and before Bolt turned off the light at the front door, he strode the length of the hall and stood in front of the parlor door and tried to open it. Tried hard. Nothing happened.

He turned to Quentin and shrugged. "See?" he said.

"Oh, I believed you," said Quentin.

"Well come here and try it yourself," said Bolt.

"I don't think so."

"You went *in* that room, you said. I'm just asking you to try the door. I'm right here beside you."

"Well, that takes care of the trespassing charge, and breaking and entering. But I keep thinking, what's on the other side of that door, holding the handle so you can't turn it?"

"Look," said Bolt, "we've already established that there's nobody but you and me in this house solid enough to leave a footprint."

Quentin walked slowly toward Bolt, who stood back to give him access to the door. Quentin paused in front of it, then reached out to touch the handle.

A single shining word appeared on the door:

NO

Behind him, Bolt gasped. Quentin turned to face him. "You see it?"

Bolt was backing up, just as Quentin had done a few days before, when he first saw the writing.

Someone else had seen it. Quentin knew it was absurd in the face of whatever danger lay behind the parlor door, but at this moment he was almost giddy with delight at having a witness. "It's just words," Quentin said. "It won't hurt us."

"Just the same," said Bolt. "I think I'm done here for now."

That was fine with Quentin. "Let's go get some lunch."

The chief's fingers trembled as he locked the door of the house from the outside.

"You keep this locked all the time?" asked Quentin.

"Always."

Deadbolt, handset. Two locks.

"Well, it wasn't locked when Madeleine and I came here," said Quentin.

"She had the key?"

"She doesn't leave footprints, Mike," said Quentin. "I don't think she can carry keys."

"Well, this deadbolt needs a key, inside or out," said Bolt. "And it was locked when I got here, after your call."

"And there were no other footprints but mine?"

"None."

They looked at each other for a long moment.

"I think," said Quentin, "that we can safely conclude that there's something or someone in this house that can lock and unlock doors."

Bolt reflected on this for a moment. "You know, trying to open that parlor door was about the stupidest idea I ever had."

"Chili," said Quentin. "Lunch. And then the old lady's rest home."

"Anyplace will do," said Bolt as he shambled down the snow-covered steps. "As long as it isn't here."

The chili was hot, but this was Mixinack, not San Antonio, so it wasn't hot enough to stop Quentin from telling his whole story to the one person on earth who had to believe it. Then they got in Quentin's car and started driving north, despite the thickening storm.

13
Salad

It was a hundred-mile drive up the valley. The snow was deep and the plows were out in force, as the towns of the Hudson Valley locked down for yet another major storm. "We need some relief," said Chief Bolt. "About time we had another winter Olympics in Lake Placid. Only sure way of preventing snow for a whole winter."

"You're just getting old," said Quentin. "I still love the snow."

"You're just from California," said Bolt. "If you grew up shoveling it, you wouldn't think it was so nice. You sure you know how to drive in it?"

In answer, Quentin accelerated and then did a sharp enough lane change on the highway to set the car fishtailing a little on the snow. He handled it immediately, stabilizing the car and drifting back down to a safer speed.

"Next time just answer with your mouth," said Bolt. "I don't need a demonstration of stunt driving."

"I spent a winter in South Bend and another in Duluth and another in Laramie."

"Sounds like you need a new travel agent. Turn off at the next light."

"Left or right?"

"Right puts us in the railroad right-of-way, so I guess left."

"Since we're out of your jurisdiction, can I tell you that nobody likes a smug bastard with a badge?"

"I don't want to be liked, Quentin, I just want to get some of this chili out of my system."

"How far are we from the rest home?"

"They put these things close to the main highways so the families won't have any trouble visiting. Not that many of them do. Left at the next light. Then the next right and it's on the right."

"What's it called?"

"I don't remember. It's the only rest home there. Looks like a big motel, only less parking and no neon."

"It looks more like a prison than a motel," said Quentin, when it came into view.

"Yeah, well, you haven't seen many prisons, then."

"I meant except for no bars on the windows."

"And no twenty-foot fences and guard towers and floodlights and checkpoints."

"So when did I say I was an expert on anything?" said Quentin. He pulled the car to a stop in a parking place. At least he was pretty sure it was a parking place. There were plenty of choices but no visible lines. Now that he was here, he wasn't sure what he hoped to accomplish. Bolt said she was in a coma, or at least not coherent. If that was true, there was no hope of learning anything useful from her. Yet she had called him, asked him to find her. Or had she? How did he know the message was really from her? Up against an illusionist like the User, how could he ever be sure what was real?

The snow was real, he was confident of that. Thick and cold as it worked its way up his pantlegs and down into his running shoes.

The front door of the rest home was unlocked, but there

was no one at the reception desk. There was a bell. Chief Bolt rang it, but nobody came.

"Hello?" called Bolt. Quentin walked on into the main hallway and looked left and right. Nobody.

"They can't all be out on a field trip," said Bolt.

"Probably shorthanded, in this storm," said Quentin. "It's four o'clock. Maybe everybody's fixing dinner."

"Dining hall's straight ahead, kitchen's off to the left," said Bolt.

Sure enough, the cook and two attendants were frantically making dinner. "Forget looking for people and pitch in and cut up lettuce for the salad!" cried the cook.

"Yeah, right," said Bolt.

"Why not?" said Quentin. "It's not like we have an appointment."

"I could do this at home!" Bolt protested.

"Yes, but here we'll be doing it out of pure virtue." He was already washing his hands.

"Thank you!" cried the harried cook.

"Does this mean I can go back to bedpan duty now?" said one of the attendants.

"Break's over, back on your heads!" said the other. Nobody laughed.

Quentin took a big knife and started hacking at the lettuce. Soon Bolt was beside him, peeling and slicing cucumbers. "I always feel like I'm emasculating something when I do this," said Bolt.

"Didn't know you cops lived such metaphorical lives."

"Told you I was a poet."

They chopped for a while in silence, except for the songs the cook began but never finished. A line or two of some Elvis song or a Four Seasons tune in full falsetto, and then she'd peter out, humming and getting the melody wronger and wronger until it was some other song which she would drift into singing till she ran out of lyrics.

"I know why we're doing this," said Bolt.

"Oh?"

"Because you're scared of the old lady and you're putting off meeting her."

"That's why *I'm* doing this," said Quentin.

"Yeah, well, I have no will of my own."

"No wonder you send the other cops out to run your speed traps. 'No, Officer, I was only going twenty-five.' 'Oh, sorry, my mistake, what was I thinking?'"

It took longer than Quentin thought it would. Ten minutes, twenty, thirty, but finally it was done, three huge bowls of green salad, with cucumbers, radishes, cherry tomatoes sliced in half, carrot shavings, and garbanzo beans. It actually looked pretty good.

"If only some of the customers had teeth," said Bolt.

"They all have teeth," said an attendant, "if they remember to bring 'em." By now he was in full sweat, taking trays of chicken out of the oven and putting more in.

"Hate to chop and run," said Bolt.

"You were a great help," said the cook. "I was really joking when I asked you to help, and I probably broke sixty regulations by letting you do it, but I usually do this with a staff of four, some of which know what they're doing."

"Bon appetit," said Quentin.

Out in the dining room, a few residents were scattered around at the tables, though no food was being served. Apparently they brought the ones in wheelchairs early. And some of the slow walkers probably needed a head start. Short-handed as they were, the attendants were running around like country club towel boys.

"Hard to believe this," said Quentin. "Working so hard, and no tips."

"Yeah, well, that's because the nurse who runs this place is a cast-iron bitch," said Bolt.

In a moment the nurse in question charged into the dining room heading for the kitchen. At first glance she seemed middle-aged, but that turned out to be the uniform and her businesslike air and her complete lack of makeup. Actually she couldn't be much over thirty, maybe younger, and if she hadn't stopped cold and given Quentin and Chief Bolt a hostile look, she might even have been attractive. "My evening shift can't get through the blizzard," she said, "but I still get visitors."

"We made the green salad," said Quentin.

"Oh, get real," said the nurse. "There *is* no salad fairy." She brushed past them and went on to the kitchen. At the door she stopped and called out to a big Polynesian-looking attendant, "Bill! Escort these two guys to the reception area, would you?" Then she disappeared into the kitchen.

As Bill the Polynesian approached, Bolt pulled out his badge and held it up. Bill took a few more steps as he recognized what it was, then gestured for them to sit down wherever they wanted.

The nurse emerged from the kitchen in a slightly better mood. "I shouldn't let non-employees handle the food, but I can't think of what you could do to poison a green salad," she said. "Mrs. Van Ness says you washed your hands."

"Could have done surgery," said Bolt.

"I know you," she said to him. "You're the cop from Mixinack who used to visit Mrs. Tyler."

"It's nice to be recognized."

"Who's the other salad fairy?"

Quentin rose to his feet. "Quentin Fears," he said.

"Sally Sannazzaro," she said. "I'm the medical officer and acting superintendent of this medium-care facility." They shook hands. "Are you a lawyer?" she said. "You don't look like a lawyer."

"Good," he said. Why had she thought he might be a lawyer? "You don't look like the medical officer and acting superintendent of a medium-care facility, either."

"Yes I do," she said pointedly.

This is going so well, thought Quentin.

Bolt took a step toward the door. "You won't be feeding

the bed-care patients till later. Mind if we go visit Mrs. Tyler right now?"

"I mind very much," said Sannazzaro. "I don't allow unsupervised visits of my total-bed-care patients." To Quentin she added, "They're helpless and every visitor is a potential heir in a rush."

Bolt's face reddened. "I'm an officer of the law."

"I remember that and I don't care," said Sannazzaro. "Don't rattle my chain, Chief. You always want to see her alone and we always get mad at each other so let's skip straight to the part where you do what I say without any further argument so I don't have to get another restraining order."

"You have *never* had a restraining order against me!"

"Wasn't that you?" She didn't seem interested in them anymore. "I have places to go." She headed for the door.

"I always prefer a woman who knows her place," said Bolt loudly.

She didn't even look back at him.

"Why are you goading her, Mike?" asked Quentin.

"She just brings it out in me."

Sannazzaro was brusque, but she was under a lot of pressure tonight and certainly didn't need to deal with visitors.

"It's no surprise when women like that never get married," Bolt added.

This wasn't like Bolt. He had always been barbed, yes, but Quentin had never seen him mean. Till now. "Knowing men the way I do," said Quentin, "I'm surprised women ever marry."

Bolt answered with a sneer. "You didn't tell me you were so politically correct. Is somebody keeping your balls in a freezer in case you need them later?"

Was this even the same man? "It doesn't take balls to call hardworking women bitches and make their lives harder," said Quentin.

Bolt's face got ugly then, but instead of answering he

stalked off to the reception area. Quentin only caught up with him when he sat down and picked up yesterday's paper. Quentin didn't try to talk to him, just sat and read the latest *Time* while Bolt cooled off.

But Bolt didn't want to cool off. Quentin had barely gotten into the story about the new fat substitute that caused anal leakage before Bolt was talking again. "I can't believe she still has it in for me."

"What?" said Quentin. It had seemed to him that it was Bolt who had it in for her.

"That crack about never knowing who was an heir in a hurry."

"I thought that was interesting, that they have to have a rule like that. Do you think there are a lot of murders in rest homes?"

"No," said Bolt. "That was nothing but a jab at me. The first time I visited Mrs. Tyler here, some nurse had moved her pillows around and she looked uncomfortable. So I pulled out one of the pillows to plump it up and for a split second I set it down so a corner of it was across her face while I was reaching under her to lift her up and get the pillow under her, you know, and at that *exact* moment Nurse Ratched walks in and jumps to the conclusion that I was smothering Mrs. Tyler."

"Life's embarrassing moments," said Quentin.

"I explained it but she treats me like a pariah."

"Was there ever a restraining order?"

"She threatened one, but it never would have stuck. I mean, if I don't visit her, who will?"

"Rowena?"

"She thinks her mother murdered her brother."

"Do you?" asked Quentin.

Bolt glared at him. "So you think I was trying to kill her so Rowena would be grateful to me? Rowena's happily married to somebody else and so am I. And she's not vengeful. She left home to get her freedom. She didn't have to kill her mother. I can't believe I'm defending myself to you. You expect me to believe *your* version of how you spent your first night in Mixinack, but now you're suspecting me of trying to kill a helpless old lady who gave me every break I ever had in my life."

"I didn't suspect you of anything, Mike," said Quentin. "You're jumping to conclusions way too fast."

"Am I?" The paper went back up in front of his face.

For the next hour, the only thing said by either of them was when Bolt muttered, "We make the salad and they don't even offer us a soda pop." Instead of letting himself be annoyed at Bolt's petulance, Quentin decided to be annoyed at *Time* for the way every reference to the budget deadlock seemed to blame Congress instead of Clinton. At least they could try to be impartial, he thought.

He knew that he was only trying to fool himself into ignoring his own fears. Things were completely out of his control. He had thought Bolt might become a friend, but the way he acted with Sannazzaro reminded Quentin of the way he had acted earlier that day in the kitchen at the Laurent house, when he threatened to beat Quentin up. I don't have any allies in this, he realized. None of the people I trust really believe in what's happening, and those who believe in it all have their own agendas. Bolt. Grandmother. What did the old lady want? Someone who could make words appear on a door a hundred miles away wasn't helpless even if she did spend her life in a rest home bed.

Nurse Sannazzaro finally approached them at quarter to seven. "I'm sorry you came on such an impossible night," she said. "I would have asked you to come back tomorrow, but I know Chief Bolt drives up all the way from Mixinack and so you'd want to wait."

"Thanks," said Quentin. "Can we see Mrs. Tyler now?"

Sannazzaro studied his face. For what? What kind of judgment was she making? "Forgive me, gentlemen, but I have to ask you—see her for what? She doesn't speak. I'm not sure she even knows what people are saying when they speak to her."

"But she's not in a coma?" asked Quentin.

"No," said Sannazzaro. "Nor is she paralyzed." Again she sized him up, as if to decide whether he was worth the trouble of explaining. Apparently he was. "It's like she simply doesn't care enough to pay attention to her own body or her own life."

"Depression?" asked Quentin.

"Despair. I've seen it before. Doesn't respond to Prozac. The only surprise is that she hasn't died yet. Usually once a resident loses all hope, death comes quickly. But Mrs. Tyler has lingered in this state for years now. You're wasting your time." She did not need to add: And mine.

"Ms. Sannazzaro," said Quentin, "I honestly don't know what this visit will accomplish. But it was my idea to come here, not Chief Bolt's. He just came along to show me the way. I don't mean any harm to Mrs. Tyler or anybody in her family. But I'd like to *try* to talk with her. That can't do her any harm, can it?"

Sannazzaro considered this. "I guess you're right."

They followed her out into the corridor.

"She couldn't have stopped us anyway," said Bolt, obviously intending Sannazzaro to overhear him. "This isn't a prison and there's such a thing as habeas corpus and privacy rights."

Quentin wasn't a lawyer, but he was pretty sure that neither legal principle applied in the case of two non-family visitors without an appointment on a busy understaffed night at a rest home. But he said nothing to Bolt, not in the testy mood he was in tonight.

Sannazzaro also ignored Bolt. "I hope this won't take too long, Mr. Fears. We have a lot of baths to give tonight."

They followed her to an elevator and went up to the top floor, then down to the end of a corridor. "Our bedridden patients don't need to be particularly convenient to the recreation and dining areas," Sannazzaro explained. "They also have fewer visitors than anyone else, so it makes sense to put them in our remotest locations."

Mrs. Tyler had a room to herself. She lay stretched out on the bed, her hands at her sides. She might have been arranged that way by an undertaker. No human being would voluntarily assume such a symmetrical position.

It took a moment, looking at her, to be sure she was the same woman he had seen at breakfast in the Laurent house.

"I found you," said Quentin.

The old lady's eyes opened for a long moment, then closed.

"Well, I'll be," said Nurse Sannazzaro. "She actually noticed you."

Quentin sat down next to her and took her by the hand. "It's good to meet you in the flesh, Grandmother," he said.

"Grandmother?" asked Sannazzaro.

"Can't you at least *pretend* not to be eavesdropping?" snapped Bolt.

Sannazzaro stood in the doorway, silent now.

Not moving his lips, Quentin formed words carefully in his mind. Can you understand me? Can you read my thoughts the way Madeleine could?

No answer. Not even the fingers squeezing his hand.

"You wanted me to come," Quentin said quietly. "You wanted me to find you."

"She's a turnip," said Bolt impatiently. "Now you've seen her, let's go."

It bothered Quentin that there was no hint of affection for her in his words. Back in Mixinack, it had been obvious that Bolt really cared for the old lady. But now . . .

"Sorry if I'm boring you," said Quentin. "What do *you* do when you visit? Play chess with her? Go on walks?"

"I sit and hold her hand," said Bolt.

"And he plumps up her pillows," said Sannazzaro dryly.

Bolt glared at her. Quentin was surprised that a medical officer would taunt someone like that—especially someone who looked after a helpless old lady without being paid for it. Though come to think of it, he wasn't sure but what Bolt *was* getting paid out of the estate. All that mattered right now, however, was communicating with Mrs. Tyler, and the hostility between Sannazzaro and Bolt wasn't helping.

"If we can't all be friends," said Quentin, "can you both just shut up? Of course I mean that in the nicest possible way."

"It's stuffy in here," said Bolt, standing up. "Will you call your lawyers if I ask for leftovers in the kitchen?"

"Eat anything that isn't actually on the floor with a footprint on it," said Sannazzaro. "But not until the cook brings it out to you in the dining room. It really is against state health regulations for you to be in the kitchen."

Bolt got up and shambled to the door. "Of course, you both know that I'm really going to the john. That chili keeps coming back to me in waves."

For Quentin, the chili had seemed far too mild to cause any discomfort. But then it was only New York chili, and besides, he hadn't eaten half as much as Bolt.

The door closed behind Bolt.

Quentin turned back to Mrs. Tyler. "We're not going to be alone," he said quietly, "so if you're going to talk to me, now would be a really good time."

But she said nothing. Not even a blink or a squeeze of his hand.

Quentin sighed and leaned back in his chair, letting go of Mrs. Tyler's hand. "What a waste of time," he said. "I'm sorry, Ms. Sannazzaro."

"I do appreciate your help with the salad," said Sannazzaro. "We don't get much volunteer help here, as you might guess. Most of our residents are alone or forgotten. Living on their savings or the sale of their houses. Many of them never had children. Those who did generally seem not to have had very devoted ones. I'm afraid I've become cynical, but the only people who visit our bed-care residents seem to be heirs who need money, hoping to get a better estimate of how long the stubbornly nondeparted are going to keep on depleting the estate."

"I'm not an heir," said Quentin.

"But you called her Grandmother."

"That's how my wife introduced her to me."

"I don't know which lie is more obnoxious, Mr. Fears, that you claim to be married to her granddaughter or that you claim you were ever introduced to Mrs. Tyler."

"'There are stranger things on heaven and earth than are dreamt of in your philosophy,'" Quentin quoted. "Please open your mind to the possibility that I might be an honest man who was himself deceived."

"Why do you care what I think?" asked Sannazzaro.

That was a good question. There was more to it than trying to get along with the keeper of the gate. He wanted Sannazzaro to think well of him. He delivered his answer in the first words that came to mind. "Because you seem to be an honest person who performs well under pressure and genuinely has the best interest of the residents at heart." And then he thought of a few things he didn't say: That she wasn't trying to get anything from him. That she made snap judgments but then wasn't afraid to change her mind. That she said and did what she thought was right without apology but also without unnecessary harshness.

"It's obvious you don't care what *I* think," said Quentin, "and normally I could say the same about myself, but the truth is I don't like it when good people think ill of me. Actually, I don't like it when bad people think ill of me, either, but there's not much I can do about that without becoming one of them."

Sannazzaro smiled. It was better than a face-lift. "How good are you at telling the difference?"

"No better than anyone else," said Quentin. "I tend to trust people until they prove me wrong. I get fewer ulcers than the people who trust nobody."

"Not to mention saving yourself from a colostomy," said Sannazzaro. "Different generations seem to express stress through different body parts. Our parents got stomach disorders. Our generation seems to be more rectally oriented."

"Now there's a pretty thought."

"So you really thought you were being introduced to Mrs. Tyler?"

Quentin looked at the old lady and nodded.

"And your wife said she was Mrs. Tyler's granddaughter?"

"She took me to Mrs. Tyler's house and said it was her grandmother's."

"Where *is* your wife, Mr. Fears?" asked Sannazzaro.

Quentin chose his words carefully. "She left me under conditions that suggest our marriage wasn't quite as honest and openhearted as I thought it was."

"Well, then, you won't be surprised when I tell you that Mrs. Tyler has only one child, her happily married daughter Rowena, and *she* has only one child, a little girl named Roz. Ten or eleven years old by now."

"You know them?" asked Quentin.

"I have Mrs. Tyler's records. And my memory of our long conversations. She wasn't like this when she first came here. It was very sad to watch her slip away into this dreamy state after only a few months."

"Did you like her?" asked Quentin.

"Oh, yes. Not demanding, not complaining." Then Sannazzaro smiled wryly at her own words. "I suppose those are the virtues of the comatose, as well. No, what I valued about Mrs. Tyler was her grace and strength. I got the impression that she had seen the worst that life has to offer and still managed to find joy somewhere, hidden in the folds of despair."

"But then the despair won."

"I don't know about that. She's still alive. So I like to imagine that wherever she's wandering, she's not so much lost as simply contemplating the daisies she found in the midst of the wasteland."

"'A host of golden daffodils.'" He quoted impulsively, almost before the thought came to mind. As if, talking with

Sannazzaro, he had just opened a doorway into his mind and whatever he free-associated came tumbling out.

"Wordsworth," said Sannazzaro. At least she recognized the source. "'I wandered lonely as a cloud that floats on high o'er vale and hill, when all at once I spied a crowd, a host of golden daffodils.' What a stupid poem, don't you think? Here I thought I had the only high school English teacher who made students memorize and recite bad Romantic poetry."

"You probably did. I just read things and some of them stick in my memory, kind of randomly."

"You mean you picked up Wordsworth voluntarily?"

"Until I got married I had a lot of time on my hands. For a while I tried to work my way through the entire Penguin library."

"What stopped you?"

"There's an awful lot of really dull stuff masquerading as English literature."

"I always think of books as being like people," said Sannazzaro. "Even the dull ones are worthy of decent respect, but you don't have to seek them out and spend time with them."

"The disadvantage with people," said Quentin, "is you can't put bookmarks in them and set them aside till you want them again."

Sannazzaro gave a hard, sharp bark of a laugh, then raised an eyebrow. "On the contrary," she said, "I've had people do that with me lots of times."

"Feeling a little dog-eared?"

"Aren't you?"

"At the moment," said Quentin, "I'm feeling well-read."

To his amazement, she blushed slightly and looked away. Somehow things had got too personal. He could see her put on her business face again. "Well, Mr. Fears—"

"Please call me Quentin. Like the prison in California."

"Minus the 'San'?"

"You've got my 'San,'" Quentin said. "Doesn't your name mean St. Nazareth?"

"Holy Man of Nazareth, I think. Mostly it means my mother and father. Hardworking people and they loved me but it was my brothers who were meant to go to college."

"You were supposed to marry and have babies?" asked Quentin.

"Or disappear. They welcome me home for holidays but nobody ever, ever asks me what I do or cares when I tell them anyway. My married sisters and my sisters-in-law, though, there's always plenty to ask *them* about. They're ranked according to the number of babies they've had or are about to have. They've got quite a competition going."

"Babies are good," said Quentin, perversely. He had already convinced Chief Bolt that he was politically correct; now was he trying to make Sannazzaro think he was a neanderthal? Was he simply too tired to care what he said?

No, that was a lie. He liked Sannazzaro and so he didn't want to be polite with her, he wanted to be honest and so he said what he believed.

"I know babies are good," said Sannazzaro, predictably irritated. "I didn't say they weren't."

"I didn't say you said they weren't," said Quentin. "I just thought about babies and how my wife has left me and I'm not going to be watching our babies grow up around me. I'm just feeling sorry for myself. My babbling has kept you here when you have baths to give. Sorry."

He started to get up, but to his surprise Sannazzaro waved him to sit down, and sat herself in the other guest chair, the overstuffed one at the foot of the bed. "We're not going to be able to keep to the regular bath schedule tonight anyway. As soon as I go out there, the attendants will feel I'm putting them under pressure and everything will get tense for them. The truth is they're all working overtime and they want to go home and in a few minutes I'm going to dismiss all but the one who's really supposed to be on shift tonight."

"Your night shift is only one?"

"Supposed to be four after the dinner rush is over and then two after everybody's tucked in. But I'm staying the night so we'll be all right. And I've got to admit I enjoy a couple of minutes of visiting with somebody who isn't afraid of me."

He wasn't sure that was true—she *was* an intimidating person. But not because she wanted to be, or tried to be. Rather she was so direct, so forthright, so clearly uninterested in making a good impression that it gave her the upper hand. Quentin liked this about her. It made him curious. "I've never heard of a nurse being in charge of a rest home. Usually isn't it a salesman type who can sucker people in?"

"This really is a good rest home, so our residents aren't suckers," said Sannazzaro. Before Quentin could protest his innocence, she went on. "But you're right, it used to be a salesman type. Then they caught him with his hands in the till and his fly open in some of the residents' rooms—I don't know which was worse in the owners' minds. Anyway, they needed a fully trained replacement immediately. I was already here as medical officer. So I've been acting superintendent since October of '94."

"Why don't they just make it official?" asked Quentin.

"Because I don't want the job and I keep turning it down."

"So why don't you quit running the place and go back to your nurse duties?"

"Because if I do they'll bring in another salesman type to run the place, and I'd hate going back to that nightmare."

"So you won't take the job, but you won't give it up," said Quentin.

She laughed. "It sounds just as stupid to me, but what can I do? They're paying me at the nurse level plus a bonus, which saves them money, and in the meantime I don't have some cost-cutting moron glad-handing the public and stealing from the patients. Except that I'm tired all the time and don't have a life, things are going great."

Again Quentin found himself speaking on impulse. "It's a good thing we both know that I'm depressed and recovering from a spectacularly failed marriage, or I'd offer to take you away from all this." Quentin wondered at his own words. Was this flirtatious conversation for its own sake? Or did he unconsciously mean something by it?

Fortunately, she took it as a joke rather than a come-on. "Just don't say anything about the Virgin Islands or I'll take you up on it and you'd be stuck with a cast-iron bitch who doesn't look all that good in a bikini."

"Now you've done it. Now I'm thinking of you in a bikini."

They laughed.

Quentin was relieved that it was just a flirtation between two tired people who knew nothing would come of it. But he hadn't had many ventures into the world of flirtation, and most of what he'd seen had been while waiting to meet partners in upscale bars where all the flirters were so drunk that it didn't take much for them to think each other clever. It kind of gave him a thrill to play at it with a sober person whom he liked. But it also made him feel guilty. Even though he knew Madeleine wasn't real, he still felt married and he was a faithful husband.

"You're thinking of your wife," said Sannazzaro.

"Yeah, well, I was thinking that I still feel married."

"I'm glad to hear it. I've known too many men who never felt quite married no matter how many wives they've been through. Their own and otherwise."

Remembering again where they were, Quentin looked at Mrs. Tyler's closed and silent face. "I wonder how Mrs. Tyler felt about her husband."

"Loved him," said Sannazzaro. "But he died young. She told me that she thought the death of their first child, a boy, was too hard on him. He lost heart. Like I said—when people truly despair, they don't live long."

"She seems awfully old to have her oldest grandchild be only ten."

"I think the little girl is eleven. But yes. Mrs. Tyler married late. Maybe that was part of her husband's despair. She was forty before she started having babies."

"What was the delay?"

"What is it ever? She married Mr. Tyler only six months after she met him. He was more than ten years younger than her. She always assumed that he'd outlive her, which was fine, she didn't want to be a widow."

"Bummer," said Quentin.

"And *you* meant to be a father," said Sannazzaro. "Nobody's life ever goes according to plan."

"So why do we keep on planning?"

She thought for a moment. "Because that's how we know who we are. By what we intend to be. By what we try to become."

"And fail."

"I don't say 'fail,' Mr. Fears. I say we aim and miss. But we still hit something."

"Ouch."

She smiled. But she had been serious, and he could see that his joke disappointed her.

"Sorry," he said. "I think what you said is right. I'm just kind of caught up in the target that I missed. I haven't even looked to see what I might have hit. Maybe the arrow hasn't even landed yet. And please call me Quentin."

"Minus the 'San.'"

"That's what I'll call *you*."

"Call me Sally," she said.

"Sally, may I call you?" he said. And there it was. He wasn't content for this conversation to amount to nothing.

She looked at him for a while before saying, "When you know what's happening with your marriage, I wouldn't mind a phone call now and then."

He smiled. He liked a woman who knew how to spell out the rules. He also liked it that she had the same rules he did.

She smiled back.

He got up to leave, and so did she. He was reaching for the door when he saw words appear on it.

DON'T GO

His hand hovered over the doorknob.

"Well?" asked Sannazzaro. Sally.

He looked at her. She didn't see the words. Too bad. It would have been nice if he could tell her what was really going on. But without the evidence of her own eyes, like Bolt had had, she would never believe him. And he didn't want her to think he was crazy. He wanted very much for her to like him because he needed a friend who was good and decent and lived in the real world and didn't charge him three hundred bucks an hour.

"Sally," he said. "I want to talk to Mrs. Tyler. Alone. I know she won't hear me, but it would mean a lot to me. I'm not going to hurt her. If you want affidavits about my character, call my lawyer, his number's on my card." He handed her one. "Or call my parents and they'll tell you I was always a good boy."

"Maybe I should call your neighbors," said Sally.

"They'll just tell you I'm a loner who keeps to himself." He grinned.

She shook her head. "Quentin, I don't know why I should trust you. You're such a smooth operator. You're not telling me the truth. And you came here with slime on your shoes."

Apparently she *really* didn't like Bolt. "The way Bolt acted here tonight, I've never seen him like that. If I'd known the way things stood between you, I never would have brought him. Everything I've told you is true but you're right, I haven't told you everything because I don't want you to think I'm crazy."

"So. Convince me you're not crazy."

"Sally, I saw Mrs. Tyler in a house in Mixinack a few days ago. She slept through breakfast but in the parlor she looked me in the eye and said, 'Find me.' That's why I'm here."

213

"This isn't helping."

"You can see why I didn't tell you, but it's the truth. Crazy things are happening but I know I'm *not* crazy because every now and then somebody else sees the same things I see. Earlier today I saw writing magically appear on a door in that house in Mixinack—and Bolt saw it too."

"Better not use Bolt as a witness of your sanity, Quentin."

"And when a limo driver dropped me and my wife off a few days ago, he saw lights on in the house and a servant waiting to meet the car, just as I did. Only the next day I found out that the power hadn't been on in that house ever since Mrs. Tyler came here. And the only footprints in the snow were the driver's and mine."

She shuddered. "This isn't funny, Mr. Fears," she said.

"You asked for the truth," said Quentin. "But when I tell you the truth, I stop being Quentin and become Mr. Fears again."

"I don't believe in ghost stories."

"That's good," said Quentin, "because my wife's not dead and neither is Mrs. Tyler."

Sally looked at him for a long moment, her expression shifting among conflicting emotions. Then, abruptly, she reached for the knob and drew the door open.

Bolt practically fell into the room. He laughed nervously as he recovered his balance. "I was just coming in."

"You were listening at the door," said Quentin.

"I thought it was funny," said Bolt, "you trying to convince *her* of some idea that doesn't fit into her narrow little nurseview of the universe."

Quentin wanted to deck him. "Of course she doesn't believe me. It isn't believable."

"So why did you tell her? You had her eating out of your hand."

Quentin felt unutterable contempt for Bolt. Where was the man he thought he knew back in Mixinack? Did he really think that the conversation between him and Sally

214

was nothing but manipulation? "Let's get out of here," said Quentin.

"About damn time," said Bolt. He shot Sannazzaro a triumphant glance. Quentin took his arm and almost dragged him out of the room.

"What's the rush?" said Bolt. "You were sure taking your time before."

"For a while today I thought I liked you," said Quentin. "But I was wrong."

"Ah, the rest home witch has enchanted you, has she?"

Instead of jabbing an elbow into his mouth, Quentin strode on ahead.

"Mr. Fears! Quentin! Wait!"

He stopped and turned. Sally Sannazzaro had rushed into the hall from Mrs. Tyler's room.

"Quentin, she spoke! She told me to bring you back!"

Quentin turned in surprise to look at Bolt. Bolt looked angry, even ashamed. "She's lying," he whispered. "The old lady is brain dead. She's a vegetable."

"Bolt, I know that she's not, and so do you."

"She's *dead*," muttered Bolt. And he didn't come with Quentin back up the corridor.

Quentin paused in the doorway to meet Sally's gaze. "I wasn't lying, Sally," he said.

"I trust Mrs. Tyler as a judge of character," she answered softly. "Apparently you have the gift of bringing people back from the dead."

"Wouldn't *that* be nice."

"I'll leave you alone with her, but don't let Bolt in here, Quentin."

"I won't."

Then he went inside and closed the door behind him. Mrs. Tyler turned her head and looked at him. "Thank you for coming," she whispered.

14
Old Lady Tyler

Her voice was husky from long disuse. When she gestured
with her hand it seemed almost translucent in its frailty. She
tried to roll over, and it looked as if her body was too heavy
for anything to move it; then he helped her roll on her side,
to face his chair, and he could feel how light she was, as if
she had been shaped of air. Had she no bones? What was it
that tied a creature so insubstantial to the earth? Gravity
could not possibly hold her here.

"You've borne up well," she said.

He shook his head. "I've hardly been eating the last few
days."

"Keep up your strength."

He didn't need motherly advice from this woman. He
needed answers. But now that she was speaking to him, he
couldn't think of what to ask.

"Why didn't you speak till now?"

"It's not safe for me to stay in my body," she said. "Eter-
nal vigilance."

"That's the price of liberty, as I recall," said Quentin. "You
don't look free to me."

"But I'm not dead."

"Who wants to kill you?"

"Rowena."

"Your own daughter?"

"We had a falling-out."

"I guess."

"*She* picked you, not me," said Mrs. Tyler.

"Picked me for what?" asked Quentin. "Why can't *she* just open the treasure box?"

"It's evil of her to call it that."

"What is it, then?"

"A coffin. A prison. The gate of hell."

"Yeah, I'm sure I would have opened it for her if she called it *that*."

"You must never, never open the box."

"Was it you that stopped me before?"

"I helped you stop."

"But I was trying to open it."

"You thought you were. But a wiser part of you was afraid to open it. A wiser part of you was already learning not to trust the succubus."

Until this moment it had not occurred to Quentin that that's what Madeleine had been all along. A succubus. An evil spirit sent to seduce a man in his sleep. He knew of the myths and legends, but he'd never heard of any stories in which the succubus stayed around long enough to marry the man.

"What's in the box?" he asked.

"Pray to God that you never have to know."

"That's not an answer."

"I didn't bring you here to answer your questions. You don't know enough to ask the questions that matter. And I can't stay long inside my body. It's too dangerous. Too much can happen while I'm not watching."

"All right, tell me what I need to know."

"Rowena keeps my body locked down on this bed, and when I send my spirit wandering, she shadows me. Wherever I roam, there she is, blocking me from this, blocking me from that. I try to watch her closely, but I didn't even know you existed until the succubus brought you to the house and she started raising the dead."

"Why me?" Quentin asked. "Do you *know* why?"

"All I can do is guess. Everything depends on how much she knows. Rowena was such a rebellious child. She hated me as soon as she was old enough to pluck memories out of my mind. She didn't understand what happened, and she wouldn't let me explain. She told me my mind was too loathsome for her ever to want to enter it again."

Daughters entering their mothers' minds. "What *are* you people?"

"Oh, Quentin, how dim are you really? We're witches. The real ones, not the silly ignorant women who prance naked and try to turn our affliction into a mystical religion. It's not something you can choose. Most people have only the faintest touch of the power. A glimmer now and then, that's all they get of the other side. But *we* grow up looking at the spirit as well as the body. We can see, we can touch everyone, both spirit and body. We hear words spoken aloud, but at the same time we can also hear the thoughts behind them. We can walk on our legs, but we can also send our spark out flying. We can see the living, but we can also see the dead, and when we know where they're anchored we can call them and make them come to us."

Quentin thought back to Sunday school, to the one story from the Bible that had a witch in it. The witch of Endor.

"That's right," said Mrs. Tyler. "It always bothers Christians and Jews that their scripture has such a tale in it. How could a woman who had chosen evil have the power to call a great prophet back from the dead? So they say it was fakery. Or it was Satan, pretending to be Samuel. But *we* know what she did and how she did it. All the dead are within reach. Saul knew Samuel. He must have had some relic of the old prophet—some of his hair. Maybe he even dug into his grave and took a piece of him. Brought it to the witch, and she used it to call him, and Samuel spoke to Saul through her. Maybe Saul was like you—he could see a little, if he really tried. It happened then, and that's how it happens now. That's how she called Jude and poor Simon and Stephen and foolish old Minerva."

"Dug into their graves?"

"Maybe not. They were all tied to the house, so she might not have needed relics. But why do you think Christians have always made such a big deal about relics of the saints? The power to call back their spirits—it was forbidden for them to use it, but they also coveted it. If you had a genuine piece of the finger of St. Peter, you could call him to you. There's nothing silly about it."

"So how did *I* call my sister Lizzy? I didn't have any part of her."

Mrs. Tyler was astonished. "You called back your sister? You called the dead yourself? When?"

"When I was a boy. The age your granddaughter is now. My sister was on the edge of death and I wasn't letting them take her organs for transplant. I sat alone beside her hospital bed, the way I'm sitting here beside you, and she came to me. Or at least she spoke inside my head. And told me that it was all right to let her go."

"You don't have to tell me the whole story. I see it *now*. Oh, my. Oh, no."

"What?"

"She *hid* that from me, the little spider. It changes everything."

"Changes what?"

"She knows more than I thought. She's not ignorant, she's just stupider than I ever imagined."

"What is it that she knows?"

"You aren't in thrall. She doesn't own you. Oh, why didn't I see it? Of *course* she sent a succubus instead of just enthralling you."

"Trust me, I was enthralled."

"On the contrary, you were enchanted, but not enthralled. You're still free."

"I guess."

"She thinks she can control the beast through you. Because you're so strong. And free. If you're enthralled when you let the beast out, it won't pay attention to you, it will go straight for her. But if you're free when it touches you, then it will want you. She's counting on your strength to draw it to you. It flows to strength. She thinks that when it's all inside you, taking possession of your body, then she can enthrall *you* and she'll control *it*."

"Control *what*?"

"The beast that took my little boy."

Quentin remembered the story Bolt had told him. "Rowena told Chief Bolt that you murdered your child before he turned two."

"I know she thinks that's what she saw in my memory, but it was *not* my boy that I killed. She didn't understand."

"Didn't understand what?"

"*It* had taken control of little Paul before his first birthday. Paul was beautiful and brilliant. He was going to be a glorious child of light. So few boys have the power, but he was the bright and shining one. But the beast saw him and came and stole his body. It took me a while to realize it. I thought at first that maybe some witch had enthralled my child, and I tried to find the link and break it. But the link was inside him. The thing owned his body, and finally I realized that it wasn't my Paul anymore, it was the beast using his stolen body. Paul was gone and I would never get him back. When the beast takes your body, it's *his*. There's no remnant of you left."

Now Quentin understood. "So Rowena did see you kill the boy."

"She saw my memory of cutting the living heart out of the *beast*. But she was a child. Of course she thought it was my little Paul. To try to stop me, the beast made his body cry and beg in Paul's little baby language. 'No, Mommy, don't hurt me, Mommy.' Rowena saw that. But *I* had seen the truth. He did things that none of *us* can do. He moved things with his mind. He destroyed things. We found them: a fly embedded in the midst of a pane of glass; locks opening without keys—ah, you've seen evidence of that? It was the beast."

"What's this beast? You mean the book of Revelation?"

"I mean the dragon. There might be many of them, but I've never heard of more than one upon the earth at the same time. It comes to a body that began human, but once the beast has it, the shape changes to whatever the beast desires. It came to Adolf Hitler when he was trying to paint in England, and it owned him from then on until it had no power left except to poison the body it dwelt in. It was in the ancient conquerors who built up piles of skulls and spread fear through the world. It loves death. It also hungers for strength. The stronger the human whose body it steals, the stronger the beast is until the human body dies."

"So it can be killed."

"How many suffer and die before it falls? Yes, it can be killed—eventually. And in this age, who is pure enough to kill it?"

"Pure? Like St. George?" Quentin couldn't help laughing. It was the cliché of romantic stories—slaying the dragon to save the maiden.

"Why do you laugh? Why do you think Rowena chose you?"

"Not because of my purity," said Quentin.

"What do *you* know about it?" said Mrs. Tyler. "You have to be pure to hold on to any of yourself in its presence. Her plan doesn't work if you're not pure."

Quentin laughed again, only bitterly this time. "She's going to be disappointed."

Mrs. Tyler ignored him. "If she had let me teach her,

she would know that you can't control the beast. She must have seen my memory of the powers that Paulie seemed to have. How could she not have understood, if she saw so much?"

"Maybe she didn't believe about the beast," said Quentin.

"She knew the powers she herself had. She knew my memories were true. What other evidence did she need?"

"Maybe she thought you had gone insane, and this was a paranoid fantasy about your own son being possessed by the spirit of a dragon. If all she saw in your memory was a few special powers that he had, and then you overreact and kill him—"

"It wasn't Paul, it was the—"

"How did you *know* it was the beast? Were you really sure?"

"Of course I was sure! What kind of monster do you think I am?"

"I don't know. What kind of monster do *you* think you are?"

"What are you saying?"

"Why did you wait until he was nearly two before you did it? If you were sure?"

"Because it was my son's face. Because it was my son's voice. Because *it* was trying to hide itself from me until my son had grown stronger and I no longer would have the power to resist. And it almost worked, I almost waited too long. It almost had the power to stop me. But I got my vengeance. I didn't set it free. I locked it up."

"Inside the treasure box."

"One time it was hidden in a bottle and cast into the sea, but bottles float to shore and are found."

"A genie?"

"It doesn't grant wishes except its own," she said. "Another time it was hidden with a corpse inside a mummy case in Egypt, but thieves found their way into the secret chamber and it was free again. Killing it solves the problem

223

for today, but then it's free to find another host. I was not going to let it do to another mother what it had done to me."

"Had you ever seen this beast before?" asked Quentin.

"Of course not. But I knew the lore. Unlike Rowena I learned everything from my mother. And from my grandmother. I knew what to look for."

"Had any of *them* seen this beast?"

"Don't you dare accuse me of what you're accusing me of."

"I'm not accusing you of anything," said Quentin. "I'm just saying that maybe the reason Rowena didn't believe it was the beast was because deep down in your heart of hearts, you weren't sure either."

"Do you think I would have cut into that precious body if I had the slightest doubt?"

"Somewhere in the back of your mind you fear that you went mad and murdered your own son."

"No!" But it was not a word, it was a wail. Somehow from that frail body there came such a cry that it must have been audible in every room in the rest home.

Then, suddenly, her body went slack. She rolled onto her back and lay there, body symmetrical, eyes closed. Her spark was gone again.

But not far. On the wall the word was blazoned so brightly it almost blinded him:

LIAR

"I wasn't accusing," he tried to explain again. "I was just trying to figure out why Rowena could search your memory and still believe that you murdered him."

GET OUT

"All right." He went to the door and opened it. He could hear pounding footsteps and the jammering of many voices. Of course the others in the rest home had heard Mrs. Tyler scream. There was Sally Sannazzaro, rushing toward the room, a look of horror on her face.

"Sally," said Quentin, "it's all right! I didn't hurt her; I just said something that made her angry. She's asleep again."

I HOPE YOU DIE

The words covered the corridor wall like a mural. He turned and on the other side it said:

I LOVED MY BABY

"I know you did, Mrs. Tyler," he said softly, knowing she could hear him, knowing that she wasn't listening.

Sally pushed past him into Mrs. Tyler's room. Only when she had satisfied herself that the old woman was still breathing did she come back out. He was afraid she was going to beat him up on the spot.

"All we did was talk," he insisted, holding up his hands to forestall her.

"Get out," she said. "You're never coming back here, do you understand me?"

"Sally, I didn't hurt her. She called me here. She wants my help, and I want to help her. I just said something that made her angry because it was true."

Mrs. Tyler's answer fairly burned on the walls, the same word, over and over:

LIAR

LIAR

LIAR

"But she'll get over it," said Quentin, "and when she does we need to talk again."

"Not a chance," said Sannazzaro. "Now get out, you and your friend Bolt. You've caused enough trouble in this rest home."

"All right, I'm going."

"I've already punched the alarms to bring the police and paramedics. So you'd better go fast."

"Thanks for waiting to find out the truth before calling in the cavalry," Quentin said angrily. "I didn't violate your trust."

"My trust ended when my friend screamed. It sounded like you were tearing her apart with your bare hands!"

Quentin burned with frustration at having lost Sannazzaro's friendship so unfairly. Yet even her snap judgment of him made him want to be closer to her. Because she was the opposite of Madeleine. Instead of being exactly what he wished for, shaped to his every desire, she was completely herself, and whatever she gave him she would give him freely, as an equal. Most people Quentin knew were at least a little bit like Madeleine, trying to outguess him, trying to give him whatever he wanted to get on his good side. So he could never be sure who they really were. He might not understand Sannazzaro, but whatever she was, it was real. He wanted to reach out and shake her and shout at her until she believed him: I'm real, too. I'm as real as you are. But then, maybe he wasn't. Maybe you had to be as pure to stay in the company of good people as to survive among beasts.

Chief Bolt sauntered out of the elevator. "Anybody dead?" he asked cheerfully.

"You are, if you don't get out of here right now," said Sannazzaro. "I'll kill you myself and call it self-defense."

They got in the elevator, Sannazzaro with them. "I'm going to see you out the door and into your car and driving away."

Wordlessly they rode down. But as she followed them to the door, she thought of something else to say. "I'm going to have a guard posted at her room. Her estate can afford it and I'm going to make sure you never get in there again."

Quentin stopped just outside the glass front door, the snow blowing around him. He could hear the sirens of the approaching emergency vehicles. "Sally," he said, "I kept my word and did no harm. When you want me back here, just call me. I'll come."

Sannazzaro closed the door in his face and locked it.

Bolt was already waiting beside the car. "Get in, bone-head, we don't want to be here all night answering questions."

Quentin didn't want to stay with Bolt, but there wasn't much choice right now. There was only one car that would get him away from here before the police arrived, and Bolt had to be in it. Quentin had a hard time opening the door, trembling as he was with rage and frustration and weariness and fear at the things that Mrs. Tyler had told him, at Sannazzaro's unfairness. No, it wasn't that at all. He was trembling from the cold. That's all.

He backed the car out of the stall and headed for the parking lot entrance.

"Don't turn right, you fool, turn left!"

"But that's where the sirens are coming from."

"We don't want to look like we're running away from them, Quentin. Do we?"

"Fine, whatever, you're the cop." Quentin pulled out onto the snowy road and drove back the way he had come. They were passed by an ambulance and a firetruck. But no police. Sannazzaro hadn't called the police after all. Or else the police were slower than the others. He didn't linger to find out.

Not till they got back on the freeway did Bolt finally ask the obvious question. "Now do you mind telling me what the hell happened?"

"I should ask *you,* Bolt. What got into you back there?"

"What are you talking about?" said Bolt. "I didn't do anything. *You* were the one who got to talk to the old lady. Fill me in."

Back when they were eating chili together, Quentin had told him everything he knew up till then. But now, having seen the way he acted with Sally Sannazzaro, wondering if there might be something to Sally's belief that he had tried to smother the old lady—now Quentin didn't feel like telling him anything.

"She didn't make any sense," he said. "She was delu-sional. I don't know what she thought I was, but she got frightened and screamed."

"Well, since she's been a turnip for several years now, do we count screaming as an improvement or a deterioration?" asked Bolt. The wry tone was back in his voice, now. He was himself again. Or maybe he had been himself back in the rest home. How could Quentin know?

"I liked Sally," said Quentin.

"Yeah, she's a real charmer."

Quentin looked up at the freeway sign announcing the next exit. Only it didn't say the name of a town.

GO AHEAD

Go ahead?

"I got news for you, Quentin," said Bolt. "From what I know of women, Sannazzaro doesn't like you."

She did, though, for a little while.

The sign that should have announced restaurants at the next exit had also been altered.

OPEN THE BOX

"Of course, what do I know about women?" said Bolt.

The sign promising gas stations now said:

I WANT YOU TO

Go ahead, open the box, I want you to. Gee, thanks, Grandmother.

The little exit sign had also been changed.

DIE

"By the way, have you been noticing the signs?" said Bolt. "Have you?"

"Somebody doesn't like you," said Bolt. "Can Sannazzaro do that?"

"I doubt it," said Quentin. "It's the old lady. She's a witch.

Rowena's a witch. My wife Madeleine was a succubus."

For a moment Bolt was angry. "Rowena's not a witch!"

"Just think about it for a second," said Quentin. "Those words aren't going up on those signs by themselves."

"It's the old lady."

"Yes, it's the old lady. But the other stuff *wasn't* her. Rowena's the one who keeps her tied down to that bed. It's a war between witches, fighting over a dragon, flinging succubuses around to win the cooperation of the occasional man. Don't think for a minute that just because you loved Rowena, she isn't one of them."

"Yeah, well, what do *you* know about Rowena?"

"Nothing. I know absolutely nothing about anything, Bolt."

"Me too."

"You can say that again. If you hadn't been acting like a prick back at the rest home, Sannazzaro wouldn't have gotten so angry at me."

"I don't know what gets into me when I'm around that woman," said Bolt. "If there's any witch in this whole business, it's her."

I'm not calling them witches metaphorically, Quentin wanted to say. I'm telling you that the woman you love probably had you enthralled, under control. That's probably what was happening to you back in the rest home.

But there was no point in saying it. Because if it was true, Bolt wouldn't be able to understand it.

"Anyway, it's been a long time since lunch," said Bolt. "If by some chance one of these signs actually says something about food instead of carrying your hate mail, you up for dinner?"

How could he think of eating?

But now that he mentioned it, Quentin was hungry too. "You sure the police won't be looking for us?"

"We've changed counties now," said Bolt. "That sign that said *liar* about eight times was the county line. Besides, I don't think Sannazzaro really called the cops."

"No, I guess not."

"See? She likes you, Quentin. Not calling the cops on you—man, that's love."

Quentin had to laugh in spite of himself. Bolt was back to himself again. Things would settle down at the rest home, too. Sannazzaro would realize that she overreacted. Mrs. Tyler too. Everything would be fine.

In the meantime, what had he learned? He thought of all the stories of witches he had heard and read. The warty noses and pointy chins were obviously just prejudice against age. The magic potions were the stuff of alchemy, or the lore of folk medicine, which was used to both cure and curse. But the idea of witches calling upon the dead, sending succubuses to sleeping men, collecting macabre body parts from people they knew, all of these must have had roots in true incidents. Even the stories of witches worshiping Satan . . . for what might happen if this beast that Mrs. Tyler talked of should succeed in taking control of an adult body? There were plenty of people who worshiped Hitler. Caligula made himself a god. What if the beast took over some poor devil of a druid? What would that look like to people who didn't understand what those witches were doing, or who the man they worshiped really was? For the lifetime of the man it inhabited, the beast might well make witches into his personal slaves, holding bacchanals that would fit even the most bizzarre medieval accounts. Witches, succubuses, dragons, the devil. To some people they would always be myths. But not to the people who were born with a greater ability to commune with spirits living and dead.

What about me? Quentin couldn't help but wonder. He certainly had nothing like the power of these women, but he had some. He had called to Lizzy without realizing it—and without having any relic of her, either. The moment he imagined having a relic of her, he thought of what that would have entailed, taking some fragment of her body. Wasn't that just what the transplant doctors had done? Organs of her body had been scattered across the country and kept alive, binding her spirit to them until at last they died. He shuddered in revulsion.

"Turn the heat up if you're shivering," said Bolt beside him.

Quentin thought of how Bolt, poor man, was in love with a witch and never realized it. Rowena kissing him in the kitchen. Quentin had been pretty thoroughly enchanted by a succubus; how much stronger must it have been for Bolt, who kissed the witch herself? Was that the exact method a witch used to enthrall a man? The kiss that wakens the sleeping princess. The kiss that turns the frog into a man. A kiss before dying.

He tried to sort through all that Mrs. Tyler had told him about thralls. A man with no will of his own. The beast would leap right past him to the woman who owned him. So if Bolt was enthralled, that would explain why Rowena couldn't use him to open the box. It would expose Rowena as surely as if she opened it herself. But what *could* a thrall do? Had she sent him to try to murder her mother? Maybe he wouldn't even know that was what he was about to do? His rational mind would have to make up some alternate explanation for his own actions, such as wanting to rearrange the old lady's pillows. He loved and honored Mrs. Tyler; he couldn't possibly imagine killing her. Even if he found himself in the act of murdering her, the idea would be inconceivable to him.

Dangerous people, these witches. As dangerous when they loved you as they were when they hated you. That is, if they ever really loved anybody, instead of just using them.

Quentin pressed the long-distance speed dial number for Wayne Read on the cellular phone. It didn't really matter now if Bolt heard him or not. Rowena and Mrs. Tyler and half the witches in the world could be listening in on all his conversations and he'd never know it.

The salutations over, Quentin got to the point. "If you don't have the address for the so-called Duncans yet, I have more information. The wife was born Rowena Tyler. And their address is probably in the file of Mrs. Anna Laurent Tyler at the Willoughby Retirement Home." He gave him the address.

"We're still checking out other leads too," said Wayne. "If you were just there, why didn't you get the address yourself?"

"I didn't part on good terms with the management."

"So how is our investigator going to get the information?"

"It doesn't have to be admissible in court, Wayne."

"You've been reading too much detective fiction, Quentin. Most private investigators have no burglary skills whatsoever."

"Most *burglars* have no burglary skills. Just walk in during business hours, take the file, Xerox the sheet with the address, and walk out. They're shorthanded right now."

"Quentin, you live in a fantasy world."

"We all do, Wayne. I just found out I was married to a succubus who was created by a witch. It's year-round Halloween now."

"We'll find a sane way of getting the address."

"Thanks."

"By the way, Quentin, you asked me how to go about divorcing a woman who doesn't exist?"

"I thought it might be a problem."

"No problem at all. No divorce needed. There wasn't a marriage."

"What do you mean?"

"All the documents—license, certificate—she never signed them."

"I watched her." But of course that meant nothing; Quentin knew it as he said it.

"It's your signature on both lines of every document. You're married to yourself, Quentin."

"At least I know I'll be faithful."

"Good-bye, dear lunatic. Try to stay uncommitted for a little longer—at least until you've paid my bill."

"I'll do my best."

Bolt laughed when Quentin hung up the phone. "Listen, if Rowena doesn't want you to find out where she is, nobody's going to get a true address."

"So I guess we'll have to hope she *does* want me to find her."

"I don't imagine you'll take me with you."

"Believe me, Bolt, if she wanted you to go to her, I wouldn't be able to stop you."

"Damn straight," said Bolt, pretending to be joking.

Rowena existed in the real world somewhere. Sooner or later, Wayne Read's investigators would find her; if she still had a use for Quentin, she would let them find her. The creator of the succubus that Quentin had loved and lost—yes, he would have something to say to her when they met.

233

15
Snow

It usually wasn't hard for Quentin to wait for other people to do their work. His career for many years had consisted of giving people the money and support to make a go of something. He would get periodic reports about how things were going; he would meet with them now and then; but by and large he let them do what they loved to do, what they had dreamed of doing, and waited until it was fairly clear how things were going to turn out.

In a way this was the same thing. Caught up in other people's dreams, waiting to find things out. The trouble was that he wasn't sure what the dream was, or who was the dreamer, or whose nightmare it would be when all was done.

He toyed with the idea of waiting in Mixinack for Wayne's report—Bolt even offered to let him stay on the couch in the study of his big old Victorian house. But Mixinack was the place where the treasure box was, and it wasn't the treasure box Quentin wanted to get into at the moment.

What *did* he want? After dropping off Bolt at his office to pick up his car, Quentin drove south on a road denuded of traffic by the storm. The advisories on the radio begged people to stay off the highways during what they were already calling the "Blizzard of '96." The airports were closed. Quentin wouldn't be catching a flight tonight. He should have looked for a motel and holed up to wait out the storm. Instead he kept driving south. Not because the weather would be better there—word was that the storm would do a better job of shutting down Washington than the budget impasse. The people that the grande dame had known as the Duncans, who were almost certainly Rowena Tyler and her husband and child, lived somewhere in the DC area. And they were the people he had to see. To find out how much of Mrs. Tyler's story was true. To find out what they really wanted of him. And to get some idea of how to extricate himself from all this.

Because he did want to get out. A few days ago, all he wanted was Madeleine. Now all he wanted was his liberty. A man who has loved the perfect lover isn't likely to find a substitute very soon. Rowena could give him that lover back, possibly, but he had a feeling her price for such a service would be too high. So why look for her and her family? Why not drive west until he found some open airport and fly on to California, to Hawaii, to Tokyo or Singapore. He thought of places he had always wanted to see but never took the time for, because there was no one to see them with. Jerusalem. Kilamanjaro. Machu Picchu. The Great Barrier Reef. The Himalayas. Tashkent. Timbuktu. There was no more reason to wait for a companion. Either he would see them alone or not at all.

But was there really anyplace on earth where he could be free of this? Maybe they would give up on him and find someone else to do their bidding. But was that better than having him do it? After all, their next victim might be a man who did have some connection to the world. A husband, a father, someone whose destruction would leave a hole. While Quentin knew that even if this business killed him, what difference would it make? His will had been changed to turn everything over to his parents. They would allow Wayne to follow through with all the existing partnerships, and then they'd do a pretty good job of philanthropy, getting rid of his entire fortune before they died, except for whatever they needed to make sure they finished out their lives in comfort. His death would leave the same hole in the world that a fish leaves when it's pulled wriggling out of the ocean.

So why should he turn this over to somebody else? Quentin was expendable. Be a good soldier, he told himself. March the march, up to the front, take aim, and fire your best shot. Then die if you must. But let it be with a bullet in front, not in the back. Facing the enemy.

Oh, aren't we getting dramatic? He laughed at himself and changed to another radio station as the previous one faded into the white static of the falling snow.

The Jersey Turnpike was closed. He started searching for alternate routes and ended up, about three in the morning, driving the deserted streets of downtown Philadelphia. A policeman pulled him over.

"Don't appreciate the joyriding, mister," said the cop. "Can't you see it's dangerous out here?"

"Got no place to go, Officer," said Quentin. "The airports are snowed in and I want to get back to DC."

"Find a motel and get to sleep."

"Then my car will be covered in snow and I'll be stuck in a city that's closed down tight."

"Better than having us dig you out of a snowbank three days from now, stiff as a board."

"Officer, will it be OK if I promise to find a safe place to bed down, and then just keep driving where I want? Or are you going to follow me and arrest me for trying to get home?"

The policeman looked at him with disgust. "Do what you want." Then he went on back to his patrol car.

Do what I want. Well, that's great advice. But what if the thing I want most in all the world can't be done? Because I want to go home, Officer, and home isn't that apartment in

Herndon and it isn't my folks' house in California. Home is where the people who live there need me to come home to them, and worry about me when I'm gone. There's no such place on this earth, no matter how far I drive.

What's so wrong with feeling sorry for myself? Better that than trying to get other people to feel sorry for me. And *somebody* sure ought to, because my life is definitely in the pitiful range, if it hasn't already dropped on down into disastrous.

Oh, Lizzy, why did you have to go riding that night? Or why couldn't I have gone with you? Why couldn't we have done the transplant the other direction? It was a brain you needed, and mine was OK. You would have done so much better with it than I ever have. Why couldn't they transplant my life into you, so you could live it for me?

"Buck up, Tin," said Lizzy.

She was sitting beside him, shifting her weight in the seat to get comfortable.

"You're a pretty good snow driver. *That's* something they didn't bother teaching us in driver's ed back in high school."

"Thanks," said Quentin. "Sorry. I didn't mean to call you."

"No sweat. Truth is that I like it when you do. Time doesn't pass out there the way it does for you, so you can't exactly get bored, and there's plenty to do, depending on how you define *do*, but I gotta say I miss having a body. I never really used it, Tin."

"I was just thinking that myself."

"No, you were thinking that you were as useless as the turd of a dog who just died."

He laughed in spite of himself.

"You were thinking that you're the guy who really needs a hand grenade to land in his foxhole so he can dive on it, save his buddies, and have the President give the Medal of Honor to his parents, along with eight boxes containing his remains."

"Lizzy, is there any way through this thing?"

"There are a thousand ways through this thing, Tin. But they might all end up with you dead."

"Is that so bad? You're doing OK."

"Sure. Death's all right. But not worth going through any extra trouble to get here. You miss everything when you're here, Quentin. Even the pain. Even the despair."

"So is Mrs. Tyler right? Will the treasure box kill me?"

"Treasure box. What you mean is, is the beast real? Well, I didn't know what to call it till just now, diving into your memory to see what the old lady told you about it, but I'd say that's a pretty fair description of the bad thing in that house."

"She put it in the box. It isn't good to let it out."

"I don't know, Tin. As long as it's in that box, it's going to keep trying to suck people in to get the box open. But if it dies, maybe it'll be a while before somebody calls to it. Opens up to it and lets it in."

"Come on, Lizzy. Last time it got sucked into a year-old baby."

"She was lying to you, Tin."

"It wasn't in the baby?"

"Oh, it was, all right. But it didn't just happen along. Didn't just *come*. She called it."

"Man, that's even worse than what I said to her."

"She didn't realize that's what she was doing. She thought she had this brilliant baby, and so she wanted it to learn everything. She was pushing."

"Like those people who try to get their kids into college-prep nursery schools?"

"I guess."

"Or flashcards. They make their babies learn words from flashcards."

"She got the kid to call things it didn't have the brains to control. I don't care how smart a one-year-old is, Tin, walking and talking and all, it doesn't know how to deal with something as old as life itself. It came and the baby was gone, just hanging on to its own body like a passenger hanging from the back of the bus, begging the driver not to close the door."

"How did you learn all this, if the old lady doesn't know it?"

"After the passenger's been dragged long enough, he starts begging the driver to close it. Cut him loose. Even if it means he crashes onto the pavement."

"You found baby Paulie."

"I didn't like anybody else in that house. Baby Paulie was lonely and scared. I didn't realize how he was connected until now."

"So he *was* still there."

"Only sort of. Mrs. Tyler wasn't wrong. Best thing she could have done was cut him loose from a body he'd never have the use of again. If only she'd actually done it, instead of leaving him lingering, attached to that treasure box. But of course now it's too late. When that box opens, somebody's going to find themselves looking down the throat of the beast. And Paulie will still be along for the ride, as will the person the beast devours."

"Me."

"I hope not," said Lizzy. "Please don't."

"So I should run."

"I don't know. Maybe you should stay and win."

"Can I?"

"These witches are powerful, but you're not nothing. You've got some strength in you. And there's something else, too. You aren't trying to get something out of this."

"What, survival is nothing?"

"No, you don't even really care about that, either. One thing's for sure about all these guys, the witches and the beast. They *want* something. They're so hungry it hurts to be around them. They think that being hungry is the same as being strong. So the less you want, the weaker you look. Maybe that'll protect you."

"How hungry was Paulie when the beast took *him*?"

"Very, very hungry. Babies are nothing *but* hunger, and his mother was teaching him what to be hungry for. You can bet that even if the beast hadn't come, he would have grown up to be a monster."

Quentin laughed. "Yeah, I've seen children like that."

"No joke, Quentin. Monsters aren't born, they're made. By monster parents, or they make themselves by their own desires. But they don't come out of the womb deformed. There's always a path that leads away, even if they don't take it."

"Our parents weren't perfect either, Lizzy."

"But they were good people, and we knew that, we saw it. That's enough, if the child also wants to be good."

"And you learned all this by being dead?"

"No, Quentin. I learned all this by looking into your memories and seeing what you've learned without even realizing you learned it."

"What, is this like Madeleine? Am I talking to myself again?"

"Ever since I died, Quentin, when you talk to yourself you're talking to me. I'm in there. I'm part of you. You didn't have to steal some relic of mine, the way those witches do. I gave you my heart long before they cut it out of me. Along with my kidneys and my corneas."

"Nowadays they take livers and lungs, too."

"Car parts, body parts—automobile accidents are the great growth industry of America."

"I know you got *that* out of my head," said Quentin. "I read that somewhere."

"Quentin, you *are* hungry for something."

"What?"

"For a good life. For a life worth living."

"Sure I am. Who isn't?"

"But what if the price of that was killing somebody else?"

"Come on, Lizzy."

"Sometimes good people have to do terrible things. Mrs. Tyler had to decide what to do when the beast took her baby, no matter whose fault it was that it got invited in. Mom and Dad had to decide to let them cut me apart and kill my body so some good use could come from it."

"I've never forgiven them for that, either."

"They've never forgiven themselves, either. But they went on living, like Mrs. Tyler goes on living. Because that's what good people do. They make the terrible choices sometimes, and then they live with the results, because they did right, or at least the closest thing to a right choice that they could find."

"So who are you telling me to kill?"

"The beast, Quentin."

"But you said when the box opens . . . "

"Find the beast and kill it. Send it back out into darkness."

"It'll just find somewhere else to come in again."

"Maybe not for a long time. And then someone else will have to find it and kill it. But you will have done your part here and now."

"Lizzy, I've never even hit anybody in anger in my life."

"Don't be angry now, either. No matter who it is, no matter what they've done to you. Even the beast itself—don't be angry, don't be hungry for revenge. Because if it takes *you* down its throat, then you'll be the one begging for someone to cut you free."

"Like you begged me."

She shrugged. "Look. Baltimore signs. That's close to Washington, right?"

"Like halfway from Philadelphia, maybe. With this snow I may never get there. I'm insane to be pushing on through like this."

"No, you're close now. You're going to make it."

"Lizzy, why can't you stay with me all the time? Just to talk to? Think what we could do together. The life we could live!"

242

"Nothing you do can turn it into a life for *me*. And if I'm here with you, it won't be a life for you, either. You called to me a lot, after that first year, but you didn't see me showing up, did you? Not till you were in real trouble. The rest of the time I left you alone."

"I didn't want you to leave me alone, Lizzy."

"Sometimes we get what we don't want."

It was hard to see, his eyes awash with tears of longing and regret. "Lizzy, I'm scared."

"Good idea."

"And it hurts. Losing you. Losing her."

"Take an aspirin," said Lizzy. She always used to say that when he complained.

"We take Tylenol now. And whatever it is. Advil."

She joined in the old game. "Excedrin. Anacin."

"Bufferin. Goodey's Headache Powders. Lizzy, don't leave me, please."

In that moment she was gone. He paid the toll and went down into the tunnel that would take him under Baltimore. Somewhere on the other side of the tunnel was the witch who had sent Madeleine to him, the witch who had led him to the treasure box, the witch who wanted to feed him to the beast.

16
The User

It was just before dawn when he got onto the beltway around Washington. With the blizzard there was so little traffic that he made better time than usual. The snow made everything feel silent, though Quentin knew that inside the car the noise was the same as always. He rounded a curve and the Mormon temple loomed, brightly lit as always, but even more dreamlike and fantastic in the falling snow. Right where the temple looked most like a Disneyland castle, some-one had written in huge letters on an overpass *Surrender Dorothy!* The letters had been plastered over, but patches of lighter gray marked where they had been, which made him think of the caption and smile.

Then he thought of the Wicked Witch of the West flying over Oz to write those words in the sky and the smile faded. No flying broomsticks for these witches. But still they flew. Who knew how many witches were observing him here in this car as he drove? Hi, Rowena. Howdy, Mrs. Tyler. Showing me off to the coven? Look, here's the boy! You should have seen him bouncing around with that succubus we sent him! Married her, poor sap! Can you believe it?

What fools these mortals be.

He got off the freeway at the toll road, which had been recently plowed but no one was driving on it, not westbound anyway. He was alone in a white world. One tollbooth was manned, but he drove through one of the coindrops because he didn't even want the human interaction of paying toll. Now that he was near home, his sleepiness was almost overpowering. He started chanting exit names. Wolf Trap Farm Park. Hunter Mill. Wiehle. Reston Parkway. He got off at the Fairfax County Parkway, threw another quarter into a coindrop, and now there was some traffic. If one lonely pickup truck spinning its wheels at an intersection counted as traffic.

He pulled the rental car into a snowfilled parking space and walked past his own car, which had snow piled up to the windows. Most of the other cars were also covered, untouched since the blizzard started. No one in their right mind would have been out driving in this. The sky brightened a little as he climbed the stairs to his condo. The sun must have risen behind the snow and clouds. He let himself into his apartment, stripped off his clothes, and fell into bed.

He woke just after noon. The phone was ringing. He answered it in his sleep.

"Wake up, Quentin!" the phone was shouting.

"What?" said Quentin. "Who is this?"

"For the ninth time, it's Wayne Read. Quentin, are you awake now? Say something coherent please. This is a test."

"Hi, Wayne."

"What did you do, drive all night through a record-setting blizzard? Have you got the brains of a roach?"

"Roaches all stayed in for the storm."

"Smart roaches. If you're not going to wake up, Quentin, don't answer the phone, let your machine take it."

"Didn't know I'd answered it. What do you want?"

"I have the name and address you wanted. They really are called Duncan but the number's not listed and they don't own the house so it wasn't easy finding them. Ray and

Rowena Duncan." He gave the address. "The investigator there in DC says that it's a townhouse complex in Sterling, at Sugarland and Church. Sugarland crosses Dranesville Road at the last light before Route 7. Does all this mean anything to you?"

"Yeah."

"Have you written this down, or should I call again later?"

"I'm writing it." He fumbled for a pencil. Then he realized that if he opened his eyes, the job would be easier. "It's bright. Sun must be shining."

"Yeah, the blizzard is over for now. It's on the news. In California they love talking about eastern blizzards. It makes us all feel smart."

"Californians need that now and then," said Quentin.

"Well, you *are* one, so you'd know."

"How'd you get the address?"

"Very clever detective work indeed, Quentin. Our guy in Manhattan drove up to the rest home, walked in, and asked the superintendent for the address of the next of kin of Mrs. Anna Laurent Tyler. The superintendent—I think you know her—"

"Sally Sannazzaro."

"Thanks, I didn't want to try pronouncing it myself. She asked who wants to know. He said he was representing Quentin Fears and she said OK and gave it to him. She also gave him a message for you."

"If it's along the lines of drop dead, save it for later."

"No, it's along the lines of sorry I was such a bitch, and Mrs. Tyler says sorry too, and please come back she wants to talk to you."

"She called herself a bitch?"

"A direct quote."

"Did the words 'cast iron' come into it?"

"She didn't elaborate, but I'm sure you can pick the metal you want."

"So I guess she's not mad at me anymore."

"Quentin, I would say that was the gist of the message. But I can repeat it if you want."

Quentin didn't know why he felt so relieved, but he was almost giddy with it. "That's good. That's really good."

"Have you been drinking?"

"Driving all night. I'm still not awake."

"A word of advice. Don't go seeing these people until you *are* awake."

"Sure."

"See a movie. I recommend something light and stupid. Take your mind off your troubles. Not *The American President,* that's too stupid. Not *Sabrina,* it'll just break your heart that you're not in love. Broke mine anyway. Unless of course you *are.*"

"Am what?"

"In love."

"Wayne, am I paying three hundred an hour for this?"

"Three fifty. I'm paid to give good advice. *Twelve Monkeys* will make you wonder if you're crazy, don't see that one either."

"Do you actually see all these movies?"

"I have to do something while my wife is going around to country bars, Quentin. I don't like my job well enough to work late every night. Though I'll admit that your recent activities have kept me hopping. Sort of information central here. I keep getting reports from all fifty states about how Madeleine Cryer never existed there, either."

"Sorry. You can call that part of the search off. Nobody's going to accuse me of killing her. They've got more to fear from an investigation than I do."

"Too late. I've already got all the reports and all the bills. Thanks to fax machines, every invoice is instantaneous."

"So pay 'em. You need me to send you another check?"

"No, I've still got plenty in the account. Quentin, get up, take a shower, go to a movie. Some mindless sequel. *Grumpier*

Old Men. Father of the Bride Two. No, I take that back, that might depress you too."

"Good-bye, Mr. Ebert."

"Siskel. For Pete's sake, Quentin, I run every day. Good-bye."

Quentin got up, showered, armed himself with a broom, and went out to clear the snow off his car. He didn't have a shovel but the ice chipper from the rental car helped him get the deepest stuff, which had frozen. Most of the other cars in the lot had already been cleared off. A lot of spaces were empty now. People must be going back to work. Or else just getting out of the house before they went insane. Plows must have come through because the roads were drivable and traffic looked about normal.

He took the broom back up to the front door but didn't even bother unlocking it to put it inside. Nor did he go in to get the address he had written down. He wasn't ready.

Instead he took Wayne's advice, sort of. He drove to the Reston Town Center and put the car in the parking garage and walked to the theater. A big handmade sign in the window said *Yes!!!!! We are open!!!!* Quentin walked up to the box office and asked what was worth seeing and the ticket seller said, "*Twelve Monkeys* is the greatest movie ever made," so Quentin bought a ticket and went inside. It wasn't the greatest movie ever made but it was very good and every bit as disturbing as Wayne had said it would be. The message seemed to be, you can't change anything and you'll end up dead so why try? But it was certainly heroic, almost noble along the way. And everybody struggling to figure out what was real and what wasn't, Quentin absolutely knew what that was like. Also, the movie left him wondering how they decided that Bruce Willis got three naked butt shots and a fleeting moment of frontal nudity in the battle scene, while Brad Pitt only had one butt shot while he bounded around on beds in the mental hospital. Was there some hierarchy of nudity in Hollywood? The more millions you get, the more you get to moon the audience?

It was with thoughts like this that he walked through the dazzling sunlight to the Rio Grande, which was doing decent business for four-thirty in the afternoon. He sat down and looked at the menu while the couple at the next table talked about how nice it was to get out of the house, a lot better than having the police discover them later after they murdered each other, and should we get two orders of pork tamale appetizers or just split one, and where are the chips, didn't the waiter hear them when they asked for more chips? Quentin looked up at them—a red-cheeked dark-haired woman and her husband with blond thinning hair—and he said, "I'm not eating my chips, do you want them?"

They seemed horribly embarrassed at having been over-heard and refused his offer with thanks and apologies. But Quentin had meant it. He had momentarily forgotten that at a restaurant everyone is supposed to pretend there's an eight-foot wall around each table. Except the waiters, of course, who are supposed to pretend that each table is the only one they're waiting on. Like living in a small town. Notice me when I want to be noticed, but why are you prying when I want to be left alone?

The waiter brought the other couple their drinks and then came to Quentin's table to get his order. As Quentin spoke to the waiter, he saw the couple raise their glasses to him in a cheerful toast. He smiled back at them. OK, so maybe sometimes the walls *did* come down.

He ate, he went home. The sun was setting. He couldn't put this off forever. He got the address and drove to the dwelling place of the witch who had chosen him to be her enchanted tool.

There should have been a flame leaping from a chimney, or the silhouettes of devils dancing on the window shades. Instead it seemed a perfectly ordinary northern Virginia townhouse, in a row of five with varied façades in a feeble attempt at individuality and charm. Much like Quentin's own. The porch light was on.

I know you're expecting me, he said silently. I know you've been watching me, you've been waiting for me to work up the courage to come here. So go ahead and open the door and end the pretense.

But the door remained closed.

He climbed the steps and rang the bell. After a reasonable wait, a man came to the door. "Yes?" he said.

"Mr. Duncan?" asked Quentin.

"Yes. Do I know you?"

"My name is Quentin Fears."

"I'm sorry, but I'm not expecting you. Should I be?"

"Are you serious?" asked Quentin. But to all appearances the man was completely oblivious as to who Quentin was and what he was there for. "Mr. Ray Duncan?"

"Yes." The man was growing a bit impatient.

"Your wife is Rowena Tyler Duncan?"

"What about her?"

"And her mother is Anna Laurent Tyler?"

"Yes." Now he looked concerned. "Has something happened to her?"

"I'd like to come in, if I might, and talk to you and your wife together."

"Who *are* you?" Ray demanded.

"I was at the rest home yesterday, talking with Sally Sannazzaro. With the airports closed I had to drive the whole way to talk to you today."

"If you have a message from Ms. Sannazzaro, why didn't she simply call?"

Quentin was through talking. Whatever game these people were playing, he was fed up with it. He stood and waited in silence.

Finally Duncan's curiosity overcame his suspicion. He opened the door wider and invited Quentin inside.

It was your ordinary overdecorated living room. Perhaps a little bit too *Architectural Digest,* but not so much as to offend the eye, as long as you stood with the fireplace at your back. Quentin took that position, but not for aesthetic reasons. It gave him a view of the front door, the passage to the kitchen and dining room, and the stairs leading up to the bedrooms.

"Have a seat, Mr.—Pierce, was it?"

"Fears, Mr. Duncan." Quentin sat in the red paisley chair, moving the white pillows from it and laying them on the floor. "Is your wife at home?"

"Fixing dinner."

Quentin thought of the breakfast he had at the Laurent house in Mixinack, and had no pity. "Please bring her out here."

"State your business, Mr. Fears."

Quentin's patience was done. "I've come here this once. I won't come again. And I won't stay another minute unless your wife faces me now."

"Faces you! Sir, you can pick yourself up and head for the door or I'll—"

A woman appeared in the passage between kitchen and dining room. "What is it, Ray?"

"Don't come out here, Ro. In fact, call the police, please. We have an intruder here who—"

But the woman ignored his instructions and came on through the dining room to the living room.

Quentin could not help but think that he had seen her before. For that matter, now that she stood beside her husband, they both looked vaguely familiar. But she especially—he *had* seen her. Spoken with her? Whatever the occasion, it wouldn't come to mind. Perhaps it was simply that she bore some resemblance to Madeleine. After all, Rowena created the succubus, it had to have some of its creator inside it.

Inside *her.* Whom was he trying to fool? He still thought of Madeleine as a woman, as his wife, despite his best efforts to expunge her from his heart.

"Rowena Tyler Duncan," said Quentin. "My name is Quentin Fears."

When she showed no reaction to his name, he went on. "I spoke with your mother last night."

Rowena's face darkened. "What do I care?" She turned to leave the room.

"And I rode back to Mixinack with Mike Bolt."

She stopped and, slowly, turned back to face him. She looked agitated. "Our old gardener."

"Chief of police in Mixinack now," said Quentin.

"I'm glad to hear it."

"Married and has several children."

Rowena nodded.

Ray Duncan was a bit nonplussed. "Who's this Mike Bolt guy? What are you talking about?"

"A childhood friend of mine," said Rowena.

"Oh, don't be so modest," said Quentin. "She enthralled him years ago. In the kitchen of her mother's house, as I heard the story."

"What do you want," Rowena whispered fiercely.

"Don't be coy," said Quentin. "I'm not here because of what *I* want. I'm not the one who's been playing games, Rowena. Quite the contrary. So drop the pretense and tell me what you want so we can decide what to do about it."

Rowena and Ray looked at each other. Whatever passed between them, it did not make them more cooperative.

"Sir," said Ray, "you seem to know more about us than we're comfortable with, but I assure you that we have no idea who you are."

He seemed so honest that for a moment Quentin wondered if perhaps he *had* been fooling himself. But Mike Bolt had seen the writing on the signs, and on the door back in the Laurent house. And Madeleine had disappeared, leaving no footprints. It was real, it had happened, Mrs. Tyler admitted it, and Rowena *was* a witch.

"I know more than you think," said Quentin. "I know that Rowena looked into her mother's mind many years ago and saw a memory of what seemed to be a terrible crime. And for all I know, it *was* a crime, a monstrous, indecent act. The murder of Rowena's brother, Paul, when he wasn't yet two years old."

Rowena covered her face with her hands.

"Ro, is this true?" Ray seemed genuinely appalled.

"Your wife, Mr. Duncan, is quite aware that her mother believed that it wasn't Paul she was killing, but rather something that she calls 'the beast.' It's Mrs. Tyler's belief that this creature took possession of her young son's body, and from then on her true son was already gone and could never be recovered. All that was left was for her to kill the beast. But not quite kill it. She kept it imprisoned somehow in a box that is kept in the parlor of the family mansion on the Hudson. Am I getting this right, Rowena?"

Her face still buried in her hands, Rowena nodded.

"But for some reason, Mr. Duncan, Rowena has decided she wants that box open."

Rowena looked up, startled. "Oh, no. Oh, please, no."

Ray was alarmed as well. "What is it, Ro?"

Rowena leapt to her feet and rushed to the foot of the stairs. Then, changing her mind, she hurried back to her chair and sat down, wringing the tail of her shirt. "It's none of your business," said Rowena. "Nor Mother's!"

"Oh, that would be my opinion, too, if you hadn't drawn me into it with that whole charade that's been ruining my life for the past year."

"Charade?" asked Ray.

"Why don't *you* tell him, Rowena? He might accept it better coming from you."

Rowena looked confused, but then apparently made up her mind. "You tell it, Mr. Fears. Tell us both."

"Madeleine," said Quentin. "My wife. The succubus that you created, Rowena. Are you honestly telling me that your husband has no idea that you're a witch?"

Ray rose to his feet and started for the kitchen. "I'm calling the police."

"Stop, Ray," said Rowena.

"The man's insane, Ro."

"No, we have to hear him out," she said. "We have to find out what's been going on."

Ray leaned against the wall, clearly furious at having been vetoed by his wife.

"You believe your wife Madeleine is a succubus created by a witch, Mr. Fears?" asked Rowena.

"She took me to the house you grew up in. I was made to believe that it was occupied. I met several of your dead relatives, and a couple not so dead. Your mother was there, in spirit if not in body. And your brother Paul, though of course Madeleine called him 'Uncle Paul.' Just as she called Mrs. Tyler 'Grandmother.'"

And then Quentin stopped. Because, while his words clearly caused Rowena great pain, it was just as clear that she was hearing of all this for the first time. And now it finally dawned on Quentin that if Madeleine had been created by Rowena, why wouldn't Rowena have made her a woman of her own age? She was more or less the same age as Quentin. And Rowena could easily have supplied all the memories needed to make Madeleine completely convincing as a child of the sixties and seventies, like Quentin.

Instead Madeleine had been ignorant of many things she should have known. She covered it by pretending to have had a sheltered childhood, but in fact Madeleine could not have been the creation of a grown woman. Especially not in the parlor, where she had become a petulant, spoiled brat, acting like a child of . . . ten.

"Your daughter," Quentin said softly. "Of course she's also . . . one of you."

"A witch," said Rowena miserably. "Ray, go wake up Roz."

"Ro, you know how she hates us to waken her from a nap."

"What's she doing?" Quentin asked. "Flying around spying on people?"

"She doesn't understand how dangerous it all is," said Rowena.

Ray was at the foot of the stairs. "What are you talking about?"

"Please, Ray. Go get her."

Ray sighed and trotted on up the stairs.

Rowena faced Quentin and spoke earnestly. "My daughter is a remarkable girl, Mr. Fears. Very talented and . . . strong. Maybe if I had let my mother teach me, I could have controlled her the way my mother was able to control me during my childhood. A child with such powers, such knowledge—it takes extraordinary care to keep them from running amok. But I couldn't trust my mother on anything, not after what she did to Paul."

"You never knew Paul."

"Yes I did," said Rowena. "He came to me every day as I was growing up."

Quentin knew the truth at once. "That wasn't Paul, Rowena. That was the beast."

She shook her head, then burst into tears. "I don't know," she said. "I just knew that I didn't want Mother to . . . if she was the kind of woman who killed disobedient children, then how could I bring my daughter under her care? I haven't been able to control Roz for years now. I'm afraid sometimes that she's controlling *me*. She studies things, figures them out, and . . . whole days disappear and I don't know what happened. I know she rules her father. He's completely enthralled. When I did that to Mike, I had no idea, I didn't know what I was doing. I've left him alone ever since —"

"Then who's been sending him to try to murder your mother?"

Rowena's hand flew to her mouth. "Oh, no. No, she couldn't."

"Yes I could, Mother," said a petulant child's voice from the stairs.

A young girl slowly came down the stairs, her hair looking a bit slept-in, but otherwise neat as a pin. Quentin could imagine how she had looked during her nap—arms at her sides in perfect symmetry, nothing moving, the way Mrs. Tyler lay while her spirit was off keeping watch or whatever it was she did with it. Rewriting traffic signs, for instance.

Then the girl's face became visible as she finally got to a low enough step, and Quentin realized why Mr. and Mrs. Duncan had looked so familiar. He had seen all three of them before. In the Giant food store on Elden Street, right before his first hallucination of Lizzy.

"That's right, Quentin," said Roz. "You didn't like me, as I recall."

"I thought you were an insufferable spoiled brat."

Roz gave her best cutey-pie grin. "Well, I showed *you*, didn't I?"

"Showed me I was right."

"Showed you what real power is!" Her smile turned vicious. "You had your treasure of a sister in your mind. Comparing her to *me*. So I made you see her. Drove you crazy with it."

Quentin glanced at Rowena, sitting in her chair, and Ray Duncan, who had followed his daughter down the stairs and was now sitting on the couch. How were they taking this?

They both sat staring off into space.

"I shut them down," said Roz. "There's no reason for them to know all this."

"You created Madeleine just to torture me for daring to think what's obvious to everyone who sees you?"

"No, stupid. I showed you your sister because of that. But then, when you were sitting there watching the vision I made for you, what should happen but she turns up!"

"Who?"

"Lizzy," said Roz. "Your dead sister. Her spirit. Well, I

257

wasn't calling her. She didn't even notice me. It was you who called her. What a joke on me! You had some of the power! Who would have guessed it?"

"Nothing like what you can do."

"Yeah, well, I'm kind of remarkable. The way Uncle Paul was. Only Mother didn't kill me the way Grandmother killed her precious baby boy. That's a nice thing to find in the family closet."

"You only got your mother's memory of it, with all her misunderstandings."

"I would have gotten Grandmother's memories directly, but I knew how strong the old lady is. She and Mother were battling it out constantly. That's how I learned half of what I know, watching their struggles to keep each other from watching them. It was easy to take control of Mother—she was completely off her guard. And Father, of course, is just a human."

"And therefore not worth considering."

"I need him for a phone call now and then."

"You're telling me you just improvised all this?"

"Come on, why not?" said Roz. "You were stronger than most humans. I thought about that for a few minutes and I realized that maybe I could use you to open the treasure box for me."

"Is that what your mother calls it?"

"Mother has no idea what it really is or how to use it. Power beyond belief. Grandmother filled her with horror stories about it, but that's because neither of them has a spark of creativity. Me, I think of all kinds of things that no one has ever thought of before. Least of all the dragon. It can be killed, which only sets it free to possess somebody else. It can also be captured, which is what Grandmother did. But I've done research neither of them thought of doing. There *are* books, if you know how to sort the nonsense from the truth. I'm only eleven, but I'm—how to say it mildly?—the school system calls me 'gifted.'"

Quentin wanted to smack that smug little mouth.

"So much for your being a nonviolent kind of guy, right, Quentin?"

He also hated the way she called him by his first name.

"What would be better?" she asked. "Should I call you 'Tin'?"

In that instant, she stopped being a little girl. She was transformed into Madeleine. Quentin's heart leapt in spite of all he knew.

And then she was Madeleine naked, prancing around the room like a stripper in some cheap movie.

He had done it before; he could do it now. He forced himself to know that she wasn't real.

She didn't go away.

"It's harder to get rid of me," said Madeleine, sitting in Ray's lap and twirling his hair, "when there's a real person inside the shell."

Harder but not impossible. Quentin remembered the bratty little girl and after a shimmering moment there she was, sitting on her father's lap, twirling his hair.

"You're a terrible lover, you know, Quentin. Any woman who ever sleeps with you is going to have to fake every orgasm."

It was obscene hearing language like that from a child.

"Your fault, Quentin," she said. "I wasn't interested in any of that stuff till *you* started pawing at Madeleine that night in your living room. It was obvious I was blowing it, so I had to read up and spy on Mom and Dad and figure out what this sex crap was all about. I finally got it, though, didn't I? Made all your fantasies come true, didn't I?"

Quentin looked away from her in shame.

"Oh, come on, here you are, you wanted to face me, didn't you? So face me. Be a man. Buck up."

"You don't want me to be a man," said Quentin. "You want me to be a tool."

"But we *did* have fun, didn't we? Playing with politics like

259

we did. We made a great pair, spending your money to change the face of American politics. Whoever rules America rules the world. If you'd had the stomach for it, I might have forgotten all about the treasure box and gone for the big game. Not the '96 elections, but by the year two thousand we would have been ready. Both candidates for president would have belonged to us. But you just couldn't do it. Couldn't follow through. I knew from then on that you'd be nothing but trouble. So . . . plan B."

"The treasure box."

"It was really plan A all along, I knew that," said Roz. "I knew you'd wimp out because that's the way you are, soft at the core, like Mother. You just don't have the heart to do anything powerful. Even keeping her like this—I couldn't do it if she had any spine at all. She's a witch! She could shuck off my control if she wanted to. If she even knew I was doing it. But she keeps thinking that she loves me, and that makes it easy to control her. The way I could control you as long as you loved Madeleine."

"But you couldn't get me to open the box."

"That was Grandmother. She didn't know it was me, of course, because I cover everything I do with Mother's spirit. Just some of it, to serve as my mask."

"So it's you controlling Mike Bolt. Through your mother. And you constantly blocking Mrs. Tyler from seeing what you're doing."

"Easy easy easy."

"But you can't do everything at once."

"I don't have to. I just follow the people who matter. The people who amount to anything."

"You're afraid, though," said Quentin. "Or you wouldn't be trying to kill your grandmother."

"Of course I'm afraid, bonehead. This is powerful stuff we're dealing with. This dragon, it's no joke! And Grandmother can interfere. I want her out of the way. She's overstayed her welcome by about a decade."

"By coincidence, your lifetime."

"She's a baby-killer, Quentin. She deserves to die." Roz giggled. "Come on, get in the spirit of this."

Quentin shook his head. "I came here thinking that maybe we could do business. Maybe we could work out a way for me to get you what you want and have done with it. But no, I don't think so."

"I'm not worthy?" she said with mock regret.

"Who needs a beast with you in the world?"

The words didn't even seem to sting her. "Everybody's a critic. Well, let's see. That means Quentin Fears doesn't want to go back to Grandmother's house and open my treasure box for me. How sad for me! Poor Roz doesn't get her way! Boo-hoo! Boo-hoo!"

Come on, you evil little witch, get to the point.

"Impatient, huh? Like I said, I only follow the ones that matter. For instance, that investigator your lawyer hired here in DC. While you were in talking to the grande dame, I was out at his car, enthralling him. He's mine, Quentin. So he gave you the address of this house, sure—when I was ready."

"Ready? You were taking a nap."

"You went to a movie and had dinner. I had things to do. The point is—you remember, I was making a point—the point is that your little investigator, he also ran an errand for me."

Quentin felt sick, though he had no idea what she might have made the fellow do.

"He went to a graveyard in California and did a little digging," said Roz. "Got me a nice chunk of your sister's body. And since I also knew her name—you didn't know that was needed, did you?—since I knew her name, I was able to summon her. He just got back with it this morning. I've got your sister all locked up tight. A prisoner just like the dragon. Only *she's* not powerful at all. She can't get out, not even a little bit of her. She just exists inside her—well, let's just call it her *home*, why don't we?"

"The beast already has you."

"I'm stronger than the dragon. That's what Mother and Grandmother have never taken into account. What if somebody comes along who's so strong she doesn't have to kill the beast, or imprison it? I'm the one who will *tame* the dragon, and ride it wherever I want."

"Cowboy in the rodeo," said Quentin.

"And you'll help me, Quentin. It'll be in your body that the dragon lives while I'm riding it. I think that's only fair. I gave you the best year of your life. Well, not quite a year, but close enough. Once I got the hang of it, you had better sex than any man ever gets, night after night. And I was good company, too. The perfect wife. I paid in advance for the use of your body now. You won't suffer, you know. In fact, you and your precious Lizzy will be reunited. When your body dies, anyway. Nothing lasts forever, right? You have my word that after the dragon has your body, Lizzy comes out of the—place. Free again. So you get paid again. Come on, Quentin, it's a good bargain. Your sister for my dragon. Plus the happiest year of your life. You can't ever say you were cheated."

Quentin felt as if he were already dead.

"You may even get some vicarious pleasure out of seeing how the dragon and I use your body. You're thinking that I'm pure evil, I know that, but you're wrong. I'll use all that power to do good. Unite the world under one strong ruler. Peace on earth. Good will toward men. Hitler was Hitler before the beast got him. Caligula was already a strutting little bastard."

What do you think *you* are?

"Sticks and stones, Quentin. That's all I ever wanted power for. To do good for everybody. You'll see, this is all for the best. You were lucky to be chosen. And when I get old enough and reach puberty, I'll probably mate with your body, so that your children will inherit the kingdom of the whole earth. Like the book of Revelation promises—a thousand years of peace."

"It also promises devastation."

"That all depends on how stubborn people are about resisting me. You can't make an omelet without breaking some eggs. Don't wince at the cliché, Quentin. It only became a cliché because it's true."

Quentin rose to his feet and walked on leaden feet toward the door. "I won't help you," he said.

"Oh, Lizzy will be so sorry to hear that."

"She'll understand."

"But you don't understand, Quentin. This isn't something temporary. If you don't help me, I'll never, never let her out."

Quentin stopped in the doorway. "Your lifetime and never are two different spans, little girl. You only *think* you're immortal."

"I don't have to live forever. I just have to bury your sister's dwelling place in the backyard, and—tell me, Quentin—who's going to dig it up? How many thousands of years before erosion finally exposes it? And even then, you don't know what her container is made of. But I'll give you a hint. It isn't biodegradable."

Quentin could hardly breathe, he was so filled with impotent rage.

Roz got up from her father's lap and skipped to the stairs. "I'm just a little, little girl," she said. "You shouldn't be so mad at me."

"I want you to die," said Quentin.

"Someday I will. Now say good-bye to my parents."

She bounded on up the stairs.

Almost at once, Mr. and Mrs. Duncan came back into focus. Ray looked quite startled. "I must have dozed off, for heaven's sake! What was I thinking of?"

Rowena, however, had an unutterable sadness on her face as she looked up at Quentin.

"I can't deny it anymore," she said. "My daughter rules me, doesn't she?"

"Only because you love her," said Quentin. "Though how and why, I can't guess."

Tears flowed down Rowena's cheeks. "Because she's mine. Because I'm not my mother. I *love* my children."

"Your mother loved her children too," said Quentin. "But give your mother credit for this much: The beast *stole* her child. She didn't raise hers to be a monster."

"Do you dare to judge me?" said Rowena.

Quentin shook his head. "I don't judge you for what you've done, or haven't done. But if you let her do what she's planning, then I blame you, yes."

"I don't care what you blame me for," said Rowena. "I'm not my mother!"

"Too bad for the human race," said Quentin. "Too bad for your daughter. She *thinks* she can control the beast."

Suddenly Rowena and Ray went slack again. Roz appeared at the top of the stairs.

"That's enough, Quentin," she said cheerily. "A little learning is a dangerous thing."

"And absolute power corrupts absolutely," Quentin answered.

"Bite me," she said. Then she gave him a little wave. "Open the door and out with you, babe."

He wanted to think of something he could say that would wither her with its brutal cleverness. But nothing came to mind. And there was no point in trying to talk to Rowena and Ray, not when they were in this condition.

"Roz," he finally said.

"Yes, Tin, my pet?" She spoke the term of endearment so ironically that it cut him to the heart. Because he *would* be her pet, if she won her gamble. If she lost, he would still be the dragon's mount, the beast's own steed, and Lizzy would never get out of prison.

"Maybe I'll do it," he said.

"Lizzy will be so glad to hear it."

"You've got to bring Lizzy with you. Whatever you've got her in, bring it."

"Not a chance," said Roz. "You think I'm stupid? I'm just a widdow widdow girr." Her baby talk made him want to smack her all over again. "We wouldn't want nasty badums to stwangow me, would we?"

"As if I could."

"Just in case you get any ideas about that," she said, "remember that *I'm* not an illusion like Madeleine was. If it comes to a fight between us, I'll win. You can't fight a witch, Quentin. You aren't that strong."

"If I decide to do it, how do I let you know?"

"I'll know, you big silly goof." She did her cutesy giggle again.

"What makes you think you'll succeed this time, when last time you failed?"

"I have a better plan."

"For instance?"

"I'll be there myself this time," she said. "And there'll be a little less interference."

"You're no match for your grandmother, if that's what you mean."

"I'm a match for anybody," she said. "I'm younger than Alexander was when he inherited his father's kingdom."

"You're not as smart as you think you are."

"You're not smart enough to judge. Now go away, Mr. Fears. My parents get so stiff and sore when I put them out like this, sitting up."

Quentin opened the door and left, the door ajar behind him. He was halfway down the steps when he heard her. "That was a childish gesture, Quentin! Leaving the door open! What a big baby!"

He ignored her and returned to his car.

There had to be a way to stop her. The trouble was, he didn't know enough to have any hope of discovering it. But that was all right. Mrs. Tyler wanted to see him again. She would help him figure out what to do to get Lizzy free without turning loose the beast upon the world.

Though he also knew that if it came to a choice between Lizzy's freedom and saving his own life, or even saving the world, he wouldn't even have to think about it. His own life was worthless to him now. And the world? The world could take care of itself. The dragon had been abroad in the world before, and the world survived. Besides, even dragons don't live forever. Peter, Paul and Mary didn't know what they were talking about.

Dragons die, yes. Wouldn't that be a joke on Roz and the beast, both? If he took a huge dose of poison just before opening the treasure box? Let the dragon have his body, and then it drops dead!

But that wouldn't get Lizzy out of the prison. He had to have a better plan than that. Mrs. Tyler would know what he should do. He had to get back to Mrs. Tyler.

17
Hair

Quentin called the rental car company and explained why the car he rented at La Guardia was about to be left at Dulles. The clerk he talked to had a singsong nasal voice, which would have been annoying enough by itself. What really drove him up the wall was her air of complacent superiority and utter unwillingness to admit the tiniest shred of merit in Quentin's position.

"That car isn't authorized for return at another airport, sir."

"But that's where it's going to be returned."

"But you can't return it there, sir."

"But that's where I am."

"You signed a contract promising to return the car to La Guardia."

"There was a storm. La Guardia was closed down."

"A contract is a contract. Don't you keep your contracts, Mr. Fears?"

"I'm trying to return the car. You have an office at Dulles."

This cycle was repeated about three times before Quentin finally lost patience. He didn't raise his voice. In fact, he spoke more quietly. "Let me explain it to you very simply. You don't have a choice because I didn't have a choice. La Guardia was closed and I had to get to DC. Now I'm here, and I'm flying back to New York from Dulles. FAA regulations won't allow me to check the car as luggage."

"You signed a contract, Mr. Fears. If you don't intend to—"

Quentin was fed up with being accused of breaking his word. "I'm saying this only once. If you want to talk instead of listening, that's fine with me."

"Go ahead, Mr. Fears."

"I paid for the collision damage waiver. That means if I *wreck* the car I don't have any problem about not returning it. Also, if the car is stolen I'm off the hook. So either you can have your people at Dulles accept the car, or I'll leave it at a Seven-Eleven with the keys in the ignition and the motor running, and you can have your insurance company reimburse you. Which will it be?"

"You'll have to speak to my manager."

"I have a better idea. *You* speak to the manager. If he or she has any questions, here's the number of my attorney."

Quentin put his kit into a bag along with his last clean shirt, socks, and underwear. He'd buy more if he needed it. He also took his cellular phone, and on the way to the airport he called Wayne Read and told him about his problem with the rental car company.

"Quentin, you shouldn't let clerks like that get to you. The madder you get, the more they enjoy it."

"I know, Wayne. They get a little power and it goes to their heads. I just don't want to be delayed."

"I'll call them. Don't worry about it."

"I'm five minutes from Dulles."

"I'm very, very quick."

He was. The car return people accepted his contract without a quibble. "That's just fine, Mr. Fears. All taken care of."

Sometimes it was very nice to have money and lawyers. Why ordinary people didn't strangle arrogant bureaucrats more often, Quentin didn't know. But then, bureaucrats *were* ordinary people. Maybe most people simply understood about having to obey stupid rules at work. They went along because they didn't want to cause some other poor schmuck any trouble. Everybody had to do what it took to keep their jobs.

Yeah, but they didn't have to take so much pleasure in it.

As he walked through the airport he thought, So I have money and that means I can buy my way free of a lot of petty annoyances. Somebody bothers me, I can have my lawyer deal with it. Is that evil, somehow? To have that much power? How much power do you have to have before you're a monster? How easy do you have to make your own life at others' expense before you're evil and deserve to be destroyed?

Sitting on the plane, Quentin decided that he hadn't crossed the line. Yet. He knew he wasn't a tyrant. Yet. But he also knew that the line wasn't very clearly drawn. When did Roz cross it? Because he was pretty sure that she had. Controlling your own parents, using them as tools, creating a succubus to seduce some poor sap into sacrificing his body so you can try to harness an even worse monster than yourself—all those things were over the line.

At the same time, he had to recognize that once he turned things over to Wayne, there was no guarantee that it would all be handled kindly and politely. For all he knew, Wayne was the lawyer from hell, calling the head of customer relations and explaining that Quentin Fears, who had enough money to carry out a hostile takeover next week, was being harassed by an ignorant clerk in the New York office and could he please be allowed to return his car at Dulles? And then the company bigwig got on the phone and took care of everything. Part of which might be the serious chewing out of that clerk at La Guardia. Or maybe a bad evaluation. Or maybe losing her job. Maybe because she had messed with the wrong man, with Mr. Big Shot Millionaire, that clerk was going to go home and tell her widowed mother and three younger siblings, of whom she was the sole support, that she had lost her job.

Just because I don't see how it's done doesn't cleanse me of evil that's done in my name, with my money. Maybe the only difference between me and Roz is how far over the line we've chosen to go, and how honest we are about what we want in the world. I tell myself I never sought power, that I don't care about money, that I'm just going about doing good.

The woman at the car rental company in New York was a jerk. She probably didn't lose her job or even hear about the matter again. But Quentin didn't know. Just as Roz had no idea of what she was doing to the people she controlled. That private investigator who flew to California and somehow managed to dig up the grave of a girl who died decades ago and take some part of her body—he couldn't stop himself, but now he had to live with having done it. Roz didn't care. Roz didn't wonder about it. But was that the only difference between them—that she didn't have a second thought about it, but he wondered and felt a little guilt?

Besides, how did he know she felt no guilt? Maybe she was racked with it all the time, but went ahead because she knew she was *doing good.* She would unite the world under one government. She would end all war. No more Bosnias or Rwandas, Somalias or Chechnyas. Lebanon at peace. Chiapas without corruption or oppression. Colombia without the *cartelistas.* Joyous celebrations of liberty in Tiananmen Square. The end of mismanagement in Zaire. The end of assassinations in Haiti. If these were the dreams of Roz's heart, then who was he to say that the few lives she ruined weren't a fair price for the good she would accomplish? How was her action any different from a government drafting soldiers and sending them off to die in a noble cause? There *were* noble causes. Why couldn't this child's cause be noble, too?

Almost he could make himself believe that there was no moral difference between himself and Roz. That he had no right to judge her. That it really came down to a contest for survival. The law of the jungle. On her side, powers far beyond any that Quentin could bring to the battle. On his side, whatever advantage came from age and experience over the shortsightedness and impulsiveness of youth. But morally, no real difference between them. Or worse—that the hopes of the world rested on her victory, and if he succeeded in thwarting her, the one bright hope for the future would be extinguished.

No no no, he shouted inside himself. That isn't right. That's all a lie. But he couldn't think of how he could ever be sure.

Is *she* the one putting these doubts into my mind? Trying to get me to come along willingly? The succubus wasn't enough, so let's try hoodwinking the boy.

But it didn't work that way. These witches could make people see things. They could enthrall them and force their obedience. They could cause people to forget things. But they couldn't enter Quentin's mind and force him to think a certain way, or he would never have been able to win free of his belief in Madeleine when she returned to him in his bed. These doubts came from his own mind. He was still his own man, alone inside his head.

Roz can't make me think a certain way—but she *can* see what I'm thinking. And that means that if I'm to have any hope of stopping her, I can't allow myself to think of my own plan. Which means I can't *have* a plan. Which means I might as well give up, because she *does* have a plan and I'm one of the pawns.

Aw, don't sell yourself short, Tin, old boy, he told himself. You're at least a knight. Maybe a bishop. Maybe even a rook.

But not the queen.

And the king was locked inside the treasure box.

That's my mistake, he realized. Roz is not the enemy. No matter how much I hate and fear and resent her, no matter how I might want to avenge my humiliation at her hands, the real danger is the one who stole Paul Tyler's life from him and waits now for the lid of the box to open so he can leap to another body and take control. The beast seduced Rowena with its lies. How did he know it wasn't also seducing Roz? Come to me, I'll serve you, you can rule over me. You're the one with the power. I'll jump into that Quentin Fears's body and then you enthrall him and you've got me. Good plan! Good plan!

Roz is not the enemy. Roz is being fooled by the beast as surely as I was fooled by Madeleine.

And truth to tell, in the contest between Roz and the dragon, Quentin might not even qualify as a pawn. Even as the game unfolded, he wouldn't understand what he was seeing. They were out of his league.

At La Guardia he rented another car—from a different company this time, because he didn't want to think again about what he might or might not have done to that clerk. He drove north on roads now banked with snow like canyon walls on either side, where the plows had pushed it all. No scenery, just the white lights of oncoming cars, the red lights of the cars ahead, and the looming walls of filthy snow.

As he neared Mixinack, he read Mike Bolt's number off his card and phoned him. Maybe it was crazy to go back to him, knowing that he had been under Roz's control. But now that Rowena was more aware of what was going on, Roz wouldn't have such free access to him. As long as Bolt stayed away from the rest home, he was a good man. A friend. And he had a right to know how this all came out.

Bolt answered the phone.

"This is Quentin. I'm about five minutes out of Mixinack. You offered me a place to stay. The couch in the den or something."

"It's midnight," said Bolt. "Are you serious?"

"I met Rowena today. She's living in Virginia."

"Is she . . . what you said? Is she your enemy?"

"She's a witch, Bolt. But I'm not good at picking out bad guys and good guys today. We'll talk about it when I get there."

"Is she coming here? Will she come to Mixinack?"

"I think so," said Quentin. "For all I know they beat me here."

"You really drove back to DC last night in that storm? They said nobody was getting through."

"They were off by at least one. They always are."

"And you're already back."

"Yeah, well, I'm a frequent flier."

"So come on over." Bolt reminded him of how to get there. And then: "Is she still beautiful?"

"Rowena?"

"No, her dog."

"Mike, you're married."

The joking tone was gone when he answered. "Please. Tell me."

"She's beautiful, yes." Though Quentin was quite certain that she would look even more beautiful to Bolt than she looked to him.

"I wasn't crazy to love her, was I?"

"Bolt, we're all crazy to love anybody. But it drives us even crazier if we don't."

"Was that, like, a wise and pithy saying?"

"You better have it posted on your fridge before I arrive."

As he negotiated the side streets of Mixinack, which hadn't been as thoroughly plowed as the highways, Quentin finally found the moral certainty he had been wishing for and despairing of all the way there. It was Lizzy. Lizzy held hostage. The right and wrong of it just didn't matter in the face of that. He would do what it took to get Lizzy out. And that meant staying alive himself, alive and free. Because he was pretty sure that whether the beast won or Roz did, Lizzy's bright spirit would be forgotten in her prison cell if Quentin wasn't there to find her and let her go.

* * *

Bolt's wife was up when he got there. Quentin saw at once that she had been asleep; her hair was tousled despite the brush that had been passed over it a couple of times, and her eyes were heavy with weariness. But she met him with a smile when Bolt introduced them. "My Leda," he said, casting an arm across her shoulder.

"Caf or decaf?" she asked, shrugging off her husband's arm and playfully jabbing at him with her elbow.

"No coffee," said Quentin. "You shouldn't have gotten up, I didn't want to be any trouble."

"If you didn't want to be trouble, you'd've stayed in a motel," said Bolt. "Come on, Quentin, how many times you think we have millionaires sleeping on our couch? Let us play the openhearted host."

"You're very kind. Decaf then, or hot chocolate."

"Which? Got 'em both," said Leda.

"Chocolate then."

She made hot chocolate for all three of them, and then pulled a half-finished quart of vanilla ice cream out of the freezer. They all put a dollop of the ice cream into the hot chocolate and then took spoonfuls of it, ice cold and scalding hot at the same time. As he ate, Quentin noticed the swans all over the kitchen. Swans of wicker, porcelain, stuffed fabric, wood; painted on pots, printed on paper and framed, embroidered on cloth, patterned in the wallpaper.

"Leda and the swan," said Quentin. "I guess that means the swan is you, right, Mike?"

"The god in disguise who comes and carries off the beautiful damsel," said Bolt. "Zeus. God of lightning and thunder. Thunder*bolts,* right?"

"Careful," said Quentin. "It makes Hera jealous."

"Yeah, well, there is no Hera," said Bolt. "The woman who

gets up at night with my kids, she's the only woman for me."

She smiled at him, wan with fatigue, but pleased none-theless at what he said. "Look at him, this is my romancer," she said. "The swan could pick *me* up, I don't think it could fly. God never made no swan that big."

Quentin could hear how she exaggerated the Bronx in her speech as she modestly refused her husband's worshipful words. A sweet woman, a good woman. And Bolt did love her. Too bad how he was in thrall to a witch whose daughter now had control of her and of the men she happened to pos-sess. If Rowena wanted him, he'd walk away from Leda with-out a backward glance. And yet he'd know that he had done it. Could he bear living with that? Roz certainly wouldn't care; would Rowena?

They finished the chocolate. Quentin refused to talk about his plans. He didn't have any. He couldn't afford to have any. Drive to the rest home? Stay here waiting for Roz to arrive?

Leda went back to bed after rinsing the mugs. Bolt showed Quentin to his room. Not a couch, a fold-out bed, nicely made. A TV with a remote. "Not the Ritz," said Bolt.

"Beats Motel Six, though," said Quentin.

"Good night, then. You won't need no alarm in this house. We'll keep the door closed, but the pitter-patter of little feet will probably sound like World War II."

"I won't mind."

Bolt turned to go.

"Mike. Would I be wasting my time if I asked you for the loan of a gun?"

"You don't need a gun. Guns just go off and hurt people."

"You know what I'm up against."

"You can't shoot women who don't leave footprints, Quentin."

"The ones I'll be with, they leave footprints."

"Have you ever fired a gun?" asked Bolt.

"I promise you I won't shoot it around any civilians."

"What's to stop them from taking it away from you and shooting you with it?"

"I've got to have something, Mike."

"I'll get you something for self-defense. But don't even think about lethal force, Quentin. If there's any lethal force needed, I'll do it."

"You plan to be there?"

"Wouldn't miss it."

"But will you be a free man, Mike?"

"What do you mean?"

"Rowena owns you, Mike. Her mother said so."

"Her mother's lying," said Bolt cheerfully. "I owe her a lot, but what she says about Rowena, you just got to consider the source."

No point in arguing with him. Maybe Mike would be an asset, maybe he wouldn't. But since Quentin refused to think of any plan besides to wing it, he didn't let himself consider the question.

"Aw, don't look so glum, Quentin. Just think—you've been seduced by a succubus and now you get to have a show-down between the witches and the macho guys."

"Sweet of you to include me with the macho guys," said Quentin.

"That's what it means to be . . . pals." Bolt grinned.

"Not just guys, but pals." Quentin laid his hand on his heart. "I'm touched."

Bolt shook his head. "Yeah, well, just remember that if one of us has to die in that house tomorrow, I sure hope it's you."

"I know Leda wouldn't have it any other way," said Quentin.

Bolt closed the door behind him as he left. Quentin undressed, and as he crawled onto the creaking, sagging fold-out bed with the paper-thin mattress he knew it would be the worst night of his life. He was asleep in three minutes.

* * *

In the morning, Quentin pulled on his clothes and staggered into the kitchen, where Leda was making pancakes and slapping them down on the kids' plates. "Don't you want to use the bathroom before you eat?" she asked.

"If the pancakes are ready now," he said, "I'm not going off to the bathroom and letting *these* guys eat them all."

The kids laughed and Leda introduced them and they ate breakfast together. Not until they had charged off to school did he realize that he hadn't seen Bolt this morning. Why hadn't he noticed? It was incredible that he hadn't noticed.

Roz, what are you doing?

"Where's Mike?" he asked, dreading the answer.

"Oh, he had some errands he had to run. He told me to tell you that's the burden of the working man. Also I'm supposed to give you this." She handed him a small spray can. Nothing was written on it by the manufacturer, but a label saying "MixPolDep" had been affixed to it. "It's Mace. The real thing, not pepper spray. Tear gas. He says don't use it outdoors because it's bound to blow right back in your own face, and if you use it indoors make sure your hand is no more than a foot from your target's face."

"He really thinks I'm a klutz, doesn't he?"

"I don't know about that," said Leda, "but he gives the same instructions to new cops when they start working for him."

"I can live with that," said Quentin. "Thanks for the breakfast. Best meal I've had in a week."

Which was true. What he had thought he was eating in the Laurent mansion was better, but it wasn't, strictly speaking, a meal.

"Should I wait for him to get back?" Quentin asked.

"He says do what you need to. If you aren't waiting for him at the department, he'll drive on out to the house. Don't start without him, he says."

"Fair enough," said Quentin.

Then dread stabbed through him and he thought, I wasn't going to let Bolt out of my sight. I've got to go looking for him. He's already got at least an hour's head start on me. Got to call Sally and warn her that Bolt is on the loose.

But he didn't call her. He went to the bathroom and showered and shaved and got dressed in the last of his clean clothes. Maybe it would be the last time he'd ever need clean clothes anyway.

For a moment, as he left the house, he remembered vaguely that he had some kind of errand to run. Something that had seemed very urgent when he thought of it back in the kitchen, right after breakfast, but what was it? Couldn't remember. Well, if it was that urgent it would come back to him.

He drove to the police department. The receptionist said, "Chief Bolt was here a minute ago. He stepped out for a minute. He says for you to wait."

Only then did he remember his urgent errand, and in that moment relief swept over him. Bolt had just stepped out. Everything was going to be fine.

He opened the door and found Sally Sannazzaro waiting in Bolt's office.

She jumped to her feet. "I can't believe it," she said. "Mrs. Tyler said I'd find you here. I thought she meant that Chief Bolt would tell me how to reach you, but no, here you are!"

"It's fate," said Quentin. "You drove all the way down here? You must have left at five in the morning."

"I left at eight. The roads are clear and it's later than you think."

"Thanks for not holding a grudge," he said.

"No, I was terrible. Bolt just gets under my skin. Maybe he fools you with a nice-guy act, but I swear he's evil."

Quentin shook his head. "When he's himself, he's a good guy. He loves his wife and kids."

"Well, I guess I've only seen him when he wasn't himself,"

said Sannazzaro. "What about you? Are you yourself right now?"

"I hope not," said Quentin. "I'm trying to work up the courage to do some really stupid and dangerous stuff today."

"If you know it's stupid . . ." But she didn't finish the sentence. They both knew that sometimes stupid, dangerous stuff had to be done.

"What brought you down here?" asked Quentin.

"I'm on Mrs. Tyler's errand," she said. "Somehow she knew you'd be here."

"Amazing woman. I guess this means she's talking to you again."

"She's so alert since you visited. Even more than when she first came to the rest home. She assures me that you didn't cure her, but Quentin, I—can I call you Quentin again? Still?"

He had a sudden impulse to say, Only if I can call you Mrs. Fears. But he didn't say it. He knew at once that this sudden desperate desire he felt for Sally Sannazzaro was nothing but eve-of-death syndrome. The same need that made soldiers on the verge of war want to marry someone or sleep with someone, to leave seed behind in case they didn't come back.

She misunderstood his hesitation. "So you're still angry?"

"No, I'm not angry at all. I don't know what I'm feeling. Please call me Quentin."

She rested her hand on his for a moment, to cement their reconciliation.

Then she took a large manila envelope out of her purse. It had been folded in quarters to fit. She unfolded it, opened it, and pulled out a Ziploc bag filled with gray hair.

"She sent me her *hair*?" Quentin asked.

"I didn't say she was sane, Quentin, I just said she was alert. I can't explain it to you—she got up, found the scissors, and hacked her hair off before I even got there this morning. She looks dreadful but she said you'd know what it was for. And if you don't, there's a note."

"What does it say?"

"She didn't tell me I could read it."

He thought of the grande dame, complaining when he didn't seal the note he was leaving with her, and he smiled.

"You think I read it anyway?"

"I smiled because I knew you didn't," said Quentin.

She rolled her eyes. "That was mean," she said.

"Mean?"

"Of course I read it. One of my residents cuts off all her hair, gives it to me in a plastic bag, and tells me to take it to a millionaire in a town where he doesn't live so how do I know he's even there, and you think I didn't read the note?"

By now Quentin had it open and was reading it.

> Dear Quentin,
>
> If this is with you, then I am with you. Wear it over your heart. It isn't much, but it's all I can do for you now. Don't let it touch your skin. If it touches your skin, it won't be able to resist taking you, even if it wants her more. It's in your hands. God be with you.
>
> Yours sincerely,
>
> Anna

"You read this?" asked Quentin.

"Does it make any sense to you?"

It hadn't at first. Until he realized that when she said not to let it touch his skin, she didn't mean her hair, she meant the beast. Or did she?

"She's crazy, isn't she?" asked Sally. "I love her, but the old lady's gone bananas, hasn't she?"

"Is that a clinical term?" asked Quentin.

"It's a serious question. I knew she was mentally gone as soon as I read it. But I couldn't let it go. I knew I had to come down here and show it to you."

"She's not crazy, and you know it," said Quentin.

Sally hesitated a moment, then nodded. "I know. But I want to know what this is for."

Quentin opened his shirt, then took it off. "Bolt must have some duct tape in here somewhere. He's too macho to have nothing but this wimpy office tape."

Sally joined him in opening drawers and file cabinets. "So you aren't going to explain anything?"

"Sally, all I'll do by explaining is make you think I'm even crazier than Mrs. Tyler."

"Here it is. This file drawer is like a tool cabinet."

"Help me tape this bag over my chest, would you? And don't bother with the cheap joke about putting hair on my chest. I know how stupid this looks."

"Quentin, I don't know what you think you're doing, but this isn't exactly a bulletproof vest, you know." One thing Quentin really liked about her: She might be complaining, but at the same time she was still taping.

He had to tell her the truth. It wasn't fair to leave her in the dark. And if he was going to lose this struggle, he didn't want Bolt to be the only one who knew what was at stake. "Mrs. Tyler's a witch, Sally. She can send her spirit out of her body into the world. Wherever some relic of her physical body is, she can focus and be drawn to it. I'm wearing this so when I confront the devil, I'll have her power between him and my heart."

Sally shook her head. "OK, don't tell me." She patted the bag on his chest, now outlined with duct tape. "You were right, it really does look stupid."

"Her daughter Rowena is also a witch," said Quentin. "Mike Bolt worked for the family as a kid, and she kissed him and enthralled him so that whenever she wants to, he's her complete slave and does whatever she commands. That's why he tried to smother Mrs. Tyler. He probably didn't even know he was doing it."

Now she knew he wasn't joking, but that didn't mean she belicved it. "Come on, Quentin." She wound the tape all the way around his torso several times. "Why would Mrs. Tyler's daughter send some guy to kill her?"

"Because Mrs. Tyler killed her son, Paul, when he was a baby, and Rowena knows it and never forgave her." There was no point in trying to explain about Roz and the treasure box and Madeleine. Even this much was obviously more than Sally could believe.

"This story is crazier than Ross Perot, " said Sally.

He pulled on his shirt and buttoned it over the bag of hair taped to his chest.

Sally was still trying to find something believable in Quentin's account. "Chief Bolt really did intend to kill Mrs. Tyler?"

"He doesn't intend anything," said Quentin. "It all depends on what the witch who controls him wants him to do."

"You're the one with witch friends, Quentin. When is the next time he's going to try it?"

They stood looking at each other for a long moment, there in Chief Bolt's office, as they thought of at least one possible reason why he wasn't there in the office with them. Why hadn't they realized it before?

Quentin opened the door and rushed out to the receptionist. "Where's Chief Bolt?"

"He doesn't report to me, Mr. Fears, it's the other way around."

"Can't you raise him by radio?"

"He didn't take a radio car."

"I thought all police cars had radios."

"The radio cars are all needed for on-duty officers," she said. "He was going out of the city anyway, what does he need a radio car for?"

"Out of the city? Where?"

"Check with me Friday when he has me type up his mileage report for the week."

Sally put her hand on his arm. "Quentin, I'm going back to the rest home."

"If he's really there, Sally, you can't stop him yourself. You get in the way, he'll plow right through you."

"I'll call the police," she said. "I'll call them as I go."

The receptionist looked puzzled. "What are you two talking about?"

"Nothing to do with you," Quentin reassured her. "Thanks for letting us use Chief Bolt's office."

"Oh, he said you should make yourselves comfortable if you showed up."

"Our*selves*?" said Quentin. "He was expecting both of us?"

"Sure. Sally Sannazzaro and Quentin Fears. He wasn't sure you'd come in, Mr. Fears, but he said *you* were coming for sure, Ms. Sannazzaro."

Sally looked at Quentin with fear in her eyes. "There's no way he could have known that."

"I've been telling you the truth, Sally," said Quentin. "Whatever the witch who controls him needs him to know, he knows."

"I wish I had time to ask you why all this is happening," said Sally. "Wish me luck."

"Good luck, Sally." But he could see in her eyes that she already knew it was too late.

"Good luck yourself," she said. Then she practically flew out the door. Quentin heard her sensible nurse's shoes make ringing footfalls as she ran down the corridor out toward the parking lot.

With a sick feeling, Quentin followed her out into the hall, more slowly. Maybe he should go with her, head north, try to stop Mike. But it was obvious to him that Roz was manipulating things this morning. If she allowed him to go north, it was because it didn't matter—she had blocked him easily enough this morning, just by making him forgetful. In all likelihood, Mike had left an hour before, while Quentin was still showering. It would be easy for Roz to fool the receptionist into thinking Bolt had "just" stepped out even if he had never come in this morning at all. If Roz wanted Mrs. Tyler dead, it was already too late.

Quentin's only hope was to make sure that if Mrs. Tyler died today, she didn't die in vain. His job was to go ahead with whatever awaited him at the Laurent house. The Duncans were undoubtedly there already. Roz was an eleven-year-old kid. She wouldn't wait. They probably left for Mixinack before Quentin was through arguing with the rental car clerk on the phone. They probably arrived at the house before he even woke up this morning.

One thing for sure, though. They wouldn't start without him. He was the one who had to be there to open the box. That made him the guest of honor. He got in his car, pulled out onto the main thoroughfare, and headed south for the Laurent house.

18
The Dragon

Sally Sannazzaro was on the phone the minute she got her car out onto the road. "Chief Todd, this is Sally Sannazzaro. I'm down in Mixinack, and I have reason to believe that an armed man is going to attempt to kill one of my residents."

"This the same guy from the other night?"

"Yes."

"The police chief from Mixinack?"

"He's made an attempt before."

"It's pretty ugly when one police department arrests the chief of another one."

"We can sort it out later."

"How do you know he intends violence?"

"While we're talking about this, he could be shooting her. The resident in question is in room 368, that's third floor, the end of the south wing on the left, her name is Anna Tyler, she's an old woman, bedridden, completely helpless."

"Why would he have it in for a—"

"Don't just send a couple of patrolmen as if it were a domestic disturbance call or something. I have reason to believe Chief Bolt is having a psychotic episode. He's going to be extremely hard to stop."

"I sure hope you aren't just crying wolf, Ms. Sannazzaro."

"I sure hope I *am*."

She disconnected the phone. It was out of her hands. All she could do was drive north and hope she was wrong, hope that Quentin was as crazy as his story and Chief Bolt was just out in Mixinack somewhere running a speed trap or something.

But Quentin Fears didn't seem crazy. He seemed like the soul of rationality. A nice guy. How many millionaires stop to help a rest home make salad on a stormy night?

Got to stop thinking about the salad. Got to stop thinking about Quentin Fears. Drive, that's all I can do right now, drive north. Taping the old lady's hair over his heart. But that's what she asked for. And Chief Bolt *did* try to smother her. Can three people share a psychosis? Am I bringing the total to four?

Mike Bolt opened the glass door and walked right past the reception desk. There was no reason to skulk or hide. She didn't see him. None of them would see him. He was invisible. Two attendants walked past him as he stood before the elevator. His gun was in his hand—nothing subtle about what he was doing. But they didn't notice he existed.

Deep inside him, some lost part of himself was crying out, "I've got a gun, you fools! Somebody stop me!"

Outside, sirens wailed. Cars crunched through ice-crusted snow. Car doors slammed. The elevator door opened. Mike stepped on and punched the 3 button. He watched four policemen charged into the rest home, hands on their guns. Mike was in plain sight, framed in the closing elevator door, but they didn't see him. One of them inquired at the reception desk as two others took off at a run along the corridor, one left, one right. The fourth ran straight for the elevator, but instead of trying to get on as the elevator door slowly closed, he punched the up button. The door reopened, but the policeman didn't get on. He just stood there, tapping his foot impatiently, waiting. Finally the door closed completely without the policeman ever having seen the man he was there to find.

That lost inner part of Mike Bolt fell silent in despair.

Quentin pulled into the drive at the Laurent house, a place far too familiar to him now. He remembered how nervous he had been the first time, in the back of the limo, worried about meeting Madeleine's family. Would they like him? What a joke. But still he wished that he could go back. That Madeleine could be real, that the life he thought he had could be the real life.

A Lincoln Town Car with Virginia plates sat in front of the house, its engine idling. The doors were closed and it seemed unoccupied. As Quentin walked past the car on the way into the house, he glanced inside and saw that the driver's seat had been leaned back as far as it would go, and Ray Duncan was lying there, eyes closed. He must have driven all night to get here. The witches were leaving him outside to sleep. Apparently he wasn't going to be useful in today's little drama.

But he wasn't asleep. Or perhaps the crunch of Quentin's feet in the snow had wakened him. He gave a little wave and sat up. Quentin walked around the car to the driver's side as Ray rolled down the window. "Ro and Roz are already inside," he said. "I'm taking a nap."

Thanks for introducing me to the wonderful world of the obvious. "Must have been a tough drive."

"I like it," said Ray. "Makes me feel useful." He grinned.

I wonder if I looked as pathetic as this when I was Madeleine's lapdog. "Well, don't let me keep you awake."

"I just hope you like the house. Beautiful place but too big for us to keep up. I don't know what the rush is for, but I'll tell you, I'll be glad to get it off our hands. Rowena always gets so upset when you talk about it—either moving in or selling it. But last night after you came over to talk about buying it, well, she changed her mind. I shouldn't tell you this, but let's just say that we're pretty motivated sellers."

Quentin smiled. "We'll see."

A pair of driving gloves lay on the seat beside Ray. Quentin remembered what Mrs. Tyler's note said. Don't let it touch his skin. Maybe he shouldn't open the treasure box with bare hands.

"You going to need those gloves for the next little while?" asked Quentin.

Ray looked down as if noticing them for the first time. "No, you need them? Go right ahead." He handed the gloves through the window. "Got climate control in here, but I bet the house is an iceberg."

The house is whatever your daughter decides it is. "Thanks, Ray."

He heard the window rolling up behind him as he walked around the car and up the stairs.

Roz and Rowena were waiting for him on chairs in the entry hall. Rowena sat like a lady; Roz had her feet up over the arm of the chair. "Took you long enough," said Roz. "You flew and we got here first."

"Didn't know it was a race," said Quentin. To Rowena he said, "Hope you didn't have any trouble getting in. But of course you have a key."

"No, we don't," said Rowena. "The door was open."

"Chief Bolt locked it when we left here the other day."

Roz sighed. "Why are we discussing locks and keys?"

"Because, as your mother will tell you, the thing inside that box is stronger than you think," said Quentin. "Don't open it, Roz."

"I'm not going to. You are." Roz grinned saucily.

"Haven't you explained it to her, Rowena?" said Quentin. "That thing is supposedly trapped inside the box, but still it has power enough seeping out to lock and unlock doors. It's not like you. It has the power to make changes in the physical world. It's so far out of your league that it's insane of you to think you can control it."

Roz got up and started skipping around the room. "Grown-up talk. It's a good thing for you I need you to be free. When my parents lecture like this, I shut them up. I feel sorry for other kids who have to listen."

"Hasn't it occurred to you that maybe the beast is deceiving you as surely as you deceived me? 'Come on, it's not so strong, you can control it, you can ride this horse,' just a bunch of lies to fool you into doing what it can't do for itself—break your grandmother's seal and get out?"

"No, Quentin. Stupid impossible ideas don't occur to me." She looked down at his hands. "You won't need those gloves."

"It's cold in here."

"How stupid do you think I am? I said, *you won't need those gloves!*" Her face grew nasty and dangerous-looking, filled with rage.

"I think I do," said Quentin.

She transformed before his eyes into a monstrous travesty of a woman, long nails reaching for him, sharp teeth brandished in his face. "Take off the gloves," hissed the monster's voice. "Nothing will happen until you do. Lizzy won't be free until you do."

It was no good. She could find even the most pathetic sort of plan in his mind. Quentin pulled off the gloves.

"Nice to see you for a moment without the cute façade," he said. Immediately Roz returned to her little-girl self.

"Ha ha, break my heart," she retorted. "And don't think I'm not perfectly aware of Grandmother's pathetic attempt to thwart me. I've taken care of *her* already."

Quentin felt sick at heart. He'd been right about not having a plan, because whatever fragments of a plan *had* occurred to him or to Mrs. Tyler had been foreseen and forestalled. Poor Mrs. Tyler. Did Roz mean the old lady had been pinned down to her bed again? Or worse? Could Roz really make her mother's poor thrall commit murder?

"I could make him bite his own feet off," said Roz. "The only reason I don't do it with you is because the dragon won't ride in you if you aren't free."

"Let's do it," said Quentin.

As if in answer to him, the door to the parlor flew open, slamming against the wall. For a moment Roz looked startled, nervous. Then she turned back to him and grinned at him. "The steed may buck, but in his heart he still wants to be ridden."

"That may be the stupidest thing ever said by anybody," said Quentin.

"Say what you want, Quentin. I won't have to hear it much longer."

"Where's Lizzy?" asked Quentin.

"Out in the car. As soon as we finish, I'll set her free."

"What if you're wrong? What if you lose your gamble in there?"

"Then it won't matter much *what* happens to Lizzy, will it?"

"I'm not doing it if I'm not *sure* she's getting out."

Roz turned into Madeleine, looking sweet and shy. "If you don't do it, Tin, I'm afraid she won't have *any* chance of getting free. We'll just have to bet on my success, won't we?"

Quentin closed his eyes, refusing to see Madeleine.

"Harder to get rid of the illusion when I'm inside it, isn't it, Tin?"

He turned his head away.

The voice was Roz's when it came again. "Let's stop playing games. The door is open. It's time."

He opened his eyes. It was Roz again. She gestured for him to lead the way into the parlor.

This room wasn't as ratty-looking as the other rooms in the house. No windows had been broken. The dust was thick but no spiders had made webs, no rats had gnawed at it. The place was still. Only Quentin's own footprints led into the room. The treasure box, sitting on its pedestal, seemed to glow just a little. To throb with inner light.

Mike Bolt came out of the elevator and walked down the corridor. One of the two cops who had run for the stairways when they first arrived was already coming out of Mrs. Tyler's room, as the other jogged up to join him. "He hasn't been here yet."

"If he's coming at all."

"Well, we're supposed to keep watch on the door."

"Wild-goose chase, just like the other night. I don't know why they let psycho nurses run a place like this."

As they complained, Mike walked right between them. They didn't see him.

He went through the open door of Mrs. Tyler's room. She lay on the bed, her eyes open. She was struggling to rise from the bed, but each time she arched her back, she fell right back onto the sheet. She stopped struggling and turned her head to look at him. "I guess she's got us both, hasn't she, Mike?" she said.

He raised his pistol, aimed it at her head, and fired once, twice. Each time, the force of the bullet threw her farther toward the edge of the bed. Thrice. The fourth bullet knocked her off the bed. A bloody smear across the pillow marked the passage of the old woman's head.

Mike turned around and suddenly the presence that had engulfed and controlled him was gone. He looked down at the gun. What was he doing with this gun? Why was he in this empty hospital room? He stepped through the door and looked down the hall.

Two policemen were standing there. Mike called to them. "Where's Mrs. Tyler? Isn't she supposed to be in this room?"

"Who the hell are you? Where did you come from? Get out of there!"

Mike stepped back into the room as he heard them rushing toward him. He saw the blood on the pillow. He walked to the foot of the bed, looked behind it. There she lay on the floor, obviously dead, her head almost completely blown away. He looked down at the gun in his hand. He remembered firing it.

"Mrs. Tyler," he whispered. "Oh, sweet Lord, no."

"Drop it! Drop it *right now.*"

The men in the doorway were pointing their guns at him.

"Did I do this?" he asked them.

"Drop it and get your hands on your head."

Mike leaned down as if to lay down the gun. But when he was fully bowed, his arms in shadow, he brought up the gun to his mouth and blew out the back of his head before the policemen could respond. He flopped back against the wall, arms flailing. The policemen fired then, by reflex, filling him with bullets. But he never felt them. He was already gone.

Quentin stood before the box. "Why are you standing so far from me, Roz?" he asked. "Afraid?"

"Prudent," she said with a smile.

"You mind my asking you what's actually in this box?"

"From what I've read," said Roz, "it could be either the baby's heart or its head. I'm betting it's the heart. I don't think even my late grandmother would have the stomach to cut the head off her own baby."

"She's not dead!" cried Rowena.

Quentin turned to see the woman standing in the farthest corner of the room, in the shadow. She was cringing as if in pain. Or as if she was hoping to avoid pain.

"Is too, Mother," said Roz. "I used your power over that boyfriend of yours. Hope you don't mind. He *was* a crack shot. I wanted the job done right."

"It's a lie," whispered Rowena. "Murdering your own grandmother."

"Isn't that what you always taught me, Mother? How evil Grandmother was? The baby-killer. Now I've evened the score. If you don't believe me, ask Quentin. *He* has a relic of hers. He can call her now." Roz turned to him. "Go ahead, Quentin. Call her by name."

"Mrs. Tyler," he murmured.

"By her *name*," said Roz.

"Anna Laurent," he said. "Anna."

Mrs. Tyler stood across the box from him, just as she had when he was here before.

"Is it true?" he asked. "Are you dead?"

"Yes," she said. "Poor Mike. He's so worried about his family."

"Listen to her," said Roz. "Pretending to care about the man who killed her. She doesn't care about him. She doesn't care about anything. Except that she *lost*! She never even knew it was me she was fighting."

Mrs. Tyler turned her head and gazed levelly at Roz. If she felt any surprise, Quentin couldn't see it. But then, could you surprise the dead?

Roz was still gloating. "Always thought it was her own stupid weak daughter fighting her. Look at your daughter, Grandmother!"

Now Mrs. Tyler looked at Rowena, and her eyes softened. Love? Pity, at least.

"There she is, your softhearted daughter, the one who couldn't *bear* the idea of hurting anybody. Well, *I'm* your true child, Grandmother. I have the kind of strength you had— only more of it! What I did to you was nothing but justice! Can you deny it?"

"I don't deny anything," said Mrs. Tyler quietly. "Oh, Rowena, if only you had believed me."

Rowena was looking out the window, tears streaming down her face.

"How sad for the old ladies," said Roz. "All caught up in their little drama. Well guess what, ladies. This isn't about you. You were either tools or obstacles, that's all. Mother was a tool, and I used her. Grandmother was an obstacle, and I pushed her out of the way. Because what I'm doing really matters in the world. I was always too large to live in your little soap opera. I was born bigger than your minds could even comprehend. So stick around and see what power is *for*."

Mrs. Tyler looked at Quentin over the treasure box and gave him a tight little smile.

"Do it, Quentin!" cried Roz. "Open my treasure box."

Mrs. Tyler nodded slightly.

Roz laughed. "Oh, Grandmother, do you *really* think you're still a player in this game?"

Quentin reached out and gripped the sides of the box. He had been in this pose before, but then he had had no notion of what was inside it. Now he felt the nakedness of his skin as he touched the warm, soft wood.

"Lift the lid," said Roz.

This time there was no Uncle Paul to stop him. He lifted the lid a little. For a moment nothing happened. He looked up at Mrs. Tyler. As he did, a long slender red artery snaked out from under the lid and attached itself to one of the veins on the back of Quentin's right hand.

He cried out in fear, not pain. He reached with the other hand to pry it away, but the artery was now a part of his own body, and when he pulled on it, his hand moved with it. Two more arteries snaked out and attached to his left hand.

"Should've kept the gloves," Roz jeered.

Quentin tried to resist, but his hands weren't obeying him very well. He wanted to leap away from the box, but his hands reached for the lid in spite of his strongest effort. His hands flipped the lid open.

It was like opening the inside of a human chest. A lacy network of veins and arteries was attached to the lid and the walls of the box, and more and more of them reached out to attach to Quentin's hands and bare forearms.

Roz started walking toward him, smiling but also terri-fied. "Good," she said. "Possess him. Possess him."

"Stop it, Roz," whispered Rowena.

"Too late, Mother," said Roz. "Once it starts, it can't be stopped."

With terrified eyes, Quentin looked at Mrs. Tyler. She appeared solemn but not afraid. Watching him.

A huge heart rose up out of the box, drawn up by the arteries now attached to Quentin at a dozen points. It was beating, but not rhythmically.

"Hurry," whispered Roz, coming closer. "Take him."

"The heart only has a couple of minutes," said Mrs. Tyler, her voice as mild as if she were giving an explanation to a class. "Inside the box it couldn't die, but outside it has to have a host. Don't fight it Quentin. Take the heart to your chest."

In an agony of fear Quentin looked at her. It was all he could do to keep his hands from seizing the heart—and now she was telling him to surrender? To let the heart have him?

"Only a couple of minutes, and then it will have to stay where it is," said Mrs. Tyler. "Put it on your chest."

Quentin stopped fighting the impulse. At once his hands flew to the heart, seized it, ripped it from the network of arteries in the box. At once the unused veins withered and shriveled until they looked like last year's kudzu vines. The box no longer throbbed.

Quentin's hands hesitated only a moment. Then they snatched the heart to his own chest, where it clung to the cloth of his shirt, beating, beating.

"Done," said Roz.

"Done," said Mrs. Tyler.

"Roz, don't!" cried Rowena.

"And now to make you mine," said Roz. She came closer. "Bend down, Quentin, so I can kiss you." Suddenly she was transformed into Madeleine. "Kiss me, Tin. Kiss me one last time."

She was close to him. In front of him. He could see Mrs. Tyler behind her. With her hands she mimed prying something free of her chest. He understood at once. But did he have the strength to do it?

Alone he didn't. If the beast hadn't wanted to go to her, he never could have done it. But it did want to go. And because of Grandmother's hair between Paul's disfigured heart and his own flesh, the last remnants of her power had been there to help keep the beast from taking full possession of him. Quentin reached up his hands, took hold of the heart, and ripped it away from his body. With Madeleine right in front of him, the same motion pushed it into her chest.

In that instant she changed back into Roz, only where Madeleine's chest had been, there was the naked skin of Roz's face. The heart was already attaching to her in a dozen, in scores of places. And the veins were dropping away from Quentin's hands. He backed away, free of the thing, but unable to stop watching what was happening to Roz.

The heart slid down her face, under her jaw, to her neck, and down inside her shirt. Roz was terrified. "Mother!" she cried. "Help me! Mother!"

"Now you know," Mrs. Tyler said to Rowena. Her voice was thick with bitterness. "Now you know why I did what I did."

"Can't you stop it?" Rowena whispered.

"I already did, once, when it possessed my little boy," said Mrs. Tyler. "But at present, inconveniently, I'm dead."

"Mother!" Roz's voice was more frantic. "Mother!" she screamed. And then the voice became a gurgle.

Roz stumbled, fell to one knee. Her shape began changing. Her arms shriveled and drew up inside her sleeves and disappeared. Wings broke the fabric of her blouse, tearing it open across the back; they spread wide, a ten-foot, then twenty-foot span, lithe as black silk, thin as paper. Quentin could see the light of the window through a wing. Her head rocked back, her jaws opened. A huge serpentine tongue flicked out once, twice, and then her face collapsed into a new shape. The head of a dragon. It opened its jaws to reveal a vast array of teeth, and roared.

Into the roar there came another sound. A popping sound. One. Two. Three.

The dragon shape collapsed. It was Roz again, only there was a bloom of blood on the side of her head, and another on her belly. She looked over her shoulder at her mother with terrified eyes. "Mommy," she whispered.

Rowena fired again, knocking Roz down to the floor. Only the girl's torn clothes showed how the dragon had transformed her a moment ago. The heart hung limply throbbing at her throat. It was feverishly trying to get away, but it was weak now. Rowena fired into the heart.

"Don't waste bullets on that thing," said Mrs. Tyler. "It already had possession of Roz's body. That's the body that has to die."

Sobbing, Rowena sent her last two bullets into her daughter's head.

Eyes open, Roz rocked onto her back and died.

"You had to do it," said Mrs. Tyler. "You had no choice. You can live with this, Rowena. I know you can, because I did."

Rowena, her eyes dead, turned to Quentin. "Get out of the house. Get out or die."

Only now did Quentin realize that the beast had not gone. It didn't have a living body now, but it still had some power to move things in the physical world, as it had when it was in the box. The floorboards under Roz's body buckled as if some immense gopher were burrowing there. The rippling moved like a wave under the pedestal; the box fell and crumpled. The wave passed under Quentin and threw him off his feet. Now the walls were rippling, as paintings leapt out and fell to the floor, as plaster split away in chunks and slid down the wall.

"Get out," said Mrs. Tyler. "Both of you."

Quentin got up, tried to take Rowena's hand to help her. She shoved him away. "I just killed my baby," she whispered. "I'm not leaving her."

With the room bucking like a horse, Quentin staggered for the door and hurled himself into the entry hall.

If anything, it was worse out here. The foot of the stairway had come loose and was now pawing at the ground like a cat's foot, daring him to try to get past without being caught and crushed. There was no way he could reach the front door.

He ran for the library. Books were flying from the walls, smacking him like a flock of suicidal birds. There was no passage there. The dining room. The stairway snatched at him as he passed, but he made it inside. But as he stood there, panting, the dustcover on the table came to life and fluttered toward him as if to engulf him in a net of fine embroidery. It blocked all doors leading from the room. So Quentin ran for the tall window and threw himself through it like a high jumper, back first, shattering glass around him into shards like icicles.

He landed in leafless bushes, prickly and thorny, but it was kinder than the glass would have been. Scratched and bleeding, he pulled himself free and ran around to the front of the house. Ray Duncan was standing in the open door of the Lincoln, staring horrified at the house, which was trembling and, here and there, bulging with the passage of the invisible beast.

"What's happening? What's happening?" he demanded when he saw Quentin.

"Get in the car and drive!" cried Quentin.

"Rowena's in there! Roz! My little girl!"

"Roz is dead and Rowena won't come out. Come on, man! Save yourself!"

"Roz!" cried Duncan. "Rowena!" He ran up the stairs to the porch.

The moment he reached the front door, the front wall suddenly burst as the stamping foot of the stairway lunged out, knocking him down, then smashing him, again, again, his lifeless body flopping under the stairs like a mouse under a cat's paw.

Quentin left the Lincoln and ran to his own car, got in, started it, backed it all the way out to the highway. Then he stopped. "Lizzy," he said. Roz had said they brought Lizzy's prison with them.

He tried to drive back into the property, but the wheels spun and his car slid sideways. He stopped, got out of the car and ran, slipping and sliding on ice and snow, toward the house. As he ran, he plunged his right hand—still bloody from the veins that had been attached to it—into his jacket pocket and pulled out his cellular phone. He punched in 911, pushed SEND. "Tell the Mixinack police to get down to the old Laurent house! I don't know the address, they'll know where it is! The Laurent house. Send fire trucks. Ambulances! No, I can't stay on the line."

He jammed the phone back into his pocket as he reached the Lincoln. The house was shuddering on its foundations. The top story collapsed into the third floor. Glass burst and flew out in all directions. He reached in through the driver's door and fumbled to remove the key from the ignition. Got it. He ran back to the trunk and opened it. Then he flung the key toward the porch, where Ray Duncan might have dropped it as he ran for the house.

There was only one suitcase in the trunk of the car. He yanked it out, flung it open on the snow, and pawed through it. Only a few articles of clothing, a few kit items. A champagne bottle. Had Roz really been that certain of having a celebration afterward?

He opened every zipper compartment. He found only a couple of boxes, one holding stationery, the other some gold chains and pearls. There was nothing else that could hold a relic of Lizzy's. Roz lied. She didn't have Lizzy's prison with them.

Then he looked again at the champagne bottle. Picked it up. Could some part of Lizzy possibly fit inside?

Suddenly Mrs. Tyler was standing before him.

"Get away while you still can."

"I have to set Lizzy free."

"Get away."

She was gone.

Quentin got up from his knees, still holding the champagne bottle, and ran down the lane toward his car. Behind him, the roof of the house fell through the last three stories until they were all pancaked on the foundation. The first of the police cars wailed toward him. He waved them into the lane, but they hadn't even emerged from the trees before the house burst into sudden explosive flames. Fire leapt out and engulfed the Lincoln, the suitcase lying open in the snow. The roof collapsed one last time, falling into the foundation. Flames, sparks, and debris flew into the air and settled back down in burning pieces all over what had once been the lawns and the drive. The police drove in, followed by firetrucks. They set to work subduing the blaze, but clearly there was nothing left, no possibility of survivors.

Quentin broke the champagne bottle with a stone. In the broken glass he saw it: The shriveled, skeletal hand of a teenage girl. "Lizzy," he whispered.

She sat in the snow in front of him, leaning against the car. Tears streamed down her face. "Thank you, Tin," she said.

"Lizzy, she had you—"

"Good work, Tin. I'm free and the beast is gone."

"Are you sure? It had control of the house, it was—"

"Only as long as there was still life in her body. Now that she's dead, the beast lost its connection to the world. Mrs. Tyler found me and told me everything. She knows so much, Quentin."

"Yes, but she's dead. And Roz's parents are dead, and what good did it do? The beast will just come back somewhere else."

"Not till someone invites it," said Liz. "Maybe not for a long time. You've done all you could. You stopped it here, before it could get a foothold. That's all that anyone can ever do."

"Lizzy, what if I hadn't found you?"

"But you did. Mrs. Tyler led you. As soon as she found me, she made you realize." Lizzy glanced around. "They're coming to question you. Don't let them see you talking to me—they'll think you're crazy. And don't leave my hand here, Quentin. I don't want to be tied to this place."

She disappeared. He reached down and picked up her desiccated hand and put it in his jacket pocket.

A policeman sauntered over to him. "You the one called this in?"

"I was here to see the house," said Quentin. "They drove up from Washington to show me the house."

"Somebody was in that place?"

"I just got here. I was out at their car, talking to Mr. Duncan, when the roof started collapsing. He yelled about Rowena and Roz being inside and he ran for the house and it caught him. I called for help but it was too late for any of them. Should I have gone in, Officer? I was so scared, I drove out here and my car got stuck but then I ran back and I thought I should try to help them but the house was collapsing and—"

"No, no, you did the right thing. If you'd gone in there you'd just be dead, too."

"It crushed him right there on the front porch." It took no effort at all for Quentin to let the emotion pour out, to dissolve in tears—of relief, of exhaustion, of grief for the good people who had died. All of them—even Roz. She was just a child. She never understood what she was doing until it was too late. Ray Duncan never understood anything at all.

"Here, man, come on, sit down, get in your car and sit down for a minute." The policeman opened the door and helped him in. "Wait here, will you? We've got questions, but there's no rush, you can get ahold of yourself first, OK?"

Quentin sat there, getting control of himself, as a fireman approached the cop who had been talking to him. "I can't believe a house could collapse like that. Must've had termites out the wazoo."

The cop shook his head. "Just before this call came in, we got word. The old lady used to live here, she still owns the place. She got her head blown off in a rest home upriver. Our own chief. Used to work here as a gardener. He went crazy and killed her and then blew off his own head." The cop looked away for a moment, as if to contain his own emotions. "Family man, decent guy, good boss, good *cop.* You never know."

"The owner of this house just got killed?"

"It's like the old lady's revenge, the house collapsing like that. It can't just be a coincidence, she gets murdered and then her house caves in."

Quentin spoke up from the car. "I think they were her family."

The cop and the fireman came closer. "What?"

"The Duncans. They said their mother owned the house, they were selling it for her. She was in a rest home up the river, they said."

"You mean the people inside the house were her kids?"

"And her granddaughter. All the family she had in the world."

"Dear God in heaven," murmured the cop. "The whole family in a single hour, a hundred miles apart."

"Nobody's ever going to believe a story like that," said the fireman. "Straight out of the *The X-Files.*"

They went on talking. Quentin closed his eyes. It was over. The ending was lousy, but it could have been worse. For him. For everybody.

Except Mike Bolt's family. It was hard to think how it could possibly be worse for them.

*   *   *

Sally Sannazzaro pulled up to the barricades in front of the rest home. The policeman recognized her, waved her in. They were bringing two bodies out of the building, both with sheets draped over their heads. News cameras flashed. TV crews shone floodlights that made it brighter than day on the bodies.

Chief Todd was standing by the ambulance. He waved her over, then thought better of it and walked to meet her as she got out of her car. "Nobody can figure out how he did it. My boys got here first, they verified that she was OK and then they stood watch at the door and they *swear* nobody could have got by them. But he did. Not one of them heard the shots, they just saw him standing in the doorway with a gun and she was already dead."

"And Bolt?"

"They couldn't even disarm him before he blew his own head off. That didn't stop them from pumping about eight more rounds into his body. Ms. Sannazzaro, we screwed up. I don't know how, because these aren't my worst guys. I don't know whether to fire them or drown them like puppies, I'm so mad. I'm so sorry."

She patted his shoulder and turned away. Tears ran down her cheeks. "I don't think it could have been stopped, Chief Todd," she said. "I think it was going to happen no matter what."

"I know you got a thousand things to take care of inside, the whole place is in an uproar, your staff will sure be glad to see you. I'll come by tomorrow and ask you some questions, all right?"

"Fine," she said.

She started for the entrance of the rest home. The newspeople noticed her and started firing off questions. She passed the ambulance as they loaded the second body onto it. She didn't pause to see which one it was. It didn't matter now.

All she knew was that there was only one person on God's green earth who could explain this all to her, and he was a crazy man wearing the dead woman's hair in a plastic bag taped to his chest.

19
Into the Grave

Police questioning in two towns kept Quentin in the area for the next few days, and by then there was no reason to leave before the funerals. Besides, Sally Sannazzaro was there, also answering questions for the police, and then, after hours, assailing him with questions of her own.

Poor woman. She was trying so hard to believe him. Not a skeptic like Wayne Read, she nevertheless had no evidence for her own eyes, as Mike Bolt had had. It didn't help that immediately before he told her the true story, she read through his litany of deceptions to the police as he gave a more believable version of Mike Bolt's activities prior to going on his murderous mission.

Yet she stayed with him as much as possible during the days of inquisition and grief. It finally occurred to him that she stayed with him, despite her doubts, because she needed him right now. He was actually good for something that didn't involve money or opening boxes containing mythical beasts.

Before Mike Bolt's funeral, as he and Sally sat with Leda Bolt in her living room, he felt how empty and powerless his money was when pitted against real problems. Yet it could do something. He promised her that all her children would have a college education, that they would never lack for anything. If it was hard for them to continue living in Mixinack, he would pay for them to move anywhere they wanted.

"Why are you doing this?" she asked. "You barely knew Mike."

"I knew him better than anyone but you, in those last few days of his life. He became my friend. How long do you have to have a friend before you can help his family after he dies?"

She burst into tears.

In a few moments her crying softened and he spoke to her again, his hand on her bowed back. "Leda, it's going to be hard for you, but even harder for your kids. I don't know how to tell you in a way that will make you believe me, but it's true, and so I'm going to say it anyway. If you tell your kids that their father was a good man, through and through, that will be the truth. If you tell them that even though it was his body that held the gun and pulled the trigger, their father never chose to kill Mrs. Tyler, and if he chose to kill himself it was only because he thought he *had* killed her. But it wasn't him. It was someone else, someone who is dead now, too, using his body against his will. Your children are not the children of a murderer or a psychotic. Their father was sane and good. You married a fine man and he loved you with his whole heart and you made him happy. You should all be proud of him."

Leda cried all the harder as she turned and threw her arms around him and clung to him. He held her as she wept. Across the room from him, her hair bright in the light through sheer curtains, sat Sally Sannazzaro, watching him, tears on her own cheeks. She nodded to him. He had done well.

Quentin and Sally stood together beside Mike Bolt's grave with the Mixinack police department, the entire dozen of them, defiantly loyal to him no matter how he met his end.

They knew without Quentin telling them that it wasn't the Mike Bolt they knew who did what was done at that rest home. And from the way they gathered around Leda Bolt and her children, Quentin suspected that the family would not be leaving Mixinack; they would be well watched over here.

Later that day, Quentin and Sally were perhaps the only mourners among the curiosity-seekers gathered at the four new graves in the old Laurent family cemetery. The walled graveyard was the only structure left standing on the Laurent estate. Quentin had already set Wayne Read to work buying the place. He planned to fence it from the road, fill in the foundation of the house, and let it go wild. A little nature preserve. A small, untended graveyard. Let the dead tend each other undisturbed. Let no house grow in this place for a hundred years. Somewhere the beast would be on the prowl again, searching for another heart, another host. But not in this place. This place had had the last of the dragon.

Finally it was over, and at the end of the day it came down to this: Quentin Fears and Sally Sannazzaro on the sofa of her apartment. It was time to face her unbelief in him. Because he didn't want to walk away and leave her in her doubts. "Sally," he said. "I didn't make this up. I'm not stupid enough to make up something this crazy. Until this century, most people believed in witches. The things that've happened here this week, the things that happened to me over the last year, they would have been a marvel or a horror, but not a surprise. We were just born in the wrong time, that's all."

"I don't know about that," said Sally. "I think a time without witches is better."

"But this *isn't* a time without witches. I wish it had been."

"It is now," said Sally. "In *our* lives, anyway."

"I hope."

"I'm taking your word for it that you're not insane."

"I was hoping you didn't make it a habit to invite psychos for long conversations over ice cream in your apartment."

"Ben and Jerry's soothes the savage breast a lot better than music," she said. She took another bite of Wavy Gravy.

"I have to ask you something, Sally," said Quentin.

"Go ahead. I don't have to answer."

"You're not a witch yourself, are you? Pretending to disbelieve my story so I won't suspect what you are?"

"Why do you ask? Are you feeling enchanted?"

"Maybe a little."

"That's the aftermath of grief and shock. You want to cling to somebody."

"True. But when the shock is over, and the grief is under control, won't I still want to cling to somebody? Isn't that, like, normal?"

"But you might be more selective in whom you cling to. I'm not a witch, Quentin, but people have called me similar things."

"Yeah, well, I'm a lonely recluse. It's either you in my life or I turn into Howard Hughes. My last chance. Save me, Sally."

"Are you really, *really* rich, Quentin?"

"Yeah. And thanks to Madeleine, I have political connections all over the country, too."

"Screw 'em. Let's just leave. Now that the funerals are over. Let's leave the country and go to Europe. South America. Africa. India. China. Australia."

"Are you serious?"

"Separate rooms, Quentin. I'm not that kind of girl. But you can afford it, can't you?"

"First class all the way."

"Let's see if we like each other when we're not making salads or running rest homes or watching decent people destroy themselves and each other."

"As long as you don't mind stopping in California first," he said. "I've got to put something back where it belongs."

She knew what he was talking about. She nodded and looked away as her eyes filled with tears.

"Do you have a passport?" he asked.

"No. How good are your political connections?"

"Get the picture taken and we'll see how fast the system can be made to work."

She reached over and took his hand. "If you ever take me to meet your parents, Quentin, I promise not to get along with them too well."

He laughed and looked down into his ice cream dish. "And if I ever think that you remind me of my sister Lizzy, I promise not to mention it."

She smiled. "Even if it doesn't work out, Quentin, I'm still glad I know you."

"Once you duct-tape a Ziploc bag to a man's chest, there's no going back."

She leaned her head on his shoulder. It felt very good. The weight of it. The smell of her hair. Her hand in his. It was different from the way it had been with Madeleine. There wasn't the same sharp thrill to it. It was quieter this time. But it was also better. Right from the start, it was better. If he had ever known a woman like Sally, perhaps he couldn't have been so completely fooled by a fake.

Or maybe he was being fooled again. After all, Madeleine had been created by an eleven-year-old girl—a gifted one, to be sure, but she got everything she knew about sex from books or from Quentin's own head. An adult witch with real experiences could do a better job, couldn't she?

He tried very hard to doubt Sally Sannazzaro's existence. To pretend that the pressure of her hand, the weight of her head, all was illusion. That her strength and kindness were drawn from his own need. That her temper and sternness had been created only to make her more plausible in the aftermath of Madeleine.

But when he opened his eyes, she was still there, looking up at him.

"What are you doing?" she asked.

"Trying to make you disappear."

She thought about that for a moment. "It isn't going to work," she finally said.

"Good," he said. And then he kissed her. It wasn't a perfect kiss. They bumped noses. They laughed. "If you're a fake," he said, "don't ever tell me."

And so they would go on, apart or together as love and chance and time might decree, surrounded always by the silent, beloved dead, and answering their silence with the shout of life. That was the invisible treasure box that Quentin had been given long ago but only now found and opened. There *was* power in it; the kind of power that disappears when it is taken, yet grows as fast as children when it is shared.